D0772368

Sairish Hussain was born and brought up in Bradford, West Yorkshire. She studied English Language and Literature at the University of Huddersfield and progressed onto an MA in Creative Writing. Sairish completed her PhD in 2019 after being awarded the university's Vice-Chancellor's Scholarship. *The Family Tree* is her debut novel and she is now writing her second book.

The Family Tree

Sairish Hussain

ONE PLACE. MANY STORIES

HQ
An imprint of HarperCollins*Publishers* Ltd
1 London Bridge Street
London SE1 9GF

This edition 2020

1
First published in Great Britain by
HQ, an imprint of HarperCollins*Publishers* Ltd 2020

Copyright © Sairish Hussain 2020

Sairish Hussain asserts the moral right to be
identified as the author of this work.
A catalogue record for this book is
available from the British Library.

ISBN Hardback: 978-0-00-829745-9
ISBN Trade Paperback: 978-0-00-829746-6

MIX
Paper from
responsible sources
FSC
www.fsc.org FSC™ C007454

This book is produced from independently certified FSC™ paper
to ensure responsible forest management.

For more information visit: www.harpercollins.co.uk/green

Printed and bound in Great Britain by
CPI Group (UK) Ltd, Croydon, CR0 4YY

For my grandmothers,
Anwar Jan and Riaz Begum.
Thank you for your warmth and wisdom.

PART ONE

One

February 1993

He clutched the tiny bundle in his trembling arms, rocking gently back and forth, careful not to make a sound. The streetlamps were glowing outside. He could see the dull orange light burning through the misted window. It was 4 a.m. and Amjad wondered if he would get any sleep now. He doubted it. Sleep provided a merciful cover and it had been blown only a few moments before. The sound had travelled ruthlessly down the hallway, determined to trouble him. He considered turning over on the couch and placing something over his ears. His arm throbbed as he eased it from under his weight, and his fingers twitched longingly as he contemplated reaching out for a cushion.

Minutes later, Amjad plodded up the stairs. He dragged his feet, step by step, one arm using the banister to pull himself up, the other still throbbing and limp by his side. He paused for a moment, balling up his fist in determination. He needed all the strength he could muster, all the resolve in the world to reach the top of those damn stairs.

Five little fingers were now wrapped tightly around his pinky. His daughter's face rested peacefully against him, her tiny chest rising and falling. Amjad had wrapped her up in his wife's shawl and tried not to think of the disgraceful thoughts he had entertained just moments before. The ones where he'd wanted to block out Zahra's frantic wails with a beige corduroy cushion.

Amjad held Zahra close. Even then, amidst all the pain, he could not help but smile as he looked at her. He had managed to soothe his newborn baby, despite desperately needing consolation himself. It was the first of a series of 'moments'. For the next few weeks, Amjad would find himself comparing his two lives. The previous one, in which he could simply call out and his wife, Neelam, would come rushing into the room to assist. And this new one, where his voice would reverberate against the dark walls and disappear into nothing. They would never stand together over Zahra's cot and exchange tired smiles, fingers interlocked as Neelam's head rested on his shoulder. They would never shush each other as they eventually tiptoed back to bed, Neelam telling Amjad off for stepping on a creaking floorboard.

Amjad wiped his eyes. It had all changed. The mud under his fingernails proved that. Only yesterday he had thrown the earth into his wife's grave and cried silently at the mosque beside her body. Now it was just Amjad. Amjad, rocking back and forth in a darkened room, clinging on to Zahra.

She would never know her mother. Her little face would never be cupped by Neelam's hands. The tips of their noses would never touch. The injustice of it all crushed him and Amjad wanted to fight against it. Was there no one he could protest to or demand an explanation from? No complaints form, no senior institution he could persuade to overturn their decision, to let his wife live?

Amjad thought he saw a pair of eyes peeking through the bedroom door. It creaked open and ten-year-old Saahil teetered into the room. His long, uncombed hair shrouded his tiny face and his big, doleful eyes looked to Amjad, desperately.

'Come here,' Amjad whispered, arm outstretched.

Saahil walked closer and leaned in to his father. His shaky little hand gently stroked Zahra's head. Amjad felt his heart break.

'My beautiful little boy,' he said as he enveloped his son. They all huddled together for some time. Zahra, wrapped in the silky smoothness of her mother's shawl, and sleeping soundly against her father's chest. Saahil, small and as fragile as a baby deer, struggling to take his first steps in a new world, a world without his mother. And Amjad, holding them all together. He must stop feeling sorry for himself, he thought. He was determined to protect his children from anything. Pain would have no place in his household. He would fling it out the door at its first appearance.

The dull orange glow shed light on the family's silhouette in the darkened room. A raindrop slid down the window.

Two

The nagging started a year after Neelam's passing. As they approached the dreaded first anniversary, Amjad's mother seemed to grow in confidence.

'You need to marry again,' she said, peering at him expectantly through her jam-jar glasses. 'Are you listening to me?'

Amjad rolled his eyes. 'Do you want to eat saag aloo tonight, Ammi?' he asked, jumping up from the sofa and heading towards the kitchen.

Food was his second-best tactic at diverting the conversation of marriage. Running out of the room was the first. On this occasion, despite combining them both, Amjad knew he wasn't going to get out of it so easily. His mother's voice followed him into the kitchen. It grew shrill and spiky, almost as if it had developed fingers and clipped him around the ears.

'Don't change the subject,' she snapped.

Amjad flinched at the sound. He knelt down and opened his cupboards. His scowl turned into a beam as he admired his fully stocked shelves. As soon as Ammi announced that she would be visiting, Amjad had rushed out to replenish the groceries. He didn't want a repeat of what had happened on her last visit. She'd opened the cupboards to find nothing but baby food, sweet corn and an out-of-date tin of tuna. As expected, a rant had ensued.

This time, the kitchen was well stocked with fresh ingredients. Amjad reached in and sliced open a brand-new sack of potatoes. He eyed some tinned spinach but remembered that he'd bought a fresh bag for tonight's supper. Ammi wouldn't be impressed with anything that came out of a tin. He placed both items on the worktop and realised that Ammi was still talking.

'The kids need a mother,' she called out. 'You can't do it all by yourself.'

Amjad sighed and realised that Ammi wasn't going to drop it. Reluctantly, he headed back towards the lounge and peered around the door. He saw his mother's slightly magnified eyes focus on him through her glasses. She sat up straight, raring to go. Amjad took a seat opposite and watched her adjust the loosely draped scarf around her neck impatiently. He braced himself.

A year after Neelam's passing was, according to Ammi, a reasonable timeframe in which to mention marriage. It was her way of being tactful. After all, it was the last *first* of that year. Each hurdle had been planned by Amjad to reduce the trauma for them all. He'd fretted over what to do for Saahil's first birthday without his mum. An answer came in the form of Ehsan, Saahil's best friend at school. They'd spent the day playing together at a trampoline park before ending with a sleepover at Ehsan's house. It was for the best, to keep Saahil away from home. A home without Neelam. Amjad was quite sure that Saahil hadn't completely forgotten about his mother's absence on his birthday. He was, in fact, just better at surviving. Children always were, everyone told Amjad.

Eid was another major hurdle. As the day approached, Amjad just wanted to be as far away as possible. An empty home on Eid would feel like a betrayal to Neelam, but the smell of her cooking would not fill the rooms. There would be no samosas

7

crackling as they entered the hot oil. Or lamb biryani steaming when removed from the oven. Neelam's soft voice would not nag Amjad to smarten up his clothes for when the guests arrived. Or scold Saahil for making the living room untidy again. How, then, could Amjad spend Eid there?

Ammi seemed to offer a solution by inviting them to her house. She called Javid, Amjad's brother, and ordered him to drive up from Birmingham to spend the day with them. Amjad, however, had received another invitation from one of his closest friends, Harun, who also happened to be Ehsan's father. Despite Eid being a non-negotiable day of the year to spend with family, Amjad did the unthinkable and rejected Ammi's offer. As expected, she hit the roof, scolding him for wanting to spend Eid with non-relatives. But there was a generosity in Harun's invitation that Amjad was grateful for. It offered him exactly what he needed at the time: a complete and utter change. He wanted new conversation that didn't involve pity for himself and his children. He wanted to eat food that was cooked by Harun's wife, Meena, knowing it would taste different. He wanted Saahil to have an amazing time playing with his best friend. True, there wasn't much to Eid except for excessive amounts of eating and tea drinking, but Amjad knew that if he had taken the children to Ammi's house, they would all be searching for the only person missing in the sea of faces.

Every landmark Amjad came through felt like an achievement. But the anniversary of his wife's death and daughter's birth loomed over him as it drew nearer. He needed to cross over and guide his children through this final push. Almost like another birth, there was trauma, pain, a determination to squeeze through, and a great gasp of air. They would all come out on the other side, hurting but still alive.

'Anyway, what about you?' Ammi's voice rang in his ears. 'Do you want to end up all alone? You need someone you can grow old with.'

Amjad sighed. 'I'm not going to marry a stranger from Pakistan and bring her over here to clean the house and look after my kids. They've got me and you, they don't need anyone else.'

'Well, I'm not going to live forever!' Ammi screeched. 'I'm an old woman.'

'You're only fifty-nine,' Amjad laughed.

'You don't listen to anything I say,' she said, ignoring him. 'You won't even let me move in and help you out.'

Amjad smiled patiently. He watched his mother peel pomegranates for Saahil who stuffed the seeds into his mouth quicker than they appeared on the plate. Every now and then, her henna-tipped fingers ran over his face affectionately. Amjad was pleased with how the bond between grandmother and grandson had strengthened over the past year. But he still needed to stand his ground on this subject.

'Look, Ammi,' he said, slightly tired of having to explain himself yet another time. 'You've lived in the same house since you came to this country. You've got friends and neighbours, your own little community. It would be difficult for you to change homes after thirty years. Plus, I don't want my house turning into a royal souvenir shop,' he said, with a mischievous glint in his eye.

Ammi had always been a staunch royalist. Royal memorabilia littered her home, most of which were gifts bought for her by Amjad's father. Teapots, cups and saucers, plates, bowls, brooches, card holders for her bus pass, keyrings and even books she couldn't read a word of. You name it, Ammi had it.

'And anyway,' Amjad continued after seeing the royal joke

hadn't gone down too well with his mother. 'It's good to stay independent for as long as you can.'

He really didn't need another guilt trip for not letting his mother move in with him. As the eldest son, it was considered his duty to look after her in this way. Since his father had died a few years ago, Ammi was constantly reminding him of how old she was. It was a cunning little tactic that Amjad believed was quite popular amongst Asian parents. He'd recently exchanged notes with some of his friends to find out what their ageing mothers and fathers got up to. They were all familiar with the older generation's mindset of being at death's door at the age of fifty-five, and needing looking after.

'Ah yes,' Ammi retorted. 'And I suppose when I can no longer stay independent you will chuck me into a nursing home like goray do away with their parents.'

'Well, like I said, you're fifty-nine. No care home would have you!'

Ammi glared at him. Amjad suppressed a smirk.

'I really don't know what the problem is,' he said, deciding enough was enough. 'You're here quite a lot anyway. You stay overnight. I pick you up and drop you off whenever you want.'

Ammi argued back and although Amjad didn't say it, the constant pestering was the main reason he didn't want his mother living with them. Whenever she came over, she would settle herself down in her favourite spot, all fluffed up like a hen ready to roost. Her head darted with precision in all directions, and her beady eyes remained forever watchful. Maybe he was imagining things, but Amjad felt as though she was always waiting for some slight error to be made, evidence that he needed to marry again. After all, a woman would not put ketchup in the curry instead of using fresh tomatoes as Amjad often did. Or tie Zahra's nappy the wrong way around. Although Amjad knew she meant well, the last thing he needed was to be pecked to death over silly mistakes. He would sigh with relief when he dropped the old woman off on her own doorstep, guilt stabbing at him as he drove around the corner and out of sight. Especially as he remembered how much he had relied on her during the months following Neelam's death.

Had it not been for his mother, Amjad doubted he would have survived the shock. He knew his children craved a nurturing female presence, and only Ammi was able to provide that. Her warmth revitalised them whenever she entered the house. She swept through each room, dusting things down, lighting fires and throwing open curtains. Life returned to the home as Ammi's voice rang through it. The children laughed and played. When Ammi took charge, Amjad would shuffle off into a corner, glad he no longer had to be the strong one.

And of course, there was Harun and Meena. Such was their friendship that Saahil had been with them the night Neelam went into labour. Harun's cheery voice had answered Amjad's call from the hospital. The expectation of good news diminished the moment Amjad told Harun that his wife had haemorrhaged after the delivery. Amjad could still remember the stuttering disbelief in his friend's voice. He could still hear the muffled outburst of grief in Meena from the other end of the phone. They had reassured him that they would take care of Saahil for as long as he needed. And their support did not stop there.

As Amjad adapted to his new life without Neelam, he realised that he needed help with everything. If Ammi wasn't there, then Meena was always on hand to teach him how to look after a newborn. She showed him the proper way to bathe an infant and how to mix the baby formula correctly. She was the first person Amjad would call late at night when Zahra cried and wouldn't settle. Meena shooed Harun away to carry out other jobs. Amjad remembered staggering down the stairs on those first painful mornings without his wife. He'd find supermarket bags full of food on his kitchen worktop. He knew it was his friend, Harun, who had left them there during his daily school run with Saahil and Ehsan. Meena was always available to babysit the children. Harun was there in other ways. Amjad could call him up and jump into his taxi at any time. They would go for long, quiet drives. It was just what Amjad needed to clear his head. Harun never refused him or asked why. He just drove in silence.

Slowly but surely, Amjad was able to lift his eyes from the ground. Ammi, Harun and Meena had got him through the last twelve months and now, he had developed a pretty decent system. It took time, with many accidents and failures along the way. Saahil had adjusted to his new role and was always on stand-by whenever Amjad attended to Zahra. Nappies, baby bottle, dummy, he ran to fetch whatever Amjad ordered. When Zahra began crawling, Saahil followed her around the room as she scuttled between table legs and put random objects into her mouth. He stood patiently against the kitchen door as Amjad was known to forget about the shuffling baby and fling it open from the other side. Now that Zahra was trying to walk, Saahil would distract her as his father ironed his school uniform and tidied the house.

Making dinner was also a joint effort. Unlike Neelam's finely chopped onions and selected spices added to the curry in a timed manner, Amjad just threw it all in and hoped for the best. He'd never really cooked before in his life and had initially turned for help to Ammi who was delighted with an opportunity to boss him around.

'Remember to brown the onions!' she'd shout at him from the lounge.

Fifteen minutes later, Amjad would empty fragments of charred onion into the dustbin. How brown were they supposed to be? Ammi just had a knack for things. He didn't. He'd quickly hide the burnt pan in a cupboard and pull out another one before Ammi waddled into the kitchen to inspect his progress. He preferred learning how to cook at Ammi's house. She would eventually get impatient and send him off to watch TV. She'd rustle something up in no time, and fill some Tupperware for him to take home. On these days, Saahil would eagerly run down to the roti shop a few streets away and buy four chapattis for a pound. Of course, the days Amjad could not muster the energy to cook, he would get some fish and chips for dinner or simply reach out for the faithful can of Heinz beans, always available to throw over some toast.

No shop-bought rotis were allowed in the home if Ammi was around. She would knead the dough and roll out the chapattis herself. Amjad would tear off a small piece and give it to Zahra to nibble on. It was, however, another opportunity for Ammi to check his cupboards, which almost never met her standards.

'No ginger!' she'd remark. 'How can you make curry with no ginger?'

Twelve months later, though, this was becoming Ammi's biggest weapon to use against him. The lack of garlic or ginger only suggested one thing:

'See, this is why you need a woman in the house,' she'd squawk. 'And if not me, then it's time you got married again!' Amjad would block his ears.

'So,' he said, glancing at Ammi with the hope that the conversation of marriage was over. 'Is saag aloo okay then?'

Ammi sniffed and began muttering under her breath. Amjad grinned and went back to the kitchen, as if to get started. Instead, he stood by the sink and stared out of the window. After taking a year out from work, tomorrow Amjad would return to his job as a warehouse operative on a part-time basis. He would drop Saahil off to school and Zahra off at Ammi's in the mornings and be home by noon. His return to work felt like definitive proof that his family were now more than just managing. Saahil no longer stared into the distance, still and despondent. He was actually excited to start secondary school. The offer letters notifying them of which school he'd been placed in would be arriving in the post in the coming weeks. And Zahra was beautiful. She was taking her first steps and saying words other than 'dada'. Amjad was still going to be their father, but also a man who worked and had his own independence. A year later, and Amjad realised that there were other things to think about now.

Neelam was still a part of their lives, but her love manifested itself in other ways. The shawl she had grabbed and wrapped around her shoulders on the night of Zahra's birth remained a constant presence in their daughter's life. It was the last item of clothing that Neelam had snatched from the bed, just as the contractions grew in strength. The last source of comfort his wife had felt, the last bit of fabric her fingers had caressed. It was the same shawl that Amjad wrapped his newborn inside, on the night after Neelam's burial. It was a silk-blend pashmina shawl sent to Neelam from her mother in Pakistan. Against a teal blue backdrop, a border of mustard yellow florals snaked their way around the fabric. The shawl was finished with a heavy yellow fringe on either side. Amjad was determined to keep it as close to Zahra as possible, almost as though it was a gateway to Neelam's love. Now, she wouldn't settle without it.

One day, Amjad held up the shawl against the sunlight. The images on the pashmina changed and took on a new life, like the stories found in stained-glass windows. A mustard-coloured blossom tree stretched the length of the shawl. Silhouettes of small birds flitted from branch to branch. Amjad peered further and placed the symbols in his own mind. Now, a year later, and all he had to do was point to each bird.

The two small ones at the bottom of the tree, facing one another.

'Me... Saaheeee,' Zahra would say.

Another bird, standing on the same branch, but some distance from the first pair.

'Ehsi.'

A larger bird, flying high, with its wings spread protectively.

'Dada.'

Higher still, and a rather plump one that could easily have been dozing.

'Ammi.'

'And this one Zee...' Amjad would ask eagerly. 'What about this one?'

It was the lone bird situated right at the top of the tree, the silhouette of its beak facing down. Amjad would hold his breath, hoping she'd remember.

'This one?' he'd ask again.

Zahra would usually take her time, unable to put a face to the name. She'd always get there in the end though.

'This... my mummy.'

Three

The theatre with its elegant domes and imposing columns was the first structure that welcomed people into the city. As they swerved past and through the series of roads which would lead them out of the centre, it gave them a false sense of grandeur to the city they were about to enter. The theatre appeared out of place. It didn't look as if it belonged there. It was too flamboyant, too flashy for such a simple town. Derelict factories and abandoned warehouses eyed the building enviously from afar. Whenever Amjad drove past the theatre, he felt ashamed because in his thirty-five years of life, he'd never actually been inside. Nor had any of his neighbours or colleagues. People like him didn't go to the theatre. He assumed posh folk from nearby towns like Leeds, York and Harrogate were the most frequent visitors. People who regularly spent evenings at the theatre. Saahil had been once with a school trip to see the pantomime. He'd been nagging Amjad ever since to take him again. Amjad insisted he would, if and when he had the time.

Reminders of a glorious past were evident everywhere. The city housed an old factory which was once the largest silk and velvet manufacturer in the world. Amjad read about it in the newspaper when it had recently closed down. It surprised him that a mill town in Yorkshire could have such significance. It made him appreciate the forlorn-looking building more. The only impact it made now was its imposing, smokeless chimney that could be seen from almost every spot in the city. Even now, it was an impressive structure, built in the 'Italianate style' the newspaper informed him.

Amjad was parked opposite the mill now, waiting for Saahil and Ehsan to come out from another blackened gothic building: their primary school. It looked like it may have been a church in the olden days. Now though, it sat in a parade of shops including a halal butcher, a travel agent offering Hajj and Umrah packages, and plenty of windows displaying mannequins wearing glittery salwar kameez.

Amjad watched as Saahil and Ehsan pulled off their blazers and heaved their rucksacks from their backs. They ran towards his rust bucket of a car, smiles erupting on their faces as they spotted Zahra gurgling away in the baby seat next to him. Amjad set off and took a right turn down a long street. Within seconds, he was in his old neighbourhood. After all, where there was a factory, there was living accommodation built for its workers. It was almost a maze. One street after another with rows and rows of terraced houses. Amjad headed straight into the puzzle, stopping at one give way after the next, braking harshly to allow other cars to pass through the narrow streets. He drove past littered back alleys filled with scraggly children. Patterned salwars hung from washing lines. Tracksuit-clad youths stood around outside grimy kebab shops. Amjad sighed with relief. *Thank God we got away from here*, he thought once again. He checked his rear-view mirror, the crown of the factory's chimney still visible. Saahil and Ehsan were sitting in the back, tugging at their school ties and whispering away in hushed voices. Amjad craned his neck and tried to listen in on their conversation. He caught Ehsan's eye.

'Ask your dad,' Ehsan said, nudging Saahil. Saahil cleared his throat.

'Abbu, what's so good about the other school, the one you wanted us to go to?'

Amjad sighed. The long-awaited school admission letters had arrived at the beginning of the month. When Amjad had opened Saahil's, he was devastated to see that his son had been placed in the local failing comprehensive, the one he'd dreaded him going to. Ehsan's letter revealed the same fate. It was only a mile away from the school Amjad wanted the boys to attend, another comprehensive but one with a much better reputation. There was no complicated selection process, no exam, no interview. All offers were to be made based on the pupil's catchment area. It didn't matter then, that Amjad had worked seven-day shifts to save up enough money to move his family away from what was known as the 'Paki ghetto'. He couldn't exactly change his child's skin colour. He'd said this bitterly to Harun. Not that either of them let Saahil and Ehsan hear them. They didn't want the boys to start thinking like that at such a young age.

'That one's for white people,' Ehsan said, without waiting for an answer.

Amjad jerked the car with surprise.

'We haven't got a place there coz we're Pakis. Think about it. All our goray mates have got in.'

Saahil looked confused. 'But how can there not be any white kids at this other school?'

'Oh yeah, there will be,' said Ehsan. He leaned closer to Saahil and whispered, 'Council estaters.'

'Ehsan,' said Amjad, frowning in the mirror. *Kids these days are so smart*, he thought, trying his best to appear shocked at his statement. He saw Ehsan shrink back in his seat.

'Sorry, Uncle,' he said. 'But I'm just *sayin'*… It's true.'

'What did I say to both of you the other day?' Amjad said, stopping at some traffic lights. 'At least you'll be together. And if you work hard, you can succeed anywhere. You just need to really concentrate and… and try.'

'What does "special measures" mean again, Abbu?' asked Saahil.

'It just means the school is erm… struggling… a bit,' Amjad said, choosing his words carefully.

'Hmmm,' said Saahil, not sounding too fussed. 'At least we can mess about at this crappy school.'

'Saahil!'

'I'm just joking, Abbu.'

'We can't mess about,' Ehsan said, his face scrunched up with worry. 'You know what my dad's like. He says I'll end up washing dishes at a restaurant if I don't study hard.'

'He's right. And *you*,' Amjad said, pointing to his son in the backseat, 'you'll be stacking shelves at Morrison's. That's what happens if you don't concentrate at school. Look at me: if I'd listened to my dad and studied properly, I'd be a lawyer or a pharmacist now.'

Saahil nodded dutifully. Ehsan continued frowning.

'I don't wanna be a shelf-stacker,' he said. Amjad saw Saahil grin and roll his eyes.

'As *if* that's gonna happen,' he whispered into Ehsan's ear.

Amjad smiled to himself approvingly as he parked up outside his house. Here it was, the home he had inhabited for less than six months with his wife. After struggling to conceive again for nine years, Neelam had announced her second pregnancy to much jubilation. Amjad was determined to make a fresh start. He could see the area they lived in deteriorating further and wanted better for his family.

They couldn't move too far away as they needed to be close to a mosque. Amjad had always skipped his lunch break on Friday afternoons to pray the special Jummah prayers. Men poured into the mosque at noon, sometimes accompanied by their young sons whose floor-length robes flapped around at their ankles. Fathers and sons walked together; Saahil with Amjad, Ehsan with Harun.

The best he was able to afford at the time was a charming terraced house less than two miles and a fifteen-minute drive from their old place. It was further away from the city centre. As Amjad drove through, the takeaways became less visible, the streets became greener. There were English families on the street too, as well as black and Indian, fulfilling Amjad's hope of living in an area where his children would play with kids of different backgrounds. Not that everyone was so welcoming. Amjad remembered being glared at by their elderly white neighbour on the day they had moved in. He'd almost mouthed 'sorry' as he'd carried a cardboard box apologetically through the door, a pregnant Neelam following him. At her insistence, Amjad placed two hanging baskets at each side of the door. He sometimes still imagined her standing by the doorway, scarf draped loosely over her head, one arm extended to arrange the flowers and the other placed protectively over her baby bump.

Amjad thought about quickly shoving some fish fingers into the oven for the boys' dinner when a taxi pulled up behind them. It was Harun.

'Sorry, I got held up in traffic,' he said, smoothing down his creased shirt.

'You didn't have to rush,' Amjad replied, unstrapping Zahra

from her car seat. 'Anyway, come in, we'll have a cup of tea.' They all went inside.

Harun still helped Amjad with school runs to save him from dragging little Zahra out in the cold. Saahil could walk home as the school wasn't far, but Amjad didn't like the idea of him sauntering home with the rest of his friends, kicking discarded takeaway cartons in his path and replying to racist graffiti on the walls. Besides, Harun's increased help since Neelam's death had become a regular opportunity for a cup of tea. As much as Amjad loved his children, it made a nice change not to have to gurgle away in baby language to Zahra twenty-four-seven, or have to tell Saahil off *again* for banging his football against the wall. Harun's company always relieved Amjad of the bitterness he felt at being a widowed dad who constantly changed nappies, prepared baby food, ironed uniforms and made dinner. Harun reminded Amjad he was still a young man who could obsess over cricket and football scores, talk about cars and share Bollywood music cassettes. He was Amjad's contact with his previous life.

'Keep it down,' Harun shouted at Saahil and Ehsan as Amjad prepared the tea. They always saved their meetings to make proper Pakistani chai, not the watery English tea they usually drank for quick convenience. Harun stood in the kitchen with Zahra in his arms as Amjad boiled the milk in a pan and threw in a few teaspoons of loose Yorkshire Tea, lots of sugar, cardamom pods and some cinnamon sticks. When it was ready, they both settled on to the couch as Saahil and Ehsan played with Zahra.

'Ah!' Harun shouted, making them all jump. 'I notice a new marking on your door.'

Amjad glanced back and grinned. 'Yep, we had a ceremony on her birthday a few weeks back.'

Harun was of course referring to the first foundations of a growth chart inked into the kitchen door. Saahil was the first to be marked on his tenth birthday. Neelam was alive then, and they had just moved into the new house. She'd held the ruler against the top of Saahil's head and Amjad had made the marking in a blue felt tip pen.

Saahil, 10 yrs, 14/09/92

He was precisely fifty-five inches. Ehsan had been eyeing the chart enviously ever since and so, a couple of months later, on his birthday, Amjad had done the same. The marking was made on the same side of the door, as the boys wanted to race each other up the wall.

Ehsan, 10 yrs, 01/12/92

He groaned when he realised he stood at just fifty-two inches and vowed to come back stronger, and taller, next year.

A couple of weeks ago on Zahra's first birthday, Saahil insisted on marking her height too. Amjad forced a smile and thought of Neelam as he held Zahra against the opposite side of the kitchen door. Saahil made the marking with a pink felt-tip pen.

'Keep her head straight, Abbu!'

And there it was, written in slightly shaky handwriting:

Zahra, 1 yr, 20/02/94

She was a healthy twenty-nine inches.

After admiring the growth chart, Harun glanced at Amjad, who had suddenly gone very quiet.

'You're not still worrying about the new school are you, Amjad?' he asked, slouching over his mug, the bad posture gained from his job as a taxi driver.

'No,' Amjad lied. Harun raised an eyebrow at him.

'They're both clever boys,' he reassured. 'They'll be fine.'

Amjad looked unconvinced. 'I know they are, but the school's reputation…'

'They're getting a new head teacher,' Harun reminded him. 'And apparently it's someone who's already transformed one of the schools in the area. I did tell you that, didn't I? Try to be a little optimistic, will you?'

'Sorry, but I can't. I just have a bad feeling about the whole thing.'

'Amjad,' Harun said, impatiently. 'I don't know what your problem is. You need to stop worrying.'

Amjad bit his tongue. *Maybe you don't have to worry, mate,* he thought as he watched Harun sipping his tea. Harun carried an ordinary man's burdens. Bills, mortgage, work problems. But at least he had a lovely wife at home who he could talk to. Somebody who could share the worrying with him.

Harun continued: 'You were born here and can help your boy. Look at me…' He paused for a moment, keeping one eye on Amjad as he grinned. 'I still sign my name with a thumbprint.'

Amjad laughed along with him, feeling slightly guilty for his negative thoughts. Harun came to England when he married Meena. After receiving just a basic village education, Harun had worked in a cotton mill before taking up taxi driving. He struggled with his English sometimes and mostly conversed with Amjad in Urdu. Not because he didn't understand the language at all; Ehsan was constantly blabbering away in English to his father, but Amjad sensed Harun was too embarrassed to speak it in case he got it wrong. Or maybe because of what his accent would sound like.

'Yeah, well,' Amjad began, trying to justify himself. 'I was never clever enough at school. We didn't have much money either growing up. Just took whatever job was available.'

If Harun's feet hurt from pounding at the pedals in his taxi all day, then Amjad's shoulders ached from stacking heavy boxes at the warehouse. He didn't want that for Saahil. And he knew Harun didn't want that for Ehsan.

'It's not like that for our boys,' Harun reminded him. 'Times have changed. Insha'Allah, they'll both make it to university. You wait and see.'

There was no doubting the boys were good academically. Amjad watched them on occasion working through their homework together. They sat with open books facing them, brows furrowed as they tackled difficult sums. They seemed to bounce off each other. Throwing sassy remarks in each other's direction in a far more intelligent way than when Amjad was their age. He couldn't have chosen a better best friend for Saahil himself. It also seemed as though his regular outbursts of 'you don't want to end up like me' had had some impact. Saahil actually wanted to do well at school. So did Ehsan. Amjad overheard them a few times speaking of what they would do once they 'got rich'. He smiled as he eavesdropped on their big plans. They consisted of nothing more than driving fancy cars for the time being, but it didn't matter. Amjad held on to that flicker of ambition, he wanted to nurture it, to tell Saahil he could do and be anything he wanted. In fact, it wasn't that Amjad worried Saahil wouldn't try hard on his own despite being shunted into a failing school. His insecurities were more personal. He just didn't want to mess up.

It was one thing feeding and clothing your kids, and another making sure they were well prepared in life. If he could just make it until they were old enough to look after themselves, he'd be happy. If he could just witness the lives they would go on to create for themselves, he'd be content. If all he could do was encourage hard work and determination in Saahil, it was enough. After all, if he popped his clogs unexpectedly, then at least Saahil would be well-equipped to look after his baby sister.

Amjad felt silly worrying over the timing of his ultimate demise. But death just took people. He'd seen that for himself. The thought of his children alone and unsupported choked him up with fear. He needed to raise them well and give them everything they would need to be okay, for Neelam's sake.

Amjad knew that when he did eventually join his wife in that other place, he wanted to be able to meet her eyes when he got there.

Four

Saahil's heart sank as he watched his Abbu peer into the rear-view mirror. A parallel park was about to take place just outside his new school. They were gridlocked, with cars jam packed in all corners. Some parents braked in the middle of the road and let their children go free in the morning rush hour. Not Abbu, though. Since they had started secondary school a week ago, Abbu made sure he found a parking spot every day. He wouldn't let Saahil and Ehsan go anywhere without a daily 'Be Good' lecture. Saahil knew that Ehsan was thinking the same. He had slumped slightly in his seat, knowing what was to come. Abbu would tell them to concentrate in class. To keep their heads down. To report anything suspicious to teachers. Not to answer back to bullies. To be kind and helpful to all. It was basically a masterclass in how to get your arse kicked in.

Abbu tugged at the handbrake before turning around to face Saahil and Ehsan who were sitting in the back seat. Zahra gurgled away happily in the front.

'We know, Abbu,' said Saahil, before his father was able to speak.

Abbu smiled. 'All I was going to say was that if you see Mr Dixon, pass on my regards.'

Ehsan tried to keep a straight face. He pulled up the collar of his blazer to shield his smirk. Saahil rolled his eyes.

'He won't even remember you, Abbu.'

'Of course he will. We had a brilliant discussion yesterday.'

The school had hosted a 'welcome meeting' for new parents the night before. Ehsan's mum and dad were unable to attend, which meant that Saahil had to endure the whole thing alone with Abbu. They all sat together in the bland school hall, which made Saahil feel like as though he was waiting for assembly to begin. It was even worse. The evening basically consisted of teachers trying their best to convince the new parents that the school wasn't as much of a shit tip as they had heard. They gave one boring presentation after the next and depicted pie charts of progression coupled with empty slogans about 'determination' and 'excellence'. That sort of thing.

'Any questions, please ask!' they shouted in their shrill, over-enthusiastic voices.

A session of mingling occurred, and of course, Abbu headed straight for the principal. Saahil stood around like a spare part, smiling occasionally whenever Abbu motioned towards him proudly. Mr Dixon nodded patiently as Abbu listed off all his concerns. Saahil wasn't really listening, but he heard random snippets of his father's rant about the 'quality of teaching' and 'student behaviour'.

'I mean, how is it going to affect our kids' futures when colleges find out they've been educated in a special measures school?' Abbu had asked. 'And what can *we* as parents do to help?'

Mr Dixon nodded his bald head sympathetically before quietly taking out a piece of paper from his pocket. He made a spectacle of unfolding it and smoothing out the creases.

'Names,' he'd said, before pausing for effect. 'We've only been back at school for a week, and these are the names of nine pupils I just expelled this morning.'

Abbu's eyebrows shot up his forehead. Even Saahil was transfixed.

'They were caught fighting with knives on the premises.'

'Oh.'

'I have experience in this, Mr Sharif, and I run a tight ship. I promise you,' he'd leaned forward dramatically, 'I *will* turn this school around.'

Abbu was sold. Since then, he'd not stopped talking about his discussion with the glorious new head teacher. He beamed as he unlocked the car doors, looking more relaxed than Saahil had seen him in a while, and motioned for him and Ehsan to get out.

'Bye, Zee,' said Saahil, reaching into the passenger seat and squeezing Zahra's plump little hand.

Once Abbu was out of earshot, Ehsan turned to Saahil. 'If you see Dixon, don't pass on your dad's regards unless you're alone and there's no one else around who can hear you.'

'Yeah, I know, I'm not stupid,' Saahil sulked. 'Dixon probably won't even remember him. How many parents did he meet yesterday?'

'Everyone's getting carried away,' Ehsan began, swinging his rucksack over his back. 'The school's not *thaaat* bad. They're just making it into a big deal.'

They walked past the sixth-form centre, a small one-storey block that was separated from the rest of the school building, and saw a group of older boys smoking outside the entrance. They towered over Saahil and Ehsan and turned to face them as they approached. Saahil immediately noticed the difference in uniform. He and Ehsan were dressed immaculately. They looked like perfect posters boys for the school. Sharp black blazers, crisp white shirts and black and red stripy ties. Judging by Ehsan's lethal side parting, Auntie Meena had even attacked his hair with a wet comb.

None of the older lads were wearing blazers. They wore mismatched black jumpers that were without the school logo. Sleeves were rolled up casually. Some did not wear ties and others had them hanging down by their chests, shirts unbuttoned. The boys slouched against the door of the sixth form and followed Saahil and Ehsan with their eyes.

'You two in Year Seven?' asked one of them through a puff of smoke escaping his mouth.

Saahil nodded.

They all looked at each other and chuckled. Saahil and Ehsan passed them quickly but heard one of the boys drawl, 'Fockin' get smaller and smaller every year, don't they?'

They headed into the tired-looking school block that was almost as drearily decorated as a hospital. It hadn't stepped out of the Seventies with its cream walls, brown furniture and creaky staircases. The boys pounded up to the top floor within seconds and joined the back of the queue for their Maths lesson. Maths first thing on a Tuesday morning wasn't so bad. Partly because it was the subject that Saahil and Ehsan were best at. Not that their new teacher had noticed. Mr Ali would refer them to the correct page of a textbook and spend the rest of the lesson yawning and stretching behind his desk.

According to the seating plan which had been devised a few days earlier, Ehsan was to sit directly in front of Saahil. As expected, Mr Ali gave them a page number and told them to get on with it. He leaned back on his chair and reached out for his telephone. The students nudged each other and waited for the familiar pattern of Mr Ali's morning routine: a phone call to his wife.

'Forgot to ask,' he mumbled as he scratched his protruding belly. 'What you making today?'

A muffled voice spoke at the other end of the phone.

'Oh no, not daal again,' he snapped. 'How about...'

'Aloo gobi, sir?' a boy shouted from the back of the room.

Mr Ali jumped as the class burst into laughter. His face reddened as he slammed down the chunky white receiver and told them all to be quiet. Ehsan swivelled around to face Saahil, grinning. He always did this so that the two of them could work through the sums together.

'This looks like a hard one,' he said, squinting at the fraction.

Saahil had already tackled it. He pushed the book towards his best friend. 'Quick, copy my answer.'

Ehsan did. 'Nice one,' he said.

'What do you think to number two?' Saahil asked, looking up from his workbook. He noticed that Ehsan was distracted.

Following his gaze, Saahil spotted the gaunt, pale figure of Kyle, a boy they knew from primary school. He remembered the time when Kyle had stood almost nose to nose with him and snarled in his face, 'My dad said that your granddads came over here to work in the mills and factories, they came over here to do our dirty work.'

Since the new school was overwhelmingly Asian, Saahil had noticed the same white kids had now lost their bravado. They looked uncomfortable most of the time and were still adjusting to being a minority. Kyle was one of those unlucky ones who had been shunted into the school 'full of Pakis'. He lived in the surrounding council estate and had lost the geographical lottery, just like the rest of them.

'Times have changed, haven't they?' whispered Saahil, noting that Kyle was now the only white boy in the Maths lesson. It just wasn't in his nature to have to pretend not to exist. *That* would still take some getting used to.

'Don't think Kyle will be a problem anymore,' Ehsan muttered. 'What d'ya think?'

Saahil thought back to the few timid white faces he'd encountered over the past week. 'Don't think any of them will be.'

From the corner of his eye, he saw Mr Ali stand up lazily and reach for his red pen. The marking ritual was about to begin. Their teacher would make his way around the class, hovering over each pupil like a big bug, his insect-like tentacles jabbing ticks and crosses against each student's work.

'Shit,' Ehsan said. 'We're only on question two!'

Mr Ali spotted him. 'Oi, turn around and face the front. I won't tell you again!' he yelled, sending Ehsan swivelling back round to his own desk.

When Saahil hurried out of the classroom door, Ehsan was already waiting for him. They sprinted down three flights of stairs and out of the school building. The boys headed for the main gate with the rest of the crowd, expecting Abbu's car to have already arrived promptly at 2.55 p.m. This time though, it wasn't there. The boys hung around for an extra fifteen minutes, growing restless as cars came and students disappeared into them.

'Could have walked and been home by now,' Ehsan sulked. No sooner had the words escaped his lips than Uncle Harun's silver Toyota Corolla screeched to a halt in front of them.

'Hurry up,' he shouted, as Saahil and Ehsan scrambled into the car as quickly as they could. 'I have another school run scheduled in ten minutes.'

The boys belted up as Harun set off in haste. He didn't get very far. The taxi joined the nicely forming queue of cars that were inching their way out of the road. He sighed and dropped his shoulders.

'That's me late for Thomas,' he said, referring to the school boy he was contracted to pick up and drop off home every day.

'Where's my Abbu?' asked Saahil.

'Held up. Your sister had a… ahem… accident in the car seat just as he was about to set off for you both.'

'Well, I don't know why you don't just let us walk home,' Ehsan began. 'Then none of you would be rushing around like maniacs.'

'You can once you've settled in,' Uncle Harun replied.

'"Settled in?"' Ehsan mouthed to Saahil before shaking his head in disbelief.

Saahil made a face in agreement, and wondered when the fussing over the new school would stop. Uncle Harun raced out of the junction, earning him a few horn blasts from angry drivers.

'Oh, bugger off,' he mumbled.

'Can Saahil come to ours?' Ehsan asked his dad.

'Yes, of course.'

The boys grinned at each other. Within five minutes, they were driving down the familiar sloped street of small semi-detached houses. Some were red-bricked, others were painted white. No autumn colours were present along the road, as all the houses had solid concrete gardens and brightly painted doors, red, green, blue and black. Harun swerved around potholes causing Saahil and Ehsan to bump into each other, laughing. He braked sharply.

'Right, out you get… Quick! Quick!'

The boys scrambled out and Ehsan grabbed the house key from his father's hand.

'Go eat something or… something,' Harun said. 'Yep. Bye.'

He made to pull away before stopping to wind down the window.

'You mum will be home at four o'clock,' he shouted through it.

'Okay,' Saahil and Ehsan said together. Saahil felt stupid immediately. *He* wasn't the one being addressed. It stopped him in his tracks, and he realised how much he missed being told the same thing by Abbu. That his mother would be home soon. Or home waiting for him. Saahil's face reddened with embarrassment and he hoped Ehsan hadn't noticed the mishap.

Uncle Harun set off down the street, disappearing behind the cars that lined the pavement. Saahil looked on as Ehsan pretended to be really interested in watching the taxi reach the end of the road. A few seconds passed by before he turned to Saahil.

'Are you okay?' he asked, quietly.

'Yeah… fine.'

Ehsan nodded enthusiastically without making eye contact.

'Let's go attack the biscuit drawer then,' he said, throwing his arm around Saahil.

They set off together towards the red-bricked house, crossing through the wobbly fence that was missing a gate. Ehsan entered the key into the emerald green door and turned the lock. They bustled inside, Saahil's eyes still adjusting to the newly decorated living room. Despite the pastel blue that tinged the room, there were contrasting patterns everywhere. Auntie Meena had gone to much effort to pick out the flowery wallpaper, the navy frilly curtains, the cornflower blue striped carpet and the paisley patterned settees. Saahil and Ehsan threw their bags and coats on to a heap in the middle of the floor. Without taking off their shoes, the boys headed straight for the kitchen through a sliding pine door.

The decor calmed down slightly in the kitchen which was mostly white and beige, but Saahil spotted some ivy stencilling on the tiles around the windows.

'Did Auntie do this?' he asked, running his fingers over it.

Ehsan nodded.

Saahil watched as his friend filled the kettle with some water. He stood on his tiptoes and arranged two mugs on the worktop. After adding teabags, he waited patiently with his arms folded as the water began to boil. He reached for the sugar canister and added generous teaspoons into each cup, spilling the tiny white particles all over the beige kitchen worktop.

'Oops,' he said, with a giggle.

Saahil busied himself with rummaging through the large biscuit tin. He pushed aside cream crackers and chocolate chip cookies until he found what he was looking for – a packet of Fox's Sports shortbread biscuits. Ehsan grinned with delight and carried both cups of tea into the living room. They sat down on the settee with a thud and set the tea on the table. Ehsan tore the packet of biscuits open too eagerly causing a wonky tear down the middle. Some fell out on to the table. Saahil picked one up.

'Hockey player,' he said, studying the stick man carved on to the top of the biscuit.

'Oh, I've already eaten mine,' Ehsan said, his mouth full.

Saahil pulled his tea closer towards himself. It wasn't for

drinking. Its only purpose was for dunking in the biscuits. Two at a time.

Ehsan flicked through the telly and found *Arthur,* a new cartoon programme about a human-like aardvark and his antics with his family and friends. They knew full well that they were too old for it, but watched it anyway.

'Don't tell anyone we still watch this,' Saahil reminded Ehsan.

'I know.'

Fifteen minutes later, their episode of *Arthur* finished. Ehsan's eyes were still glued to the TV as he absentmindedly reached inside the wrapper for another biscuit. He found nothing. They'd demolished them all. He flicked it away impatiently and drummed his fingers against the pine coffee table.

'What?' Saahil asked, but he already knew what his best friend was thinking.

'Shall I check to see if we've got those orange-flavoured custard creams?'

'Yeah!'

Ehsan hurried to the kitchen as the phone rang.

'Grab the phone,' he shouted back to Saahil. Saahil answered it, as he had done many times before, to find Auntie Meena's worried voice at the end of it.

'Are you okay, beta?'

'Yeah, Auntie, I'm fine.'

'Can you tell your uncle that I'm going to be home late?'

'I will—'

'Have you eaten?' Meena interrupted. She didn't wait for an answer. 'There's some leftovers in the fridge if you're hungry. Or you can make some toast. Or a sandwich.'

Saahil felt Meena's warmth envelop him through the telephone.

He smiled as he listened to her fussing over them. Although she reminded him of his own mother, Saahil couldn't help but notice the differences between the two women. Unlike Auntie Meena, Saahil's mum had been from Pakistan. She had mostly worn salwar kameez, didn't work or drive, and spoke English with an accent. Meena, on the other hand, sounded like one of his schoolteachers. She had a job as a receptionist, had her own car and wore English clothes. When his mum was alive, Saahil had often wished she could be more like Auntie Meena. He'd wished she could drive him to McDonald's when Abbu wasn't there, or swing her handbag over her shoulder and twirl her car keys around her fingers as confidently as Meena did. But Saahil remembered his mother always shrugging off Abbu's suggestions of driving lessons.

'She lacks confidence,' Abbu would say to him later.

Saahil didn't really understand what that meant at the time, but he had seen the same reluctance in Uncle Harun sometimes, who was also from Pakistan. The same hesitation in doing things that neither Abbu nor Meena possessed.

'Don't worry, Auntie, we've already eaten,' Saahil reassured.

He turned and winked at Ehsan.

'Oh good,' Meena said. 'Well, I'll see you soon.'

As Saahil replaced the receiver, there was a soft thudding on the front door. Ehsan had just shoved two orange creams into his mouth and motioned for Saahil to get it. Saahil fiddled with the key before swinging it open. He looked down to find a pint-sized visitor.

'Zee!'

Zahra stood by the door clutching Nelly the Elephant, her favourite cuddly toy. She rushed forward to get inside. Saahil

36

helped her up the step and smoothed down her baby blue frock as she hurried past him. Abbu and Uncle Harun were wandering down the garden, chatting.

'Come on,' Abbu said, beckoning Saahil out of the house.

'Oh no, you're coming in for chai,' Harun said, pulling Abbu by the arm.

'We'd best get going—'

'No, no, you're coming in for tea.'

'Ehsan, quick!' whispered Saahil, turning to his best friend. Ehsan, however, had already picked the bags and coats up from the floor and tidied away the biscuit crumbs.

'You better have loose tea leaves,' Abbu said, closing the door behind him.

'Shut up, you'll get what you're given,' Harun retaliated.

Abbu laughed and slapped his friend on the back. Zahra had already headed for the toy box that was hidden at the side of one of the settees. She almost knocked over the floor lamp as she pulled out a tub of plasticine. She nudged Saahil to open it for her.

'Have you both eaten?' Harun asked them.

'Yeah, we're full,' said Ehsan, hiding the empty biscuit wrappers behind his back.

Abbu followed Uncle Harun into the kitchen.

'Semi-skimmed milk!' Saahil heard Abbu say. He could see his father's backside sticking up in the air as he bent down to inspect the fridge. 'Haven't you got whole?'

'God, you're turning into your mother,' Harun replied.

Saahil leaned into Ehsan. 'If they ask,' he said, 'school was absolutely fine.'

Ehsan nodded before a ferocious knocking made them both jump. Ehsan scowled. 'Who is it now?' he said, before heading for the door. He swung it open. Saahil recognised the man as one of the dodgy neighbours. He often saw him racing up and down the road in growling sports cars.

'Yo, is your dad in?' the neighbour drawled, twirling his gold neck chains around in his fingers.

'Yeah, I'll just go and get him…' Ehsan said, before raising his voice. 'Abbu, Uncle Naveed is here!'

The man at the door grimaced, flipping his cap on front to back. 'Don't call me "uncle" dude, call me Nav,' he muttered, smoothing down his bomber jacket.

Harun greeted Naveed at the door in Urdu. Naveed replied in English.

'Check out my new motor, bro!' he said, waving his arms around in wild hip hop gestures.

'Very nice, Masha'Allah,' Uncle Harun said.

Abbu slid the kitchen door to a close and joined them. He craned his neck to see what all the fuss was about. Saahil watched as his father's eyes widened at the sight of the car.

'Come, come,' Naveed said, practically pulling both the men out of the house. They all walked to the end of the garden. Naveed jumped into his car and revved the engine.

'Vroom vroom, bro!'

'It's ugly,' Saahil whispered to Ehsan, as they both looked at the monstrous red car parked outside the house. Ehsan nodded in agreement.

'Check out the spoiler,' Naveed said, caressing it with his fingers. Abbu and Uncle Harun were offering their own expert opinions. They inspected the alloys, they lifted the bonnet.

'Come for a quick spin, yaar!'

'No, no,' Abbu said. 'The kids are on their own.'

'Oh, don't be boring,' Naveed shouted, slapping Abbu on the shoulder.

Abbu scratched his head before looking back towards the house. 'You go,' he said to Harun. 'I'll watch the kids.'

Uncle Harun squinted at Saahil and Ehsan as they stood in the doorway. 'They'll be fine – we won't be long.'

'No, I need to watch Zahra.'

'I'll whizz you around in two minutes, brother!'

'Yeah, come on,' Harun said. 'What's wrong with having a bit of fun once in a while?'

Abbu hesitated but Harun nodded encouragingly once more. Saahil saw all three heads nod in agreement. Abbu jogged back to the house.

'Saahil, watch Zahra.'

'Where are you going?'

'Just for a quick drive.'

'How long are you gonna be?'

'Watch Zee, okay?'

Saahil groaned. 'Fine,' he sulked. Watching Zahra was getting to be a full-time job.

They looked on as both their dads got into the car like excited teenagers and sped off with an ear-splitting roar of the engine.

Ehsan turned to Saahil. 'We've got five minutes. Shall we go and blast some music?'

'Yeah,' replied Saahil, struggling to shake off his annoyance.

Ehsan walked towards Zahra with his arms splayed open. She was sitting on the carpet, lost in her own world, mixing red clay with green, blue with yellow.

'Leave her,' Saahil snapped. 'She's playing.'

Ehsan turned to him and frowned. 'We can't leave her down here on her own.'

'She'll be fine.'

Ehsan shook his head and tried to pry the plasticine from Zahra's little fingers. She ignored him, her small face screwed up in concentration. Ehsan held her gently by her arms but she resisted.

'Don't, she'll start crying. She wants to play here,' Saahil said again. He was already halfway up the stairs.

Reluctantly, with one glance back at Zahra, Ehsan followed. They ran upstairs and went straight to Uncle Harun's room. That was where the cassette player was kept. The room was cluttered, with Auntie Meena's shoe boxes piled up against the wall. Saahil knew that only one humble drawer belonged to Harun. They laughed about it often. Ehsan busied himself with finding the cassette player whilst Saahil pulled out the stool from the dressing table. Auntie Meena's make-up was arranged methodically in colour order.

'Found it,' Ehsan said. He placed the stereo on the bed and turned the volume to max.

'I used it last,' he reassured. He pressed the play button with attitude expecting Public Enemy to blast from the player. Instead, a cheesy Bollywood love song blared from the speakers. Ehsan blocked his ears, looking mortified.

'What the heck is this?' he shouted.

Saahil laughed his head off and began acting out the melo-dramatic dance moves he'd seen in countless Bollywood movies. Ehsan guffawed but an almighty bang made them jump. Ehsan quickly stopped the music. They listened intently, ears pricked up. Another clang and the pair of them sped to the top of the stairs. The front door was open and swaying in the wind.

'Didn't you close it?' Ehsan asked, whilst running down the steps.

'I did... I thought I did.'

Saahil glanced into the living room to check on Zahra. The plasticine lay abandoned on the floor and she was nowhere to be seen. He decided to go into the kitchen to look for her, but a sound stopped him in his tracks.

'Saahil!'

Ehsan's cry sent shivers up Saahil's spine. He ran to the door and his eyes focused on a bounce of black curls and a frilly blue dress. A giggle escaped Zahra's lips as she stood waving at them from the middle of the road. An engine roared and the car carrying Abbu and Uncle Harun hurtled down the hill towards her.

Five

Saahil thought he'd never seen his Abbu like this before. He watched as his father clung on to Zahra as if his life depended on it, his eyes bloodshot and staring ahead. Zahra sucked her thumb and blinked obliviously, her head resting against Abbu's chest. She was wrapped up in the shawl that had once belonged to Saahil's mother. Abbu's fingers tightened around Zahra as she snuggled closer to him, her little fist crumpling the fabric as she buried her face in the shawl's silkiness.

At first Saahil thought he'd never seen his father *this* worried, this helpless. But he had. Nearly two years ago, on the night after his mother's burial, Saahil remembered waking up, tiptoeing to his father's room, and finding Abbu rocking back and forth with Zahra in his arms. Only this time, Zahra had grown and both her legs dangled either side of Abbu. This time, Saahil was to blame.

Two other people were also present in this nightmare. Uncle Harun paced his living room. Ehsan's leg was pressed against Saahil's. They were sitting together on the sofa, arms folded, unable to meet anyone's gaze. Not even each other's.

The commotion that had taken place just a few moments before had calmed down now, but Saahil would still be remembering the almighty screech of the car brakes for days after. The vehicle's heavy doors were thrown open. Uncle Harun had got to Zahra first and scooped her up in his arms. Abbu checked her over quickly, repeating her name over and over again. Even Naveed stood frozen to the spot, his hands covering his mouth in shock. Then, all three heads had turned to face Saahil and Ehsan who were standing by the door.

Uncle Harun had charged towards them, roughly shoving them back into the lounge. He slammed the door shut in Naveed's face.

'What were you doing?' he shouted. 'How did she get out of the house?'

The boys bumbled their way through the questions, each forced to make up different excuses.

'Where were you?'

'Upstairs,' Ehsan said.

'No, we went into the kitchen,' Saahil lied.

'Why was the door unlocked?'

'I thought I'd shut it.'

'Didn't you hear her?' Harun yelled.

'We had music on,' Ehsan cried.

'No, we didn't,' Saahil retaliated, angry with Ehsan for always having to be truthful.

The scolding continued for at least twenty minutes. Saahil kept throwing glances at Abbu, who was surprisingly quiet. He had just sat down on the settee, hugging Zahra tight. Ehsan squeezed Saahil's arm. They huddled together, eyes cast downwards.

'None of your stories match up,' Harun said, shaking his head in disbelief. 'That means you deliberately left your sister downstairs alone.'

Ehsan began sobbing. Saahil felt bad for not being able to comfort him. None of this was his fault. Uncle Harun started pacing again. Zahra had fallen asleep in Abbu's arms.

'It's my fault, Amjad,' Harun finally said. 'I told you to come with me and Naveed. One of us should have stayed behind.'

Slowly, Abbu shook his head. 'It's no one's fault but mine. She's my daughter. I'm responsible for her.'

'But you're at my house,' Harun insisted. 'And anyway, she's like my daughter too.'

'No, I shouldn't have come. Sometimes I forget...' Abbu's voice trailed off as he glanced at the boys. 'I rely too much on Saahil to keep an eye on her when I have jobs to do. But this wasn't a job, this was just... me being silly.'

'Amjad—'

'No, it's true.'

Saahil felt a lump rise in his throat. He tried to remember the last time he had seen his Abbu do something carefree and fun. Even if it had just been taking a ride in a fancy car. Saahil couldn't. And now because of him, Abbu felt like he was being punished for not being a perfect dad for just five minutes.

'I'm sorry,' Saahil managed to utter, his voice croaky. He felt all eyes shift towards him.

Uncle Harun sighed. He motioned for Saahil and Ehsan to make some space and sat down between them.

'Just be more careful next time,' he said, placing his arms around their shoulders. Ehsan leaned into his father. Saahil did the same but glanced again at his own dad. Abbu had stood up, placing Zahra over his shoulder. Her body was limp. She was sleeping, but Saahil dreaded to think what might have been because of his stupidity. Abbu rearranged a cushion and lay Zahra down on the settee.

'Shall we not tell Meena about this?' Uncle Harun asked, sheepishly. 'She'll bloody kill me.'

Amjad nodded. 'Don't tell Ammi either.'

'Okay.'

They remained silent for a few more minutes. Harun slapped his hands together and forced a smile. 'Now, where were we?'

'Tea,' Abbu sighed. They went off together into the kitchen. Saahil and Ehsan waited for them to go before rushing to sit by Zahra's side. She was in a deep sleep, her chest rising and falling. Saahil reached out and stroked Zahra's cheek.

Two weeks later, Saahil and Ehsan arrived at school on Monday morning. As they walked through the playground, they noticed the change in atmosphere. Everyone was making their way to lesson promptly. Heads were down. No slouching. No mismatched uniform. Police were still walking around the premises.

For the past week, a group of Year Eleven boys had run riot regularly throughout the building, setting off fire alarms and causing the entire school to evacuate. Fifteen minutes later, as the students were back and settled into class, another fire alarm would cause them to evacuate again. This happened no less than five times. Teachers despaired as they tried to catch the culprits. Pupils rejoiced with each sounding alarm, hoping the heroes who had disrupted their lessons weren't caught.

But last week things had gone too far. During a particularly dull English lesson, the fire alarm had blasted in their ears once again. This time, though, it was no fake. A letter was sent to parents explaining what had happened. As expected, Abbu hit the roof. Saahil had listened to his frantic phone call to Uncle Harun.

'This is outrageous!' he shouted. 'They set the head teacher's car on fire.'

'Little bastards,' Uncle Harun replied.

Saahil clearly remembered making his way towards the fire exit on that day. The heat radiated through the window; he could feel it before he saw it. The flames had engulfed an object in the distance and teachers were circling the staff car park in a protective barrier. One of the vehicles was on fire. It was parked away from everyone else's cars, in a specially designated spot.

'Is that…' Saahil had whispered to Ehsan.

'Yeah, Dixon's,' he confirmed.

They'd spotted their principal being comforted by the assistant head teacher. She had her hand on his shoulder. His fingers were pinching between his eyes, against the bridge of his nose.

When Abbu had put the phone down to Uncle Harun, Saahil only made matters worse.

'Chill out, Abbu,' he'd said.

'*Chill?*' Abbu's voice grew high-pitched.

'Yeah. They set the *car* on fire. Not the head teacher.'

Unfortunately, these words provided little consolation to Abbu. Saahil couldn't understand why. He realised it was best to avoid the conversation at all costs. But Abbu wasn't going to forget this in a hurry. And neither was the school.

Three lads from Year Eleven were eventually caught and expelled. The police were also involved, but it was far from over. Saahil's teachers wore permanent frowns throughout the rest of the week. Ofsted was being mentioned in worried undertones. For the first time ever, even the senior students were hesitant to put a toe out of line.

This morning, though, something was different. Saahil noticed that the teachers were standing in corridors and leaving their lessons unsupervised. They talked away in urgent whispers. Saahil and Ehsan walked past their young English teacher, who was sobbing outside her classroom door and being comforted by others.

'Who died?' Saahil asked Ehsan, who snorted in response.

The boys entered their Maths class and sat down in their seats. Ehsan swivelled around again to face him as Mr Ali called his wife. He was covering his mouth and talking in a low voice. Saahil guessed that this time, the topic of conversation wasn't daal. He nudged Adam, the lad sitting next to him.

'What's going on?' Saahil asked. 'Everyone looks really worried.'

'Haven't you heard?'

'Heard what?'

'We're stuffed, that's what,' Adam replied.

'Why?'

'Well, put it this way, Mr Dixon isn't going to be turning our school around any time soon… He resigned this morning.'

Six

Amjad should have known that it was his brother ringing him at eight o'clock in the morning. The ringtone felt sharper, louder and even more headache-inducing than normal. Not unlike Javid himself. Amjad narrowed his eyes as he went to pick it up, gearing up to give the caller a telling off for ringing so early. He never got the chance as Javid's booming voice filled his ears.

'It's a bit early—' Amjad began, but as usual, Javid talked over him.

'So, you're coming over to ours for Eid then, yeah?'

Amjad wasn't trying to be awkward, but that did not sound like much of an invitation. He quickly glanced at this year's fasting schedule. There were only a couple of days left to Ramadan.

'Well, are you inviting me? I'm not just going to turn up, am I?'

Javid let out an exaggerated laugh. Amjad held the phone an inch away from his ear so not to burst his eardrums.

'Of course I'm inviting you,' Javid said. 'Who else is going to drive Ammi down?'

Amjad bit his tongue and decided not to respond. He hadn't spoken to his brother in over a month. He didn't want to be the one to start an argument, no matter how much Javid rattled him.

'I mean, we'd come over to your house,' Javid continued. 'But there's barely any space for us all to fit.'

48

'Well, you shouldn't have had so many kids then,' Amjad retorted, thinking of the five spoilt brats Javid and his wife had produced.

Javid roared with laughter again. Amjad could almost feel the spit flying from his brother's mouth and spraying all over him.

As soon as he'd put the phone down, Amjad began plotting ways to get out of it. Spending Eid with his brother was his worst nightmare. Eid in the gloomy month of February would be a miserable affair anyway, but *this* Eid marked the end of Ramadan, which did deserve a bit of a celebration. He would have to put up with Javid flouncing around in his fancy new four-bedroomed detached. The last thing Amjad wanted to do was listen to his brother bragging about his kids and his wife and the council job he'd only managed to get because he had a friend on the inside.

After he'd finished the school run and returned home, Amjad rang Ammi to see if he could talk her out of going.

'Javid invited us over for Eid,' he mentioned, as casually as he could.

'Yes, lovely,' Ammi replied.

Amjad let out a silent groan. He could almost hear the beam on her face. She had a much more favourable opinion of Javid than he did, but that was largely because she'd given birth to him and was programmed to love him regardless. Still, Amjad thought he'd give it his best shot.

'I thought we were going to have a quiet Eid,' he began, feeling incredibly stupid for even saying that. Eid was never quiet. 'And your knee has been playing up, it'll get really stiff if we're driving all the way to Birmingham. It's a two and a half hour drive.'

'You don't want to go, do you?' Ammi said, in her quiet, lethal voice.

'No... I never said that. I'm just thinking of you.'

'Well, whether you want to go or not, you're not getting out of it this time.'

Amjad sighed. How could his mother see right through him? It was decided then, or rather, decided *for* him. Eid would be at Javid's house, and Amjad could hardly wait.

He sat down with a cuppa and thought about how Eid used to be with Neelam. The preparation would start weeks before with her choosing outfits for them all. She would show the new clothes excitedly to Amjad. Three sets of salwar kameez: a boring white/grey/brown one for him, a small one for Saahil with fancy buttons and collars. And, the most important of all, a sparkly, colourful one for her that was bang on trend for ladies' fashion. Amjad would always feign interest and nod along encouragingly, before going back to reading his newspaper.

On the day, Amjad would wake up early whilst Neelam and Saahil slept. His salwar kameez was always ironed and laid out on the bed. So was his leather waistcoat, which only made 'special occasion' trips out of the wardrobe. His wife would have everything ready for him when he woke up for Eid prayers.

His return from the mosque was always his favourite part of the day. He'd walk in through the door and be greeted by Saahil, who'd come bounding into his arms. His little boy would be ready with his new clothes and slicked back hair. Neelam would already be cooking in the kitchen. Kebabs, samosas, lamb biryani. There would be mouth-watering smells of cumin, coriander, ginger and garlic and the sounds of bubbling and frying. The heat would be intense. Neelam would still be wearing her old clothes for now, a plain salwar kameez with the scarf draped over her body like a sash and tied in a knot near her hip. Amjad would embrace his wife and greet her.

'Eid Mubarak,' she'd whisper back in his ear.

Since her death, Amjad had lost interest in Eid. But the clothes shopping was now his responsibility. He would usually make one stop at the first kids' store he set eyes on. He would pick a frock for Zahra without putting too much thought into it. She was a beautiful little girl, no matter what she wore, and a healthy thirty-seven inches. The growth chart inked into the kitchen door was coming on nicely. They'd made a new marking only a couple of days ago on her birthday:

Zahra, 3 yrs, 20/02/96

At a solid sixty-one inches, Saahil was old enough to choose what he wanted to wear. New jeans, new shirt. Amjad paid for whatever he wanted, within reason. His and Ehsan's measurements were also creeping higher on the growth chart; last year's markings were noted with a brand-new blue felt-tip pen:

Saahil, 13 yrs, 14/09/95

Ehsan, 13 yrs, 01/12/95

Much to his disgust, Ehsan was lagging behind at an unsatisfactory fifty-nine inches.

Amjad hadn't bought a new outfit for himself since Neelam died but if he was to spend it with Javid this time, he would have no choice but to make an effort. He could feel his stress levels rising as the shopping trip drew nearer.

Saahil looked bemused when Amjad told him that they wouldn't be going into town, but were heading for the big shopping centre in Leeds.

'Pushing the boat out, Abbu,' Saahil mocked.

'Well, I don't want you looking less polished than your cousins,' Amjad replied.

They arrived in Leeds after a twenty-minute drive and parked in the shopping centre car park. Saahil began tugging at Amjad's sleeve as soon as they walked out of the lift and into the mall. 'There are these new trainers—'

'Nope, you're wearing smart shoes this time.'

'Smart? Why?'

'I want you to buy a suit,' Amjad said.

'A what?!'

'Come along.'

They ventured into a department store. It wasn't exactly Amjad's usual shopping spot.

'Don't knock anything over, Saahil,' Amjad said as they hurried past the perfume and make-up stands. There were women everywhere testing lipsticks and pouting in mirrors and sniffing perfume samples. Amjad searched for the escalator.

Once they got to the kids' section, Amjad decided to tackle Saahil first.

He refused point-blank to wear a suit jacket.

'Why don't I just wear my bloody school uniform instead?' he sulked as he trailed behind Amjad towards the 'Boys 11 to 16' division.

'I bet Zakariya will be wearing a suit,' Amjad said, referring to Javid's eldest child. He was thirteen, the same age as Saahil.

'Yeah, well Zakariya is a geek.'

After some more bickering, they opted for a navy three-piece set: shirt, waistcoat and a little bow tie.

'It's quite expensive, Abbu,' said Saahil, twirling the price tag in his hands.

'It doesn't matter, it's a one-off,' Amjad said, settling Zahra down on the cushioned seating area. 'Now, watch Zee whilst I go and find a frilly dress.'

Saahil suppressed a grin as Amjad stomped off towards the 'Girls 2 to 4' section. He was the only man in the sea of women. They looked relaxed and leisurely. Amjad looked focused and a little bit grumpy. He came back with a handful of items, puffing and out of breath.

'Which one?' he asked, wiping sweat from his brow.

'This one.' Saahil pointed at a blue dress decorated with golden stars.

'No, I want something more… princessy,' Amjad said, not quite believing he had just uttered those words. An elegant mother wheeling a pram past gave him a funny look.

'What about this puffball thingy?' whispered Saahil.

'What puffball?'

'This skirt thing that's sticking out.'

'Nah, don't like it.'

'Are we going for pink?' Saahil asked, in a business-like fashion.

'Yep,' Amjad replied. 'Pink, glitter, that sort of thing.'

Saahil turned to Zahra, who was looking at them both, bewildered.

'Zee, which one do you like?'

She shuffled forward on the seat, Nelly the Elephant tucked under her armpit. Amjad showed her each frock in turn, but nothing elicited a response from her. He shuffled from one foot to the other.

'Gosh, this is hard work,' he sighed.

'Pick one, Zahra,' Saahil groaned.

Her little fingers reached out and pointed to a silvery lilac dress that was embellished with sequins, a sparkly waist belt and a beautiful mesh skirt. Amjad swivelled it around to face him. He had a good look.

'This is perfect,' he said, smiling. 'Well done, Zee. We need matching shoes now.'

Saahil returned with a few suitable pairs for Zahra to try on. Amjad sat down on the seat beside her and held up her leg, his big fist almost completely covering it.

'Maybe a lovely headband too,' suggested Saahil, holding up a series of sequined bows, ribbons and flowered accessories. He placed them next to Amjad and zoomed off again around the shop floor. Zahra began fidgeting as Amjad tried to put the shoe on her.

'No, Zee. Be a good girl.'

He adjusted in his seat and heard something pop. A sharp object pierced his bottom.

'Ouch!' Amjad jumped up to find that he had snapped one of the headbands in half. Zahra jumped off the seat giggling and ran off around the corner barefoot. She disappeared behind a rack of babygros.

'Abbu, what have you done?' Saahil asked, as he inspected the broken headband.

'Go and get your sister and let's get out of here,' Amjad sighed. 'I think that's enough shopping for one day.'

Saahil did as he was told. Amjad scooped up the sparkly shoes and gathered together the unwanted dresses. He didn't want the shop assistants to think that they were messy buggers. In the distance, he heard Zahra starting to wail.

'Abbu, help!' Saahil shouted. 'She's having a tantrum.'

Amjad peered around the corner and saw Zahra lying on her back, kicking her arms and legs. He hurried over to assist his children, wishing Eid would hurry up and be over with.

*

When Saahil woke up on Eid morning, he grudgingly put on his waistcoat and silly bow tie. He resented having to wear stupid clothes and drive down to Birmingham to see cousins he didn't really like. But when he spotted Abbu's face at the breakfast table, he immediately forgot about his own little demonstration. He couldn't decide who looked more miserable and realised he had to be on his best behaviour.

They attended Eid prayers together. Saahil spotted Ehsan and Uncle Harun briefly at the mosque and ran over to them.

'We're rushing Harun, sorry,' Abbu said. 'Have to set off for my brother's as soon as we get back.'

'Wish me luck,' Saahil said to Ehsan as he was dragged away from his best friend.

Zahra began wailing almost as soon as they set off down the road. She scrunched up the mesh skirt of her dress and pulled at the neckline of her glittered bodice.

'Where's her blanket?' Abbu roared. 'You were holding it last, Ammi.'

'Excuse me, I gave it to Saahil.'

'No, you didn't, Ammi.'

Everyone continued bickering about the so-called 'blanket', which was actually the yellow pashmina. In recent years, Zahra had now christened it 'birdie blanket,' which annoyed Saahil a little. It was his mum's shawl, not a bloody bed sheet.

'Great,' Abbu sighed. 'She'll never settle now.'

He glanced back at Saahil. 'I don't understand, she picked that dress herself,' he added, as though Zahra was a twenty-year-old woman, not a three-year-old toddler.

'Maybe it's itching her,' Ammi said, sitting grandly in the front seat.

Saahil tried to attend to his little sister. She pulled off the flowery headband she was wearing and threw it on the floor.

'I hope she doesn't cry all day,' Abbu sighed. He turned to Saahil. 'And *you*, don't show me up in front of your uncle.'

'I won't.'

'Give salaam properly to him and—'

'Properly? How do you give salaam properly?' Saahil mocked. 'You just say this, "Salaam".'

'Don't you get clever with me!'

'Concentrate on the road,' Ammi screeched.

Saahil felt slightly guilty for giving Abbu attitude. He watched as his father sulked and drove them towards the motorway. He looked smarter than Saahil had ever seen him. Instead of wearing a boring white salwar kameez, Abbu had opted for a dark grey. The leather waistcoat had taken another trip out of the wardrobe and Abbu had finished off the look with a black topi.

'Too much?' he'd asked Saahil when he'd tried it on in the morning. 'It was one of my dad's fancier hats.'

Saahil liked the way Abbu's finger caressed the geometric patterns and small shards of mirror that had been intricately sown on to it. It was circular in shape apart from the arch-shaped cut-out which exposed the forehead.

'It's wicked, Abbu,' said Saahil.

'Good. And it will annoy Javid when he sees that I'm wearing one of our father's hats.'

Ammi's snores started piercing the air around halfway through the journey. Abbu tutted and turned off the radio. Saahil and Zahra giggled in the back but subsided after a stern look from Abbu. Slowly, a slumbering Ammi began slipping closer and closer to the edge of the seat. Abbu was too busy concentrating on the road to notice. Her head thumped against his shoulder making him jump and swerve. A car horn honked and Ammi jerked awake.

'My knee,' she complained instantly.

Saahil saw Abbu catch the words before they came tumbling out of his mouth. He cleared his throat and opted for a more polite way of putting it.

'Well, this is why I was worrying about driving all the way down here. But you insisted we came.'

'Not to worry,' Ammi said, adjusting in her seat. 'I can stretch.'

With incredible flexibility, Ammi stretched out her leg and placed her bare foot on the dashboard. She cracked her toes with satisfaction.

'Ammi, no,' pleaded Abbu. 'Not on the dashboard. Everyone can see your foot. We'll pull up next to people and they'll—'

'They'll what?' Ammi asked, without a care in the world. 'Keep driving and stop moaning.'

Saahil craned his neck to catch sight of the offending foot, but Zahra threw Nelly the Elephant at his face. He threw it back and it landed on the floor. Zahra began crying.

'Abbu,' Saahil shouted over her. 'Are we nearly there yet?'

All Saahil had heard about for the past couple of weeks was Uncle Javid and his new four-bedroom detached house. He was half expecting a palace to pop up when they turned around the corner and parked up in a vacant space. Saahil noticed that there was a driveway next to an immaculate patch of grass. Two cars were parked there. Saahil could imagine himself and Ehsan running around outside on the tarmac and Zahra sitting on the grass with all her toys. Maybe Abbu would lounge on a garden chair, reading a newspaper and drinking tea.

Uncle Javid must have heard their roaring engine. He walked out of the door and stood with his arms wide open.

'Welcome!' he shouted expansively.

Javid rushed forward to assist Ammi as she got out of the car seat. Saahil glanced at the doorway and saw Auntie Farhana. She was still wearing plain clothes with a pinny tied around her waist and huddled behind her were Saahil's cousins, all five of them. Saahil felt a pang in his chest. He noted all the small hands gripping her legs and hips as Farhana reached down and picked up Aleena, who was the same age as Zahra. He turned to look at his own sister, who was sitting quietly and waiting for Abbu to unbuckle her from the booster seat.

'Amjad!' Uncle Javid boomed. It was more like a chest bump than a hug as both men squared up to each other. Saahil wasn't being biased, but he definitely thought his Abbu looked way smarter. Uncle Javid looked bland in his black trousers and white shirt.

Once inside, everyone hugged, kissed and greeted each other 'Eid Mubarak'. It was only when Saahil pulled back did he take into account the lavishly decorated living room. If he thought Auntie Meena had gone overboard with the contrasting patterns, she had nothing on Uncle Javid. At least Meena had stuck to one colour theme. Here, there were maroon frills, navy stripes and purple florals.

Uncle Javid beamed as he stood centre stage.

'Masha'Allah, the house is lovely,' Abbu said, though Saahil could sense a sarky undertone.

Ammi was fussing over all her grandchildren. They practically stood in a line, from big to small, in front of her so she could inspect them. The two girls, Aleena and Humaira, were dressed like small Christmas trees, a green one and a red one. They wore bindis on their foreheads, and struggled to keep the flowing chiffon scarves in place, fidgeting on the spot and constantly readjusting. The outfits were adorned with sequins and embroidery that looked almost painful. Saahil imagined that if he passed his hands over the fabric, he would probably need a few plasters to cover up the cuts on his fingers.

The boys were not as bad. They wore traditional salwar kameez and sparkly waistcoats, leaving Saahil a new-found sense of appreciation for his checked shirt and bow tie.

After the initial niceties, everyone parted off into their own little groups. Aleena and Humaira zoned in on Zahra, who was clutching on to Nelly the Elephant and eyeing the two girls suspiciously. Saahil kept one eye on her and one on the two boys stood in front of him.

'How's it going, Zakariya?' Saahil asked, leaning into his cousin.

Zakariya grimaced. 'It's Zak, actually,' he replied in a posh accent.

It was going to be a long day.

Ammi had charged into the kitchen to inspect Auntie Farhana's cooking. Saahil could see Ammi stirring a pot here and clanging a pan there. She tasted some curry and frowned. He could see Farhana waiting with bated breath. Ammi wore a disapproving expression and made a gesture with her hands.

'More salt, it doesn't taste of anything,' she ordered.

Farhana looked deflated and hurried for the condiment drawer.

'Why don't you go and sit down?' she said as she returned. 'You'll be tired…'

'Where's the rice? And have you started frying the kebabs yet?'

Ammi turned away to nosy at the worktops. Saahil watched as Auntie Farhana took a deep breath and followed her mother-in-law with resolve.

Abbu and Uncle Javid were still arguing about which route he took to get there. 'You see, if you'd turned off at Junction 24—' Javid said.

'But that's the long way around.'

'No, no,' Javid replied, wagging his finger. 'There's a shortcut—'

'Well, I'm not familiar with those roads.'

'If only you'd called me before you set off—'

'Look, I got us here, didn't I?' Abbu said. 'Now put a sock in it.'

An hour later, Abbu tapped his stomach. 'Any chance of food, Farhana?' he said, smiling. She was probably his favourite member of the family. Quiet, humble and the complete opposite to Javid.

'Almost ready,' she replied. 'I probably would have been done half an hour ago but...' She motioned towards Ammi with her eyes who was dicing cucumber and tomatoes into small pieces and mixing them into a large bowl of natural yoghurt.

'Are you sure I can't help with anything?' Abbu said. 'Ammi, why don't I do that?'

'No,' she snapped. 'You cut them up into clumsy-sized pieces.'

Abbu shrugged apologetically to Farhana, who nodded, grateful for his attempt.

Saahil was preoccupied with Zak, Bilal and five-year-old Hamid, who didn't want to miss a thing. He kept jamming his head into tiny gaps to get a better look and grabbing and snatching at all the figurines Zak had laid out before him.

'You can't borrow any of these,' Zak warned Saahil before he had even opened the box.

Small figures of every type of comic-book superhero and villain were now lined up meticulously in front of him. Batman. Joker. Superman. Catwoman. And Saahil's favourite, Spiderman. He reached out to touch one.

'They're collectables, you see,' Zak said, shooing Saahil's hand away.

'Right, put all this mess away,' Uncle Javid boomed. 'Dinner's ready.'

Saahil turned away and saw Abbu give him 'the look' from across the room.

'Auntie, can I help you bring the dishes to the table?' Saahil asked in his politest voice possible. Farhana pulled his cheek with affection and gave him the drinking glasses and two bottles of Coke. Saahil carried out his task then watched as the rest of the dishes and bowls were brought to the table. His stomach grumbled with anticipation. The starters were lamb kebabs, vegetable pakoras and chicken spring rolls with mint sauce.

'I always like to bring the food out in stages,' Uncle Javid said, grandly. 'Not like these other Pakistanis, who dump everything on the table in one go, even dessert. So uncultured, they are.'

Saahil could see Abbu racking his brains to see if he'd ever done that during an official Uncle Javid visit. He seated Zahra on his lap and offered her small bite-size pieces to nibble on. Saahil looked around to see his cousins piling the food on their plates. They were passing ketchup around instead of the mint sauce.

'Don't spill any on your clothes, please,' sighed Auntie Farhana.

After the appetiser, Uncle Javid insisted they have a break for an hour.

'Digest this properly,' he ordered. 'Then we can move on to the mains.'

Ammi disapproved. 'Stop acting like a gora,' she said to him. Abbu rolled his eyes and offered to wash up the dirty dishes in between.

'Why don't you go and change into your Eid clothes?' Abbu said to Farhana. 'I'll take care of this.'

Farhana wouldn't have it. 'You're our guests for today,' she said.

The group grew restless, counting every minute down until Javid's hour rule was over. Ammi muttered under her breath about 'wasting time'. Farhana hung about the kitchen, occasionally stirring a pan there and arranging a dish here.

'I'm still hungry,' Bilal wailed.

'I think we've digested now, Javid,' Abbu said.

'Another ten—'

'Nope. Farhana, let's do this.'

Abbu and Ammi bustled forwards to assist Farhana whilst Uncle Javid stretched luxuriously. Chicken and potato curry was being ladled over lamb pilau.

'We have spinach and paneer too,' Javid shouted over the group. 'I always like to serve a vegetarian option too.'

'*You* like to serve?' Abbu asked. 'You haven't lifted a finger all day. Farhana's done all the cooking.'

Ammi took a mouthful and asked for the salt. Saahil and his cousins took a bite before simultaneously coughing and spluttering for water.

'I barely put any chillies in so don't start!' Auntie Farhana said, wagging her finger at them all.

'It's wonderful, thank you,' Abbu said, pointedly to her.

Ammi stirred the serving dish and commented on the excess oil but otherwise, praised the cooking. Grains of rice littered the floor as the children rushed away from the table. Saahil received another 'look' from Abbu and helped Farhana take the dishes to the kitchen.

'Another hour's break this time, I'd say,' Uncle Javid half said, half burped.

'Let me know when I can go to the toilet too, Javid,' joked Abbu. Javid roared with over-the-top laughter and patted Abbu on the back.

'What's for dessert?' Saahil asked. 'Please,' he quickly added after getting a stern eye from Abbu.

'Gajar ka halwa.'

'What's gajar?'

'Carrot,' Farhana replied.

'Oh… nice,' replied Saahil, thinking it didn't sound very appealing. 'My mum always made trifle for us.'

'Forget trifle shifle,' Javid said, waving his arm dismissively. 'This is proper authentic, home-made—'

'Actually, we got this from the shop,' interjected Farhana.

'Did we?' Uncle Javid said.

'Yes, *you* bought it this morning.'

'Oh, must have slipped my mind,' he laughed nervously.

'And for the record… I love trifle too, Saahil.' Farhana winked at him.

'Yes, yes, very nice. What's on the telly?' Javid grabbed the remote and turned on a Bollywood music channel. 'Oh, Amjad, look! It's our favourite!'

Amitabh Bachchan was singing an epic song about friendship whilst frolicking in a stolen motorbike and sidecar with partner in crime, Dharmendra. Abbu smiled and joined his brother on the sofa. They sang along and copied the gestures. Saahil knew it was a very famous olden-day film from the Seventies. Abbu had tried to get him to watch it several times. He turned away smiling and found Zak and Bilal beckoning him into the other room.

'Let's jump on the sofas,' Bilal whispered, excitedly.

'Er, okay.'

They burst into the room next door. It was super clean and neat, and Saahil could tell that it hadn't really been lived in. Fancy ornaments were placed methodically throughout and an elaborate flower arrangement lay centre stage on the coffee table. Saahil sat on the edge of the sofa. He sank all the way in and realised why the boys wanted to jump on them. They were very soft and bouncy. Zak, Bilal and Hamid began leaping from one sofa to another, competing over who could jump the highest. There was a knock on the door and Humaira walked in with Aleena and Zahra.

'Girls aren't allowed in here,' Zak announced, flushed pink in the face.

'Shut up,' Humaira said, pushing him out of the way.

Abbu's words about good behaviour played on Saahil's mind as he watched his cousins have a blast around him. They were getting giddier and giddier. Jumping around and pushing and kicking each other from one sofa to another. Saahil stayed put in the corner and had his arms around both Zahra and Aleena protectively. Bilal took a running jump and almost fell on top of them.

'Oi, watch out okay?' Saahil warned. 'These two are only little.'

Bilal barely hung around to listen. Aleena wiggled out of Saahil's grip and ran towards the rowdy bunch. He called after her, not realising that Zahra had also slipped through his fingers. Saahil stood up to grab hold of them both. In the corner, Bilal pushed Zak and he fell back. With a thud he landed on top of Zahra.

'Zee!'

Zak stood up quickly as Saahil picked Zahra up from the floor. She didn't cry, but looked shaken and rubbed her arm.

'You idiot,' said Saahil, squaring up to his cousin.

'Well, why was she in the way?' Zak shot back.

'In the way? I told you to be careful—'

'Piss off.'

Saahil grabbed him in a headlock and a scuffle ensued.

'Fight, fight, fight,' the boys shouted.

'Stop it this instant,' Humaira shouted, her arms folded. Zahra and Aleena began crying.

The door was thrown open and Abbu stormed into the room followed by Uncle Javid. They tried to separate the boys, each grabbing their own kid as both Zak and Saahil's limbs shot out in half-hearted attempts to hit each other.

'Stop it right now,' Abbu said. 'Both of you.'

Saahil did, but Zak didn't.

'What happened?' Javid asked.

Both Saahil and Zak started shouting over each other at once, both relaying their own version of the story.

'Okay, okay,' Abbu said. 'Let Zak speak first.'

Saahil knew Abbu was attempting to be diplomatic.

'He tried to strangle me,' Zak screeched.

'Yeah, because you fell on top of Zahra and nearly squashed her.'

'So Saahil hit you first?' Javid asked. 'He started it? Is that what you're saying?'

'Yeah.'

'Well, Amjad,' Javid said, looking down his nose at Abbu. 'I did try to advise you about discipline—'

'Excuse me, you haven't even listened to what my son has to say.'

'Well, it doesn't really matter. If he started throwing punches—'

'No, I didn't!' Saahil shouted.

'—then there's obviously some anger issues.'

Abbu's eyes were widening with shock. 'You are unbelievable, Javid.'

'Now, that low-achieving school isn't helping. If you'd listened to my suggestion and gone for the private school—'

'I don't want your stinking suggestions.'

'I even offered to contribute towards fees—'

Abbu turned a beetroot colour. 'How dare you?' he whispered angrily.

Javid took his glasses off and wiped them, smiling condescendingly.

'We are leaving,' Abbu announced. He grabbed Zahra and put his arm around Saahil. They turned away from the room.

'*Amjaaaad,*' Javid said. 'Now don't start sulking.'

It was so quick that Saahil didn't even see it coming. Abbu turned and punched his brother square on the nose. Javid fell back and hit his head against the edge of the door. The children drew a collective gasp. Even Abbu looked shocked.

'What on earth is going on?' Ammi asked, waddling down the hallway.

Abbu turned to her. 'We're leaving. If you want to stay, you are welcome to.'

Javid rushed forward to his mother like a little boy. Saahil was pleased to see a droplet of blood oozing from his nose. 'Amjad just punched me!' he cried.

'Why, what did you do?' she asked, casually.

Javid began spluttering. 'But... but... he punched me.'

'You deserved that and more,' Abbu shot back.

Ammi reached out and touched Javid's face to inspect. 'It's just a small cut. Now the carrot halwa is ready.'

'I don't want carrot halwa,' Javid almost screamed with frustration.

'Neither do I,' moaned Abbu.

Abbu and Uncle Javid began relaying details of the fracas to Ammi like two squabbling boys.

'Stop!' Ammi held up a hand and glared at them both. It was almost as if an imaginary ladder had appeared and she had grown a foot taller as the two men shrank. Abbu dropped his shoulders and looked to the floor. Javid clutched his cheek.

At that moment, Auntie Farhana opened the door. 'Dessert, anyone? I think the hour is up?' She peered at Javid and frowned. 'What happened to your nose?'

'I punched him,' Abbu said.

'Walked into the door,' Javid added, hastily.

Farhana laughed and motioned them back into the living room. 'There's more than enough for everyone.'

They lumbered in and took their seats as plates were handed around. Saahil looked at his dessert. Well, it was definitely carroty, and tasted absolutely divine. The sound of spoons clinking plates was all that could be heard. Zak glared at Saahil from across the room. Javid glared at Abbu. Silence ensued.

'Well, this is awkward,' Saahil whispered to his father.

'Finish the halwa and let's get out of here,' Abbu replied.

'Okay… nice punch, by the way.'

Abbu winked at him.

Half an hour later, Abbu strapped Zahra into her car seat. She had fallen asleep. They waited around as Ammi kissed everyone

one by one. Zak stuck a finger up at Saahil when nobody was looking. He responded with two.

'Amjad,' Uncle Javid muttered, 'can I have a word please?'

Saahil watched as they both headed some distance away from the car. There was some mumbling, shuffling and nodding, both men failing to make eye contact with each other. It ended with a hesitant handshake and then Uncle Javid initiated an awkward hug. Abbu responded and patted his brother on the back, though Saahil could see him purse his lips during the embrace. Saahil sighed with relief as he waved the family goodbye. That was Eid over and done with for another year. He couldn't wait to go home and tell Ehsan all about it.

Seven

August 1997

Whenever Saahil would think back to the soundtrack of the summer of 1997, he would remember only one song. It had been driving him mad over the school holidays and thanks to Zahra, it blared from the speakers for the fifth time that day. Mel B let out a wild laugh before the Spice Girls zig-ah-zig-ahhhed their way to Saahil's ears. He had to stop himself from tearing his hair out.

Approximately ten minutes ago, Saahil had watched Zahra's eyes flickering towards the stairs. He'd braced himself, knowing what was to come. As soon as Abbu announced that he was going to start making dinner, Zahra began inching towards the steps. Abbu disappeared off into the kitchen and from the corner of his eye, Saahil saw Zahra scramble upstairs. The door handle turned and clicked and the stool was dragged across the floor. Saahil heard the cassette player ticking as his little sister jabbed at the buttons. He'd counted to ten before following her, and then flung open the door. Zahra had been in the same position as she usually was: standing on the stool and reaching towards the cassette player. Her small finger hovering over the play button, she gave him a sly grin before pressing down.

And here they were again. The same scenario played out numerous times over the summer. Saahil helped a dancing Zahra off the stool. He took a seat at the edge of the bed and waited as

69

his little sister waved around her arms and wiggled her bum at the music. He checked his watch, willing for it to be over.

'Next one,' Zahra said, flushed in the cheeks.

'No, that's enough, Zee. Five times already.'

Before she could protest, Saahil switched off the player and scooped Zahra up in his arms. They thundered down the stairs and into the kitchen to find Abbu stirring a pot.

'What were you doing?' he asked. 'Told you to chop these onions for me.'

Immediately, Zahra flung her arms up in the air and shouted, *'If you wanna… my lover!'*

Abbu's eyebrows shot up his forehead. Saahil clamped his hand over his sister's mouth.

'Zee,' he mumbled into her ear. 'Told you not to say that.'

'Yes,' Abbu said, placing his hands on his hips, wooden spoon in one palm. 'And I told you not to get her that tape just yet.'

Saahil was flustered by the accusation, but he had a good comeback. 'Well, you're the one who bought her a Spice Girls pencil case and stationery to match.'

'Girl power,' Zahra shouted, thrusting her fist up in the air and hitting Saahil on the nose. Abbu shook his head and told them to get ready for dinner.

'Won't be long as I'm only throwing in this tin of mixed vegetables,' he said. 'Just need to brown the onions.'

Saahil followed Zahra into the living room. She was still singing and dancing. It was the latest obsession that the family was having to accommodate. A couple of months ago, Zee was crawling around on all fours, pretending to be Simba from *The Lion King*. One time before that, she wouldn't get out of the bath in the hope she would develop a tail and turn into the Little

Mermaid. Zahra's imagination was already running wild and now she was going to be starting school. A pleated grey skirt and white blouse hung behind her bedroom door. Smart black shoes lay in a box under her bed. And of course, there was the primary school bag and Spice Girls accessories. Though Saahil wouldn't admit it out loud, he did think their songs were catchy. Zahra's favourite was Mel B. Saahil took a fancy to Ginger Spice.

Zahra was already attending nursery in the afternoons so Abbu was quite relaxed about her starting school. He'd had a wobble the other day though, when all the uniform was bought and all the organising was done. He sat down on the sofa looking lost and forlorn.

'What's up?' Saahil asked.

'Well… it's started, hasn't it?'

'What has?'

Abbu shrugged. 'The daily grind. For the rest of her life it's started. Primary school. Secondary school. College. University. Job.' He ticked them off with his fingers.

'Yeah,' said Saahil. 'That is quite depressing. But we all have to go through the same thing.'

'I know. Wish she could stay like this forever, though,' he'd said, motioning towards her as she slept soundly on the couch.

Saahil nodded in agreement. They began ticking down the days on the calendar. New term began on Wednesday. Saahil would go back to the joys of GCSEs and Zahra would start learning her ABC.

After a change of head teacher for the second time around, Saahil's school seemed to be making progress. Another team of principals had been drafted in to tackle the failing institution. An even more useless disciplining system was introduced, the first step being a 'think sheet'. Students were ordered to sit away in a corner and reflect upon their bad behaviour by filling in a form. They'd all quickly devised a set way of filling out the ridiculous thing.

How have you disrupted the lesson?

Talking.

What will you do differently?

Not talk.

'Apparently, the new heads have experience doing this,' Uncle Harun repeated to Abbu for what felt like the hundredth time. 'They've transformed two schools in Leeds.'

'We've heard it all before though, haven't we?' Abbu replied.

The two of them had relaxed considerably in the years following the burning car episode. After seeing that Saahil and Ehsan's grades were climbing, both dads realised that their own advice was true: kids could succeed anywhere if they worked hard. Both Saahil and Ehsan were predicted straight 'A' grades in their results. They had the option of moving away for A Level studies, but both had opted to stay put. Remarkably, Abbu and Uncle Harun hadn't protested. Neither had Auntie Meena.

Saahil didn't care anymore about what people thought of his school. Throughout his time there, he had seen classroom chairs being hurled at teachers who dodged them calmly and continued teaching. He'd seen petite female teachers jump straight into fist fights between burly sixteen-year-old lads and try to restrain them. Saahil's teachers probably worked twice as hard as staff at any other poncey school. And not *all* the kids were so bad either. Saahil and Ehsan were good. They were aiming high and had survived without any major incidents. Though they hated school at times, both boys couldn't imagine being anywhere else.

Once Zahra stopped dancing to the Spice Girls, she pointed to the calendar that hung on the living-room wall. She had chosen it especially as each month featured a different breed of fluffy kitten.

'You wanna tick off another day?' Saahil asked.

Zahra nodded.

'Okay, even though it's only five o'clock.'

Saahil grabbed a pen and picked Zahra up. She made a wonky cross against Saturday 30th August. Just four days until she started school. She wiggled in his arms with excitement. Saahil wondered if he'd been this eager to begin his education. *It's not all that, Zee*, he almost said.

'Food's ready,' Abbu called from the kitchen.

'Let's go help,' Saahil said to his sister. He placed her on the floor and she ran off as soon as her feet touched the ground.

When his mother's bespectacled face swam into view, Amjad thought he was being woken up for school. *Five more minutes*, he wanted to say, burying his face into the pillow.

'*Amjad*,' she hissed. He felt her hand tapping his shoulder urgently.

'Ammi!' he shouted back, coming to his senses. He drew the duvet close to his chest in shock. Ammi shuffled on her feet and pulled away. What was she doing in his bedroom in the middle of the night? The curtains were drawn shut but a small beam of light shone through signalling the arrival of the morning. Amjad rubbed his eyes and sat up in bed.

'What are you doing? Why are you here?' He reached out and checked the alarm clock. It was 7.30 a.m. Ammi remained distant and stayed in the shadows. She cleared her throat and mumbled something indistinguishable.

'Is everything okay?' Amjad asked, suddenly serious. A panic began brewing in his chest.

'Yes, yes. Of course,' Ammi replied.

'So what is this? How did you even get here?' he asked, knowing that *he* was the one who always chauffeured his mother between their homes.

'I… er… got a lift from the neighbour.'

'At seven o'clock on a Sunday morning?'

'Yes.'

'Which neighbour?'

'Does it matter?' she snapped. 'Are you getting up now?'

'Well, I suppose,' Amjad replied bitterly, thinking he could have done with a lie-in. 'Are the kids asleep?'

'Yes.'

Amjad made to get up but he stopped and looked at his mother's face in the dark. She wasn't making eye contact with him.

'Ammi, what's wrong?' he asked. 'Something's wrong, I know it is.'

'No… nothing.'

'Tell me the truth. What's going on?'

'Come downstairs first.'

Amjad's heart began beating fast. He knew this talk. It was the same talk the doctors had used before they told him that his wife had died. *'Sit down first, Mr Sharif.' 'Take a seat first so we can discuss this…'*

'Has something bad happened?'

'No… well, not to us.'

'Not to us? But something bad has happened?'

'Erm—'

'Tell me now.'

'I'll show you if you come downstairs.'

Ammi's voice wobbled and she clapped her hand over her mouth. Amjad stood, confused, not knowing where this was going.

'Ammi?' he asked, this time more urgently.

His mother broke down into tears. She spoke through sobs. 'Something terrible has happened to this country.'

The TV was already playing when Amjad stumbled down the stairs with Ammi. He knelt down on the floor, his eyes glued to the screen. He couldn't bring himself to blink. The sombre-looking newsreaders were talking, but the words seemed to wash over Amjad. Besides, he couldn't hear them. Ammi was speaking quickly in Punjabi, explaining how she had discovered the news.

'I woke up to pray Fajr namaz at five o'clock. I don't know why, but I like to keep the TV on in the background whilst I get ready otherwise it's so eerie and quiet. As soon as I switched it on I saw… this.'

Amjad turned up the volume on the remote control. But it wasn't going to change the words that were emblazoned on the bottom of the screen: PRINCESS DIANA KILLED IN PARIS CAR CRASH.

'I couldn't be alone,' Ammi sobbed. 'I called a taxi and came here.'

Amjad sat his mother down on the sofa and placed his arm around her. He kept one eye on the TV as reports flew in from various sources. For now, they were staring into a dark tunnel in Paris. It was cordoned off by police and surrounded by onlookers. The newsreaders welcomed 'those joining us now for today's

75

breaking news' not in their usual sharp, business-like tones, but in a stuttering disbelief. They took extra-long pauses, looked flustered and slightly out of control, almost as if they didn't want to say the words.

'Shall we move our attention to the papers?' said the reporter as he turned to a guest seated to his left. He looked relieved to be sharing the screen with another person. The guest journalist held up a front page and began his analysis.

'I'll make tea,' Amjad mumbled, suddenly feeling hollow. He left Ammi on the sofa and went into the kitchen. He watched the kettle as it boiled. The sound of the telly travelled to his ears. He wondered how people all over the country would react as they woke up on this lazy, summer Sunday morning. How were they *meant* to feel?

'So young and beautiful,' Ammi was saying as Amjad carried in two cups of tea. Amjad looked at the screen and saw footage of Diana walking through a minefield. It cut to her riding a water-park slide with the young princes.

Half an hour later, they heard movement upstairs.

'I better go check on the kids,' Amjad sighed, glad for the excuse to get out of the room. 'When you hear us coming down, Ammi, just turn it off for a bit. I don't want them seeing this yet.'

Amjad plodded up the stairs and creaked open Zahra's door. He saw a flash of pink and found his daughter wrapped around his leg in a tight hug.

'Morning,' he smiled.

'Morneee,' she replied, her small face beaming up at him.

He picked her up in his arms and opened Saahil's door. His son was sitting up in bed.

'Why are you lot awake so early? And why can I hear Ammi?'

'She's here. We're all going to have breakfast together.'

Saahil grinned. 'Double breakfast?'

'Yeah,' Amjad nodded, knowing that if the kids stayed over at their grandmother's, she would feed them a proper breakfast. Toast, fried eggs, tomatoes and beans. A sharp contrast to the sugary cereal that Amjad hastily poured for them.

Saahil jumped up and rushed towards the door.

'Take your sister,' Amjad said.

Saahil took her by the hand and walked her down the stairs. Amjad watched them go and sat alone on the bed, taking deep, slow breaths. He couldn't understand what was wrong with him. But then he thought about a person he always believed he had zero in common with: the Prince of Wales, waking up his children in the early hours to tell them that their mother had died. Four years ago, Amjad had done that too.

The flowers gathered outside Kensington Palace. Men and women sobbed on camera whilst talking about the beloved princess. Ammi's relatives called from Pakistan to offer their condolences. Harun rang Amjad to tell him that Meena had been crying all week.

'You know she loved Diana,' he said.

Amjad had never known anything like it. Even journalists were debating whether it was all just getting a bit 'too much'. Why would people grieve for somebody they didn't know? Amjad couldn't explain why, but he also felt a deep sadness for Diana, a woman he had been quite indifferent to in real life. Yes, he always thought she was beautiful, always admired her humanitarian work, but Diana was someone he had never met or known. But sorrow lay heavy over his chest for the rest of the week. He could see it on the faces of friends and passers-by. Amjad thought about the two young princes, motherless, like his own two children. He thought about a youthful life cut short. Like his own wife. People up and down the country were mourning the crossovers and parallels of their own lives.

Ammi spent more time at their house. She dabbed her eyes whenever the news showed footage of Diana gliding around in her different gowns. Ethereal and otherworldly she was now. Ammi insisted on pulling out an unused 'Charles and Diana' tea set. It was, of course, another romantic gift from Amjad's father. The photo printed on each piece of china was of the seemingly happy couple back in 1982. TO COMMEMORATE THE BIRTH OF THEIR FIRST CHILD, read the saucers. It even had a pair of cherubs on it.

When pictures emerged of the mangled black car found in the Paris tunnel, Ammi rushed off to pray. She began admonishing Amjad every time he put his foot down in the car for the rest of the week.

'Drive carefully,' she snapped. 'Look what happened to poor Diana.'

The night before Zahra started school on Wednesday, Amjad recalled a thought he'd been having throughout the summer holidays. When he took Zahra to her first day at school, would she be the only kid there not to have a mother? The events of the weekend seemed to retune his brain. After all, if it could even happen to princes.

They'd already tackled nursery, so there was no crying on the Wednesday morning when Amjad dropped Zahra off. He felt a pang in his heart when she was all ready in her uniform, smart coat and school bag. He grabbed the camera from the cupboard and took two snaps of her. When they arrived, all the parents gathered around at the entrance of the brightly decorated classroom. They appeared strong on the surface, but Amjad sensed that some would probably cry in the car on the way home. Zahra stood and waved at Amjad before rushing off, eager to get started. He felt lighter as he drove home. That was until he switched on the telly and was met with more mournful news coverage of the death of the princess.

Amjad was most surprised at Saahil's reaction to Diana's passing. He had delivered the news gently to his son, not thinking there would be much to it. Saahil would express sorrow and move on quickly. On the Sunday morning when the news first broke, Saahil nipped out to buy sweets for Zahra. He'd returned with a couple of tabloids bearing the headline: DIANA DEAD. Amjad had reacted badly. He hated the bluntness of the words. The insensitivity. Saahil shrugged and hid them out of view. But over the next few days, he seemed to withdraw into himself. He was the first to switch on the TV in a morning, listening intently to details of the country's grief. He asked questions about William and Harry. Why were people bickering over the silence of the Queen? What was all the fuss about the flag that flew over Buckingham Palace? The night before the funeral, Saahil brought home another newspaper. The front page displayed images of the young princes reading floral tributes to their mother outside Kensington Palace. Saahil stared at the photos. Ammi always liked to point out how he was the same age as Prince William. Amjad often joked how that was as far as their similarities went.

'Well, I suppose we have something else in common now,' said Saahil, not taking his eyes off the pictures. 'Both our mums are dead,' he finished abruptly.

Amjad frowned. 'I've told you not to talk like tha—'

'What? You want me to put it nicely?' He glared at Amjad, who had never seen him like this before. 'I'm going to sleep in tomorrow,' he said. 'You watch the funeral if you want.'

Saahil didn't come downstairs all morning. Ammi used up an entire box of tissues as the world tuned in for the final farewell. She gasped when she saw the two boys appear and walk behind the funeral cortege.

'They're too young for this,' Amjad kept saying. Prince Harry looked so small.

In the afternoon, Saahil's voice travelled down from the top of the stairs. 'Is it over?'

'Yes, you can come down now,' Ammi replied.

Whilst he was eating a late breakfast, Amjad stroked Saahil's hair.

'Are you okay?' he asked.

Saahil nodded and avoided eye contact. Amjad didn't know what to say. He knew that 'deep talk' was the last thing that Saahil wanted. It would make him feel even more uncomfortable than he already was. But that didn't stop Amjad from feeling completely incompetent as a father. They spent the rest of the day keeping out of each other's way.

That night, Amjad tucked Zahra into bed and turned out her lights. As he inched out of the room, he saw Saahil hovering by the door.

'I'm just going to finish this homework in my room,' he said. 'And then I'll go to sleep.'

'Okay.'

They stood awkwardly for a few seconds. Amjad thought about saying something, but Saahil's body was already turned in towards the direction of his bedroom, perhaps in the hope of a quick exit.

'Goodnight then,' Amjad said, deciding against it. He began making his way towards the stairs. But before he knew it, Saahil was hugging him. They had stopped doing 'goodnight hugs' a while ago, what with Saahil now being a super-cool teen. Amjad was completely taken aback. They both giggled nervously and Saahil quickly retreated into his room in a flash.

As Amjad drank his decaf tea alone in front of the telly that night, he couldn't stop thinking about the hug. When he woke up in the morning, his mind settled on it once again. It was only a silly hug. But by noon the next day, Amjad knew what was bothering him about the embrace.

It was the tightness of it.

Eight

Three empty plastic bottles were lined up on the dining table. The fourth had toppled over and rolled on to the floor near the doorway. If Zahra bounded towards it without looking, she would trip over and fall, but Saahil couldn't muster the energy to go and pick the bottle up. He was sitting at the dining table poring over huge textbooks, stopping for frequent swigs of Red Bull and Lucozade and wondering whether they were beginning to lose their effectiveness. He'd have to switch back to coffee and try not to spill any over his books. There were already a few noticeable stains on some of the pages. The last time, he had completely missed his mouth as he'd brought the cup to his lips.

Saahil lowered his head and let the cold page touch his cheek. He envied those losers at school, the ones he and Ehsan used to laugh at. They were probably sitting at supermarket checkouts right now, sliding loaves of bread down those slopey things and arranging groceries into plastic bags. Saahil would gladly swap lives with them. Here, he'd say, take the bloody Engineering degree and let me have a go on the till.

Not that he'd be saying that tomorrow after his final exam. But that was twenty-four hours away and Saahil was exhausted. He had almost dozed off when Zahra jumped on top of him from

82

behind. He jerked awake as her skinny arms wrapped around his shoulders.

'Zee, why did you do that?' he asked, wearily. She appeared at his side, chewing gum loudly and still wearing her school uniform. She grimaced and pinched her nose.

'You stink, Bhaijaan,' she said.

'Oh, thanks.'

'When did you last have a shower?' she demanded. 'And don't tell me you don't have time. I have loads of homework too, but I still have a bath when I need to.'

Zahra's eyes travelled over the pile of open books on the table. She squinted at the tiny writing, the technical graphs and complicated Maths symbols.

'Your homework looks well boring,' she added.

'Well, it doesn't matter if it's boring,' said Saahil, tugging her plait lightly. 'It's gonna get me a wicked job and then I'll have loads of money to spend... on myself!'

Zahra's smile evaporated.

'Anyway, where's Libby?' Saahil asked, clearly hoping her little school friend would arrive at any moment to distract her and let him continue with his work.

'She might not be coming today.'

'That's a first,' said Saahil. Libby was always at the house within an hour of them both finishing the school day.

The doorbell rang.

'Oh, that may be her,' Zahra said, eyes lighting up.

'No, it's probably Abbu,' Saahil replied, checking his watch.

Zahra giggled her way to Amjad as he appeared at the door. He responded with equal enthusiasm prompting Saahil to smile and roll his eyes. He stood up, stretching and yawning.

'Pull your pants up!'

Saahil winced.

'Nice to see you too, Abbu.'

Amjad kicked off his shoes and Saahil heard him mutter 'stupid fashion' and 'bum hanging out' under his breath. Saahil went off into the kitchen and put the kettle on. He came back with a solitary cup of tea.

'No biscuits, Abbu. You're getting a bit podgy around the middle. I don't like it.'

Amjad scowled at his son, but not for long as Zahra had already sneaked a packet of Rich Teas to him under the table.

'How's it going?' Amjad asked, motioning toward Saahil's work. He got a groan in response. Before they could continue, Ammi came down the stairs thumbing her prayer beads in one hand. She waddled past them wrapped in layers of scarf and took a seat on the sofa. Amjad eyed her nervously.

'Are you still angry with me about the can of chickpeas?' he asked. There'd been a commotion the previous night when Ammi had sent him out shopping and he'd not listened properly to her instructions.

'You were supposed to get me two tins,' she snapped back, her beak suddenly in Amjad's face. 'And you only got one. Now I can't make samosa chaat.'

'Saahil will run out and get you one.'

'No, he won't. He's busy studying. I asked *you* to get me them.'

Amjad rubbed his temples and closed his eyes.

'Bad quality chickpeas too,' Ammi added.

'Bad quality?' Amjad said. 'Chickpeas are chickpeas. What's the big deal?'

Saahil decided to intervene. 'I'll go and get you them, Ammi. Just chill.'

'You *chill*,' she shot back.

Saahil laughed and put his arms around her. She resisted a little but a slow smile spread across her face. Ammi could never be angry with him for more than ten seconds. She often said that when he walked into a room, she would notice no one except her own handsome grandson. Saahil shrugged this off on many occasions, feigning embarrassment. This, however, was not just 'grandmother talk'. The old woman was spot on. Saahil was pretty, and he knew it.

He stood a few inches taller than Amjad and walked with a slight swagger that was neither intentional nor overdone. His thick raven hair was pushed back with no desire to be neat, though the messier it got the more attractive Saahil became. His heavy-lidded eyes always found girls. They waited with bated breath to be on the receiving end of one of his smiles. Saahil was happy to oblige, but only with a slight upturn of his lips. He didn't want to lose the cool, laidback air that surrounded him with too much enthusiasm.

As Saahil scribbled complicated symbols on sheets of paper, he wore a look of steely concentration in his eyes, his pencil scritch-scratching as it travelled across the page. Saahil spoke of success as though it was waiting around for him like a faithful pet dog. It would come rushing to him as soon as he whistled. He'd worked hard enough for it and more importantly, Saahil wanted it badly enough. He'd delivered his pizzas and mopped his shop floors to earn extra cash alongside his studies. His dark eyes gazed out at the world with a bored indifference. There wasn't much to get excited about after all. The dull, northern city he'd grown up in consisted of rows of terraced houses and the odd chimney of some derelict factory piercing a crappy skyline of nothingness. It wasn't for him. Saahil would do one out of there at the first opportunity.

Of course, he was going nowhere alone. Oh no, he wasn't going to be one of those people who just buggered off and left their families to it. They were all part of his ambitions. As Ammi and Amjad bickered over chickpeas, Saahil felt a rush of affection. Zahra, who was stood by the kitchen door, gave him a look from across the room to suggest 'here we go again'. She was quite sharp-witted for a little one. Saahil caught sight of their childhood growth chart which had climbed up the wall in spectacular fashion. Saahil was last marked in the millennium year.

Saahil, 18 yrs, 14/09/00

Ehsan, 18 yrs, 01/12/00

'You won't grow any taller now,' Abbu had told him.

A laugh escaped Saahil's lips.

'Neither will this guy,' he'd said, pointing to his best friend. Ehsan had gracefully accepted a three-inch defeat.

All seventy inches of Saahil liked to take some of the credit when it came to his sister's upbringing. She was catching up on the other side of the door. The most recent marking taken a few months ago recorded her at fifty-six inches:

Zahra, 10 yrs, 20/02/2003

Saahil remembered his dad's friends watching him fondly as he scurried around after her as a kid.

'You know what they say, Amjad. Older siblings are like parents. And especially when there is such an age gap. He'll always be there for her.'

They spoke the truth. It was Saahil who took over when Amjad could not be in two places at once. The other day he had accompanied Zahra to her school's parents' evening like the mature, responsible older brother he was supposed to be. When they arrived home, Saahil gave Zahra her first self-defence lesson to prepare her for secondary school. Amjad shook his head in disapproval as he watched the pair of them wrestling in the middle of the room like idiots.

'Be careful, Saahil! You might hurt her.'

'No, I won't. I let her win, didn't I? And anyway, she needs toughening up.'

Naturally, they didn't always see eye to eye. Saahil constantly undid Amjad's fragile attempts at discipline. Zahra would bury her face in his chest when she was being told off for causing mischief. Saahil would hold her, his chin resting on her head, the corners of his mouth twitching as he tried to maintain an adult sternness.

'Leave her alone, Abbu,' he would protest. 'She's only little.'

It was always funny when Abbu got in a huffy mood. According to Saahil, it just made him even more lovable. He wasn't as slick or sophisticated as Saahil hoped to still be at forty-five. He wasn't even cool. He was just Abbu. Quite unremarkable to an outsider, with his glasses, bald patch and beginnings of a paunch. *What does he want?* Saahil often wondered, as he watched his dad plodding around the house. *What would make him really happy?* Surely it wasn't just the fork-lift driver promotion Abbu talked about.

At twenty-one, Saahil already felt like he had everything fig- ured out. He knew what he wanted to do, and who he wanted to be. But things hadn't been so easy for his Abbu. Saahil sometimes wondered what it must have been like for him, newly widowed with two small children to look after. He had told grief to stay put in one corner and had got on with it.

Saahil slipped on his jacket as Ammi's rant about chickpeas reached fever pitch.

'Hurry,' Abbu mouthed urgently, motioning him out of the door.

Saahil smiled as he walked down the street thinking about his Abbu. He realised once again that it was quite possible for people to go through life and never think about themselves. It was possible to live completely for others. He realised that Abbu didn't actually want anything for himself. The thought had probably never even occurred to him. And that's why Saahil wanted to give him everything.

Saahil and Ehsan waited for their friends to emerge from the exam room as the rest of the students piled out of the door. They walked outside and found a quiet corner to discuss their final assessment. Saahil leaned against the wall, leg cocked casually, preoccupied with his phone.

'How did it go?' Ehsan asked them all.

'I've really messed up,' Umar said before anybody else had a chance to speak. His double chins quivered as he looked to his friends for consolation. 'I missed the last question out completely.'

'Don't worry about it now, mate,' Ehsan replied. 'It's over. You'll have done fine.'

'No, I haven't,' he said, frantically. 'I'm definitely gonna fail. Didn't I tell you I would fail?'

'Stop pissing your pants, Umar,' snapped Kamran. 'You always whimper like a bitch after every exam. Doing my head in.'

'How about *you* stop having a go at him all the time?' said Ehsan.

'Yeah, leave him alone, twat,' Saahil piped up. He didn't bother looking up from his phone.

'How did you do, Saahil?' Umar asked.

'Erm… well—'

'*Obviously* he thinks he's aced it,' Kamran said, wearing his usual malicious grin, the one he reserved only for Saahil.

'Yeah,' Saahil replied coolly, knowing exactly what to say to piss him off. 'I probably have.'

Kamran snorted and twisted his face, making the small red birthmark on his nose appear even uglier. He opened his mouth but Ehsan cut him off.

'So, we'll see you both tonight then, yeah?'

'Why?'

'We're gonna celebrate with the rest of the lads.'

Kamran shrugged. 'Fine.'

He slunk off after one last glare at Saahil, whose middle finger responded casually to the back of his head. Umar ran off behind Kamran, all flustered as he tried to catch up.

Ehsan looked at Saahil.

'He's a right weirdo, isn't he?'

Saahil nodded in agreement. Ehsan's face broke into a huge smile. 'How you feeling?'

Saahil blinked a few times as reality set in. 'I'm gonna sleep for a few days. And watch the football without feeling guilty.'

'Are you joking? I've already quit my shitty job.'

They laughed and gave each other a high five.

''Ere, have you seen those girls?' Ehsan said, motioning with his eyes to the left. 'They've been looking at you for ages.'

There were two girls sitting on a bench across from them, whispering with their heads together. Saahil had already taken a good look at them, discreetly of course. When he finally honoured them with his gaze, his expression suggested he was bored out of his brains. After a few seconds, he turned away from them indifferently, and began texting on his phone. The girls giggled stupidly and hurried off. Ehsan shook his head at Saahil's absurd reaction.

'What the…' he began. 'I don't blame Kamran. You are an arrogant—'

Saahil blocked his ears. He couldn't hear the insults but could see Ehsan's mouth moving.

'Do you know them?' he asked, gesturing towards the now empty bench. Saahil shrugged.

'Whatever, I'm sure I've seen you hanging around in a corner with one of 'em. Maybe even both.'

'Don't remember.'

'Don't remember?' Ehsan repeated slowly. 'What do you mean "don't remember"? Do you just get off with them and then forget who they are the next day?'

'Oi, I don't "get off" with anyone, all right,' said Saahil, firmly.

'Oh yeah, sorry I forgot. You're a good Muslim, aren't you?'

'Yeah, I bloody am,' he said, smirking. 'Plus, you know my Abbu, he'd chapatti pan me over the head if he found out.'

'Well, don't forget,' Ehsan said. 'I'm his informer. He's told me to keep an eye on you.'

'I know,' said Saahil, giving Ehsan a dirty look. 'But maybe it's me who should be keeping an eye on you.'

'You what?'

'Hi, Alisha,' said Saahil.

Ehsan nearly choked on his own tongue. The pretty hijabi who had tried to sneak past them unseen stopped to face them.

'Hi,' she said, rather confrontationally. Her grip tightened around the pile of books she was holding against her chest.

'You on your own?' Saahil asked.

'Yes, I'm capable of walking down the street on my own.'

Ehsan laughed nervously. 'Ignore him, he's an idiot.'

Alisha's posture seemed to relax. There was a slight upturn of her lips.

Saahil noticed and grinned. 'If looks could kill I'd be dead on the floor. But if Ehsan manages to mumble a word or two to you then suddenly you don't seem to mind.'

'That's not true,' she spluttered, her cheeks reddening as she turned away in a huff and sped off towards the bus stop.

Ehsan glared at Saahil. 'You've embarrassed her now.'

'How long are you gonna play around for?' Saahil asked. 'You smile at her from across the room and act like as though you've made progress. Get an effin' move on.'

'Well, for your information—' Ehsan began, but seemed to think better of it.

'What?'

'Nowt, forget it,' he replied.

Saahil shook his head. 'Anyway, your dad is at my house. Abbu just texted me.'

They headed off towards the bus stop together. A car sped past and honked at them. Two lads they recognised from their course sniggered through their tinted windows. Saahil opened his mouth to shout something but Ehsan grabbed his arm.

'Leave it,' he said.

Saahil kicked at a scrap on the floor and mumbled something about 'getting his own car soon'. Ehsan smiled good-naturedly.

'They're showing off, taking the piss out of us,' said Saahil.

'So what?' Ehsan replied.

Saahil looked at his best friend. 'Why doesn't stuff bother you?'

Ehsan shrugged.

'Bloody pious prick,' said Saahil, rolling his eyes.

When the boys arrived home, they found Amjad and Harun in their usual spot, drinking tea and watching cricket on the TV.

'So you're going out again tonight?' Amjad asked as the boys settled down on the couch next to him.

'Again? We haven't been out in about a month,' said Saahil.

'Well, don't get carried away, all right?' Harun joined in. 'I know you're celebrating and everything but—'

'Oh, Abbu,' Ehsan said, cutting his father off. 'Don't give us another lecture.'

The dads gave each other a knowing look. Unfortunately, Harun had seen what silly students got up to on his late-night taxi rounds – half naked, drug-taking, alcohol-drinking fiends that they were. He'd seen them squaring up to the police before passing out on the streets in pools of their own vomit. They didn't understand that neither Saahil nor Ehsan wanted to behave in that way.

'How many times do we have to say it?' Saahil said to the pair of them. 'Why would we drink alcohol? It stinks.'

'I know,' Ehsan added. 'I can't breathe when I'm near it… Isn't it yeast fermentation or summat?'

'I don't know,' said Saahil. 'It bloody pongs whatever it is.'

Amjad and Harun smiled at each other. They always enjoyed teasing them.

'Well, I'm more concerned about drugs,' Harun began. 'Boys your age, they're always getting into my taxi at night, stoned off their heads.'

'Oh, come on, drugs aren't as bad as alcohol,' Saahil blurted out.

Amjad and Harun frowned. Saahil could tell that Ehsan was resisting the urge to punch him as he quickly jumped in.

'He means alcohol is like *really* haram. Whereas drugs are, you know, not as... haram.' Ehsan's voice trailed off.

'Anything that intoxicates you is haram,' Harun said. 'Anything that makes you lose control of what you're doing.'

In which case, Saahil thought, the odd joint here and there when you were out with your mates was hardly a big deal. Not that the old boys needed to know that.

'Well, what do you want us to do,' laughed Saahil. 'Become really religious and grow beards?'

Amjad and Harun's faces hardened.

Ehsan rolled his eyes. 'Nice one,' he mouthed to Saahil. It was time for lecture number two, which went along the lines of 'don't get brainwashed and blow anything up'.

'That's not a laughing matter,' Harun said.

'Absolutely not,' Amjad agreed.

Both of them glanced at each other looking uncomfortable.

'I was only joking,' Saahil quickly said.

'Yeah, you don't have to worry about us ramming a plane into Big Ben,' Ehsan chimed in, though it was the wrong thing to say to two already anxious-looking dads. The atmosphere in the room changed.

'Talk about a mood killer,' Ehsan whispered to Saahil as their fathers talked in hushed, worried tones.

'Tell me about it,' he replied, wishing he could be transported somewhere else immediately. Only yesterday he'd had a run-in with his dad for telling Zahra to 'fucking turn it off' as the TV reminded them of what had occurred on 11 September two years ago – as if they could forget. Unfortunately, Abbu had been just within earshot. First, he told him off for swearing. Second, for swearing in front of Zahra. And then for being 'insensitive'.

Sensitivity? Everyone was past that stage. Maybe if these news channels hadn't shoved it in their faces so much over the past two years, Saahil might still react with some sympathy. They were still at it, churning out one documentary after the next, agonising over every detail, milking it for all it was worth. It was easy gawping at the telly in apocalyptic awe at the scenes, but now Saahil had to remind himself there were actual people in those buildings deciding on which was the easiest way to die: to sit around and embrace a fireball on the inside, or jump out of the window and let their bodies shatter all over the streets of Manhattan.

Saahil didn't blame Abbu and Uncle Harun for worrying so much. It would be nice, after all, to just sit back and feel sorry for the victims and angry towards the perpetrators and for that be that. To not shrink slightly every time the image of those two skyscrapers popped up unexpectedly. And they did pop up. In dentist waiting rooms on muted TVs, in conversations with smug white people. It was *always* there. Crashing, burning, smoking, and spreading like an ash cloud into every facet of their lives.

Saahil often thought back to the actual day. It niggled at him: Abbu holding Zahra close in a one-armed hug; her blinking away innocently and playing with her plait as she watched the screen. She was completely oblivious to the fact that life had probably just changed forever.

'It'll blow over,' Abbu sometimes said, trying to convince himself. Because wars just had a tendency to *blow over*. God only knew what kind of hell this would mutate into, Saahil thought. After all, they'd invaded two countries now. They could bomb as many Muslims as they wanted.

'You see,' Ehsan often said, shaking his head, 'you can't do shit like that and expect not to piss a few people off.'

'No one cares about brown civvies caught up in the middle, Ehsan,' Saahil replied, bitterly.

He remembered how the awful events had impacted their second year at university. Freshers' Week for the First Years was due to start on Monday 17th September 2001. Saahil and Ehsan were talking about what they would get up to during the week's parties in hushed voices so that their parents could not hear. After that, they'd put their heads down and work hard for the rest of the year. There was an air of anticipation and excitement, until everything changed.

A couple of weeks after 9/11, Saahil had been at a hospital appointment with Ammi. The waiting room was packed and the TV was playing the *BBC News*. Slowly, all eyes began to travel up towards the screen. So did Saahil's. People began shuffling and looking at the floor. There was no shock and disbelief. Everyone in that room had seen nothing else for the past fortnight. The screen showed the second plane flying into the South Tower and being engulfed in a burst of flames. Saahil remembered digging his fingernails into his hands, his face reddening as he tapped his foot urgently on the floor. Saahil remembered vividly the sigh of relief he'd taken when Ammi was finally called in for her consultation.

Later that day, Saahil went to pick Zahra up from school. What she'd told him as they'd walked home together made him rage to Abbu that night.

'They've been having this stupid "circle time" every day since the attack,' shouted Saahil. 'Zee told me that they're passing this cuddly toy around and whoever it lands on has to talk about their "feelings" about the World Trade Center. One of the girls,

Sonia or whatever she's called, wasn't saying much. I'm not being funny, Abbu, but I've seen this girl and her mum and dad. She lives on Springside Street, okay, and it doesn't look like she has the strongest grasp of the English language… Are you listening, Abbu?'

'Yes, yes, of course.'

'Well, Zee told me that Miss Williams goes to her, "How would you feel if your mum was in the tower?" What kind of arsehole question is that!'

'Don't swear.'

'And this Sonia kid said, "I'd be sad." Well, what else what she supposed to say? Then Miss Williams goes, "Sad, is that it? You'd be devastated."'

Abbu had looked up from his newspaper for the first time and frowned. 'Really?'

'Yeah, Abbu,' said Saahil, almost bouncing off the walls. 'That's what Zahra told me. How does a eight-year-old know the word "devastated"? See what they're doing, Abbu. Watch me, I'm gonna complain.'

He never did. Abbu tried to calm him down and stop him.

'Focus on yourself. You've got a busy year ahead at uni.'

But Saahil didn't feel the same about uni anymore either. There was a sense of foreboding, with pathetic, half-hearted attempts at partying for Freshers' Week. Not all the students were so willing to talk to him and Ehsan anymore. The friendships they'd made in the first year had changed. Many of the connections and bonds undone. Not everyone wanted to stay friends. Instead, people had gravitated towards their own ethnic group protectively.

The divide that had been set during that first week didn't change much over the next two years. Saahil and Ehsan kept their heads down and stuck to their own. They threw themselves into work. Thankfully, they'd come out on the other side, but that didn't stop Saahil from viewing the whole damn thing with contempt. It was a headache he could do without. It had no place in the ideal life he imagined for himself and his family. Things that were happening a million miles away in foreign countries had no bearing on him. But there it was. This anger. This dread. And he could see it now engraved all over Abbu and Uncle Harun's faces.

'Anyway,' Abbu said, smoothing down his clothes. Everyone cleared their throats. Ehsan stopped hiding his face. There was some shuffling around and readjusting themselves on sofas; any attempt to change the atmosphere and recover the same light-heartedness that they had all started the conversation with.

'Have you heard about Rashid?' Abbu said. Saahil saw his father nudge Uncle Harun who sat upright and nodded enthusiastically. Saahil could tell that this part of the conversation had probably been scripted between them beforehand.

'The poor bloke hasn't been to Jummah for two weeks in a row,' Harun said. 'He's too ashamed.'

'Why, what happened?' Ehsan asked.

'His son got some girl pregnant,' said Saahil.

'Really? That nerd Hassan? How did he get a bird?'

'It's not funny,' Abbu said. The boys tried to look serious.

'Sorry, Amjad, but it's this one you need to keep an eye on.' Harun grinned as he pointed to Saahil. 'He's the pretty boy. My Ehsi is too shy about that kind of stuff.'

Saahil snorted as Ehsan covered his face. He was definitely too shy. Saahil only had to encourage him to ask Alisha out almost every day. Ehsan just about managed to give her a smile and gaze longingly after her as she disappeared down the corridor.

'Me?' said Saahil, all dramatics as usual, mouth hanging open in shock.

'Yeah, you,' Abbu said. 'Your uncle's right. What did I find on your phone the other day?'

Saahil groaned. Abbu had seen a text message on his phone.

'Who's Katie?' he'd asked.

Saahil pretended he'd gone temporarily deaf.

'"You better skive lesson for me today,"' Abbu read. '"I'm only coming into uni for you."' He'd turned the phone sideways. 'I take it that's a wink,' he'd said, squinting.

'Don't read my messages, Abbu!'

'Well, it's a good job I did.' Abbu had followed him around the room jabbering away in Punjabi, the go-to language whenever a good bollocking was in need. 'Is that why I send you to university? So you can miss lessons and meet girls?'

'No... I don't know...'

Abbu's voice rose. 'If I find out—'

'Yeah, yeah, Abbu... Laters.' Saahil escaped out of the door.

Okay, fine. He liked girls. A lot. And sometimes he did have a few on the go at the same time. But he always stopped short of going into their knickers. He didn't like hypocrites, and he had his own sister to think about. She was just a kid yet, but already Saahil could see she was going to be a little beauty with her cute upturned nose and pouty lips. In a few years' time, many inadequate pricks would scurry around after her; and Saahil looked forward to breaking their balls if and when they got too close. In which case, he'd rather not go around bonking everything he saw and be able to guide his little sister with a bit of integrity.

'Astaghfirullah,' he said, touching his ears like Ammi often did. 'I don't mess around with people's daughters, thank you very much. Don't wanna go to hell, do I?' He suppressed a grin.

'What moral superiority!' Ehsan mocked, patting his best friend on the back. 'He doesn't mess around with girls because *he* doesn't want to go to hell.'

'No, I didn't mean it like that—'

'Yeah, you did—'

'Shut up, *Ehsi*. Shall I tell Uncle Harun about Alish—'

'Shhh!' Ehsan placed his hand over Saahil's mouth.

Abbu and Harun looked at each other and sighed. They both turned back to their cricket and cups of tea. Saahil smiled at Ehsan when the old men weren't looking, relieved that the conversation was over.

Nine

Saahil frowned as he watched his friend Abdul swearing his way through the crowded restaurant. The Nineties Bollywood music that played in the background did little to hide the profanity, nor did the hum of multiple conversations and the clinking of cutlery. All six of the lads already seated at the table looked around, horrified. Ehsan smiled nervously at a couple sitting near them, trying to make amends. Too late, Saahil wanted to tell him, the tutting had already begun.

'What you doing? Bloody idiot!' they asked when Abdul reached the table with Hardeep.

'He's letting that gora wind him up again,' Hardeep said, casually.

'Who?'

'Daniel or summat or other.'

'He started a debate with me after the exam about Iraq and Bin Laden and all that shit,' Abdul said as he threw himself into a chair beside them. 'All his fuckin' gora gang were there. You should have seen how they were looking at me.'

'Why do you get yourself into these situations?'

'I don't. He's in my face all the time.'

'Where do you know him from?'

'Debating society.' Everyone burst into laughter.

'Serves you right then,' said Saahil. 'Don't join a debating society if you can't take it.'

'I can take it,' Abdul said, huffing and puffing away. 'But he's always at it. Making snide comments and stuff. Making out as though we're all… I'll fuckin' punch him next time.' He pulled a plate of biryani towards him, angrily.

'Well, I hope you shut him up properly, bro,' Asif said.

'I did. I told him that Blair has done us over because Saddam might have destroyed his weapons before we even invaded. That's the latest I've heard anyway.'

'There might not be any weapons,' Kamran sneered.

'I know but… that's what they're telling us, innit? That he's got weapons of mass destruction. And he's killing his own people—'

'So we've gone to save them.'

'Yay!'

'That's what I don't understand,' Asif said. 'Why does it bother them who Saddam's killing? They only give two shits when white people die. Not us.'

'Shhh! People are listening,' Umar said, as a waiter slid past them carrying a tray of drinks.

'Don't care.'

'Wait and see,' Hardeep said. 'They'll do to the Iraqis exactly what they did to us. Barge in, take all their shit, and then scarper outta there and leave 'em to massacre each other.'

'You talking about… Partition?'

'Yeah,' he said, grimly. Hardeep was Indian. The rest of them were Pakistani. A few uncomfortable looks passed around the table.

'That was complicated,' Ehsan eventually said. 'You can't just blame all of what happened there on the whites.'

'Why not? They like blaming us for everything.'

'Yeah and it's not gonna help with you doing the same thing back, is it?'

'Well, do you know what?' Abdul said, still angry. 'When people keep telling you how shit you are that's the only response you have left.'

A few of the guys suppressed laughs and muttered to each other. A waiter hovered near their table.

'Just chill out, mate,' Ehsan said.

'I know, he's getting well paranoid.'

'You would be as well,' Abdul continued. 'They were smirking at me. I was trying my best to explain and they just smirked away. I probably looked like a right twat. I was going bright red...'

'That's what goray do,' Ehsan said, shrugging. 'Explain and justify your entire existence to us whilst we sit here and watch you squirm.'

'Exactly, they get a kick out of it,' said Saahil. 'I just act thick, pretend I can't hear 'em.'

'Anything for an easy life, eh?' Kamran sneered again and adjusted his glasses.

'Yeah, either that or you end up with constant earache,' Saahil replied. 'And anyway, sometimes you can't really blame them. It's not their fault Muslims have started blowing shit up, is it?'

'And is it mine?' Abdul shot back, his mouth full of naan bread.

'Well, no, but there's some of these idiots at our mosque who are in denial. You know, "Muslim blows summat up – it's the media's fault!"'

Ehsan laughed. 'Yeah, *everything* is the media's fault. Or America's fault.'

'So what if they blow stuff up?' Kamran said. 'Why should you feel guilty? Did your dad drive those planes into the Twin Towers?'

'Shut up, dickhead—' Saahil began, but Asif cut him off.

'Fuck 'em,' he said. 'They probably did it to themselves anyway.'

Heads turned in Asif's direction expectantly. He sighed as though burdened with the task of having to educate them all.

'Nine-eleven,' he continued. 'That was some illuminati shit.'

A few of them rolled their eyes and focused on their plates once more.

'I know you don't pay any attention to what I say,' Asif said. 'But it's true. They needed a reason to start a war in the Middle East for oil. I was reading about it on the internet, it said—'

'Get him to put a sock in it,' Saahil muttered. He stopped and looked at the neighbouring tables before dropping into a whisper, 'Or he'll start banging on about Jews in a minute.'

'Jews?' Asif said, loudly.

'Shurrup, idiot!'

Saahil thought he saw Kamran smirk.

'Don't underestimate Zionists,' Asif continued. 'They control everything and they want everyone to hate us—'

'For God's sake,' Hardeep said, grabbing Asif in a headlock. They heard him mumble a few things about 'Israel' before eventually giving up.

'*Anyway*, most people know we're not all the same,' Umar said, instantly pissing Saahil off. He was sick of hearing that tired old line. It struck him as a particularly dumb thing to say. After all, there were quite a few of them about, Muslims and that.

'What? That we're not all suicide bombers?' Ehsan asked.

'Yeah, we are actually,' Saahil said loudly. '"Kill a kafir a day"! That's our motto. That's what's kept us going for the last 1,400 years. In fact, I've got an urge to slit Hardeep's throat right now because he believes in Guru Nanak and not Allah.' He smiled as he put his arm around his Sikh friend.

'It's not funny, Saahil.'

'Yeah, stop making it into a joke.'

Saahil's smile faded. He threw his fork down on to the plate with a clang. 'Fine,' he said. 'What do you suggest we do? Cry about it?'

'Shut up.'

'You shut up.'

'Calm down, everyone,' Ehsan sighed.

Saahil watched his friends dip naan bread into their curries with miserable faces. Abdul muttered under his breath.

'Well, you guys sit here and sulk,' said Saahil. 'And I'm gonna go. I'd rather not spend the evening pondering over the many ways in which people can hate each other.'

Ehsan touched his arm as Saahil made to get up. 'Don't,' he said.

'Talk about summat else then,' Saahil replied.

'Yeah, he's right. We just finished uni, for God's sake. Cheer up.'

Saahil leaned back. A shriek of laughter erupted from a table nearby, prompting them all to turn and glance at the group of mismatched-looking friends. *Probably work colleagues*, Saahil observed.

'Talk about summat else?' someone said. Saahil was retrieved from his own thoughts by Kamran's snarling face. 'Talk about summat else?' he repeated. 'Some of us actually care about what's going on in the world.'

The lights in the restaurant were dimmed, but Saahil noticed that Kamran had been glaring across the table at him all evening. His face was flushed, and the red birthmark on his nose seemed to have absorbed into the colouring of the rest of his complexion.

'*You* care about something other than yourself?' Saahil shot back. 'Don't make me choke on my vindaloo.'

Everyone held their forks mid-air and looked to Kamran for his response.

'You're a big, fat piece of shit, do you know that?' He spat the words out, as though unable to hold them in any longer.

'What the flippin' heck is your problem?' Ehsan started, moving forward in his seat. He was definitely a born peacemaker, but when it came down to it, Ehsan would defend Saahil without a second's hesitation.

'His fucking face is my problem,' Kamran said.

'Well, it's prettier than yours,' Saahil said quietly. It elicited a few giggles from around the table.

'You think you're better than everyone. Walking around everywhere like you own the place. You think you're gonna outshine us all, don't you?'

'What's this all about?' Ehsan asked, looking confused.

'Stay away from Kiran.'

'Who?'

'Kiran. The girl you were chatting up at uni today.' He looked furious. Saahil could hear him breathing hard out of his nose, eyes fixed in a stare, fists balled up tight.

'You're not talking about that bird who was trying it on with me in the cafeteria,' Saahil asked slowly.

'Shut up! You were flirting with her. I saw you, leaning into her, holding her hand.'

Saahil burst into laughter. 'As *if* I would go after her. Even I've got standards. Girl's been around the block more times than a taxi.'

'Saahil,' Ehsan said, nudging him.

'What? It's true! And anyway, why does it bother you so much? You got a thing for her?' He smirked at Kamran.

'She's a family friend—'

'Yeah, right,' Saahil interrupted.

'And I'm looking out for her,' Kamran continued. 'I don't want you trying it on with her like you try it on with everyone else. You're just a bastard who messes girls about.'

'So fuckin' what if I do?' said Saahil, having had just about enough from everybody. 'It's not like I messed about with your sister, is it?'

Kamran stood up. A few of the lads muffled their laughter. 'Oooh, shit got serious,' Saahil heard someone say. He rolled his eyes and sniggered into his drink.

'Oi, shut up now, Saahil,' Ehsan said. 'And you, Kamran, what are you getting emotional for? You don't even have a sister. Sit down.' He was pulled back down on to his seat by his friends. They glared at each other from across the table.

'We're supposed to be celebrating,' Ehsan continued. 'Stop kicking off with each other.'

Smirks vanished as the boys nodded with a new-found earnestness. Everybody always listened to Ehsan.

Saahil squinted and half covered his eyes. The green laser lights were making his head bang. They were stuffed into a booth outside in the courtyard of their favourite nightspot, well away from the packed dance floor where it appeared most of the students had finished their exams for the year. Their heads nodded in accordance with the inadequate booty-shaking that came as 'Crazy in Love' blared from the speakers. They'd passed a spliff around. Saahil waited for everything to just float away. The anger at Kamran, the stress of exams and studying, just everything.

It wasn't long until they were all acting gormless with long, drawn-out 'whaaats' flying around the table.

'Look at all those birds, man,' Asif said. He looked at Saahil and motioned with his head. 'Go on, Saahil, you always get off with one.'

'How many times… I don't get off with anyone,' said Saahil, still holding his head.

'What about you, Umar? Why don't you go dance with one of those lasses?' Umar's eyes widened. 'No no, I don't think so,' he stuttered.

'Why not? Go and have your last bit of fun before you get your bride import from Paki-land.' Everyone laughed.

'I don't have anyone in Pakistan.' An unspoken 'you will have soon' passed around them.

'Don't be a dick, Asif,' Ehsan said.

'Yeah, just because he's fat,' Saahil blurted out. 'Oh, sorry, Umar, you know what I mean. You're a nice bloke, you can have any girl you want.'

'Oh look, Robert's coming over.'

Saahil made a face at Ehsan. That was all he bloody needed. The three guys wandered towards them, beer bottles in hand. One of them tripped over a chair leg.

'All right, boys?' Robert said, obviously tipsy but still managing to reek of self-importance. Saahil had always resisted the temptation of lobbing a textbook at his head across the lecture hall, the pretentious know-it-all. Robert eyed the series of Cokes and lemonades on the table.

'Look at you lot sipping on your sodas,' he chuckled. 'Surely you deserve a beer tonight, lads. We just finished uni.'

'So funny,' Asif said.

Robert's mate, Liam, ogled at the soft drinks too, squinting and turning his head as he tried to comprehend what was before him. He opened his mouth but Saahil cut him off.

'Just shut up,' he said.

'Yeah, but, like, don't you drink… at all? Not even on special occasions?'

'No,' said Ehsan, staring into space like a man defeated. 'Told you about a million times already.'

'He's pissed, he doesn't remember,' Asif sniggered.

'So how do you explain Kamran then?' Robert shot back, grinning from ear to ear. Saahil could tell it gave him much joy to get one over on them. 'He's sat at the bar necking it down. We saw him on the way in.'

They looked over the crowd and could see Kamran sitting on his own at the bar, drinking openly, not even trying to hide it. They glanced at each other in shock.

'What a turd.'

'I'm gonna tell his dad,' Asif said, rubbing his hands together gleefully.

'His dad drinks as well. I've seen him coming out of that pub. The Shoulder of Mutton, I think it's called.'

'What were you doing in The Shoulder of Mutton?'

'I work opposite the building, Sherlock.'

'Forget about him,' said Saahil. He looked at Robert. 'All right, mate. What did you write for question 12b on the exam? I think I got it wrong.'

Saahil checked his watch. It was nearly two o'clock and he suddenly realised how tired he was. He'd drunk litres of Red Bull the night before to stay awake and make sure he had got all his revision done. Robert was now completely wasted and had transformed into 50 Cent.

'*I want them to love me like they love Pac*,' he slurred. Everyone fell about laughing.

'Do you even know who Pac is, white boy?'

'Yeah, go and listen to your puffy Timberlake.'

'He's not *that* bad,' Umar said, nervously.

'He thinks he's Michael Jackson,' said Saahil, scowling. 'And he's not.'

'I know who Tupac is,' Robert mumbled, a few minutes behind everybody else. 'He's the dead guy.'

'Oi, he's not dead all right.'

'Here we go.'

'Yeah, Asif, move on with your life, dude. He is dead.'

'No, he faked his own death, I'm telling you.'

'And which website have you been reading now?'

'Who's dead? Sorry, alive?'

'What?'

Saahil decided to leave his friends to their debate. He'd noticed Ehsan slip away fifteen minutes earlier to answer a call. He found him hanging around the doorway of the back exit.

'You missed it,' said Saahil, as Ehsan put the phone down. 'Robert's acting black.' Ehsan smiled coyly. Saahil frowned at him with suspicion.

'Who were you talking to?'

'Alisha.'

Saahil's jaw dropped. 'When did this happen?'

'I'm sure I told you,' Ehsan smirked.

'You've told me nowt. I've been egging you on and all this time… You sly bastard.' Saahil nudged his friend in annoyance, but couldn't help smiling. He turned to face Ehsan, expectantly. 'Go on then.'

'What? There's nothing to tell. We're just… talking.'

They settled down together on the step.

'You're not pissed off about Kamran, are you?'

'Nah,' Saahil lied. 'I didn't know he fancied that girl.'

'Ignore him. He's always been jealous of you. You beat him at everything. And now he thinks you're going after his girl.'

'Whatever. They're all doing my head in. Glad to get away from 'em.'

Saahil preferred it like this anyway, when it was just the two of them. They sat in silence for a moment facing a brick wall and a few overflowing black bin liners.

'It's weird, isn't it?' Ehsan said. 'That it's over. No more studying and books and deadlines.'

'Hmmm. But from now on it's just like nine-to-five work, work, work.'

'But still, do you reckon things are going to get good now?' Ehsan asked.

'Er, yeah,' Saahil replied and turned to his best friend. There was an odd look in his eyes. One Saahil was not used to.

'We'll do it, won't we, Saahil?'

'Do what?'

'I don't know. Just everything. Everything we said we would.'

''Course we will. We'll have money. First thing I'm gonna do is take my Ammi and Abbu to Mecca. We can all go, you guys as well. That'd be so cool.'

Saahil looked at Ehsan confidently. His smile faded. Ehsan was resting on his knees, hugging them. Saahil thought he looked small. Like a little boy.

'You all right, bro?' he asked.

'Yeah,' Ehsan replied. 'I've just had a weird feeling all day.' He grabbed a fistful of his T-shirt. Directly over his chest.

'Don't worry about it, man,' Saahil said. 'We're gonna be fine. We'll show everyone. Insha'Allah,' he added quickly.

Ehsan smiled and Saahil felt a sudden urge to look after his best friend. To embrace him and tell him everything would be okay.

'Do you remember that time, Ehsan?' asked Saahil.

'What time?'

'When…when you found me at school. I was alone in the cloakroom, crying, you know, not long after… anyway, do you remember what you said to me?'

Ehsan shook his head.

Saahil continued. 'You put your arm around me and told me not to worry. And you said that you were an only child so your own mum wasn't too busy so—'

'You could share with me,' Ehsan finished Saahil's sentence. They both smiled at the memory in silence.

'She'd be proud of you,' Ehsan mumbled.

Saahil shuffled around and looked away, overcome with sadness. People had said that to him plenty of times before and he had nodded dutifully. But it was different coming from Ehsan, it carried a different honesty. After all, nobody knew Saahil like Ehsan did.

Saahil remembered how they had sat poring through university prospectuses together three years ago. They'd already decided they weren't moving away from home. Saahil knew Abbu still needed him, as much as he pretended he didn't.

'You should go,' Saahil had reluctantly advised Ehsan.

Ehsan snorted. 'I'm not going if you're not going.'

'Don't be daft. We're not kids anymore.'

'Don't care. What am I gonna do on my own?'

'You'd make other friends, stupid,' said Saahil, secretly loving him for what he said.

'Forget it.'

Saahil knew what he meant. It just wasn't the same with other people. It was silly to think Ehsan's friendship had helped Saahil get over his mother's death. But it had. Plus he had Zahra. Ehsan, on the other hand, didn't have anyone. That was probably why he was the way he was, so perceptive and attentive to everybody around him. It came naturally to him having spent so much time alone. Ehsan, Saahil had quickly realised, had too much love to give. And most of it he was the recipient of.

As they'd grown older, Saahil found cover in Ehsan's serenity, in his calm, dignified manner. He didn't swagger around like Saahil did, thinking he was *it*. Saahil remembered the many times Ehsan had saved his arse from being kicked. Like he had done again today, stepping in before Kamran could whack him one for being an arrogant prick. Saahil watched Ehsan out of the corner of his eye, sitting beside him on the step, all bunched up and hugging his knees. So what if they hadn't shared the same womb, Saahil thought. According to him, they were closer than brothers. And now they were finally going to make it, together.

'Thanks,' Saahil mumbled.

'For what?'

'Just… stuff.'

'Stuff?'

Saahil laughed nervously. Suddenly, he could barely string a sentence together.

'Just for… erm.'

For sticking by me? For always making things better? For being you?

'For everything. We've come a long way, haven't we?' Saahil finally said. *How inadequate*, he thought.

They looked at one another for a second, and then burst into laughter.

'Okay then,' Ehsan said, awkwardly.

'Shall we get back to those clowns? They'll wonder where we've gone.'

'Yeah, I suppose.'

They slunk off inside, each smiling to himself in secret.

Ten

'Let's do one,' Saahil whispered to Ehsan. 'Or we'll have to carry that idiot home.'

He motioned to Liam, who had fallen asleep on Umar's shoulder. Umar, being too polite, continued smiling awkwardly and didn't shake him off. Besides, it was nearly three o'clock and the boys were getting rowdier. Saahil was sure he could feel a migraine coming on. He just wanted to collapse on to his bed.

'We're going,' Ehsan shouted. Nobody was listening.

'Shhh, they'll blackmail us into staying.'

They made a quick getaway, running towards the entrance of the club. Ehsan laughed and turned around as they got to the door. He walked backwards, not paying attention to where he was stepping. He tripped and fell straight into a group of guys loitering about outside.

'Motherfucker! Watch where you're going!'

Saahil saw at least four pairs of hands knock into Ehsan and push him away. He fell on to his knees before Saahil quickly helped him up.

'What the fuckin' hell is your problem?' Saahil shouted.

'Wankers,' Ehsan said, wiping gravel off his palms.

'What did you say?'

Saahil looked at the gang. There were about six of them, all Asian, tracksuited up and stinking of weed.

'He called you a wanker. What you gonna do?'

'Don't act hard. Fuckin' pussy students,' one of them drawled. They sniggered at each other.

'Well, we can't all be crack dealers,' Saahil shot back.

The leader, Saahil assumed, smirked at him oddly. He was visibly stoned with three lines in his eyebrows. He didn't speak but his sunken eyes stared at them over the hook of his nose.

'Oi! What's going on?' The bouncer had been momentarily distracted. Now he came charging at them.

'Clear off! I'm warning you!' he shouted.

'It's all right. We're going,' Ehsan said. 'Come on.' He pulled Saahil away. Saahil gave the thug one last filthy look before setting off down the street with Ehsan.

'What's going on today? Everybody wants to kill us.'

'I know,' said Saahil.

'It's your fault. You keep starting fights with everyone.'

'Shut up. You're the one who smashed straight into those druggies.'

Only their laughs punctured the silence as they walked through the outskirts of the park. They were a few streets away from Saahil's house. Ehsan would probably crash there for the night. They heard a noise and turned abruptly.

'What was that?' Ehsan asked.

It sounded like footsteps and a few muffled voices. They listened for a few seconds, eyes focused on each other.

'Jinn,' said Saahil, the atmosphere too eerie to pass up the opportunity. He could feel Ehsan recoil slightly.

'Or a churail,' Saahil continued casually as they entered the dimly lit park alleyway. 'Did I tell you about that guy who was driving home really late at night a few years ago? Anyway, he saw a woman in the middle of the road and she vanished. When he looked in his rear-view mirror she appeared in the back seat. He ran off screaming like a girl. They say he even pissed himself.'

Ehsan sped up to walk closer to his best friend.

'Apparently she started talking in a man's voice,' Saahil continued. 'You know, like they do in the films.'

'Don't,' Ehsan warned.

'Anyway, do you think a churail can possess you like a jinn can?' Saahil asked.

'Shut up,' Ehsan said, looking around in the dark. 'You know I get scared.'

'Well, it's true. You need to be careful when you're walking about at night in deserted places. I've heard that jinn can fall in love with you. Become obsessed. Especially if you're good-looking like me,' he added.

'Brilliant, they'll go after you then,' Ehsan laughed.

'Oh no, they can sense fear. So you better stop shitting your pants—'

'I will if you shut your face.'

'I'm only saying it for you, mate,' said Saahil, acting all concerned. 'We'll have to perform an exorcism on you, otherwise.' He paused and let out a chuckle before continuing.

'Poor Christians. In films they always get a priest in, don't they, and everybody still ends up dead. Bless 'em,' he said, fondly. 'They try their best, I suppose.'

'Talk about summat else,' Ehsan said.

Saahil laughed and turned around to face him. Walking backwards, he noticed a flurry of movement behind Ehsan, like a group of shadows had just entered the alleyway. He flinched.

'Saahil, fuck off. What is it?' Ehsan shouted, turning around.

'Oi!' The sound made them jump. It was cold, hell-bent.

They were coming at them. Running. Hoods pulled up. Sleeves rolled back. Six in total. Saahil's eyes focused on the one marching coolly behind the gang. He had three lines in his eyebrow and his fists were balled up tight. He had a swagger, his arms rising and falling, almost as if he was carrying heavy shopping bags. They were all too fast and before Saahil could reach out and move Ehsan out of the way, he saw a glint of metal, a lean object collide with Ehsan's head knocking him sideways. A splatter of blood.

Saahil felt his nose break as the fist made contact. He fell to the floor. The pummelling began.

Someone kicked his groin. He yelled but no sound came out. He tried to curl up defensively, but as he lowered himself, a shoe made contact with his head. It sent him hurling backwards. He noticed the pattern of a trainer sole before it stomped on his face. Again and again. There was mud in his mouth. A broken tooth. They were determined to flatten his head against the concrete. One of them grew tired and started booting him in the lower back.

They jumped on his ribcage. It cracked. Saahil felt blood in his mouth. Vomit rise up in his throat.

A break. Saahil gasped for air, praying it was over. He could hear them talking. They were hanging around casually. Discussing how far to go…

'… if they die?'

'We'll blame it on you.'

Saahil heard deep-throated laughter. His watering eyes saw two people high fiving.

It started again. Prolonged. Relentless. No part of his body remained untouched by a fist or a boot. Somebody sat on top of him and punched him repeatedly.

'Hold it up, hold it up.'

Saahil felt an excruciating pain in his leg. Like it had been snapped off and tossed aside. He screamed.

Play dead, play dead.

They loitered around some more, occasionally booting him wherever they felt attention was needed. His stomach. His back. His face.

'Yeah, we'd better…'

'… someone sees.'

The smell of weed filled his nose as, again, someone sat directly on top of his chest. He – whoever it was – grabbed Saahil's jaw and laughed, 'Pussy student.' His head was slammed back against the floor.

Shapes began moving away, but not before one last well-aimed kick between his legs. When it stopped, the agony started. It travelled up his body, burning through his skin like he had been set on fire.

Saahil lay there for what felt like eternity. Growing cold as he slipped in and out of consciousness. No one would find him. He would die. He thought he knew that for sure, until he felt the presence of someone watching him. A movement in the shadow. A bristle of leaves. Saahil couldn't move his head to check to see who it was. When he finally mustered up the energy, he was too late, they were gone. Saahil wondered if they would return.

Sometime later, he saw his mother. She was right there. *Right there*. Arms splayed out for him, offering protection. She looked exactly the same as she did the last time Saahil had seen her. There was a baby bump too. And Zahra's birdie blanket! The blue and yellow colours draped comfortingly around his mother's shoulders. She wasn't in any pain, though. Nor did she clutch at her belly. Saahil wanted to crawl back to her. It had been so long.

Saahil knew that happened when you were ready to go. Someone from the other side would come and take you with them. He was one of the lucky ones; he could say Shahada before he died.

'La ilaha… ill-Allah,' he breathed.

The last bit. Say it.

'Muhammad-ur rasul Allah.'

He pushed the words out.

There.

It's over.

He let himself drift away.

Somewhere a few yards away from him, Ehsan had stopped breathing.

PART TWO

Eleven

'I wo' walking home from 'bar,' said the man, crouching down by Saahil. 'Took this shortcut. Stumbled across 'em.'

A group of people gathered around the scene. Girls wailed and were comforted by their boyfriends.

'I don't have a mobile thingy,' he continued, his bloodshot eyes visible as he looked up at the ambulance crew. 'I had to run and find someone. Luckily I saw these young 'uns.'

'Can you please move back, sir?'

'Me name's Ken.'

'Ken, can you move back.'

'I can't! He's grabbing me arm! I won't leave him.' He held on to Saahil's hand tightly.

'This one over here's a goner,' a girl said, holding her head.

'I dint see the other lad,' Ken said. 'He was in the shadow, face down. These kids found him.'

'Hurry up with the stretcher!'

'He's bleeding from his ears.'

'Please move back, everyone. Make some space!'

'I don't think he's breathing.'

The blue lights flashed and pierced the dark sky. The paramedics rushed around, their faces fraught with panic.

'Get them in the ambulance.'

'Can I come wi' this one?' Ken asked. 'He's looking at me.'

'No, you're in no fit state.' They could smell alcohol on his breath.

'But… I wanna come…'

'Talk to the police.'

'Come this way with me, sir, we'll need a statement from you.'

'Well, how do I know if they're all right?' he slurred, arm still outstretched as they rushed the boys into the ambulance.

'The police,' they shouted, over their shoulders. 'They'll keep you updated.'

'The police… yeah… the police,' Ken said. 'Oh God… Oh God.'

'Where are they?'

'Did they say they were leaving?'

'I didn't see them go.'

'I don't know anything.'

'Yeah, we know you never know anything, Umar.'

'Ring 'em.'

'You ring 'em.'

'I can't be bothered reaching for my phone.'

'It's in your back pocket!'

'I'll do it,' Kamran said. They all looked at one another.

'Why are you being so nice all of a sudden?' He ignored them and dialled Saahil's number.

Twelve

Amjad stood over the hospital bed not quite knowing what to do with himself. He patted Ehsan's bandaged head lightly.

'Bismillah… bismillah,' he repeated. There was fear all over Amjad's face. His hands shook. As he gazed at Ehsan's inert body, he didn't know what he could do to make it all better. Ehsan was hoisted up slightly, his head turned to one side. His lips were cracked and his mouth hung open oddly. There was a probe sticking out of his head, something to do with monitoring the pressure. *The pressure, the pressure.* That's all Amjad could hear them saying. A catheter was stuck to the side of the bed. They were draining fluid from both ends. Bleeding Ehsan dry.

'Plenty of sedatives,' Harun had stuttered.

'But he's already… unconscious.'

'I know but still… they said they want to give the brain as little to do as possible.' Harun had looked at Amjad desperately. Amjad could almost hear him crying out, 'You were born here, surely you understand better than me!' *No Harun, I don't.*

At that moment, Harun walked in grasping Meena by the shoulders, breaking Amjad's reverie. He almost carried her to the chair. Her eyes were swollen and she stared ahead, dazed with shock. Amjad fiddled with the plastic apron they had given him on his way in.

'I'll come back in a bit,' he mumbled. Harun nodded, wide-eyed. He looked around the room as though confused as to how he'd ended up there.

Amjad almost ran out of the room without looking round. He didn't stop until he got back to the ward where Saahil lay. He slammed the door shut behind him.

It shocked him again just how horrendous his own son looked. His face was a mangled mess of blood, swelling and bruising. His body lay limp and exhausted, like he had been trampled over by a stampede. Still, Amjad thought he saw a hopeful look flicker in Saahil's barely open eyes.

'Ab—Abbu,' he stuttered. It looked as though he was trying to move forward. Amjad turned his back to his son and poured water into a plastic cup.

'What is it?' Amjad asked, more abruptly than he had intended. There was no answer from Saahil. Uttering one word had taken it out of him.

'I was there last night, Saahil,' Amjad continued. 'Nothing has changed in one night. He's had head surgery. It's going to take time.' His voice broke.

Saahil let out a moan as he slumped back into the bed. Amjad couldn't make out if it was due to the pain in his body, or his heart.

'Have some water.' Amjad lowered the cup to Saahil's lips. He slowly turned his head away. Amjad placed the cup on the table and hung around awkwardly.

A few minutes later, and he heard Saahil's heavy breathing. He was so drugged up on painkillers and other medication that falling asleep came easily. Amjad felt relieved.

He scurried off towards the toilets. Once there, he simply

stared at his own reflection. He tried not to think of the fragmented conversation he had overheard as he'd gone to check on Ehsan that morning. Two nurses cleaning an empty room and talking in hushed voices, completely unaware the father of the 'other boy' was listening. Amjad regretted eavesdropping.

'Was he bludgeoned or something?'

'Don't know… weren't found for a couple of hours after and…'

The sound of a bed screeching.

'Definitely won't make it…'

A sigh.

'Yeah, but sometimes… it's for the best.'

Thirteen

Four weeks later and Saahil was discharged from hospital. His face emerged solemn and weary from underneath the swelling and bruising. The pain of his broken ribs remained but it didn't hurt so much to breathe anymore. The fracture in his leg was by far the worst. It throbbed and ached, waking him up at night. Saahil had lost nearly two stone in weight. He remembered all the hours he and Ehsan had spent in the gym, trying to get 'big' with definition in their arms and abs. Now when he felt his body, it was scraggly and thin, pathetically weak. So much had changed in just one month.

He'd managed to visit Ehsan twice in that time. His wretched leg failed him every time as he tried to sneak off to the ICU ward. He barely got past the nurses' station before being ambushed.

'No Ser-hil. You can't go, you're—'

'Infection risk,' he'd finish the sentence off for them. He wanted to wring their saggy necks as they shouted at him in their shrill voices.

'And by the way, it's Saahil,' he'd say. 'Saaa-hil. It's double "a".' He'd limp back to his bed in a foul mood, albeit with a twinge of guilt. He didn't really care if they couldn't get his name right. He just wanted to get one over on them. And as for those sugar-coated reports from his father on Ehsan's condition, they were driving him up the wall.

He didn't need his Abbu to tell him how Ehsan was. Saahil knew it was bad. He only needed to look at the expressions his friends wore whenever they came to visit him. The pain was etched all over their faces. He knew they would have seen Ehsan first, because by the time they entered Saahil's ward, none of them was capable of forming a sentence. Umar, Asif and Hardeep would sit quietly and stare at the floor. Saahil wanted to hit them. Why had they come if they weren't even going to look at him? Or be honest with him? Robert had visited too, bright pink in the face, arms folded, fingernails digging into his elbows, unable to speak.

The day the doctor told Saahil he could go home he hated everyone even more. Again, like an ungrateful little bastard, he resented every mended bone, all the healed flesh. He felt like trashing the place with the crutches they had provided. The crutches that would help him hop his way out of the hospital whilst Ehsan lay in the cold, unfeeling ICU ward where they fed him through a tube and turned him over every hour to prevent holes erupting in his skin.

'Are you happy to be going home?' the nurses asked merrily.

Saahil bit his tongue as Abbu gave them chocolates and non-alcoholic sparkling wine for the staff room. He felt Abbu nudge him. 'Yes, thank you,' said Saahil eventually.

Home was different. Saahil smiled mechanically as Ammi fussed over his gaunt appearance and scabby face. What would he like to eat? And drink? She had made him her special chicken soup for poorly people, was that okay with him? If not she could cook something else? Anything he wanted.

Zahra clung on to his arm and cried. He barely lifted his free hand to comfort her. He didn't tell her not to cry, that her Bhaijaan was home now. Eventually, she shuffled away into a corner.

He feigned tiredness, leaning on Abbu's shoulder as they trudged up the stairs. He stood awkward and embarrassed as his dad helped him put on some pyjamas. Abbu had helped him dress and undress at the hospital, but here at home it felt worse. Saahil's eyes, however, kept flicking over to the door. There was something there that Saahil felt as though he was seeing for the first time, something that had already been present when the family first moved in. A lock.

Saahil willed for his father to just leave, but he insisted on providing extra pillows for his broken leg. He mentioned something about physiotherapy appointments.

'Yeah, Abbu. That's fine. I'm okay. No, no, leave that. Thank you. Thanks. Go on now, you need to rest, too.' Abbu must not have even got to the top of the stairs when Saahil reached out for his crutches. Hoisted himself up. Hopped over to the door. And with great relief, did something he'd never done before. Turned the lock.

Life was measured in weeks now. And progress. Saahil obsessed over the scale. The Glasgow Coma Scale. Why Glasgow? he wondered. He became fixated over every detail about this damn scale that would, slowly but surely, climb higher until his best friend was back to normal. Fifteen. It was the most important number in the world. Ehsan would hit fifteen. He needed to hit fifteen. He would. Of course he would.

The doctors had abandoned the scale. Saahil pretended not to hear the phrase 'continuing vegetative'. *Vegetative*. He flinched like somebody had shouted a dirty word in his eardrum. At the moment, Ehsan was at six on the scale, Saahil calculated. He occasionally opened his eyes, moved his hands and arms, and whimpered.

Saahil mentioned this to the young doctor. He could tell he

was newly qualified and all smug. Probably only a few years older than him. He ummed and ahhed.

'Well, we normally only record reactions that are a *response* to something. Pain or speech. Not spontaneous or random movements and sounds. It's not quite the same thing. Do you understand?'

Saahil did not know what came over him. He grabbed a fistful of the doctor's shirt and shook him violently. 'What do you mean, "do I understand"? Do I fucking look thick to you?' he shouted in his face before Abbu flung him out of the room, apologising.

Dumb doctors. They didn't have a clue. Saahil had watched them place a pen between Ehsan's fingers and squeeze hard, waiting for a reaction. It took Saahil all his strength to not snap off *their* fingers for purposely hurting his best friend. And besides, it had only been eight weeks. Seemed like a lifetime but not really. Ehsan would definitely come back to them.

Every few days, Saahil would run into the high dependency ward and Auntie Meena would hold her arms out for him. 'It's okay,' he'd say, holding her head close to his. Uncle Harun always fidgeted around in his own corner, away from everybody else. Abbu would bring food and start arranging it methodically on the small table. Saahil would settle himself down next to Ehsan and hold his hand. Then he would stare. He would stare so hard his eyes hurt. Looking for signs, looking for any movement that had not been present the last time. Saahil hated the sounds Ehsan made. He would close his eyes and bite the inside of his lip until he drew blood. Nobody else saw, they were all too busy exercising their own methods of coping.

Abbu would always stand by the top of the bed, carefully positioning himself to avoid tubes and machines. He would pop on his mosque hat and open his prayer book. Always 'Surah

Yaseen', the heart of the Quran. It was the prayer that was often recited for the dead or dying. For comfort and for ease through the process of death. This had angered Saahil at first. Ehsan wasn't dead. Nor dying. But Abbu reassured him that the prayer had numerous other benefits.

'There's a hadith, a saying of our Prophet, peace be upon him,' Abbu told him. 'Whoever recites the prayer, or listens to it, it will enter into *their hearts as a thousand cures, a thousand radiant lights, a thousand mercies, a thousand blessings...* I'm praying for his recovery, Saahil,' Abbu reassured.

He recited the whole Surah and kept his nose buried in the book as though he was consulting an instruction manual, a matter-of-fact look on his face. Saahil noticed his eyes fill so easily with tears if he let his gaze linger on Ehsan's face for too long.

Family members wandered in and out but Saahil did not allow anything to distract him. Two months since the attack and he was desperate for anything. A twitch of the index finger, an audible intake of breath. He would take anything. He'd follow Ehsan's unfocused eyes to the corner of the room. The fluttering eyelids entangled in one spot, unable to break free and shift. Saahil would move in closer, willing him to focus. 'Come on, mate,' he'd whisper. 'Stop messing about.'

Each time Saahil returned home more disheartened than the last. 'Move,' he'd say to Zahra and stomp up the stairs without giving salaam to Ammi, without even removing his shoes or jacket.

'Saahil,' Abbu's weary voice would follow him up the stairs.

Sometimes he heard Zahra sob outside his bedroom, scratching at the door. She mewled like an injured cat. He always made sure the lock was turned tight.

Fourteen

July 2003

'Asalaam alaikum.'

'Wa-Alaikum salaam.' Amjad eyed the chubby-faced lad on his doorstep.

'Is Saahil in? I'm Umar, his friend from uni.'

'Erm, yeah, he's upstairs,' Amjad answered, but he didn't invite the boy in.

'We've been trying to get in touch with him for weeks. We just wanted to know if he's all right.'

Amjad sighed heavily. He'd turned away numerous friends over the past few weeks. A young guy called Robert had knocked on the door a couple of days ago accompanied by a Sikh lad. Amjad had made excuses through the door chain and watched them guiltily as they walked away, heads bowed. Amjad couldn't face lying to another one of Saahil's friends and motioned the boy in.

'He might be asleep but we can go see. Follow me.'

Amjad lied to the kid because he knew Saahil rarely opened his bedroom door. Only if Amjad really shouted and banged at it hard with his fist did he relent. He didn't want to create a scene in front of Saahil's friend and was still waiting for Saahil to leave the room long enough so he could unscrew the lock and chuck it away.

'Saahil, open the door. Your friend is here.' He turned the handle and to his great relief, the door was unlocked. The room was dark and the curtains were closed. Amjad saw a shape perched at the end of the bed. He glanced at Umar, whose face said it all. His eyes widened and he took a step back away from the room. To an outsider, the whole set-up appeared almost menacing.

'Sorry, Umar,' Amjad mumbled.

He hurried to the end of the room and threw open the curtains. Saahil's knees were drawn up and his head rested against them.

'Umar's here, Saahil.' There was no response. Amjad leaned down and shook his son. '*Saahil*,' he hissed.

'It's okay, I'll just sit here.' Umar pulled out the chair from the desk and sat down.

'Yes… okay. Erm, well, I'll go and make some tea.' Amjad left.

Umar cleared his throat. 'Mate,' he said, gingerly, as Saahil stared out of the window. 'We've been worried about you. You haven't replied to any of our texts or calls.'

Saahil remained silent.

'We thought you'd done summat to yourself,' Umar added, nervously.

'Topped myself?' Saahil's voice was croaky. The last word he had spoken had been a few days ago to his father. It was 'no'. He thought of his own body hanging from the ceiling. Swaying side to side. He laughed at the image but felt a sharp, searing pain in his chest. He quickly brought his hand up and held it there for comfort. It happened sometimes. An occasional, painful reminder of how they had gleefully jumped on his chest. Laughed as though they were trying to balance themselves on a skateboard. How they had kicked his arms away so they could do the job properly.

'Are you okay?' Umar made to stand up but Saahil motioned him back down.

'We went to see Ehsan,' Umar started again after a few minutes. 'It's just… Kamran's in a state.' His voice shook. 'At least they got those motherfuckers,' he continued. 'Bastards. I hope they give 'em life.'

They're not going to give them life, you idiot, Saahil wanted to say. Not that he wanted to talk about it. He was already a bit fed up of Abbu giving him updates from the police. It's not like justice would be served, would it? The copper in charge of the case had already told them the sentences would be reduced slightly as they had all handed themselves in. Well-deserved for such a noble deed. Nah, his country had no balls. Here, they ran around after criminals, kissing their arses, shaking their hands and calling them 'sir'. Saahil wanted to see them hanged or tortured or beaten to death for what they had done to Ehsan.

'What do you want, Umar?' Saahil asked, his voice toneless and cold.

'I'm not graduating next week. I'm postponing it until November. I'm going to wait for you… and Ehsan.'

'There's no need for you to postpone it, it'll just hold you back for no reason.'

'But I want to. It's the least I can do.'

'I don't have the energy to argue with you, mate. All you're gonna do is walk across the stage and shake hands with some old white geezer wearing a cloak. Just get it over with.'

Umar shuffled around. He decided to change the subject.

'Why don't you come out with us tomorrow? It'll help take your mind off things. The guys miss you. And it's not good being stuck in this room all day.'

Saahil ignored him.

'At least let me try to help you.' Umar's voice became a tad impatient. 'You've always helped me. I don't know what I would have done without you these past three years. You and Ehsan. You've always helped me with work and… and stuck up for me in front of… people.'

'Ehsan stuck up for you, not me.'

'It was both of you.'

'No, it wasn't. I only bothered with you because Ehsan did.'

It surprised Saahil how easily the words came out of his mouth. He really didn't care if he caused Umar pain. It was true, he only 'stuck up' for Umar so he could take a swipe at Kamran. Only Ehsan genuinely cared about things like that. Feelings and stuff. He was the one who made sure everyone was all right. Not him.

'You're upset,' Umar said. 'You just need to try and—'

'And what?' said Saahil, waiting for the genius answer. Umar couldn't find one.

'Hopefully everything is gonna be okay, Saahil.'

Again, the shitty platitudes he had no interested in hearing. *It's not* fucking *okay, though, is it?* he wanted to shout out. *It's never gonna be okay, not unless Ehsan sits up in bed tomorrow and starts talking.* The chances of that happening were slipping away day by day.

Only yesterday Abbu had dropped Saahil off near the entrance of the hospital and gone to find parking. Saahil had spotted someone in the distance. It was Alisha. She was sitting on the wall, her face screwed up, hand shielding her eyes as she stared up at the tall hospital block. Saahil watched her for a few seconds. Then she'd spotted him. All the worry seemed to drain from her face. She sighed with relief and made to stand up, but Saahil turned away. He saw Alisha's smile fading before he entered the doors, and left her there, alone and desperate.

Saahil had spent the whole night thinking about her. He imagined her waiting around for a sign of Ehsan. She probably didn't know which ward he was on – was unsure as to whether it was appropriate for her to go up there alone. What were Ehsan's family like? Would they understand, or start to ask questions about who she was? What if the ward was filled with family members? Would she be intruding? Saahil knew that what Alisha had needed was for him to help her. To take her up with him. Instead, he had turned away. Ehsan wouldn't have wanted Alisha to see him like that. It was probably best that she just forget about him and get on with her life.

They had beaten Saahil more. He was the one, after all, who had mouthed off the most. They had done their best to break his body, but Ehsan had received the blow to his head. Then he'd stopped breathing. No oxygen to his brain. Swelling and pressure. God knows what else. *What the fuck was he doing during that time?* Saahil asked himself. *Why hadn't he moved? Called Ehsan's name? Reached out for him?* Saahil had no recollection of anything. If only he'd moved his backside, he may have seen Ehsan lying there face down in the shadows, blood seeping from his ears.

'Please go, Umar,' Saahil sighed.

Umar stood up and walked towards the door. 'Just pray, Saahil. Keep praying. There's nothing else we can do.'

Saahil went to the window and watched Umar's stocky frame walk down the street. He took his phone out of his pocket and, ignoring the unread messages and missed calls displayed on the screen, stared at the calendar. Four months. Four months until the end of November. That would be six months in total. More than enough time for Ehsan to come round and be with him on graduation day. Just like it was supposed to be. The two of them ticking off another life event together and planning how to go about fulfilling the next.

'Bhaijaan?' Zahra was outside his room, white headscarf held in place with a safety pin under her chin. She eyed him hopefully as she clutched the Quran to her chest. He always listened to her recite after school. That was *his* responsibility.

Saahil drew the curtains closed once more and walked over towards her. He stopped short and reached for the handle. He saw the last glimmer of hope fade on his sister's little face as he slammed the door shut. Lock turned. He perched himself on to the edge of the bed once more.

He had his own praying to do.

Amjad sat down on the sofa with the cup of tea he had made for Umar. He heard the door close again upstairs. He would have to do something about that lock. It was unsafe. Amjad could barely get through to his son these days. He could not be certain there were no funny thoughts going on in his head.

Saahil had no interest in talking about what had happened. When Amjad tried to ask questions, he snapped at him and wandered off, rolling his eyes. He'd done the same thing when the nice lady from Victim Support had come over to the house. Saahil had taken one look at her and bolted straight of out of the door.

'They beat the crap out of us,' he said later to an angry Amjad. 'What's there to talk about?'

Amjad was not used to his son's cutting tone. Saahil had never spoken to him like that in his entire life. It was understandable, but it still bothered Amjad when he looked into Saahil's eyes and saw no love. Just indifference. Or annoyance. The only time Amjad had seen him smile was when Saahil met Ken, the man who'd found him and Ehsan on the night they were attacked. Ken had visited the hospital but Saahil had been too drugged up to know. After Amjad's insistence, Ken came to the house one evening for dinner. Saahil was gracious, polite and smiled along to Ken's jokes. But as soon as he'd left, Saahil retreated to his bedroom once more. Door locked.

Amjad tried to comfort him as best he could. But Saahil was not a little boy. He was a man. He didn't want to be cuddled or caressed by his dad, Amjad knew that for sure. He'd sit with Saahil sometimes, a big gap between them and pat his shoulder awkwardly. 'Everything's going to be all right,' he'd say. Saahil would barely respond.

Women, Amjad realised, did not care for such barriers. After living alone for so long he had fooled himself into thinking he could do everything. He couldn't. As he watched Ammi swoop down on Saahil, his heart panged with envy. She cradled him gently as she sobbed into his hair. He didn't resist but instead lay against her shoulder, quite still. Amjad would leave them to have their moment. He had never missed Neelam so much.

Saahil had taken to carrying around his mother's old shawl. He'd lay it over his duvet when he slept. Moped around with it draped over his shoulders. He'd asked for it especially, not long after he came home from hospital. Amjad wondered why.

'Where's Zahra's birdie blanket?'

Amjad frowned. 'In her bedroom somewhere. She hasn't used it for ages.'

'I need... Can I have it, please?'

Amjad found the pashmina and gave it a good shake. Dust swam in the air around him. It was still such a mesmerising piece of fabric, despite all the years of Zahra's scrunching and crumpling and creasing. The teal blue backdrop may have faded a fraction due to the numerous washes that were required during Zahra's toddler years, but the intricate mustard yellow stitching was as striking as ever, as was the family tree that took centre stage.

'What do you want it for?' Amjad had asked.

'Oh nothing… just remembered it,' Saahil replied, taking the shawl from Amjad and holding it against his cheek.

Of course, there wasn't the added stress of finding the culprits. Amjad sighed with relief when they had handed themselves in, though he doubted a sense of remorse had compelled them to own up to their crime. News of Saahil and Ehsan's condition passed quickly throughout the community. Prayers were held at the mosque and the story had appeared in the local newspaper. The policeman mentioned how the father of one of the thugs had brought him into the police station by the scruff of his neck. That explained it all.

Something else troubled Amjad. He'd noticed it again on their last visit to the hospital: Saahil holding Ehsan's hand against his cheek; Harun throwing a filthy look in Saahil's direction, turning his back as Amjad offered him his hand.

Resentment was understandable. Saahil was recovering, physically at least, whilst Ehsan could not even respond to his own name. Deep down, he knew Harun loved Saahil, just as Amjad loved Ehsan. They had raised the pair of them together. They were closer than brothers because Amjad and Harun encouraged their friendship. Saahil and Ehsan were *his* boys. He could not imagine one without the other.

Still, there was a problem. He thought back to a comment made by Harun a few weeks ago. 'My boy, my Ehsi. He'd never have started a fight with anyone. He was always sensible. None of this is down to him.'

Amjad had agreed. But now, he was not so sure. Maybe Harun had stopped short of saying Saahil's name. They both knew he was the gobby one out of the two. But this was different. Those bastard thugs had just been looking for an excuse to start on someone.

Amjad thought of raising his concerns; maybe it would clear the air between him and Harun. He dismissed this straightaway. He would hardly start an issue with a man who had lost everything. He'd hold tight. They all would.

Ammi walked down the stairs with her prayer mat. Amjad took it from her and headed to his bedroom. He had started praying namaz five times a day since the incident. He felt guilty for reacting in this shameless, predictable way. Praying day and night now that he needed Allah to help him. His desperation compelled him to continue, of course. A beautifully stitched image of a mosque lay out in front of him. Amjad readied himself on that mat and raised his hands to his chest. It just wasn't in their nature to give up hope.

Fifteen

November 2003

The days were shorter and darker. The wind shrieked. It was always muggy at dawn. Dull and grey. Saahil could see people sitting in their cars in the early mornings, steaming the air-conditioning full blast to de-ice their windows, blowing warm air on their hands and shivering. Saahil paid a lot attention to what was going on outside. He spent too much time staring out of the curtains at the same old streets, the same old people. Always remaining hidden.

He regretted not making the most of summer. Every year before that had been spent studying or taking up shitty part-time jobs to pay for driving lessons and car insurance. Now he was free to do whatever he liked. Ah yes, the irony of it all made him laugh to himself like a madman. Alone in a room, laughing to himself.

So that's it then, is it? Saahil wanted to ask Him. That is Ehsan's life. Twenty-one years of nurturing and feeding and loving from his parents, only to be cut short when life was supposed to truly begin. Like waiting for a flower to grow and then snatching, tossing and ripping it aside before it had chance to bloom. *You can't do that*, Saahil would think, gazing skywards with contempt. But He could. And He had. And there was nothing Saahil could do about it.

He'd suddenly feel small and insignificant. Fearful and

apologetic for arguing with God. After all, when it came down to it, when he could not sleep at night, it was to Him that Saahil whimpered. It was Him Saahil would bug. 'Ya Allah… please help.'

Those sleepless nights were the worst; he would lie awake for hours, praying for sleep. Even in states of semi-consciousness, he rarely escaped unscathed. A lovely walk along a path would lead him to fall abruptly down a set of stairs. He would jolt awake. It wasn't always stairs. Sometimes it was a boot, pounding his face, kicking him out of his slumber. For the first few seconds he'd feel relieved. It was only a nightmare. But then—

It fucking wasn't, was it?

That's when images of Ehsan would invade his thoughts. Auntie Meena wiping dribble from his chin. The clenched fists. The moaning. Saahil didn't see everything, of course, but he could only imagine. Pretty nurses slapping on latex gloves, edging towards his best friend, wrinkling their noses because of the smell. Pulling back the sheets, changing his soiled undergarments. Wiping him clean. Saahil would hold his head in despair. Dig his fingernails into his face.

It was like Ehsan had been thrown off the edge of a cliff and then, maliciously, caught just in time, just before death could have him. They had reeled him back in slowly, but only halfway. Now he was stuck between life and death. He was neither alive nor dead. He was nothing. If there was a way Saahil could go back, he would. He would kick Ehsan off that cliff himself. Cut the rope. Pull the plug. Smother him.

Saahil listened in on Abbu's telephone conversations. It was increasingly Auntie Meena who talked to Abbu, and not Uncle Harun. Saahil wondered why? The adjustments were being made in their house. The kitchen wall knocked through to make space for a hospital bed. A hoist being fitted into the ceiling. A downstairs toilet and wet room for bathing.

'They ask me,' he'd heard Harun say on a previous visit. 'They ask me if I have the strength to look after my own son.' He muttered a few swear words in Urdu. 'He's still our boy. Isn't he, Meena? We looked after him before, and we can bloody well do it now.' They all surrounded Ehsan's bed at the rehabilitation unit he had been placed in temporarily. Saahil, increasingly hovering around the end of the bed, looking everywhere except at Ehsan. Harun continued.

'I know what they want. They want me to kill my own son. No quality of life. Astaghfirullah. I won't do it! *We* won't do it. Right, Meena? Kill him off just so we don't have to look after him. That's selfish.' He paused and stroked Ehsan's forehead. Ran his fingers through his hair. 'How could he ever be a burden?' Saahil had never seen so much pain on a human face. So much love. He wanted to run along to his own father and pull at the cuff of his sleeve like a kid. *Please take me away from here, Abbu. Abbu, please.*

When it got too much, he'd come home and trash his bedroom, smash plates in the kitchen. He'd even punched a hole through the glass door in the living room, Abbu charging towards him to control the outburst and Zahra cowering in a corner, frightened. He let himself be dragged off to counselling sessions, Abbu telling him all the while that he needed help. Whatever he needed, it wasn't that. A bespectacled geeky man asking him dumb questions and jotting down his answers on a clipboard.

'How do you feel about that, Saahil?'

How the fuck do you think?

He'd choose a different adjective each time to spice things up a bit. Last time it was 'devastated'. The time before 'broken'. Just broken.

Saahil tried to control the anger, but it wasn't all his fault. His body was playing tricks on him. The night before he graduated, he awoke in his bed with the feeling that somebody had their hands around his neck. He gasped, but couldn't move his arms. Saahil fought the weight on top of him and fell on to the floor, clutching his throat. He was terrified, his eyes darting around in the pitch black. Was it a jinn? The very thing Saahil had been frightening Ehsan with moments before they were attacked? Was there something watching him as he struggled on his bedroom floor? A supernatural force, a demonic spirit?

Or maybe it was Ehsan. His trapped soul finding his way to Saahil, clutching, clawing and pulling him out of sleep. Screaming for help. Cursing Saahil for abandoning him.

He needed to get out of there. He went to the door and yanked it open, staggering into his father's bedroom. He wasn't there. Down the stairs, holding on to the banister, gasping for breath.

Abbu had fallen asleep on the sofa, still seated with his head lolling backwards. He must have risen early for morning prayers. Light was coming in through the curtains. Saahil almost fell on the couch next to him. He placed his head against his father's chest. He felt Abbu stir.

'Saahil? Saahil, are you okay?'

Tears fell, soaking Abbu's shirt. Saahil felt his dad's arms wrap around him.

'I… I can't do this, Abbu. I can't.'

Soon he, too, was sobbing into Saahil's hair.

'I won't… I won't recover from this.' Saahil had battled with that feeling for weeks. Like he would never laugh or smile again.

'Shhh,' Amjad said, holding his son tight, rocking him gently. 'I'm here,' he said. 'My little boy... my beautiful little boy.'

Saahil leaned back on his chair, slowly dipping from view. He could see Abbu, Ammi and Zahra from the corner of his eye, sitting with the rest of the families. He tried to look interested as people made dull speeches about how utterly amazing his university was. How it was at the cutting edge of research and had the best employability rates, creeping up every league table known to man. How absolutely awesome they, the Class of 2003, had it. From this moment on, they had the world at their feet. They could do and be anything they wanted. They could change the whole world. Become millionaires. Blah, blah... fucking *blah*.

Even the annoying black tassel dangling in front of Saahil's eyes was more inspiring than the drivel being spouted at them. When he looked around, he wanted to laugh at his fellow students. They were sitting on the edge of their seats like meerkats, all doe-eyed and quivering with excitement. He wasn't even supposed to be there. 'Can I just clarify,' he wanted to assert, 'I didn't fail first time around, okay. Not like these thickos graduating now, months after everybody else.'

Saahil knew he didn't need to. They all knew who he was. They recoiled when they set eyes on him. Took a step back. Pretended not to have seen him. Saahil heard them whispering away, 'Saahil... Saahil and Ehsan... attack... remember... in May... Ehsan... brain dead.'

Someone cracked a joke on stage. Polite laughter. He smiled along with everyone else, instinctively looking to his side. No, Ehsan wasn't there. He suddenly felt small and insecure, sitting up in his seat and pulling himself together, realising again just how much of his bravado and swagger had relied on his best friend. It was like he was learning new things about himself everyday.

Tutors approached Saahil nervously. 'How are you?' they asked.

'Fine,' he replied, looking straight past them.

'So sorry to hear about what happened to Ehsan,' one of them said.

'Hmmm.'

Another asked about the future. *Future*. He wanted to laugh, *What future?*

'Have you got a job lined up? No... okay, well any idea what you'd like to do?' Silence. 'Further study perhaps?'

'Don't know.'

'Ah... right.'

Abbu quickly jumped into the conversation and started talking about how lovely the buildings were. All glassy and modern. Very modern indeed. Zahra held Saahil's hand and pulled him towards the photography booths. He allowed himself to be led away by his little sister without looking back.

Ammi adjusted his graduation hat. She'd pinned his gown in place, clipped it together under his tie, smoothed down creases over his shoulders. 'Masha'Allah,' she beamed. He was ready for his picture.

Saahil held the plastic graduation roll in his hand, the dodgy nail sticking out of the back of it to keep the red ribbon in place. What a let down, he thought; Ehsan would have something to say about this.

Now how was he supposed to get the hell out of there unnoticed? He watched Abbu looking at different photograph packages, an overenthusiastic assistant trying to persuade him to buy a ridiculous number of copies of the same photo, the same pose. *They only needed one bloody picture*, Saahil thought. A space had already been vacated on the wall of their living room for the thing to hang there in all its glory.

Ammi and Zahra were sitting apart from him. He could see Ammi gossiping away, whispering into Zahra's ear. Checking out what everyone was wearing, grimacing at the tan lines streaking down white girls' legs, at the over-the-top, bright salwar kameez worn by Asian girls on such a smart occasion, where understatement was key. If Saahil told them he wanted to go see Ehsan, they would stop him. He didn't blame them. He would be the last person Harun and Meena wanted to see today of all days. But they went home for breaks, didn't they? Saahil had figured out their timings. A quick five minutes wouldn't kill anybody.

Should he return his cap and gown? No, Abbu would see and realise what he was up to. At least he could leave the stupid hat with Ammi? No, she would start asking questions. He'd hide it under his gown and sneak off. He headed towards the exit. Abbu would start looking for him after he'd made his purchase. Nobody would know where he had gone. They'd ring him and he wouldn't answer the phone. They'd worry. They'd panic.

Oh well.

'He's been sitting in his chair today. Haven't you, sweetheart? We've just moved him back now.' Saahil smiled at the plump nurse who led him to Ehsan's room.

'Look who has come to see you! It's Saahil. He's come to show you his graduation outfit.'

'No, no, I haven't…'

'Mum and Dad left ten minutes ago,' she continued. 'They'll be back in this evening. He's always on time is your dad, isn't he?'

It was comforting to hear the nurse (Mary something, it said on her badge) speak to Ehsan as though he was a child. She was motherly and affectionate, like the type of person who was always ready for a cuddle.

'Now let's make you a bit more comfortable... there, that's better. I'll leave you fellas to it now.'

Saahil actually longed for her to stay. Her presence had made the atmosphere seem surprisingly serene. There was none of the pain or hurt Harun and Meena carried around with them. Or the guilt-ridden faces he and his Abbu wore whenever they entered the room. No, today, there was just this wonderful nurse, who fussed over Ehsan as though he was the most important thing in the world.

As she wandered off, the nurse tugged at the hospital curtain. She let it go halfway so it only shielded Ehsan. It was like a straight line that cut down the two of them. Saahil was still exposed. Ehsan, closed off. Saahil didn't know why, but this arrangement made him uncomfortable. He stood up and opened the curtains fully and pulled his chair to the top of the bed. To his surprise, Ehsan's face was relaxed. If it weren't for the fluttering eyelids and croaky breathing, Saahil could pretend they were back to normal. Chilling out together. Watching the football. Talking about girls. Secretly giving Zahra sweets before dinner.

Ehsan's hands were resting over his stomach. Saahil noticed they were beginning to claw and become rigid. He straightened them out.

'Ehsan,' he whispered. Saahil's arms were folded on the bed. He leaned in closer. 'Ehsan?' There was no answer. *Please talk to me.* Saahil nudged him. *Tell me what to do. Where to go from here?* Still, nothing. *You're the sensible, clever one. You always know what to do.*

Saahil had come to accept the fact that there was no awareness. No way Ehsan could see, feel or hear what was going on around him. But still, as he looked into his best friend's face, there was that question, that impossible possibility that a little part of him remained. Those questions, they haunted Saahil at night.

Does Ehsan know?

Does he know what has happened to him?

Does he know how he has ended up?

What has become of his life?

Saahil placed his head on the pillow next to his best friend. He moved in. Closer still. Their foreheads touched. He closed his eyes.

When Harun and Meena walked into the room, Saahil stood up smiling at them.

'Asalaam alaikum,' he said. They didn't respond. Instead their eyes crawled all over him, incredulously. Saahil looked down. He felt his hands claw at the black robe wrapped around his body. His eyes rested on the graduation hat toppled over at the end of the bed.

Shit.

'I'm… I'm sorry. I—'

'How dare you?' Harun breathed.

'No, Uncle, I came straight from uni, I—'

'Why have you come here!' Harun shouted. He was shaking.

'Harun, calm down—' Meena began.

'Chup!'

'He just wanted to see Ehsan, he didn't mean it—'

'*He*,' Harun said, pointing straight at Saahil's face and making him flinch, 'is the reason your son is lying there in this state.'

'Don't be ridiculous,' Meena said, looking anxiously at Saahil.

'Me?' asked Saahil, feebly.

'Yes, you. With your big, loud mouth. My Ehsi was not a shaytan like you. He didn't start fights with anyone and gob off. This is all down to *you*.'

'Saahil, just go,' Meena cried.

Harun wasn't finished.

'Just because I tolerated you all these months for your father doesn't mean I'm going let you come here today, dressed in all your finery, and gloat in front of my son!'

'Gloat?' Saahil was horrified.

'Harun, don't—'

'No, Uncle, please, I would never—'

'I'm warning you. Don't come back here again. Get out. I said, GET OUT!' Harun lashed out and knocked a jug of water off the table. It smashed. Water seeped across the wooden floor. Saahil ran, without looking back.

Saahil tore at his gown as he stumbled out of the care home. He ran past shops and down streets, carrying the black mess in his arms, the pleats dangling to the floor. He slipped into an alleyway and fell against the wall. His arms relaxed and he watched the gown tumble to the pavement, landing in a pile before his eyes.

He realised his hands were shaking and he was gasping for air. He pulled at his tie, yanking it off so he could breathe properly. He almost slammed his head against the wall as he looked skywards. A pain spread from the back of his head but Saahil barely noticed. He was too busy running over every memory he had of that night.

Every movement he and Ehsan had made, every exchange, every retort between them and the gang. Somewhere, within those memories, he would find legitimacy in Uncle Harun's accusations.

Surely it was all his fault. It had to be. *He* was the only one capable of causing such heartbreak, not Ehsan. But the more Saahil tortured himself, the more he unpicked every memory of that night, he found nothing to suggest he had done anything to justify their response of almost killing his best friend.

When Saahil emerged, he found himself curled up against the wall. He hoped nobody would walk past and see him. Ask if he was okay. He suddenly remembered his family. Now he would have to return home and face them.

Saahil gathered his things from the ground and slowly walked off towards his house, thinking all the while that he would rather run away.

'Where the *bloody hell* have you been?'

Saahil rushed past Amjad and headed straight for the stairs.

'Why didn't you answer your phone? We were waiting around there for an hour looking for you. Oi, you little shit, get back down here now!'

Amjad made to follow Saahil up the stairs but Ammi held on to him.

'Let him go. It's no use,' she said. He sighed and reluctantly followed her to the couch. Zahra held his hand. They all sat in silence.

Sixteen

Amjad smiled as he heard the chatter coming from his living room. He added the garam masala to the curry and stirred. Everything had already been beautifully chopped: the onions, the peppers, the tomatoes and the rest of the veg. By Saahil! Yep, he'd volunteered himself. He was an expert chopper. Most of it was due to his desire to be good at anything and everything. He was such a cocky little so and so.

'Watch, Abbu, watch how fast I can do it,' he'd say as a teenager.

'Yeah, stop showing off. And please don't take your finger off while you're at it.'

Amjad opened the kitchen door and saw Saahil sitting opposite Zahra and her little school friend, Libby. They appeared to be having a face-pulling competition. The girls giggled away at a particularly contorted expression of Saahil's. He was smiling at them and it seemed to reach his eyes.

Today had been a good day. Amjad had still not forgotten Saahil's desertion at the graduation; he'd said he'd bumped into some of his friends and lost track of time. Well, anything that coaxed him back into normal life Amjad could be grateful for.

There was a knock on the door. Amjad opened it, still smiling as fresh giggles erupted from Zahra and Libby. His smile faded immediately. Harun thrust something into his hands. A black object. A hat. A graduation hat.

'I'm not here to argue, Amjad. In fact, I'm surprised you haven't already rung me demanding an explanation.'

'What? Why? Come inside.'

'Tell your son,' Harun said, 'that *my* son is brain-damaged. He can't see, hear or understand anything. So there's no need for *him* to come around showing off. Not now, not ever.'

Amjad looked down at the hat. His heart sank.

'Harun, I don't know about any of this,' he said slowly. 'But whatever happened, Saahil would never show off. How can you say such a thing?'

'Don't,' Harun held his hand up. 'I haven't got it in me any more.'

'Harun…' Amjad reached out and touched his arm. Harun pulled away.

'We're moving Ehsi home tomorrow. There's no need to visit.'

'What – what are you saying?' Amjad looked at his friend's face in disbelief. Harun fidgeted, as though he was dangerously close to the edge.

'Thank you for everything you've done, Amjad,' Harun said, his voice quivering. 'But now you have to just leave us alone. Tell *him*, he's not welcome. No one is.'

'No, I'm not letting you go like this. Come inside. I'll call Saahil. He'll apologise.'

Harun slapped the palms of his hands together and held them in front of his face. 'Please,' he begged. 'For Allah's sake, just leave me alone to look after my son.' He turned and left.

Amjad stared down at the hat, feeling incredibly stupid. Saahil had lied and he had believed him. Amjad warned him not to go anywhere near Ehsan on that day. Harun and Meena did not need reminding that their son would never graduate, despite all his hard work. He would never go on to start a career, get married, have his own children.

'Just leave them alone,' he'd warned Saahil. 'We're not going to mention it, we'll pretend it hasn't even happened.'

And yet still, Saahil had disobeyed him. He'd gone and paraded around in his graduation clothes in front of Harun and Meena. Amjad felt the anger rising up in his chest. His hands trembled. He was going to kill him.

Amjad marched into the living room. 'Zahra, upstairs, now.'

'But, Abbu, we're—'

'Now!' He watched the two girls slip away, staring at him fearfully as they headed towards the stairs, well aware that something bad was about to happen.

Saahil frowned. 'What's up, Abbu?'

Amjad threw the graduation cap. It hit him on the face. 'What's this?' he asked his son.

Saahil's gaze lingered on the hat, he touched it with his fingers. He looked at the floor.

'You lied to me. I told you not to go. I fucking told you not to go.' Saahil remained silent. Amjad never swore like that. 'Answer me,' he said, standing over Saahil.

'I just wanted to see him,' he mumbled in response.

'And could you not have gone the next day? Do you not think about anyone but yourself?'

Saahil looked hurt. 'Abbu?'

'Harun has been around, telling me they're taking Ehsan home tomorrow. And that none of us are welcome.'

'He can't do that,' said Saahil, jumping to his feet.

'Yes, he can. He's Ehsan's father, he can do what he wants.'

'I'll ask Auntie Meena, she'll let me go.'

'No, she won't. Are you not listening to me? They don't want us anywhere near them, thanks to you.'

'He's blaming me,' Saahil shouted back. 'He's saying Ehsan's a vegetable because of *me*. That I made him like that.'

'He's just lashing out. Put yourself in his position.'

'Well, he's not the only one who's hurting! What about me? What am I supposed to do?'

'What about you? You've got me.'

Saahil rolled his eyes.

Amjad stared at him. 'Ah, is that what the problem is? Have I not supported you enough these past six months? Looked after you? Don't you dare walk away from me!' Amjad grabbed Saahil's sleeve and flung him back. 'I'm sick of you running off every time you can't be bothered answering me,' he continued. 'It's time you faced things like a man.'

'Faced things like a man?' Saahil laughed. 'And how do you suggest I do that? By doing a few shifts with you at the warehouse to "take my mind off things"? It doesn't work like that.'

'And you're going to tell me how things work? You, a kid, are going to teach me a lesson about life?'

'You just don't understand, Abbu.'

'What don't I understand? Do I not love Ehsan? He's like my own son.'

'Oh yeah, whatever…' Saahil's voice trailed off. He looked away but Amjad followed him with his head so they retained eye contact.

'What? Why don't you say exactly what's on your mind? Go on.' Amjad grabbed hold of his arm.

'Get off me!'

'No. Answer me properly!'

They were yelling at the tops of their voices. Footsteps came thundering down the stairs.

'Fine!' Saahil shouted, pushing Amjad back. 'Why should you care so much about someone else's kid? That's probably why you're praying five times a day now, eh? Don't think I don't know, you're probably thanking Allah that it's Harun's son who is lying there half dead and not your own!'

It wasn't a slap. It was a punch. Amjad's fist was balled up, a speck of blood on the knuckle. Saahil, caught off-guard, fell back on to the sofa. Zahra and Libby, now at the bottom of the stairs, clung on to each other in shock.

Apart from the odd smack on the bottom when he was a kid, Amjad had never hit Saahil before. Saahil held his face and stared at the floor, surprisingly calm. A trickle of blood fell from his nose. He wiped it away with the back of his hand. He waited for Amjad to speak.

'Get out of my sight,' Amjad said. Saahil bolted out of the door. Amjad pulled a chair from the dining table and sat down. Zahra ran to him.

'I'm sorry,' he said, as Zahra cried into his shirt. He looked at Libby, who had gone bright red. 'I'm sorry, Libby, come here.' He held his arm out for her. She approached cautiously

'Are you okay?' Amjad asked, patting her on the shoulder.

'Erm... yeah,' she squeaked.

'Sorry you had to see that,' Amjad said. He settled the girls down on the sofa and put on their favourite film, *Shrek*.

'It's okay,' he said, as he floundered out of the room. 'It'll be okay.'

He leaned against the kitchen counter, watching his hands shake uncontrollably. *They need something to do*, Amjad thought.

In his fretfulness, he reached out and put the kettle on. As he waited for it to boil, he began worrying about where Saahil had gone. When would he be back? How they would carry on from this? Perhaps a break from one another was for the best?

Amjad decided to ring his brother first thing in the morning.

Seventeen

'Send him to me,' Javid said. 'I'll straighten him out.'

'He doesn't need straightening out. He just needs a change of scenery.'

Javid laughed his annoying, smug laugh. 'A change of scenery? We're two hours down the motorway, brother.'

'You know what I mean,' Amjad said. 'We just need a break… from each other.'

'Yeah, yeah,' he said, not really listening. 'The boys will come and get him.'

'Don't worry about that, I'll drop him off. Or if I can't, he'll get the train.'

'No no, you know my boys, they need an excuse to get on to the motorway and drive a hundred miles an hour.' He laughed heartily again. Amjad didn't bother to ask if his precious boys were even bloody insured.

'Just a couple of weeks, you know. It'll be nice for him to see his cousins. They can "chill" or whatever it is they get up to.'

'Well,' Javid said, in his booming voice, 'I've been saying it to you all summer. Let him come over. Don't know why you keep fobbing me off.' *Because you've driven me up the wall in a two-minute telephone conversation.*

When Amjad's nephews turned up at the door a few days later, they walked in with sagging pants and weird patterns shaved into their heads.

'Chachaaa! Amjad Chacha.' They greeted him in a bizarre handshake/hug Amjad had seen black men do on the telly. He offered the boys roti but they told him that they were going to be visiting their grandmother next.

'No Chacha,' Zakariya said. 'We're going straight to Ammi's house to have dinner, innit.'

'Yeah, innit,' Amjad could only repeat. Zahra raised her eyebrows at him.

'Where's Saahil?'

'He won't be long.' The boys decided to wait in the car. Amjad and Zahra tried to keep straight faces as they watched them saunter down the garden path. *Young people these days*, Amjad thought shaking his head. Their entire attitudes were encapsulated by the long, drawn out 'yeaaahs' they added to the end of each sentence.

Saahil came down the stairs clutching his bag.

'Have you got everything?' Amjad asked. 'They're waiting for you in the car.'

'Yeah. Allah Hafiz, then.'

'Allah Hafiz. Bye.'

Saahil fiddled with his bag. He went towards the door but stopped short. Turning around, he headed straight back for Amjad and kissed him on his bulbous nose. Amjad blinked through his glasses. He remembered Saahil doing that as a kid.

'Are you my friend, Abbu?'

Amjad smiled and touched his son's face. ''Course I am… Go on now, they're waiting for you.'

'Bro!' he heard his nephews greet Saahil. 'Come and sit. Oi, move to the back, let Saahil sit at the front.' Amjad heard them shout 'Allah Hafiz Chacha,' as they drove away.

'A few days, Abbu?' Zahra asked.

'Yep, Zee, only a few days,' Amjad replied.

Amjad wasn't sure how he felt about Saahil's absence from the home or how the big 'break' he had been so insistent on them all needing was working out. In one breath, Amjad missed his son so much it ached. His mind replayed the punch he'd landed on Saahil's cheek over and over again. It kept him up at night, thinking back to his son's face as he crumpled to the floor, hand cupping his cheek, the line of blood that fell from his nose.

At other, more troubling times, Amjad sighed with relief. He didn't miss the trauma that Saahil had embodied over the past six months, the mood swings, the violent outbursts or the whole family treading on eggshells around his son. The other night, Amjad had watched a stand-up comedy show and laughed out loud, without feeling guilty.

Pushing these thoughts aside, Amjad dialled Saahil's mobile number. Warmth spread through him when he heard his son's voice.

'Are you okay?' Amjad asked.

'Yeah.'

'What have you been up to?'

'Erm... just chillin' out.'

'Right. Is Uncle Javid doing your head in?'

'No, he's all right.'

Saahil was unusually quiet. It was like getting blood out of a stone. Maybe he just wanted to be left alone for a bit? But Amjad needed to call him, to hear his voice. It was an affirmation that Amjad *did* miss his son. He *did* want him home as soon as possible. It had only been two weeks, for goodness' sake, hardly a big deal. But the house just wasn't the same. Even Zahra moped around from room to room. The only time she was distracted was when Libby was over. As soon as her best friend left, though, Zahra started pestering Amjad to ring Saahil for her so she could speak to him.

'Give him some space,' Amjad snapped.

'Space?' she replied, confused. 'What for?'

The two weeks were almost up, and Saahil would be home soon. Amjad knew that when he returned, it would be more of the same. More hard work, more suffering. But this time, Amjad felt more than re-energised to deal with it. Better.

'What time did you say he left, Javid?'

'This morning, about nine o'clock. The boys offered to drive him, but he insisted on catching a train. Something about stopping off in Manchester to do some shopping.'

'Well, it's five o'clock now. He's not answering his phone.'

'Don't worry about it, Amjad. He's a young lad, probably bumped into his mates or something. My boys do it all the time.' Amjad replaced the phone on the stand with Javid's laugh still echoing from the handset. Maybe Saahil had pulled another stunt like before and had gone to see Ehsan? Amjad nervously dialled their number. To his relief, Meena answered the phone.

'No, Amjad, he's not here. Is everything okay?'

'He's just not answering his phone. It goes straight to voice-mail. Was supposed to be back by lunchtime.'

'Will you let me know when he gets in?'

'Yeah, I will do, Meena, thanks.'

*

'You're sure, Umar? Maybe he's sent you a message?' Amjad held the phone to his ear desperately.

'No, Uncle, I have my mobile in my hand. There's nothing from him.'

'Maybe... erm... did you have any plans to meet up?'

Umar hesitated. 'No. I haven't heard from Saahil in a while. Every call or message I sent him went unanswered... It's been a few months now.'

'Oh, okay.'

'I'll ask the other lads for you,' Umar said.

'Yes, thank you.'

'I hope you find him.'

Amjad put the phone down and flicked through the pages of his address book. Without thinking, he dialled Ken's number.

'All right, mate?'

Amjad explained the situation. 'I just wondered if he's maybe turned up at yours but then... He can't have because he doesn't know where you live... *I* don't know where you live. Sorry, I don't know why I'm ringing.'

'It's all right,' Ken reassured. 'Do you want me to come over? I can run out in the car and try and look for him?'

'No, no,' Amjad said, quickly. 'I don't think that's necessary... just yet. I'll call you later on.'

'Make sure you do.'

Amjad hung up and checked the address book again. He realised there was no one else to ring. Ammi appeared at his side and tried to grab the phone. 'Let me do it,' she shouted, like a madwoman.

'Do what? I've rung everyone.'

'Well, ring them again,' she spat.

'I'm trying, Ammi.'

'Try harder. And if not, go out and look for him.' She blinked through her huge glasses at him, challengingly, hands placed on her hips.

Amjad nodded and stood up to fetch his coat.

'Wait until he gets home,' Amjad shouted, pacing the lounge. 'I'm going to kill him.'

'Ring the police,' Ammi screeched.

Amjad turned to face her, angrily. Why had she mentioned the police?

'He'll turn up,' he snapped. 'It's only eight o'clock. It's not late.'

Zahra ran down the stairs after hearing the commotion. 'What's happening, Abbu?' she asked, fear in her eyes.

'Your Ammi is overreacting.'

'How dare you?' She descended into a rant, making sure Amjad knew just how incompetently he was handling the situation.

'I'll give it another hour.'

'But you've been to see all his friends. No one knows where he is!'

'Ammi, please, just stop shouting.'

'But it's so cold outside, look!' Ammi pointed aggressively at the frosted window.

'He'll turn up,' Amjad said, his voice also rising. 'You know what he's been like recently. There's no need to involve the police.'

'You never listen to me.'

Amjad mumbled into the receiver: 'Saahil... Saahil Sharif... Yes...
Missing... Since this morning.'

There was a pause at the other end of the phone before a
muffled voice answered, 'Okay. We'll send someone out.'

Amjad replaced the handset and cleared his throat. Zahra
looked at him in disbelief. Ammi started to wail.

The policeman who had arrived on the same night of Saahil's
disappearance had been a compassionate fellow. He'd taken the
important details: name, age, description, contact numbers of
family and friends. He'd asked for a recent photograph.

'He's kept us waiting before,' Amjad said. 'You know, since the
attack. But not like this. He wouldn't leave it this late.'

'Don't worry, love,' the officer said to Ammi, who cried silently
and wiped her eyes with her scarf. 'We'll do our best.'

The following afternoon, two different police officers arrived.
The younger one asked to check Saahil's computer and bedroom
and took some DNA from a toothbrush. The older man was
surly-faced and had a curt air around him. He said he'd come to
get more detailed information. Amjad felt uneasy straightaway.

'So you said he left your brother's house at approximately
9 a.m.?' the officer asked.

'Yes, to catch a train home. He mentioned something about
stopping off in Manchester to go shopping. But obviously you
already know that.'

'Hmmm. You said his cousins offered him a lift. But he
declined?'

'That's right.'

'So he left on his own, willingly?'

'Yeah,' Amjad paused. 'Sorry, what do you mean by that?'

'We've been in touch with the Manchester police force. They're searching the area right now.'

'Good, thank you.'

'They have, however, checked the CCTV around the train station. Haven't been able to spot anyone of Saahil's description.'

'Well, it's hardly reliable, is it?' Amjad said. 'It's always too fuzzy to see anything whenever they show it on *Crimewatch*.' The officer ignored him.

'So how has Saahil been coping since the assault?'

Amjad was caught off-guard. 'Erm, not great, to be honest. But I think we've just managed to turn a corner.'

'He's having counselling? Has it helped?'

Not really, he wanted to say. 'Yeah, I suppose it has.'

'We've been in touch with his counsellor. He told us Saahil was suffering from severe depression.'

Amjad blinked. No one had put it quite like that before. He quickly recovered. 'Obviously, they told me at the hospital, you know, post-traumatic stress…'

The policeman continued scribbling away on his notepad, without looking up.

'His best friend is in a permanent vegetative state,' Amjad almost shouted at him. 'Obviously he's depressed.'

The officer looked at Amjad and nodded. 'Of course, it must be extremely difficult.'

'What has this got to do with anything anyway?' Amjad knew the answer to his question, but pushed it out of his head.

'Has Saahil ever expressed any suicidal thoughts?'

'Suicide?' Amjad stood up. 'What are you suggesting?'

'Mr Sharif, I have to ask these questions.'

'My son would not think such things.'

'But you have to consider—'

'No no, you don't understand. We're Muslim, we don't commit suicide. It's against our religion.' Amjad knew he sounded like a madman.

'Just answer their questions,' Ammi croaked, from the other side of the room.

'Can we continue, Mr Sharif?'

Amjad nodded reluctantly.

'Has there been any tension between Saahil and family members? Any arguments in the house? Any fights?'

'No,' Amjad lied. There was no need to tell the cop about the punch. Amjad didn't think he had it in him to relay the whole thing in actual words. It had tormented him even more than usual since Saahil had gone missing.

'I'm nearly done. Did Saahil say anything unusual in the past few days? Anything to suggest he needed, well, *a break*?'

'No,' Amjad said, in an offhand way.

'When I say "a break", I mean literally "time out".'

'No. I mean yes, that's why he went to see his cousins. To have a break.' The officer jotted something down. The younger policeman came down the stairs.

'We'll keep you updated,' he said. Amjad saw the pair out of the house. Something the cop had said lingered in Amjad's head. A word.

Willingly.

'So that's it? You're just going to stop looking?'

'No, sir, but as we explained—'

'Yeah yeah, I know what you said...'

167

'Nothing suspicious has been found—'

'Suspicious?' Amjad shouted. 'Do you not know what these thugs are like? They have friends on the outside. They give orders from their cells. What if they had been following Saahil all this time? They'll be pretty pissed off that they got ten years each.'

'There's no evidence to suggest there is a link between the incident in May and Saahil's disappearance. We've investigated all avenues.'

'You're not listening to me. Something has happened to my son.' Amjad spoke through gritted teeth.

'He left your brother's house in the morning, in broad daylight. As we've informed you, the police have searched the surrounding areas and nothing has been—'

'—found, yeah, I know.'

'There's every possibility Saahil may reappear. Maybe we just have to wait.'

'Wait? It's been two weeks! He wouldn't just disappear of his own accord.'

'Sir, we can't rule such a thing out. You have to understand, your son was going through a very difficult time—'

'Yes, but he wouldn't just abandon us and not get in touch! This isn't him!' Amjad turned and grabbed hold of Zahra.

'Look, this is his little sister. He loves her to death. He wouldn't just leave her.' The police officers looked at one another but said nothing.

'You've already decided, haven't you?' Amjad said, accusingly. 'You've already decided that he's done this himself. That he's chosen to go missing. To get away from us. To get away from me.'

'That's not what we are saying, Mr Sharif. But you have to remember, Saahil is not a minor. He's a twenty-one-year-old man.'

'Hardly a man!' Amjad shouted. 'Not like me or you. He's still young. And he's vulnerable. He needs me.'

'Abbu, stop shouting,' Zahra said, tugging at his sleeve.

'Fine,' Amjad said, looking in the opposite direction. 'I know something has happened to him. You should be asking those bastards in prison. They've done something.'

'Mr Sharif—'

'We're Pakistani,' Amjad continued, waving his arms about. 'We don't just abandon our families. Our kids, they stay with us. They don't even leave the family home until they get married. They look after us and we look after them. We don't just up and leave.'

'We're doing all we can, sir.'

Amjad's face crumbled. He managed to hold it together. Only just.

'Please go,' he said.

Ammi walked the policemen out and muttered a quick 'sorry' as she closed the door behind them. She re-entered the room and touched Amjad's shoulder.

'Son?'

He turned to look at her. 'What am I going to do, Ammi?'

The weeks seemed to rage on ahead. They turned into months. Zahra watched her Abbu try to grasp hold of them. Slow things down. Pull them back. Like a rope slipping through his fingers. His hands bloody.

He barely acknowledged her some mornings. He never ate. The car keys were snatched off the drawer, the door would slam shut. Zahra would not see Abbu for the rest of the day. Not until he came home in the early hours. Where was he looking? Where to start?

Sometimes the man who looked like a scarecrow went along

too. They told her that he had saved Saahil's life. He honked his horn as he pulled up outside. Abbu would disappear off with him and not return. Often, the man, Ken was his name, would stay overnight and kip on the sofa. He would use their landline and ring people up about the 'Saahil Sharif case'. Abbu would sit on the sofa nearby, head in his hands.

Ammi moved in to look after Zahra. They clung to each other on the sofa, waiting for news. There never was any to deliver.

One day, Zahra saw her Abbu cry. He cried into Ammi's arms. *Abbu? Cry?* She hid behind the kitchen door, bit into her knuckle praying never to witness such a thing again. Her whole body quivered. The sounds he made, it stabbed at her. She woke up in the middle of the night. It was still ringing in her ears.

She went downstairs for a glass of water and found Abbu in the living room. He was staring out of the window, alone in the dark. It frightened her. It *was* still her Abbu, wasn't it? She cleared her throat. He jumped.

'What you doing up, Zee?'

'I'm scared, Abbu. I'm really, really scared.'

'Let's sit down.' They cuddled on the sofa. Zahra noticed the curtains were ajar. A dull orange glow shed light on their faces. Rain poured down the glass.

'Are we gonna be okay, Abbu?'

'Shhh…' he said. 'I'm here.'

'What's going to happen now?'

'Just the two of us now,' he said, in a trance-like state.

'Abbu?'

'Me and you.'

'And Saahil? What about Saahil?' He did not answer.

Raindrops slammed against the window.

Eighteen

Zahra could see the two guys hanging around outside the grimy convenience store. SASTI DUKAAN read the shop heading, literally 'cheap shop', and along with the fruit and veg, lay enormous thirty-six-pack toilet rolls piled up against the wall, guaranteed to brighten up any passer's day.

One of the guys stood by the doorway was the same insufferable little twerp who usually bugged Zahra during her bus wait. Qasim, he was called. Zahra had had the misfortune of knowing him since school. He'd been thrown out for setting fireworks off in the school corridors, but his unwanted affection for Zahra still remained. His gangster-wannabe ways had now landed him firmly outside Sasti Dukaan, his uncle's mini-market, where he bagged up bunches of coriander and chapatti flour for the various aunties who frequented the shop.

To Zahra's distaste, Qasim was accompanied by his pea-brained friend of a similar mould. She breathed in with resolve and ventured forward, as she usually did, to walk past them in a calm and collected manner. She'd already had a bad day, and hoped she could slip by unnoticed. The last time Qasim tried chatting her up, Zahra's Abbu had pulled up in the car and honked the horn. Qasim had slithered back inside, trying to be casual. He hadn't been as forthcoming since then, Zahra noticed, but she didn't know what to expect now.

As she approached, she heard the familiar, 'Yeah, yeah, man... yeah... innit, bro...' Their conversation stopped when they spotted her. Zahra felt them follow her with their eyes. They whispered to each other and broke out into an obvious laugh.

Zahra was not in the mood. The bus had pulled in at just the right moment meaning a quick escape was possible. The leering continued and Zahra decided to give them both something to talk about. She stuck her middle finger high up in the air behind her. She let it jog up and down to really savour the impact. When Zahra looked back at them, their stupid faces blinked. One nudged the other who quickly recovered. Zahra heard them howl 'oooooooh' as she got on to the bus and settled down in a spare seat.

She pulled out her phone and checked her Twitter, scrolling through the newsfeed of 'deep' quotes, cat memes and *Guardian* opinion pieces, looking for an aggressive enough statement to vent out a little anger. If not, she would have to tweet something herself and couldn't think of anything sophisticated enough that didn't include expletives. To her surprise, she found the perfect tweet concocted by a university friend who was embroiled in a Twitter fight with some idiot guy who had called her a 'feminazi':

I'm not here to babysit your fragile masculinity.
#blocked.

Zahra smiled and clicked 'Retweet'.

Her self-satisfaction faded when the bus jerked to a halt and she remembered why she was on her way home from work so early. She wondered what she would tell Abbu. He knew Zahra hated working at the call centre. She constantly reminded him she needed to find a graduate job now that she had almost finished her History and Politics degree at university. Maybe she could formulate an excuse from there? The real version of events was, of course, quite different.

'You told the customer to piss off, Zahra,' her manager had said.

'No, I didn't,' Zahra replied, twirling her hair and shifting in her seat. 'I waited until they'd put the phone down. Then I said it.' She suppressed a smirk.

'Management heard you because it was still recording. It's unacceptable.'

'So what?' Zahra protested. 'Everyone does it.'

It was true. It was easy to lose your temper in such a setting. She imagined her friends still sitting in the stinking call centre, leaving one answerphone message after the next. *No more crappy late-night shifts*, Zahra thought, *and no more abusive customers who couldn't pay off their catalogue debts.* Though half the time Zahra didn't blame them. Ringing people up at nine o'clock at night for five pounds in arrears was basically asking for trouble.

'Five pounds! You're ringing me up for five pounds?' they'd say in their shrill, piss-take voices.

'Er… yeah,' Zahra would reply, grimacing. *Follow the script. Follow the script.* 'It needs to be paid today. It's a matter of urgency.' She'd bite her lip in embarrassment.

Now, sitting on the bus, Zahra felt uneasy. Being unable to 'stick at it' until she'd managed to get a graduate job made her feel like a failure. It would be difficult to find something before her graduation in July, and judging by her peers, pretty impossible she would find anything suitable at all. The bleakness set in as the bus approached her stop. She let it pass by out of lethargy and eventually hit the button a stop later.

She decided there was only one person who could make her feel better. Stepping off the bus, Zahra moped her way up the street and stood outside the familiar door. Expletive-laden anger became muffled as Zahra knocked as hard as she could.

Libby's mum, Cath, answered and peeked through the door chain with puffy eyes. She always looked tired. Zahra heard a croak from inside the house.

'Who is it?' It was John, Libby's father.

Cath rolled her eyes at the sound of her husband's voice before exchanging pleasantries with Zahra.

'Is Libby in?' she asked.

'Yeah. I'll just go and get her.'

Zahra was always hesitant knocking on her best friend's door as Cath and John were almost always arguing. She waited a few minutes before Libby emerged, auburn hair piled on top of her head in a messy bun.

'Why aren't you at work?' she asked.

'Got sacked, innit,' Zahra replied, scratching her head. Libby's eyes widened.

'Ohhh,' she said, and without a word, they both set off together down the street.

Libby howled with laughter. Zahra tried to kick her from across the floor. They were both curled up with tea and biscuits in Zahra's bedroom like a pair of young grannies.

'How embarrassing,' Zahra said, holding her head.

'Don't worry, you'll get another job. You hated it anyway.'

'Yeah but, I was never in trouble, even at school.'

'Come on,' Libby said. 'It could be worse.'

'Could it?'

'Yeah, at least you don't have to clean up people's shit.'

Libby, who had nearly completed her Nursing degree, was always handy for some perspective.

'Yeah,' Zahra said meekly, suddenly feeling very pathetic. Libby looked around the room as though searching for a solution to the problem.

'Let's put loud music on and dance around like idiots?'

'No, not after last time,' Zahra said, reminding Libby of the humiliating incident a couple of weeks ago when the pair of them had tried to rap along to grime music. Neither of them heard Abbu come home accompanied with some of his work mates. They continued dropping f-bombs and other cuss words until he'd banged furiously on their bedroom door.

'Oh, shit,' Libby said, cupping her face. 'Why did you have to remind me of that?'

Zahra laughed along with her best friend. She'd done a night shift at the hospital, the bags visible under her eyes, and yet whenever Zahra needed someone to be weird with, Libby was there.

With Libby, Zahra could dunk malted milk biscuits into her tea, two at a time, and not give a shit. She could thread Libby's moustache whilst she in return bleached Zahra's sideburns. They could sit together wearing thick cosy socks tucked into their pyjama bottoms and watch Disney films, or listen to their seriously uncool Spice Girls CD on replay. They'd created their own little bubble away from everyone else.

'Your mum looked well today,' Zahra said. 'How are they both doing?'

'Still headcases, if that's what you're asking,' Libby replied.

She may have found security in Zahra's home since childhood, but to Zahra, Libby's presence was a comfort too. She didn't care that Zahra spoke an alien language to Ammi. Or that she couldn't go out drinking with her. Or that the call to prayer would explode in their house five times a day to remind Ammi it was time for namaz. Or that Zahra's family ate roti with their hands. Or that sometimes, if Abbu was feeling particularly religious, he would snub the dining table and roll out a mat on the floor, to emulate the simplicity of Prophet Muhammad. Libby had shrugged the first time she'd witnessed this seating rearrangement and, without hesitation, plopped herself on to the floor, rolled up her sleeves and tucked in, her fork lying abandoned nearby. Nope, Libby just didn't care.

Zahra sipped her tea, watching as Libby fidgeted around. She did this whenever her family was mentioned.

'Do you wanna go through *Glamour* magazine's hundred sexiest men?'

Libby perked up. Zahra set up her laptop as Libby rearranged the pillows.

'Sit down then,' Zahra said, getting comfy.

'Erm… you better hold your horses.'

'Why?' Zahra asked, a little too aggressively, eager to get started with the list.

Libby looked out of the window and smiled. 'Your Abbu is back.'

Zahra blinked. 'Bollocks!' she said, jumping up from the floor. 'Quick, think of something.'

'Like what?'

'An excuse.'

'Don't know why you're so worried; your dad's the most chilled-out person I know. It's your nan you need to worry about—'

Zahra peered out of the window. 'Oh shit. She's with him. He must have picked her up on the way home.'

'It's okay,' Libby said. 'He's helping her out of the car. We have a few minutes.'

They ran down the stairs, passing each other suggestions. However, before they could decide on a good enough excuse, the door opened and Zahra's Ammi and Abbu walked in.

'Zahra? What are you doing back home?' Abbu checked his watch as he entered the room. He looked exhausted and Zahra remembered he had taken a sleeping tablet the night before.

'Er...' Zahra began.

'Are you poorly?' Abbu hurried towards her and placed his hand on her forehead.

'No, Abbu I... er—'

Zahra and Libby glanced at each other. Ammi frowned at them both suspiciously.

'Go on,' she said, fingers tightening around her walking stick. 'Speak.'

'Well—'

'Zahra got sacked for swearing at a customer,' Libby blurted out.

'What!' Ammi screeched. Zahra turned to Libby.

'Well, you were gonna tell the truth anyway,' Libby mumbled. 'Just saved you a bit of hassle.'

'I didn't swear,' Zahra protested.

'Well... I'd best be off,' Libby announced, gearing towards the door.

Zahra found herself being forcefully led into the lounge by her eighty-year-old granny. *I can't believe what you just did*, she mouthed to Libby who smiled back apologetically.

'What happened?' Abbu asked. Zahra hated to hear the disappointment in his voice. She told the story in a speedy fashion, hiding her face as she finished. Abbu cleared his throat.

'Shut up?' he said. 'You only said "shut up"?'

'Yeah.'

'What did you really say?'

'Nothing, Abbu,' Zahra said, sheepishly. 'I promise.' Abbu did not look convinced. He raised an eyebrow.

'Well—' he spluttered.

'Sorry, Abbu. But at least I can concentrate on uni now. It's difficult at the moment what with exams and everything. I was just a bit stressed out.'

'Hmmm, I suppose. But it's not what I expected from you,' Abbu replied. Ammi snorted.

'That's all you're going to say, Amjad?'

'Erm—'

'You're too soft!' she shouted. 'People can't get jobs as it is these days. Sakina's grandson is a doctor—'

'Probably a science teacher,' Zahra mumbled.

'—and he's still waitering at a restaurant. And now your daughter had a perfectly good job and has gone and got herself sacked. Kids need to be told.'

'I'm not a kid, Ammi,' Zahra said, making a face.

'Oi, don't roll your eyes at me,' she snapped back. 'I'll sort you out—'

'Shall we eat?' Abbu said, loudly.

Ammi pursed her lips and leaned on her walking stick to get

up. Zahra smiled nervously and helped her to the dining table. The old woman's body may have deteriorated, but her mind remained as sharp as ever.

Ammi officially moved into their home ten years ago. Abbu stood outside of the house he'd been born in and sighed deeply. 'My father's house,' he'd said to Zahra. 'Where I grew up…' Ammi told him to let it go. Zahra still remembered his face; it was reminiscent of a man who had let too many things go. He'd clung on to the broken fence. Ammi dragged him away.

She'd brought along with her the contents of her entire household. Abbu decorated one of the spare rooms in the attic for her.

'You're placing your old mother in the attic?' she squawked.

Abbu insisted his intentions were honourable. 'It's a good way for you to get some exercise. We need to keep your diabetes in check; you're nearly thirteen stone, Ammi.'

'What about this room? It's spare now.' She'd reached for the handle of the third bedroom.

Abbu's hand shot out. 'Leave it,' he'd said. Ammi hung back.

Most times she got her own way. The curtains she'd presented Zahra's mum and dad with when they'd first moved into the new home were now hanging in the lounge. Abbu told Zahra the story plenty of times.

'Your mum hated them,' he chuckled. 'We put them up in the bedroom so guests wouldn't have to see them.'

They stayed hidden in Abbu's bedroom for a decade until Ammi moved in and instructed Abbu to bring them back downstairs. Wine-coloured and velvety, they almost obstructed half the light from the window, leaving the living room in a perpetual state of darkness. They annoyed Abbu because he knew his wife had hated them. They annoyed Zahra because the lack of light hindered her attempts at reading the tiny print in her textbooks. Ammi loved them though, and that was all that mattered.

Also hanging in their hallway were two mouldy portraits Ammi brought along with her. Abbu had eyed them unconvincingly.

'Surely we should only have family photos on the walls?'

'No,' Ammi said. 'They've been hanging in my house for nearly forty years. I want them up.'

Abbu fetched his ladder wearily, not having enough energy to argue back after another sleepless night. He'd hammered the hooks for both pictures on to the wall. Ammi had grinned from ear to ear. Zahra squinted. She recognised one of the portraits; it was Prince Philip and the Queen, a black and white picture with the words SILVER JUBILEE etched at the bottom. Her passion for the royal family still hadn't waned.

'Your father got me that from the car boot sale,' Ammi reminded Abbu, nostalgia twinkling in her eyes.

'How romantic,' Abbu said, grinning.

As for the other picture...

'Who's the guy in the hat?' Zahra asked, looking at the smart man wearing a triangle-shaped topi.

Ammi was horrified. 'That *guy*,' she said, 'is Quaid-e-Azam.'

'Who?'

'Muhammad Ali Jinnah, founder of Pakistan.'

'Oh,' Zahra replied. 'Cool.'

Ammi turned to Abbu, enraged by Zahra's indifferent response. She opened her mouth once more but Abbu interrupted: 'Ammi, she's only eleven. She doesn't know who Quaid-e-Azam is.'

Ammi mumbled away under her breath. 'Well, she should know. Don't you think it's important to teach your kids about our heritage?'

'Well, I—'

'Never mind, I'm here now.'

And so Ammi took it upon herself to give Zahra essential life lessons. She threw her into the kitchen at age fourteen, tied a pinny around her waist and handed her the rolling pin. Numerous chapatti-making lessons followed, with one effortless demonstration from Ammi after the next. Zahra tried to follow the same process, but things didn't always go to plan.

'Bismillah,' she exclaimed loudly. Ammi nodded approvingly. Zahra gently tore a blob of dough about the size of a tennis ball.

'Too big,' Ammi snapped. Zahra made it smaller and began rolling it in her palms into a perfect circle.

'There!' she said, holding her hand outstretched, proud of the roundness of the dough.

'Yes, move on.'

'Er…'

'Flatten it out,' Ammi said. 'And remember, the edges are the most important.'

Zahra did as she was told, but the dough stuck to her fingers and became a splodgy mess in her palms.

'Add flour,' Ammi sighed.

Zahra threw the roti into a small tub of flour inelegantly. Ammi grimaced. 'Not too much, or the roti will become dry and crack.'

Zahra could feel the pressure. She eventually laid the dough out for rolling, but this was far from the fun exercise she thought it would be. The roti kept sticking to the rolling pin and became a deformed mess. Ammi instructed her to 'add more flour' but 'not too much' causing Zahra to throw up her arms in frustration.

'You're contradicting yourself, Ammi!' she cried. 'How much flour is not too much?'

Abbu, who had come to join them in the kitchen, sighed, 'This is like brown the onions all over again.'

'Judge it,' Ammi shouted, before throwing Abbu a filthy look. 'Men,' she said disapprovingly, turning her back on him. 'They can't make roti, it requires too much skill.'

Zahra set aside the rolling pin and looked down at the square-shaped chapatti in front of her.

'Right, slap it between your palms,' Ammi instructed. Abbu adjusted on the spot to get a better look. Zahra picked the roti up carefully and tried to emulate Ammi's effortless handling of the chapattis she usually made for them. They would grow in size as they passed between each hand, rotating in a round circle. Zahra's roti, however, collapsed as soon as she picked it up. Ammi signalled that enough was enough, and decided to step in.

She started from scratch, pulling the dough into a ball, flattening it with a rolling pin, and slapping it from palm to palm. In less than a minute, a flawless, round chapatti was cooking on the non-stick pan.

'Now let's try again, shall we?' she said, handing the rolling pin back to Zahra. Zahra gulped in response.

It had taken her at least a year to master the art of making perfect chapattis. Ammi had smiled broadly and mentioned the words 'cooking', 'your own home' and, to Zahra's distaste, 'husband'.

'Ew,' Zahra grimaced. 'I don't think so, I'm only a kid.'

Ammi's face was stern. 'You won't be a kid forever. And anyway, I was married when I was sixteen.'

'Yeah, well, that was in the olden days,' Zahra replied. Abbu looked amused and gave her a thumbs-up from behind Ammi's back.

Zahra, now in her early twenties, was not a kid anymore, a fact Ammi relished. She would often hobble up the stairs and sit at the end of Zahra's bed, helping her pick out different outfits. Her hands would pass over Zahra's bosom.

'Nice, healthy,' Ammi remarked. 'Teeny waist,' she'd continue, wrinkly hands passing over the small of Zahra's back before ending with a pinch of her shapely bottom. Zahra jumped back, giggling.

'Perfect,' Ammi said. 'Just like me when I was a young girl. You've definitely inherited our figures. Not like your mother. She had a beautiful face, no doubt, but she was too skinny for my liking.'

'Do I look like my mum, Ammi?' Zahra asked. She had no memories or meaningful possessions of her mother's, apart from the birdie blanket, the shawl she used to carry around as a child. Zahra had searched the whole house trying to find it, without any luck. She could hardly picture its intricate patterns anymore.

From an early age, Abbu had encouraged her to view the stitched birds that flitted between the branches as their own family tree. Now Zahra couldn't place them in her mind. She needed to see it to understand it all again, but was too scared to mention it to Abbu. He would think she hadn't looked after it properly. But Zahra couldn't for the life of her remember where she'd last seen it. And, of all the things that were missing in her home, a shawl was the least of their worries.

Ammi, who was sometimes hard of hearing, continued talking about body shapes:

'A woman who doesn't go in at the waist is hardly a woman at all.'

Zahra had frowned. 'Ammi, that's not a nice thing to say.'

'It's true. Your friend Libby, she has a boyish figure.'

'She's athletic.'

'What does that mean?'

Zahra sighed, having given up trying to teach Ammi English words, and tried to think of an Urdu equivalent. She couldn't so instead opted for 'Sporty?'

Ammi looked at her and snorted, clearly unimpressed. Of course, the old woman was always on hand to dish out other offensive beauty tips.

'You're really fair-skinned. Not like Naseem's granddaughter who she's always showing off about,' Ammi said. 'If you put this on, though, you'll go white!' She handed Zahra a tub of Tibet Snow skin cream, Ammi's prized face cream from Pakistan. Zahra, who liked the idea well enough, had lathered it on happily. That was until she'd seen pictures of Pear's soap turning black people white in her history lesson. She'd come home and chucked the cream into the bin.

'We shouldn't subject ourselves to Western standards of beauty,' she'd said nobly to Ammi.

'That was £2.49 a tub!'

'Don't care. I don't want to be white. I'm fine as I am.'

Despite her old-fashioned ideas, Zahra could not imagine their home without Ammi.

'How's the food?' Zahra asked her, hoping everyone had forgotten about the job sacking. Ammi finished chewing before answering.

'Very good. Just the right amount of everything.'

Zahra smiled proudly as she had made the curry herself the night before.

'Of course,' Ammi continued, glancing at Abbu. 'I would add more salt in but…'

Abbu cleared his throat and said, 'Feel free if you want to clog up your arteries and have a heart attack.'

Zahra mouth fell open. Ammi grew in size.

'How dare you speak to me like that?' she shouted.

'Well, I'm sorry, but the time for niceties has gone. I say it for your own good.'

'No, you don't. You don't want me to eat well!' Ammi snapped back.

Abbu smiled as he spoke, 'Your blood pressure is way too high, Ammi. Take the salt, it's up to you. Don't you think, Zee?'

'Yeah, Ammi, it's for your own good,' Zahra agreed.

'Ah, I see. Father and daughter ganging up on me. You always do this. I should go and live with Javid, he wouldn't treat me like this!' Ammi leaned on her walking stick and shuffled back to the sofa. She sat down in a huff and muttered under her breath.

Zahra looked at Abbu, who motioned with his head. 'Go to her,' he whispered.

Zahra sneaked over to Ammi and put an arm around her big belly.

'Go away,' Ammi said, trying to resist. Zahra giggled and soon Ammi relented.

'We're only thinking of you,' she said. 'It's because we love you.'

'I know,' Ammi replied, kissing Zahra's forehead and stroking her hair.

Zahra saw Abbu out of the corner of her eye. He smiled as he watched them, tapping his foot on the floor. A few minutes later and the smile faded. Abbu was looking at the floor, lost in some thought. Zahra wondered what had reminded him this time.

Nineteen

The job-sacking had been a blessing in disguise for Zahra and she now dedicated most of her days to studying. She set off for university to meet her friends for a revision session, catching the bus at midday. She found a window seat on the top deck and plugged in her earphones. It was only a fifteen-minute drive to the uni, but always took twice the amount of time due to traffic. As they entered the city centre, Zahra noticed her fellow passengers muttering and pointing out of the window. Zahra pulled out her earphones and followed their gaze. Her eyes widened at the sight of movement in the grounds below. To an outsider, it would have hardly seemed like anything exciting. But to the locals, it was a different story.

Small figures wearing yellow hi-vis jackets were plodding around a vast area in the ground. Cranes were suspended in the air. Steel, concrete and plaster were being shifted around in different directions. The long-forgotten hole in the middle of city was finally being worked upon. It had festered like an open wound, bang smack in the centre of town – a visible eyesore for passers-by, a constant reminder of neglect, an abandoned dream in an insignificant city. New investors came and went, but plans never came to fruition. Zahra could already hear girls on the bus giggling excitedly at the prospect of the new shopping centre. The locals had waited long enough. Twelve years to be precise.

'Won't have to run to Leeds for shopping now, innit?' one of them said.

A young lad jumped out of his seat to take a better look. His mobile fell on to the floor with a thud, his headphones snapping out of the phone socket. 'Niggas in Paris' blasted from the speakers. An elderly English couple seated in front of him exchanged uncomfortable looks as the boy scrambled to silence the volume, and the cuss words. At the back of the bus, an Asian man had decided to deliver the news to his relatives…

'Yes, yes, there's cranes and everything!' he shouted in Punjabi.

Zahra grimaced as the man's voice grew louder and louder. Her gaze fell upon the elderly couple again, who were now tutting.

Zahra left the bus and headed towards campus. She spotted her friend, Sana, waiting for her at a table outside with huge textbooks piled up in front of her. Her humongous hijab gave her tiny face an ant-like appearance. Zahra spotted her easily in the sea of students making the most of the sunshine. Sana greeted her with her usual sweetness.

'Cow. I've been waiting for you.'

'Sorry, got held up.'

Sana was one of her closest friends at uni, and they could pretty much say anything to each other without worrying about causing offence.

'Your hijab is getting a bit out of control, isn't it?' Zahra said, eyeing the huge hump on Sana's head as she settled down on the bench beside her.

'Really?' Sana asked. She pulled out her phone and checked herself on the screen. She pouted and turned her head to one side. Zahra waited around awkwardly as this operation turned into a selfie. Not that she blamed Sana. If Zahra looked as well turned-out and as polished as Sana, she would take selfies on an hourly basis too. Sana had a fashion blog and was always experimenting with her clothes and make-up. One day she would come into uni wearing a turban-style hijab, long hoodie and skinny jeans, and other times, she'd float around in maxi dresses, pleated skirts and elegant abayas. Zahra glanced down at her own baggy T-shirt, ripped boyfriend jeans and Converse, feeling like a bit of a scruff.

'Do I need to tone it down a bit?' Sana eventually asked.

Zahra opened her mouth to reply when a bag was thrown on to their table making them both jump.

'Seen that prick over there?' It was Junaid, accompanied by Hasan.

'Who?'

'Him,' he replied, sitting down at the table and motioning his head towards Mohsin, one of their classmates. 'Ditches us every time and starts licking their arses.'

'So what?' Hasan said, adjusting his glasses with a shaky hand. 'He's doing a presentation with them.'

'Presentation, my arse,' Junaid replied. His eyes lingered on Zahra. Zahra saw Sana smile to herself.

'You okay, Zahra?' Hasan asked.

'Yeah, are you?' Zahra replied, wishing the pair of them would disappear.

'Hmmm,' he replied, smiling nervously.

Sana guffawed. Zahra kicked her under the table. She'd heard all about Sana's wonderful theory.

'So basically, I think they've both got a bit of a thing for you,' she often told Zahra. 'Hasan is obviously a wuss, so he can't tell you how he feels. But he's a bit better-looking than Junaid.'

'So what?'

Sana would nod understandingly. 'Yeah, what's the point if he's scared of you?'

'No, it's not even that,' Zahra replied. 'They're just…'

'What?'

'I don't know… Disappointing?'

Sana frowned. 'Well, you can't have Shah Rukh Khan running towards you in a field of yellow flowers.'

'I know, I know. But come on, Sana? They're hardly something to get excited over, are they?'

'Well, that's what normal guys are like,' Sana told her, irritably. 'Maybe they'd open up to you more if you weren't so—'

'So what?' Zahra asked, sternly.

'Er… nowt,' Sana replied, deciding it was best to end the conversation.

Junaid was still bitching about Mohsin, who caught their eye and made his way to their table, leaving behind his presentation group. *Hmmm, at least he dresses well*, Zahra thought. His hair was curly and piled on top of his head with the sides shaved and he was wearing cool, oversized glasses. And stubble. *Not bad*, she decided.

'Hiya,' he said, sitting down beside them.

'Oh,' Junaid said, pretending to be shocked to see him. 'You remembered us now, eh?'

Mohsin frowned. 'What you on about?'

'Well, you just fuck off with them goray whenever you feel like it and forget all about us.'

'Deary me,' Sana said, holding her big head with her stick-thin arms.

'I think I've been transported back to the playground,' Zahra said.

Junaid shrugged. 'Just sayin'. You can get in there with them now.'

'What do you mean "in there"?' Mohsin asked. 'We're doing a presentation together.'

'Yeah, that's what you said last time.'

'Shurrup,' Mohsin said, making to stand up.

'Just sayin',' Junaid repeated, leaning against the table. 'It's all right being best mates with them for now. But when it comes down to it, when shit kicks off, you'll come running back to your own. That's what always happens.'

'What shit is gonna kick off?'

'Do you watch the news?'

'Right, okay. Well, thanks for your wise words,' Mohsin said. He motioned to the girls. 'I'm off, guys. See you later.'

Zahra turned to Junaid. 'He can hang around with whoever he wants. No need for you to be a twat about it.'

Junaid shrugged and looked away. His gaze returned to Zahra only a few seconds later.

'It's sort of true what Junaid said,' Sana began, as soon as the boys left the table.

'About what?' Zahra asked, packing away her revision notes.

'Goray,' Sana whispered. 'It's like you and them girls in your US Politics and Society class.'

'They've been all right since… last month,' Zahra said. 'And anyway, it's only one of them really. The other two aren't so bad.'

'What happened last month?'

'The Chibok Girls.'

'Oh God, yeah,' Sana said, making a face. They'd discussed the kidnapping of the Nigerian schoolgirls at length when it had first happened, participating in the #bringbackourgirls hashtag enthusiastically. The pair of them had watched the video of Boko Haram forcing the young girls to recite the Quran through their fingers.

'What did they say to you?' Sana asked.

Zahra shrugged. 'Karen started reading the article out as loudly as she could. You know, pausing for effect and everything. After she finished she wanted to have a full-on discussion about it. Kept looking at me like she was expecting some kind of explanation.'

'Was the room full of whites?'

Zahra nodded.

'Some of them jump on every opportunity, don't they?' said Sana.

Yes, they definitely did, but then again, it's not like they were short on opportunities, were they? If Muslims weren't killing each other all across the Middle East, they were worming their way into more peaceful territories with guns, bombs and EU passports.

Zahra remembered watching the news with Abbu just before she had started university. Some people were protesting in London under a barrage of police protection. Zahra didn't really know what the protest was about, all she could see were bearded men wearing Arab shemaghs, either covering their faces or casually draped over their shoulders, shouting and waving placards in front of TV cameras.

SLAY THOSE WHO INSULT ISLAM.

BRITISH SOLDIERS BURN IN HELL.

There were even some women in the crowd wearing full niqabs and burkas, holding signs with gloved fingers. The more placards Zahra caught a glimpse of, the more irate she became.

SHARIA WILL DOMINATE THE WORLD.

EUROPE – YOUR 9/11 IS ON ITS WAY.

'Look at this, Abbu,' Zahra had said, pointing at the screen. 'How can we expect people to like us when all we do is cause trouble?'

'Most people know we're not all the same,' Abbu replied.

'Yeah, I know,' Zahra said irritably. She'd heard that line one too many times. 'But it's annoying. Now everyone who sees this will think we're all like that.'

Even slight things were sending people into a frenzy these days. The headlines were getting bigger, the scaremongering widespread. All indications as to how different Muslims were to everyone else. People were getting jumpy over the women wanting to wear veils in English schools and hospitals. Or confused as to why mass protests were being organised just because someone had drawn a cartoon and labelled it 'Muhammad'. Entire neighbourhoods were being Islamified, kids were being radicalised at their local comprehensives, Sharia law creeping into the legal system. Every movement magnified, every action scrutinised.

'There's good and bad in every,' Abbu said, in a monotone, probably bored of repeating the same phrase yet again.

He wasn't always so calm about things. Not when he watched his monthly edition of *Crimewatch*. Things particularly heated up during the mugshot segment of the programme. Abbu would lie dormant as black and white faces flashed across the screen. As soon as an Asian face appeared, with a Muslim-sounding name, Abbu would unleash the choicest of Punjabi swear words. 'Giving us a bad name,' he'd mutter, before retiring again.

Generally, however, Abbu seemed to cope with things a lot better than Zahra. He genuinely believed that things were okay just because he said 'there's good and bad in every'. *They're not okay, though*, Zahra wanted to shout at him. His coolness was a stark contrast to the fire that raged in her own head.

'You know how to change people's perceptions?' he said, realising she needed more than just a few pearls of wisdom. He held her face. 'Be kind to people. Be polite. Be the nicest person you can be to everyone. They can't hate all Muslims if they know a beautiful person like you.' He kissed her on the forehead.

Zahra took his words to heart. She'd started university eager to be nice. It was all okay at first; she'd made friends with some of the English girls thinking they would just be posh versions of Libby. There were minor incidents, like the time she'd innocently enquired as to why they had implants in their arms.

'Er, contraception,' Karen had said. 'You did know that, didn't you?'

'Oh yeah,' Zahra had replied quickly, not wanting to look like an idiot in front of Karen, a girl who looked and behaved like she'd just stepped out of a teenage Lindsay Lohan movie. She'd made a mental note to attack Libby for not telling her about it.

'So do you take the pill?' Lydia had asked. Zahra could have lied for an easier life, but she didn't. Before long, she found herself discussing the intimacies (or non-existent intimacies) of her personal life.

'So you're a virgin?' Karen said.

'Yeah.'

'And you have to wait? Until marriage?'

'Yeah.'

It was then that Zahra saw Karen give Lydia 'the look', the oh-my-God-what-a-fucking-weirdo look. Without bothering to ask Zahra how *she* actually felt about the whole thing, they'd both turned and looked at her, pityingly.

Zahra knew she'd played right into their hands. She saw the disappointment on their faces. The words 'oh, I thought you were *liberal*, I thought you weren't like *them*' were dancing at the end of their lips.

She knew what they thought about her. That her body was probably policed by a controlling family, it wasn't her own. That she was indoctrinated by religion and culture. That sort of thing. She would have liked to have pointed out that they were brainwashed too, and pressured into thinking they needed to lose their V cards by a certain age or commit social suicide. Zahra still cringed when she remembered Libby wanting to 'get it over and done with' during their college days.

'Well, I think it's nice,' Emma said, giving Zahra a hug. 'It's cute. Like Edward and Bella.'

Zahra was no *Twilight* fan, but she did like Emma – she was the sweetest of the bunch. She realised quickly, though, that the great white hand of friendship only extended when it wanted to. It wasn't the same as her and Libby, who were so used to each other that things barely even registered anymore. This was different.

It was all fine and well if they were discussing *EastEnders* or teaching each other how to achieve the perfect winged eyeliner, but as soon as the conversation steered to more uncomfortable terrain, Zahra knew where she stood. And it wasn't with them.

'I just think this whole race thing is always played upon,'

Karen remarked as she pointed to a headline involving a race row. Some people had turned up to a tennis game wearing blackface and afro wigs.

Zahra marvelled at how easy it was for privileged people to just *say* things. Things they really didn't have a clue about. To them, racism was just a bit of name-calling. And even that was one day disputed by Lydia:

'I mean, Paki is short for Pakistani, right? Well, I don't get offended if someone calls me a Brit.'

Once Zahra had recovered from the bemusement this statement caused, she said, 'There's a history behind it, you know.' The girls had blinked at her innocently as if to say, *what history?*

'It's not as simple as me calling you Lyd instead of Lydia.'

At first, Zahra thought she couldn't fault them for trying to understand her more. But even then things seemed orchestrated to make her feel uncomfortable. As though the girls were feigning interest in who she was and why she did what she did just so that they could rank in order the weirdness of the things she told them.

Zahra remembered this and decided to ask Sana if she had had any interrogations lately. They had left their revision behind and wandered into a McDonald's for the free Wi-Fi. Zahra brushed away crumbs from the table whilst she waited for her friend to return with food. There were so many kids clamouring past her with Happy Meals that Zahra wondered why they weren't at school. Sana gave them a filthy look as she settled down on the table with a tray carrying two Filet-O-Fish burgers. 'Fucking control your kids,' she mumbled.

'So, have you been questioned by goray lately?' Zahra asked.

'Nah,' Sana replied, munching on some fries. 'But I've told you the best thing to do – know your stuff. Don't flounder in front of 'em. Don't give 'em the satisfaction.'

It was like a greatest hits collection that all her Asian friends had been forced to listen to. 'Dumb Things White People Ask', it was called, a broken record that repeated the same questions over and over again.

Do you have to marry a Muslim? What if you took a white boy home? Would you make him convert to Islam? What would your parents say if you told them you were gay? Would you get disowned? What if you had a drink, would you go to hell? Do you only give charity to Muslims? How do you identify yourself, British or Pakistani? If England and Pakistan are playing cricket, who do you support?

The questions themselves were not a problem, but Zahra had identified Karen as one of those types of people who would find anything to pounce on. The more time Zahra spent with her, the more she realised that Karen was always *looking* for something. Anything to pit her normal lifestyle against Zahra's strange one. She went just far enough. Subtle. Knowing exactly what she was doing. Lydia, on the other hand, was more direct, always screeching out in her shrill voice 'Oh my God. That is sooooo weird.'

'Why don't they understand that *they* do things that *we* find weird?' Sana said.

'Yeah,' Zahra replied. 'Like when they eat steaks that are cooked on the outside and red raw on the inside. It irks my Ammi no end, does that.'

'Hmmm. Apparently they're supposed to be like that,' Sana said, fillet burger stuck in her teeth. 'You know, "rare" and "well done". That's what I've heard Jamie Oliver say.'

'Don't care. It's bloody weird.'

'What about…' Sana dipped into a whisper as the sullen-faced McDonald's worker wiped down the table next to them half-heartedly with a dirty cloth. 'When they don't rinse dishes and leave them on the stand dripping with soapy water.'

'Or that they spend hours talking to you about their cats and dogs, even though you don't give a toss.'

'I know,' Sana said. 'Well over the top. They love their pets more than they love their parents.'

Zahra slurped on her Diet Coke and nodded vigorously. 'What about when there's a really dirty scene in a movie, and goray sit there watching it with their mum and dad,' she began.

Sana frowned. 'They don't turn it over?'

Zahra shook her head. 'Karen said it's more awkward if you switch it over.'

'LOL, you should have told her that Asians change the channel even if animals are mating on a wildlife programme.'

They both laughed and carried on suggesting things to add to their list.

In truth, however, it wasn't funny. It was all right laughing about it now with Sana, but Zahra realised how easy it was for animosity to develop from these experiences. She found herself increasingly bitter, increasingly on the defensive. Any difficult encounter with Karen and Lydia would make her really angry and for a brief moment, she would decide that she quite simply hated white people. Really hated them. And she'd tell her Asian friends about what they had said to her. How insignificant and inferior they made her feel. They would shrug, 'That's just the way it is.' Well, that wasn't what she wanted to hear, though she had given out the same advice to other people plenty of times.

So she'd tell another friend until she found an aggressive enough answer, 'Fuck goray, man.' Yeah, she'd think. *Fuck 'em.*

Zahra remembered the aftermath of one of these outbursts. She'd been sitting trying to write an essay on the Third Reich when Libby had bounded into the room, 'Iyaaa! Found you some jelly beans that don't have gelatine in 'em,' her face full of joy.

Zahra could barely look her in the eye. She'd hug her best friend guiltily, insist on her staying for dinner and listen intently to all her problems by way of an apology. What if Libby knew of her disgraceful thoughts a few hours earlier?

After nearly two years of friendship with Karen and the girls, Zahra thought she had finally made some progress. Every annoying question had been asked, subtle remarks repeated until they lost their effectiveness. They all seemed to be just getting along fine, even enjoying their time together. That was until, exactly a year ago, she'd been sitting with them working on a presentation on the impact of the Great War on domestic society. Text messages appeared on her phone from her friends.

Have you seen the news?

The reaction was always the same, though it always surprised Zahra; she should have been used to it by now. Anxiety set in. Her heart palpitated. A panic rose in her chest.

Someone wearing a Help for Heroes top has been murdered in London.

The alarm bells started ringing. Zahra's fingers trembled. She prayed it was a coincidence. She prayed it had nothing to do with them. She prayed she could get out of there before Karen and the girls found out.

Unfortunately, Emma logged out of her email. The headline was on the webpage. BREAKING NEWS.

Karen, in her signature move, read the article out loud. There was nothing to suggest it was terrorist-related. Just yet. Zahra felt guilty for being relieved when a man had been brutally murdered in broad daylight. Just as she thought she was out of the danger zone, Karen's mobile bleeped.

'It's my friend. He's put "Have you heard about those two Muslims who beheaded a soldier in London?"' Karen turned to stare at Zahra dead in the eyes. Accusingly. Lydia did the same. Even Emma, who normally had Zahra's back, was lost for words. She just stared at the floor, avoiding eye contact.

Zahra only managed to whimper, 'What?'

The rest of the session was spent talking about the incident. 'This is going to be big,' Lydia kept saying, shaking her head.

'EDL are organising a march.'

'I just don't understand, though, if you can't integrate then… why live here?'

Zahra wanted to point out that for sadistic killers, community cohesion was probably the last thing on their mind. She didn't speak, but felt herself shrink in size. Zahra noticed none of them could look directly at her. She was an intruder on their grief.

'They were shouting "Allahu Akbar" as they did it,' Karen said. She had turned, with a glint in her eye. 'Is that how you say it, Zahra?'

Zahra's phone buzzed. It was Abbu.

Go straight home after you finish uni.

Another from Libby:

I'll be at your house in half an hour.

'I'd better go, guys. It's my dad, he needs me home. I'll finish my bit and email it to you.'

Zahra pelted out of the library. It was only when she got outside that she felt she wasn't being suffocated. Luckily, the bus was already waiting. After a few stops, she got off and ran the rest of the way home. As promised, Libby was already outside.

'I just got here now—'

Zahra had thrown her arms around her best friend and hugged her tightly.

'It's all right, Zee. It's all right.'

That night, Abbu looked worried sick. Ammi decided to pray some extra nafl, an optional supererogatory prayer.

'Isn't it ironic, Abbu? That Ammi is going to pray and ask for peace from the same entity whose name those men were shouting out as they hacked a man to death.'

Abbu remained silent.

'It's going to get worse, isn't it, Abbu?' Zahra asked.

'Don't think it can,' Abbu replied, turning off the TV. He was right. People didn't need to make elaborate plans to get past airport customs anymore. There was no need to construct home-made bombs or get into a cockpit and slam airliners into skyscrapers. All you needed was a target, an ordinary English street and a couple of well-sharpened knives. Simple enough things to acquire in order to turn the world upside down.

Zahra avoided Karen for the rest of the week, spending most of her time with Sana, Junaid and Hasan.

'See, it doesn't matter, does it?' Junaid said. 'You think you've finally reached an understanding with them and you can be mates, but as soon as something like this happens, all your efforts go down the swanny.'

Sana rolled her eyes at Zahra. He continued: 'And anyway, these white people like to pass themselves off as martyrs. One of theirs dies and it's like a big hullabaloo. What about us, man?'

Zahra hated to admit it, but there was an element of truth in that. When Abbu put the Pakistani news on for Ammi, the scene was almost always the same. Bored police officers standing guard over a new bomb attack on a market or a mosque during Friday prayers. Burnt-out cars and people running to fill ambulances with bloodied bodies. Or there were the excruciatingly awkward conversations Zahra had to have with her relatives in Pakistan.

'Er... so how's school?' she'd asked one of her cousins whose name she couldn't even remember.

'We haven't been in a month. Bombs are going off,' they'd reply, casually.

'Ah, right.'

Still, Zahra didn't want to hype Junaid up too much. 'Not everyone is the same,' she'd said, sounding like a broken record. 'Look at my friend Libby.'

'Yeah, yeah,' Junaid said. 'She'll probably show her true colours...'

His words faltered as Zahra had glared at him. He'd leaned back in his seat and shrugged. 'Just sayin'.'

Zahra and Sana left the McDonald's and walked towards the bus stop together. 'You ready for this last exam, then?'

'Yeah, we'll see how it goes,' Sana replied. 'Anyway, listen. There's this guy—'

'No,' Zahra interrupted.

'What? You didn't even listen to what I have to say.'

'Because I already know.'

'But he's really nice,' Sana protested.

Zahra grimaced. 'I don't know…'

She didn't really like the thought of being shunted together with someone and have to awkwardly try to make conversation. She told Sana that she thought it should just happen naturally.

'Well, at least give it a chance!' Sana snapped.

'Okay, fine, what's his name?'

When Sana told her, Zahra thought she had misheard. It sounded suspiciously like 'Rayman'. She made her repeat it several times.

'Is he Asian?' Zahra asked.

'Obviously.'

'Oh.' Zahra tried not to laugh as the bus approached. 'You mean, Reh-maaaaan?' she said, using full Urdu pronunciation.

'Yeah,' Sana replied. 'But he doesn't like it when you say it like that.'

'Forget it then,' Zahra said, stepping on to the bus and finding a seat.

'Why?' Sana asked, sitting behind her.

'White wannabe,' Zahra replied, plugging in her earphones.

Twenty

The next day, Zahra walked up the street of semi-detached houses with her Harry Potter book tucked under her arm. She checked her Twitter as she strolled along, looking for some random topic that she could maybe use to update her blog. It was approaching the two-week target Zahra had set herself to post something new, and she still couldn't think of anything good to rant about.

Zahra didn't think her blog site was very good. It didn't even have a catchy name (though Libby suggested it be named the 'Everybody is Shit Blog') or a particular theme. For the most part, it was a blog about politics and current affairs, and yet when the mood took her, she would post a funny meme to make sure it was up to date. Recently she'd written a lengthy rant against Saudi Arabia and the worldwide exportation of hard-line Wahabbism. It was followed by a post where Zahra gushed over the red-carpet Oscar dresses and then by an essay about the Black Lives Matter movement.

She continued to scroll through her Twitter as she trudged uphill to the familiar red-bricked house with the emerald green door. No matter how busy she was, she always managed to fit her fortnightly visit into her schedule. She was about to put her phone away when she spotted something on it.

A female journalist was getting rape threats for expressing an opinion. Other women were rushing to her defence. Zahra probably would have done too, but she was reluctant to get into any Twitter fights anymore. An unsuspecting Abbu had once come across her profile and seen the most horrific tweets directed at her and Sana when they'd both taken on some racists. He warned her against ever getting involved in fights online. He'd even threatened to report it to the police.

'There's no point, Abbu,' Zahra told him, casually. 'This guy lives in Edinburgh. And this one in Texas.'

Number twelve was where she needed to be. Zahra swung open the gate and noticed the car was not in the driveway. Feeling relieved, she rang the doorbell. No one answered. She knocked and turned the handle, like she had done many times before, and called out 'Asalaam alaikum' before stepping inside.

'Come in, Zahra,' a female voice responded from the kitchen. The kettle was boiling. Zahra walked the opposite way, and turned into the second door on the right.

There he was. Alone in the room, sleeping soundly in his bed. Zahra hurried towards him.

'Hello, Ehsi,' she said, smiling from ear to ear. She leaned down and kissed him on the forehead. Her hair brushed his face. His eyelids fluttered but he did not stir.

It was always when the house was completely empty that Zahra would pluck up the courage to open the door. She wandered up the stairs one day after Ammi and Abbu left home for a doctor's appointment, inched towards the silver handle, turned it and put her head cautiously through the opening as if expecting somebody to be in there.

It was almost teenagerish, as though he had been meaning to decorate and update to a more adult look. Zahra knew he would not have been happy with the bright blue walls, the single bed in the corner, the piles of boxes with boyish things spilling out of them. Zahra saw the same pin had fallen off again, leaving the Muhammad Ali poster dangling by a single tack. She pinned it back in place. It was one of the few things in her house that was easily corrected.

There was a hi-fi on one of the drawers, a big, bulky contraption that no one used anymore. All of Zahra's music was stored safely in her iPhone, the one Abbu had got her for her twenty-first birthday. Zahra reminded herself the room was still stuck in 2003, ten years ago. It had barely been touched apart from during spring cleans when Zahra would dust everything down and hoover behind the bed. Abbu never entered the room.

Zahra flipped through the CDs next to the hi-fi. They mostly consisted of Eighties and Nineties hip hop, the type he would only play when Abbu was out of the house. Though Zahra clearly remembered he would sometimes replace 'Fuck tha Police' with 'Hit Me Baby One More Time' just for her.

She found a Michael Jackson CD and skipped straight to 'Smooth Criminal'. It was their favourite. He would play it especially for her and then sit at the end of his bed and watch her dance around, smiling.

As the song played, Zahra glanced at the football posters in his room. She remembered Saahil and Ehsan swearing at the TV during a match, sometimes gaping at each other in horror, other times leaping to their feet in triumph. Zahra watched the World Cup tournaments with Abbu in 2006 and 2010. She had always tried to imagine what her brother's facial expressions would have been like had he been there with them. What smart-ass remarks would have escaped his lips? The daft sense of humour, the glint of mischief, the sullen moods – she ached for it all.

Walking to the wardrobe, she tripped over a huge textbook. *Aerospace Engineering and the Principles of Flight*, it said on the cover. She picked it up. His face had been buried in these books at one time, his fingers had flicked through the pages urgently. He'd tried his best to remember paragraphs of writing, complicated formulas, key terms and principles. All for nothing.

Zahra opened the wardrobe and reached out for the same dark blue hoodie. She hugged it as she walked back to the bed. His smell had faded from it now, but she still held it close to her in an embrace. As she sat cloaked in the sadness of the quiet room, the same thoughts raced through her mind: *Saahil was alive*. He had to be. The police would have found something. A clue. A sign. A body. They hadn't, and so, without evidence, all indications pointed to one thing: Saahil was alive.

But then, where was he? Zahra grimaced as she thought of her brother alone in a room somewhere with nobody to check if he was dead or alive. Nobody to check to see if he had eaten, if he was warm. It was the same feeling she got on those harsh winter nights where the wind knocked over trees and fences. When the rain would hit the tiles on the roof of their house, when she could barely hear herself breathe. Those nights, when Zahra would pull the covers over her head and think about homeless people who slept in shop doorways. Her brother could be one of them.

So why, then, was he living in this way? Saahil was definitely alive. So that meant only one thing: he had purposely stayed away from them for the last ten years. He didn't want to be anywhere near them. He didn't love his family, and he didn't want their love in return. He hated them.

Impossible. Zahra dismissed this straightaway as she had done many times before. There was no way Saahil would do such a thing. He loved them. He loved her. She was his baby, he'd helped raise her. Ten birthdays of Zahra's he had missed. Ten markings on their childhood growth chart. If Saahil had needed a few weeks, even months away to collect his thoughts after the attack, fine, Zahra could understand. But an entire decade? That left only one explanation.

Her brother was dead. Somebody had killed him. Those attackers had arranged for it from their prison cells. Zahra held the hoodie in her arms. She wiped her tears on the sleeve. No, no. It wasn't true. Nobody had found anything. After all, the police always uncovered the truth in the end. In films, in books, in the crime documentaries Abbu often watched late at night when he couldn't sleep. Zahra blew hard through her nose. She would punch anyone who so much as suggested that somebody had hurt her brother.

Next possibility. Zahra remembered those hellish months prior to Saahil's disappearance. He had been so broken, so tired of life. There was always the chance, the cruel reality, that her brother had simply walked off a cliff. Fallen through the sky, shattered his body. Instant death. Was he capable of such a thing? Not only to take his own life but to do so without even sparing a thought for Abbu? Abbu, who had raised them both single-handedly, Abbu, who had barely lived just so that they, his children, could do it for him. *Fuck him*, she thought, throwing the hoodie on the floor in anger.

But maybe Saahil had thought his body would be found? Zahra reluctantly picked up the hoodie. *Yes, definitely*, she concluded. He wasn't so selfish as to just jump to his death and leave them fretting for the rest of their lives about what had happened to him. But that is exactly what had happened. Saahil's plan had failed.

Zahra winced. He was dead then? No, no, that's not what she had said, thank you very much. Her brother wasn't dead.

No way. He was alive. He was definitely alive. There was no question about it.

So where was he?

'These bloody chest infections,' Zahra said, frowning. She looked at Auntie Meena, whose glasses were perched at the end of her nose as she picked away at some stitching on one of her dresses.

'Don't worry,' Meena said. 'He's pulled through worse ones. Just pray it passes quickly.'

Ehsan was wearing his nasal cannula. Today his breathing was worse than usual and could easily be heard over the racket of his oxygen tank. Zahra touched Ehsan's arm. He pulled away. Auntie Meena smiled apologetically.

'He doesn't like—' she began.

'Being touched. I know,' Zahra replied, wishing her visits to him weren't so restrictive. She couldn't take his hand in hers because it was clenched tightly around a small bean bag. Zahra wished she could embrace Ehsan, but he lay in a hospital bed, rigid and wrapped in a blanket. She just wanted to make sure that he knew she was there. Anything to let Ehsan know that they hadn't all abandoned him.

It still shocked Zahra sometimes that Ehsan was thirty-one years old. But then, she was no longer a ten-year-old kid. In just over ten years, Ehsan had changed completely. His face was no longer boyish and gentle. It was tired, coarse and almost always in a state of suffocation. An unpleasant smell surrounded him. It came from his breath and was due to all the harsh medicine he took. Meena constantly reminded her of this in an apologetical tone. Increasingly, Ehsan looked like he was ready for death. Zahra remembered how Ehsan had been short and light on his feet, but now he had gained weight. He lay like a huge burden in the middle of the room, on a bulky hospital bed. The Ehsan Zahra remembered would have hated to have been so much trouble.

'You don't have to come if you're busy, Zahra,' Auntie Meena said. 'You've got a lot on. It's only a few weeks until you finish uni, right?'

'Yeah.'

'Exactly, you need every minute you can get to prepare for your exams.'

Zahra shrugged. 'It's fine, Auntie.'

'I just don't want to you to feel as though you *have* to come. You're busy. And you know nothing changes around here.'

'I want to come, Auntie. I need to because...' Zahra's voice trailed off. How could she explain to Auntie Meena that if she didn't see Ehsan at least once every two weeks, she couldn't sleep at night? 'Well, he waits for me. He wants to know what happens next,' Zahra held up the Harry Potter book and smiled.

Meena smiled too. 'Of course he does.'

'Anyway, I'm not going to be so busy anymore. I've, erm, quit my job,' Zahra lied.

'Really? Why?'

'Well, like you said, I need to concentrate on uni now.'

'Yes. That's more important,' Meena agreed. Zahra watched her pick away at the stitching. Her hair was streaked with grey now and she squinted through her glasses like a little old lady.

'What was your job again, Auntie?'

'I was only a receptionist at a doctors' surgery,' Meena laughed. 'But still, I was good with computers.'

'Do you miss it?' Zahra asked.

'It would be nice to get out sometimes…' Meena shuffled in her seat before continuing, 'Anyway, which book are you on?'

'*Prisoner of Azkaban*. Second time we're reading it.'

'Why don't you read something other than that?'

'But he likes Harry Potter. Don't you remember? He was reading it secretly before… you know… Saahil found it in his bag and made fun of him.' They both laughed as the front door opened and Harun entered the room. Zahra stood up.

'Asalaam alaikum, Uncle.' Harun glanced at her briefly and replied 'Wa'alaikum salaam.' He still looked edgy and irritable, as though every moment was still the first time the doctors had told him that Ehsan would not recover.

'What time did the nurse leave, Meena?'

'About an hour ago.'

Harun headed towards Ehsan and sat beside him. Zahra turned to Meena. 'I'll get off then, Auntie.'

'You don't have to go,' she said, glancing at Harun. He said nothing.

'I'll come over next week. Allah Hafiz, Uncle.'

'Allah Hafiz,' Harun replied, with a half-hearted smile.

Meena walked Zahra to the door. She looked angry again but was trying to hide it. Zahra knew Uncle Harun would get it after she left. Zahra wanted to tell Auntie Meena not to worry, she'd been visiting Ehsan for ten years and was used to Harun's behaviour by now.

'Give my salaam to your Abbu,' Meena said.

'I will.'

Zahra walked down the street, the image of Uncle Harun absentmindedly massaging Ehsan's arm running through her mind.

Twenty-One

Amjad returned home and began rummaging through his work bag. He placed the Snickers bar and packet of crisps back in the kitchen drawer, not wanting Zahra to see that he hadn't eaten the snacks she'd given him. It would hurt her feelings. He always ate in the canteen with the rest of his friends, but every day when Amjad checked in his bag, he would find Zahra had provided snacks that would keep him going for the entire day.

Every day was different, she took the time to mix and match. Sometimes, it was only fruit: 'You need to be healthy Abbu,' she'd say. And other times, she would throw in a KitKat Chunky as a treat.

'Don't worry about me,' Amjad would tell her. 'You don't need to give me all these things. I eat in the canteen.'

'But it's a long day, Abbu. You'll get hungry.'

Amjad realised that no matter what he said to Zahra, she would always worry, because she was his daughter. Daughters were different. They worried. They cared about the little details. *Eat something warm today, Abbu. Don't get a cold sandwich. I've left your scarf by your coat, make sure you wear it otherwise you'll catch a cold. Remember to use the chapstick I got you, your lips are always cracked when you come home.*

There were other days when she would run towards him with hand moisturiser before he left the house, complaining his hands were dry and coarse. Or she would sit him down in the kitchen on a high chair and wrap a plastic bag around his neck.

'I'm not letting you get old yet, Abbu,' she'd say, applying the black hair dye generously to his greying sideburns.

'I *am* old, Zee. Another few years and I'll be sixty.'

'Yeah, but you're not there yet, are you?'

Amjad would smile and let her continue. Yes, daughters were definitely different. Sons, well, he'd heard his friends complaining about their boys. *Good for nothing*, they'd describe them as. Times had changed from his own mother's generation, when everyone preferred sons. Now, they all pined for daughters. And Amjad was blessed to have one.

He thanked Neelam for Zahra. When he thought back to those first few weeks following her death, Amjad held his head in shame. He had been so weary, so unsure of how to look after the new baby that he would have gladly swapped her for his wife. Amjad shuddered when he thought of those times and had come to understand that everything happened for a reason. Before Neelam died, she had given him Zahra. Zahra, who would be at home to greet him when he arrived back from work in the evenings. Zahra, whose presence relieved him of the heartache of the past. Zahra, whose existence had always prevented him from ending it all. Amjad realised that he had never loved anyone like he loved his daughter. Not Ammi, not Neelam and not even Saahil.

When he visited the mosque on Fridays, Amjad tried not to notice the same boys Saahil used to run along with were now walking with their own children. Little children they were, clambering on their fathers' shoulders or running to keep up with them, one hand clutching their mosque hats as they tried to catch up. Amjad was once like them, striding ahead with Saahil's little hand in his. Now he was like the old men. The ones with white speckled beards, shuffling along as their sons led the way in the crowd. There was only one difference, of course. No one led the way for Amjad. No grandchildren ran around near his legs. No one passed Amjad his shoes so that he would not have to bend down to pick them up. Amjad walked alone.

Only the other day he had bumped into Umar after a long time.

'Uncle,' he said, shaking Amjad's hand. 'How are you? How's Zahra?'

'We're fine, thank you. What about you? Day off work?'

'Yes, Uncle. It's been really busy at the firm.' Amjad knew Umar worked at an engineering company. He owned a BMW now and had his own house. Amjad noticed a podgy little boy hiding behind Umar's legs.

'Come and give salaam, Adil,' Umar said, picking up his little son. Amjad smiled at the boy who hid his face shyly.

'Masha'Allah,' Amjad said, placing his hand on the child's head. He'd cleared his throat, suddenly unable to speak. Umar watched him sadly and had asked if he was okay, again. Amjad made an excuse and left.

He often thought about going to a different mosque, one where he didn't come across familiar faces staring at him pityingly. There was one face he hadn't come across for the past ten years. It wasn't long after Saahil's disappearance that Harun had changed mosques. The last time Amjad saw him there was a regular Friday. His eyes focused on Amjad and he'd leaned forward as though wanting to come over to him. Amjad was sure Harun had taken a step towards him, a flicker of concern passing over his face. But then something happened. Harun's face hardened. Slowly, he'd turned his back and walked off in the opposite direction, Amjad watching him disappear through the doors. He hadn't returned to the mosque since that day.

Any visits to Ehsan were made in secret. A quick call from Meena to let him know that Harun was away for the day resulted in a mad rush to get to their house and spend a scattered hour here and there with Ehsan. Sometimes, months would go by and he would not see him. Zahra visited every two weeks, though Amjad knew Harun barely spoke to her and she would leave whenever he returned home. Part of him wanted to stride right in there and confront his old friend. What was his problem? Had they both not suffered enough? The truth was, however, that Amjad was just too tired. Too tired to argue, too tired to fight with anyone. He had Ammi and he had Zahra. That was enough.

Even to this day, Amjad could barely look at the growth chart they'd inked into the kitchen door with so much enthusiasm. Over the past ten years, he'd practically forced Zahra to take measurements on her birthday, not wanting her to think it no longer mattered. It did, but the only problem was that whenever they marked the door for Zahra, everyone instinctively glanced over to see how she compared with the boys' measurements. They'd stopped doing it back in 2000, when the boys turned eighteen. *There wouldn't have been any more markings anyway*, he often told himself, *their chart was complete*. That didn't stop Amjad from thinking about how Saahil and Ehsan's lives seemed to end with it. One day, when it became almost unbearable to look at, Amjad nearly painted over it. Ammi caught him just in time, and gave him a good telling-off.

Then there was the framed photograph on the bureau in their living room. It was of Saahil and Ehsan at around ten years of age. Saahil's mouth was wide open, one arm thrown around Ehsan and the other hand making some kind of hip hop gesture Amjad didn't understand. Ehsan was sitting with his shoulders drawn together, a shy smile spread over his little face, dignified and demure. If Amjad's eyes fell on the photograph, he would let out a chuckle at how their postures matched their personalities. Then, he would remember. In a burst of anger he would throw the picture inside a drawer and hold his head in his hands, lamenting at how things had ended up like this. It would reappear on the bureau a few days later, though, Zahra would see to that.

Amjad had scheduled another one of his yearly meetings with the imam to ask for advice. Not that there was any point, Amjad knew nothing came of them. He could tell even the imam hated them. Luckily, however, Amjad had had around five hours sleep. Enough energy to question the imam well enough and fight his corner.

When people died, you prayed for them. You prayed that God would have mercy on their souls. That He forgave them of their sins and wrongdoing. That He grant them a place in Jannah. You recited the Quran on their behalf. Last-minute attempts at salvation. But what if you didn't know if they were dead?

Once Amjad had hidden his uneaten snacks away, he quickly changed. The doorbell rang signalling the imam's arrival. Amjad rushed downstairs and greeted him. Ammi made tea. Zahra took a seat opposite them. After politely making small talk, Amjad posed the question, hoping the response from the imam would finally be different this year.

'You can't pray for Saahil as deceased,' the imam said, resignation in his voice. Despite the mosque hat and extensive facial hair, the kindness of the holy man's face shone through. He wasn't stern and unapproachable like some religious leaders, and that's why

Amjad had always liked him. The imam smiled sadly and exhaled. Amjad could tell that the whole situation pained him too. It looked as though he was searching the air for answers, but found none.

Zahra was staring straight ahead, arms folded, jaw clenched tightly.

'It's been ten years, imam sahib,' Amjad muttered. 'What do you expect me to do?'

'Pray for his safe return.'

Amjad felt his lip quiver. 'I've been doing that for ten years.'

'Yes, but there's no evidence Saahil is… no longer with us.'

'Do you think I want to bury my own son? I don't know what else to do. At least this way I can help him… somehow.'

'But it's not right. You can't pray for his soul when we don't know if Saahil is—'

'Dead, yes we know,' Zahra interrupted, harshly. Ammi prodded her with an arthritic finger.

Amjad looked around the room like a lost boy. 'So what shall I do?' He always tried to tone down the desperation in his voice, but sometimes it just escaped. He noticed Zahra glance at him, her face softening.

'You mustn't lose hope. Just pray,' the imam said.

After he left, Amjad descended into a rant. 'Pray? Wow, well, we didn't think of that now, did we? Bloody useless.'

'What do you expect from people who can't even decide what day Eid is?' Zahra said, walking around the room in a huff.

'What else can they say?' Ammi said, dabbing at her eyes. Slowly, she made her way upstairs and Amjad knew she had gone to do exactly as the imam said.

There was a knock on the door. Amjad heard the familiar 'Ey up!' as Zahra opened the door.

'Uncle Ken's here,' she said.

Ken looked around the room as he entered. 'Where's Ammi?' he asked.

Amjad frowned. 'Upstairs.'

Ken made a face before settling down on the sofa.

'Is that the only reason why you come here? So you can get fed by my mother?'

Ken cracked a smile. 'Nah. Come to see you, don't I! Anyway, what's up? You've got a face like a slapped arse.'

Amjad eyed Zahra before shaking his head. 'Nothing.'

Zahra stood up immediately. 'I'm going to try and finish my dissertation,' she said, and headed for the stairs.

'Tell your Ammi that I'm here, won't you?'

Zahra rolled her eyes and nodded. Ken turned and faced Amjad cheerfully, who glared back.

'White people,' he said, shaking his head.

'What?'

'When I come over to yours it kills you to offer me a biscuit with the cuppa you make me,' Amjad said. 'And yet you come over here wanting a curry all the time.'

'That's not true,' Ken replied, smirking, 'And anyway, your mum enjoys cooking for me.'

'Yeah, because you're so willing to be force-fed.'

It was a thoroughly odd friendship that hadn't started out so well. After Ken had saved Saahil's life, he visited him in hospital and came to the house when Saahil returned home. He had been there for Amjad when Saahil disappeared, assisting him with the police, dealing with Missing Persons and spending entire nights out with Amjad looking for him.

Ammi didn't much care for Ken at first: he was shaggy-looking with bloodshot eyes and a faint aroma of whisky. Ammi would purse her lips when he walked through the door.

Even Amjad was mildly surprised at how much time Ken seemed to have for them. After getting to know him more, Amjad discovered that Ken was divorced and had no children.

'I've only got me mam,' he'd said. 'And she dunt recognise me.'

Amjad scolded Ammi after Ken had left.

'He's lonely. And his mum is in a care home with dementia. You could be nicer to him.'

Ammi felt guilty for the rest of the evening and promised to cook for him the following day. Despite not being able to speak to each other in the same language, the pair had bonded over food, big time. Ken knew all the right buttons to press to inflate Ammi's ego.

'Yum! This daal, Ammi,' he'd say, rubbing his belly.

'Yes, please,' Ammi would reply in her broken English.

As for Zahra, she already knew to call Amjad's friends 'Uncle' out of respect. Ken was no different, apart from the fact that he was a bit paler.

Today, Amjad was actually glad that Ammi was upstairs and he was alone with Ken. He needed to talk to him about something important. He popped the kettle on and made them both a cup of tea as Ken complained about his neighbour, the council and teenagers who had graffitied his garage door. He placed the mugs on the table. Ken glanced over to the stairs to where Zahra had just been standing.

'So what's wrong wi' you all?' he asked Amjad. 'Is it about Saahil?'

Amjad looked up from his cup. He nodded. That's what he liked about Ken, he was always straight to the point.

Amjad cleared his throat. 'You know it's been ten years…'

Ken nodded as he tucked into some fig rolls.

'Well… I'm just fed up. I need to know what happened to him. You know?'

'Of course.'

'How can you not know what happened to your own son? Like… is he in pain? Is he suffering? What if he's on the streets somewhere? And if he's, you know… what did they do? *How* did they do it? Did they bury him or just dump him… what was left of him.'

'Don't do it to yerself,' Ken said, avoiding eye contact.

'No, you don't get it,' Amjad said. 'I can't go another ten years not knowing.'

He rubbed his eyes. Last night had been a good one. Four to five hours' sleep was pretty decent for Amjad. He had been wide awake for two nights in a row before that.

Ken cleared his throat. 'Erm, you haven't been popping too many of them pills, have you?'

'I took one the day before last. Why?'

'Well, you look terrible, mate.'

'You stay awake for forty-eight hours—' Amjad began.

'Sorry, sorry,' Ken said, holding up his hand. 'Just don't get it, me. As soon as my head hits the pillow—'

'That doesn't make me feel better.'

'Yeah, sorry. I'm not undermining the problem… must be awful not being able to get a good night's kip.'

Amjad opened his mouth to explain that it was a lot more than just 'getting a good kip', but decided against it. People just did not understand. What had started as a few sleepless nights after Saahil's disappearance had, ten years on, transformed into

219

full-blown chronic insomnia. Amjad just couldn't fall asleep. He'd lie awake thinking about his lost son. His dead wife.

If, by some miracle, he did drop off, he would wake up after an hour. Then he couldn't fall back again. When he did eventually drift off, he'd wake up again forty-five minutes later, needing the toilet. He'd do this throughout the night until the alarm clock would go off at seven o'clock for work.

'What's the doctor doing about it?' Ken asked.

'Giving me different pills, what else? They make me groggy for the rest of the day.'

Amjad had tried everything. From basic advice like taking a hot bath before bed, to a pointless course of Cognitive Behavioural Therapy. Zahra bought him relaxation tapes. She googled herbal remedies and made him drink tart cherry juice every day for three months. The doctor prescribed sleeping pill after sleeping pill. He'd recently been given melatonin tablets as he had reached the age of fifty-five. The first few worked before the effects began to wear off, just like the rest of them. Ammi suggested visiting faith healers who gave him religious amulets and 'holy water' to drink before bed. Nothing worked. And now Amjad was desperate.

The doorbell rang again and Zahra came down to answer it, though Amjad was sure he hadn't heard many footsteps.

'It's Libs,' she said, opening the door.

Amjad watched his daughter. 'That was quick,' he said, wondering whether she'd been listening on the stairs.

'What was quick?' Zahra asked, poker-faced. 'Me and Libs are going to my room. Call us when you're hungry and I'll make roti.'

They disappeared off upstairs.

'I think she may have heard me,' Amjad said. 'I don't like saying too much in front of her.'

'We all have to get things off our chest sometimes,' Ken said. 'Anyway, carry on.'

Amjad shrugged, 'Well, yeah. That's it.'

'Look, I know it's 'ard. But you need to think of your lass,' Ken said.

Amjad nodded. 'I do.'

'Exactly,' Ken replied. 'Regret not having some kids of me own when I see you two together.'

Amjad leaned forward and dropped his voice into a whisper. 'You can help me,' he said, looking straight at Ken.

'Excuse me?'

'With the sleep. You can help me.'

'Er... How?'

Amjad had been watching Ken. They both shared a passion for cricket, especially when England and Pakistan were competing. Amjad remembered supporting England against Harun, who supported Pakistan. The banter they had shared always brought a smile to his face.

'You coconut,' Harun would say to him. 'Supporting the goray.'

'Sorry, but this is my country. I'm not a mangy like you.'

The same banter developed between Ken and him. Amjad assumed the role of supporting Pakistan, and Ken supported England. Sometimes they would switch it around. There was nothing more hilarious than watching Ken, who was unable to pronounce the cricketers' names properly, cheer on Pakistan.

Ken only had one complaint. 'What's the point of watching the cricket without a beer?' he'd say.

Reluctantly, Amjad had allowed Ken to bring alcohol into his home. He noticed something straightaway. After two small glasses of whisky, Ken was snoring his head off, leaving Amjad watching him enviously. For weeks, Amjad had battled with whether or not he should give it a go. He was desperate enough.

'No,' Ken said, flat out.

'But it's for medicinal purposes.'

'It's against your religion, is what it is.'

'You think I want to,' Amjad hissed. 'I don't have a choice.'

Ken fidgeted in his chair. 'And what does it say in the Quran? Are you allowed for medicinal purposes?'

'Yeah,' Amjad lied. He'd asked the imam about it who had leaped back in horror at the suggestion: 'You can't solve an illness with something haram, Amjad. All diseases are from Allah. And they must be cured in the proper way. Not like this.'

Ken, who probably hadn't even read a book in his life, never mind the Quran, seemed to soften. 'Medicinal purposes, eh?'

Amjad swallowed hard, and nodded.

'I don't know,' Ken said. 'Why don't you get it yourself?'

'I can't!' Amjad replied. 'There are so many Asians around here. I can't queue up in Morrison's with Jack Daniels tucked under my arm.'

'All right, all right. I'll get you a bottle. But you need to drink it responsibly.'

''Course I will. I'm not drinking for pleasure, trust me.'

Amjad sighed deeply, eyes landing on the framed photo of Saahil and Ehsan on the drawer. Ken turned his head, following Amjad's gaze.

'You have to try and let it go…' Ken said, tentatively.

'But Saahil… He was a good kid, Ken. They both were. Him and Ehsan.'

'I know. I'd make it all better for you if I could.'

Amjad looked at his friend. 'You'll get me the bottle, yeah?'

Ken shoved another biscuit in his mouth and thought about it.

'Whatever you do, don't mix it up with your pills,' he said finally.

Zahra slammed the door shut behind her.

'What happened?' Libby asked. 'Is your dad okay?'

'No. It's this ten-year thing. Abbu's getting really stressed. Had the imam over again. You know. Same old... same old.'

'Oh dear,' Libby said, used to the cycle of events which usually unfolded in their house during anniversaries.

'And his insomnia is out of control. He was just talking about it to Uncle Ken.'

'He wants closure, doesn't he?' Libby said.

'About what?'

'Saahil.'

Zahra glowered at her. 'We can't just forget about him.'

Libby smiled sadly. 'I know what you're saying, Zee, and I know you don't like me saying this but think about it. Would Saahil leave you, *you*, for ten bloody years? It's just not possible.'

Zahra didn't answer and pretended to be extremely interested in a scrap on the floor. Libby continued: 'And in that state of mind, people can do all sorts to themselves... you know.'

'Don't even go there, Libs,' Zahra warned.

'No, I mean, like, sometimes people just go off and live their own lives,' Libby said quickly.

Zahra stared at her, fiercely. 'Asians don't do that.'

'Just an option,' Libby mumbled. 'That's all I'm saying. But to be honest with you... Well, you know what I think about it.'

Zahra looked the other way. They were both perched on her single bed. Libby prodded her. 'Are you listening?'

'What?' Zahra said, standing up and pacing the small room. 'He's not dead, all right?' Her voice quivered. 'What the hell is wrong with people? Why do they all wanna kill him off?'

'You need to face facts, Zee. They can't even find little kids like Ben Needham… and… and Madeleine McCann. Never mind responsible adults.'

Zahra whipped around. 'Responsible adults? What's that supposed to mean?'

'Sorry, but the time for niceties has gone,' Libby said, more forcefully. 'As harsh as it sounds. Sometimes you just have to let things go.'

'Let things go,' Zahra repeated incredulously.

'For your own sanity,' Libby said.

'What if I just disappeared off the face of the Earth?' Zahra sneered. 'Hmmm? What if today was the last time you saw me? Would you just *let it go*?'

'We've been over this a hundred times,' Libby sighed.

'Oh, well I'm sorry to be such a pain in your life—'

'I didn't mean it like that. But come on, Zee, you guys have tried *everything.*'

'Just because we've tried everything doesn't mean we should stop now and give up,' Zahra said. She sat down at her desk which faced the window.

'I'm not saying give up hope. Just be realistic about the situation. Saahil might be long gone, and you're still here, ten years on, making yourselves ill.'

'Well, it's worth it. He's my brother.'

Libby snorted.

Anger flashed in Zahra eyes. She turned to face her best friend. 'What is up with you today? Why are you being such a bitch?'

'I know how you feel—'

'No, you fucking don't! That's why it's so easy for you to tell me to let it go. You wouldn't be saying that if it was your brother.'

'Yeah, I would!' Libby shouted.

Zahra flinched. She stared at her best friend in shock. The room was silent for a few moments as Zahra adjusted to this new outburst.

'If it had been ten years then, yeah, I would let it go,' Libby eventually said. 'And you know what? You're so bloody adamant that your brother is still alive. So where the bloody hell is he? Where is he, whilst you and your dad float around, barely existing?'

Zahra opened her mouth to respond, but for once she didn't know what to say. Libby was normally full of reassurances, always approaching the subject with sympathy. Today, however, she was on a roll.

'You've got this distorted image of your brother as some sort of hero. Well, do you know what? He doesn't give a *fuck* about you.'

'Shut up!' Zahra shouted back. She grabbed a pencil holder and threw it. The pens flew at Libby's face like arrows. She dodged them.

'It's true,' she said. 'So you can piss off if you don't like it. Bad things happen to everyone.'

'What's that supposed to mean?'

'You'd know if you worked in a hospital. Shit things happen all the time. People don't just run off and leave their families to it. It's pathetic. Cowardly.'

'You better shut your trap Libby,' Zahra warned.

'Why? Your brother's alive, isn't he? That's what you're always saying. So be honest with yourself about what that means.'

'He might not be, though!' Zahra blurted out, tears in her eyes. 'None of this might be his fault.'

She frowned as she realised what she had just said. Libby stood up. 'That's up to you to decide,' she said.

Zahra sat down at the edge of her bed.

'Go away, please,' she said, waving her hand at Libby.

Zahra heard her friend's footsteps echo down the stairs, Abbu asking her why she was leaving already, the door slamming shut. Zahra left to shake off thoughts of how death was suddenly more appealing.

Twenty-Two

Days went by and Zahra didn't hear from Libby. She wrote out text messages, her fingers hovering over the send button. Then she remembered Libby's words, and in a fit of anger, deleted what she had written. Libby hadn't messaged her either. Zahra knew they would eventually make up, but things had definitely gone too far this time. The more Zahra thought about it, the more it made sense. She hated to admit it, but maybe Libby was right. Maybe she did just need to let it go. But that was the one thing Zahra could not do.

Feeling restless and lost without her best friend, Zahra volunteered to take Ammi to the diabetes clinic. They both walked home from the appointment, sullen-faced. Ammi had been weighed, her blood pressure, blood sugar and cholesterol were checked, all to find that everything had drastically increased from the previous year. Zahra was giving her a good telling-off.

'See, you don't listen, Ammi. Fourteen stone. That's terrible!'

Ammi grunted as she hobbled along the road, nose slightly up in the air.

'And when you go to the park with your friends, you're supposed to walk at a brisk pace. Not saunter along leisurely… gossiping.'

They turned a corner and could see the local Co-op from a distance. 'Shall we get some groceries?' Ammi asked, quietly.

'And don't think I didn't notice you stealing five Quality Streets from the tub yesterday. You hid them in your bra and took them upstairs to your room. I find wrappers all the time when I'm cleaning.'

'Oh, leave me alone,' Ammi snapped back. 'I'm nearly dead anyway. Let me enjoy the time I have left.'

'Don't talk like that!'

'Well, it's true.'

Zahra opened her mouth to respond but didn't say anything. She knew Ammi was getting on a bit. She was eighty and her health was deteriorating. But Zahra couldn't imagine life without her. God had taken her own mother before she'd even had the chance to remember her. All Zahra knew about her mum was things Abbu told her. He spoke about her in general terms, and, from an adult perspective. That was different. Zahra wanted details. She wanted little stories, funny memories. Zahra wanted to know about her mother *as* a mother. Things that maybe only a sibling could tell her. Saahil wasn't here, and so Zahra had to accept that she didn't have a mum or a brother anymore. The thought of losing Ammi as well weighed down on her.

They walked in silence into the Co-op. Zahra grabbed a basket as Ammi wandered down the fruit and veg aisle.

'How have they priced these lemons?' she asked, rubbing her hands together.

'Three for a quid.'

'What!' Ammi gasped, swearing under her breath in Punjabi. 'You can get a whole kilo for a pound at Arif's mini-market.'

'I doubt it,' Zahra said, rolling her eyes. 'What you going to do with a kilo anyway?'

'What about these courgettes?'

228

'A pound a pack.'

Ammi sighed and moved along. 'And the cabbage?'

'Ammi, I don't have time for this! I'm sorry but I need to go home and finish my dissertation. If you want something, just get it.'

Reluctantly, Ammi started putting things in the basket. They left with two bags full of shopping, but Ammi wanted to make another stop, taking Zahra into an Asian clothes shop. She felt nearly all the cream-coloured fabric with her fingers before wrinkling her nose and dismissing them callously.

'It's just for lining, Ammi,' Zahra wailed.

It took half an hour to find the right one, though to Zahra, it looked exactly the same as the first twenty she had checked.

'That's fifteen pounds,' the shopkeeper said, after cutting and measuring the material and reaching for a bag.

'Well, I've only got ten,' Ammi said. 'There you go.'

The shopkeeper laughed sheepishly. 'Auntie ji, it's expensive material, is this. Can't sell it for any less.'

'Yeah, yeah. Well, I'm not giving you anymore. Pop it into the bag. There's a good lad.'

Zahra covered her face in embarrassment but knew not to interfere when Ammi was haggling. They continued arguing.

'Auntie-ji, be reasonable, I can't knock off a fiver!'

'Leave it then, we'll go somewhere else. I can see you're really busy,' Ammi said, pointedly staring around the empty shop.

'Okay, okay.'

The man muttered under his breath as he printed them a receipt. Zahra couldn't wait to get out of there.

They continued down the street, past a mosque with some lads hanging around outside and a couple of more shops, including

Sasti Dukaan. Zahra was too busy checking to see if Qasim was safely behind his till when she realised Ammi had stopped again. Zahra saw her peering into a deli window.

'What now?'

'Samosa chaat,' she said, grinning from ear to ear.

Zahra sighed. 'Well, that's not going to do your arteries any good!'

'Please.'

Zahra hesitated. She felt she'd been harsh enough on the old woman already.

'I'll start the diet tomorrow,' Ammi said, meekly. Zahra's heart melted.

'Okay, but don't tell Abbu.'

Zahra ordered two samosa chaat as Ammi settled into a seat. She had chosen the chair facing the counter so she could nosy at the people who came and went. She watched a group of boys, similar age to Zahra, wait around for their order. She frowned.

'I never see any good-looking boys,' she sighed.

Zahra raised her eyebrows.

'For you! Silly girl,' she said as Zahra laughed.

'I want you to have a *really* nice husband. Good-looking. Plenty of money. Good job. Nice family. Willing to live close by to me and your dad.' She ticked off her requirements.

'Nice person?' Zahra added.

'Well, of course, goes without saying.'

Ammi jabbed at her samosa with a fork. 'Your granddad was really handsome.'

Zahra perked up. Conversation about the olden days was her favourite. She adjusted in her seat, eager for more.

'He wore an English suit when he came to ask for my hand,'

Ammi continued. 'The whole village started buzzing with excitement.'

Zahra giggled. She'd seen pictures of her grandfather in his youth. One of them was placed in the centre of the mantelpiece. It was a sepia-toned portrait of a man wearing a smart suit, spotted tie and a handkerchief folded in his breast pocket. His hair was combed back in an immaculate quiff and his deep, brooding eyes stared out at them moodily.

'Like a film star,' Ammi would say whenever she polished the frame affectionately with her scarf. 'In the bygone years.'

'When was the first time you spoke to each other?' Zahra asked, even though she already knew.

Ammi swallowed her mouthful of chaat and replied, 'On our wedding day.'

'What did you say?'

'He asked me what my name was.'

Zahra feigned shock but Ammi quickly added, 'Of course he knew my name! It was his way of... breaking the ice.'

'That would help, since you'd just got married,' Zahra smiled, rolling her eyes at the thought of her crazy ancestors. 'So, my granddad asked you for your name and you replied...?'

'I don't know,' Ammi smiled.

'Huh?'

'I said, "I don't know my name." I was too shy.'

They both laughed at the story, and even now, Zahra thought she could see Ammi blushing. The old woman became increasingly quiet as they ate their chaat. After they'd finished the meal, she cleared her throat.

'You know, Zahra, we should probably start thinking about the future.'

'Future?' Zahra asked.

Ammi shuffled on her seat before continuing: 'Well... you're a grown woman now.'

'So?'

'We need to start... looking around.'

'Looking for what?'

Ammi didn't speak, but Zahra realised. 'Are you talking about marriage?' she asked, smiling. 'Because if you are, you'd better not mention it in front of Abbu. He still thinks I'm "little" and asks what time I'm coming home from "school" instead of uni.'

'Little?' Ammi shot back. 'No, you're not. And anyway, these things take time. Getting to know the boy, getting to know the family. I'd say it can take up to two years before things are finalised completely.'

Zahra realised this was no light-hearted conversation. She busied herself with tidying the table, placing their empty chaat containers on top of each other. 'Why are we having this discussion?' she sighed.

'You have to get married at some point.'

'Not yet,' Zahra replied, her voice rising to match Ammi's. 'And anyway, Abbu said I can marry whoever I want – as long as he's Muslim.'

'Keep your eyes open then,' Ammi shouted, jabbing a bony finger at Zahra.

'Well, give me a chance,' Zahra said, glancing around the deli to make sure no one was listening. 'What's brought all this on anyway?'

Ammi snapped. 'My blood pressure is high! So is my diabetes. I'll be dead soon. If it was up to me, I'd stay here with you forever. But I can't.'

'Shhhh, Ammi, stop shouting. People will hear.'

Zahra's puzzlement increased when she saw her grandmother's eyes fill with tears. She reached out and held Ammi's hand.

'What's wrong, Ammi? Don't talk like that,' Zahra said, soothingly. 'And anyway I'm not an infant, I can look after myself.'

'Before I go,' Ammi sobbed. 'I want to know you have settled down—'

'Settled down?' Zahra said. 'I haven't even started yet!'

'And have your own family.'

'Settle down,' Zahra repeated, letting go of Ammi's hand. 'I can't think of a worse phrase in the entire English language.'

'I need to know you're not alone,' Ammi shouted over her.

'I'm not alone. I've got Abbu.'

'Well, you're forgetting, Zahra, that your Abbu is not going to be around forever either. It was different before...'

Ammi started sobbing louder. Zahra knew what was coming. Though her back was facing the deli counter, she could feel the eyes of other diners glancing over in their direction.

'Before you had each other,' Ammi said. 'I knew Saahil would look after you and you would look after Saahil.'

'Ammi, please... just leave it,' Zahra mumbled, reaching for her bag and hoping for a quick, clean exit through the doors.

'What's going to happen when the two of us aren't here anymore?' Ammi cried.

'There's plenty of time for all that,' Zahra reassured. 'Come on, we'll talk at home.'

'Plenty of time...' Ammi said, hiccupping. 'Says the girl whose mother died twenty years ago, in her prime.'

'Ammi! That's enough,' Zahra almost shouted. She didn't care who was listening. 'Come on, let's go.'

She stood up and walked briskly away. Ammi followed her reluctantly. They didn't speak to each other until they arrived home. Ammi went straight upstairs in silence before her bedroom door slammed shut. Zahra remained sullen for the rest of the evening. She wanted to go and comfort her grandmother, but didn't know what to say to make her feel better. Why on earth had Zahra always thought that Ammi was the strong one? An elderly lady, who had gone through four times the life that Zahra had, with many ups and downs of her own to deal with. Ammi was always strong for them, stepping in when Zahra was a baby, and again when Saahil disappeared. Maybe they had forgotten that she was struggling to cope too. All the words exchanged between them in the deli revealed her innermost thoughts. Ammi was not at peace and the thought of that killed Zahra. She didn't want to upset Abbu when he came home from work and kept the outburst to herself.

'I've just had a thought, Abbu,' she said once he'd eaten his dinner. 'Once I've finished my last exam shall we go to Uncle Javid's house at the weekend?'

Abbu frowned. 'Really? That's your idea of fun?' he said, unable to hide his bemusement. 'Well, if you're sure, I'll call him in the morning.'

'Yeah, I'm sure,' Zahra replied.

She needed to remind Ammi she had another son and that Zahra had five cousins. So she wasn't completely alone in the world.

Later on that evening, with nothing but images of weddings and marriages filling her brain, Zahra felt a tightness in her chest: if things had gone according to plan, and Saahil was now thirty-one years old, he could have been married by now with his own children. Zahra could have been an auntie!

Maybe he has, said a snide voice in her ear. *Maybe you're just not a part of it.*

Zahra quickly pushed the thought out of her head, suddenly unable to breathe.

'Sorry,' Zahra said. 'I have to go to Birmingham,'

'*Birmingham?*' Sana, Junaid and Hasan stared at her.

They'd just finished their final exam. Zahra felt euphoric at first, jumping up and down with Sana, who repeated over and over again, 'I can't believe we've finished. I can't believe it's over!' It was eleven o'clock in the morning, too early to eat or go out anywhere, so they made plans to meet up in the evening. Zahra, however, needed an excuse to get out of there.

'But we're celebrating,' Hasan protested.

'I'll see you when I come back,' Zahra replied.

'But Zee—'

'Sorry, I can't get out of it.' And with that, she left them all before they could say another word.

An hour later, she was sitting alone in her bedroom. Abbu was at work and Ammi was on one of her leisurely strolls in the park. Zahra could try and nap, she was tired enough, but she never slept during the day so knew it would be impossible. She could pack for their weekend away? Yep, she decided to get on with that. She opened her bulging pine wardrobes and began pulling clothes out and shoving them into a bag.

Zahra had lied. They weren't going to Uncle Javid's house until tomorrow morning. But the excitement of finishing her exams had quickly died down at the prospect of 'celebrations'. She just wanted to be left alone.

She felt guilty when she thought back to her friends'

disappointed faces but decided they'd get over it. It was like in the last hour she had acquired some deeper connection to her past. Because after all, Saahil and Ehsan had been here, hadn't they? *Here*, where she was now. She had finally achieved what they had.

Zahra knew how they must have felt. Joyful, optimistic and full of hope, right up until the last ten seconds before it was all snatched away from them. On the night of their final exam, her brother and his best friend had thought they were just starting out. Little did they know, it was all over for them on the very same day. How then, could Zahra follow in their footsteps with ill-fated celebrations?

Just because things had gone wrong for them didn't mean it was going to happen to her, she told herself. Still, she couldn't help but feel a desperate sadness at how things had ended up. The last thing she wanted to do was to force a smile and be jolly in front of her friends that evening. Zahra could imagine them all sitting there, cocky enough to think it was all going to map out exactly as they had planned. Cocky enough to think they were going to make it.

Zahra didn't feel that optimistic about the future right now. She'd been motivated to finish her exams, but what about beyond that? She had dreams. She wanted to achieve things people of her background didn't usually accomplish. Zahra had decided early on that she would never be happy with an ordinary job, and it irritated her when people asked her if she wanted to be a schoolteacher once they heard of her degree vocation. *No thank you*, she'd reply. If she was to teach, it would be as a lecturer at university.

'What? Dr Zahra Sharif,' Libby giggled.

Zahra frowned, but wasn't offended at being laughed at. Libby had broken the mould in her own family by being the first person to go to university.

'Maybe think of a back-up too, Zee?' Abbu said, when she'd told him.

Fine. She kept the thought at the back of her head until one day she saw an Asian TV presenter investigating the multi-million-pound market for skin lightening in the UK. The presenter had gone undercover and challenged skin-cream distributors and magazines that promoted lighter skins. Zahra was so excited by this that she spent the next few months watching every TV programme that involved reporting of this kind. Abbu thought she was going through a phase as she reran episodes of *Dispatches*, *Panorama* and *Unreported World*. Until, one day, she announced to him: 'I want to be an investigative journalist!'

His eyes widened. He'd nodded and said, 'Great!'

Abbu didn't always connect with her crazy ideas. Just like the time she told him about all of the places she wanted to travel to. Great Wall of China. Golden Gate Bridge. Taj Mahal. Pyramid of Giza. The only place she had been to was Pakistan, and that was years ago to meet her maternal grandparents. She knew Abbu always wanted to visit the Blue Mosque in Istanbul ever since one of his friends had brought him a little ornament back from his holiday. As for Zahra, the first place on her list was the Empire State Building. Or actually, the Rockefeller. The whole point was to *see* the Empire State Building, lit up at night in all its glory. After that, they could take a plane journey to Toronto and see the Niagara Falls. It was only an hour away from New York. She remembered telling Abbu about her plan.

'Yeah, Insha'Allah, one day,' he'd said. They both knew they couldn't afford to. But what had struck Zahra more was the look on his face. Holidays to America were a luxury Abbu had never even comprehended. People like him didn't do things like that. He just went to the warehouse in the mornings and came home at night.

Zahra remembered her brother's obsession with having lots of money. All the things he planned to buy them, a bigger house, a better car. Of course, Zahra wanted financial security, but more than that, she wanted to be important. It was a little egotistical to use such a word, so she never mentioned it to anyone, but Zahra wanted to change things. And more importantly, she believed she could.

Something had gone terribly wrong, and Zahra felt like she had to do something to fix it. That's why she tapped away at her blog, because thanks to the internet, there was a possibility that a few people would stumble across it and read her writing. Even if she was often plagued by self-doubt about its quality, the blog was *her* space to express herself, a space that had previously been denied to her. People like her had already been spoken for, and spoken about, fabricated to the point that there was no going back. But here, Zahra could rant. She could say exactly what she thought and not worry about the reactions of other people. She didn't need to tone it down, be less Asian, less Muslim, less female. Zahra wasn't worried that people would be put off her if they read it, thinking she was 'difficult'. She wasn't worried that Karen would like her any less for speaking her mind against them. If Zahra was sure about one thing, it was this, because she had no interest in making people feel comfortable.

Now, as Zahra sat surrounded by a circle of clothes she'd pulled hastily out of her wardrobe, she felt no excitement. No drive to achieve anything. She searched for the motivation that had propelled her throughout university. The one that insisted that it wasn't absurd for her to be as ambitious and cocky as mediocre white men. But reality was slowly setting in. Zahra knew that she would have to work twice as hard and be twice as good to be recognised as an equal. At each stage, they would try to put her back in her place. Even if she did achieve amazing things, the first question people would probably want to ask her was 'if she was going to have an arranged marriage'. Zahra wondered if she had the energy to deal with it all. Today, all she could think of was Saahil and Ehsan, and sink lower into pessimism. After all, they had had dreams too.

That was the way it was now. People approached things with apprehension. They ambled through life, joyless. Tired of routine, debt, austerity and terrible news headlines every day. Inconveniently, war was no longer just staying put in some unknown, less important part of the world. It was spilling across borders, making everyone jittery.

Only Abbu's age group watched the six o'clock news to hear about the goings-on in the country; Zahra received updates on all the world's conflicts on her phone throughout the day. She even got annoying notifications that some Facebook friend was attending an event near her that day. There was no escape from it. They were all suffering from FOMO. Most of them spent hours comparing their shit lives to Facebook friends who seemed to have it all.

The world had changed a lot in the past ten years. It wasn't the same one Saahil had grown up in. Things had spiralled out of control. If he was here now, she wasn't sure they would even relate. Libby was right.

Today, Zahra decided her brother was better off dead.

The drive down to Birmingham the next day was long and laborious. Ammi complained about her aching body parts throughout the whole journey, and insisted on stopping for a wee at nearly every service station.

'We'll never get there at this rate!' Abbu complained.

When they eventually did, it was a relief. After listening to Uncle Javid's booming voice for ten minutes, Zahra already had a headache. Luckily, her cousins motioned her into the next room.

'Well, you lot are a barrel of laughs,' Zahra said, looking around at them both. Hamid was sitting over his laptop by the desk, typing away furiously. Aleena, the youngest of the bunch, lay scrunched up on the sofa, a hot water bottle stuck to her belly ('period pain, innit'). Zahra couldn't decide who looked grimmer. She hadn't travelled two and a half hours in the car to be greeted like this.

'Sorry,' Aleena said. 'But there's tension in the house.'

'What tension?'

Aleena looked around before answering. 'Humaira turned down *another* guy.'

'A guy?' Zahra mumbled, confused. 'Oh no,' she said, realising what she meant.

Aleena nodded. 'It was a *disaster*.' Zahra loved her melodramatic expressions.

'Guess why she turned him down?'

'Why?'

'Because of his trainers.'

Zahra's mouth fell open. Hamid snorted.

'See, Zahra,' he said. 'What a ridiculous reason to turn somebody down.'

Zahra recollected her thoughts before replying: 'He came to see a girl, a potential life partner, wearing *trainers*?'

240

Aleena nodded. 'Yeah, they were those disgusting ones with those octopus-like tentacles on the soles.'

Hamid shook his head before turning back to his laptop. 'You're all the same,' he said.

'How's your mum taking this then?' Zahra asked. She was sure this would be the hundredth man Humaira had rejected, much to Auntie Farhana's distaste.

'Not good,' Aleena said. 'Humaira's gonna be twenty-nine soon, Zee.'

'Good God!' Zahra replied, mockingly.

'But you know what it's like.'

Yes, she did. She knew Ammi's little outburst a few days ago had been different. She had other things on her mind. But Zahra knew society had an obsession with unmarried women. Unmarried women who passed their sell-by date once they hit thirty.

'It's fucking unfair,' Zahra said. She eyed Hamid. 'Why isn't your mum trying to set you up?'

'I'm younger than Humaira,' Hamid mumbled, typing away on his laptop.

'How's your job search going?'

As soon as Zahra spoke, Aleena jumped up, holding her hands up in a warning, almost as if she wanted to grab the words and pull them back with a rope.

'What?' Zahra asked, confused. She looked at Hamid, whose face darkened.

'It's fucking shit,' he said. He turned the laptop towards her. 'Do you wanna know how many applications I've made, Zee? Nearly a hundred...' he pointed to the emails displayed on the screen, '... and not one reply. In months.'

'Oh. I know, it's really bad at the moment, isn't it?'

'Bad? It's impossible!' he said, his voice rising. Zahra turned to Aleena who gave her a look-what-you've-started look. Hamid continued mumbling under his breath, 'Might as well tear my degree up and throw it in the bin.'

'Don't be like that,' Zahra said. 'Insha'Allah, something will come up.'

'No, it won't,' he replied. 'I've been photocopying for nearly a year. Every day I go into work and they put me next to the photocopier. I'm twenty-four, Zee, I haven't got two pennies to rub together.'

'Don't ask what he's earning,' Aleena whispered, urgently. Zahra didn't need to. She knew Hamid, the LPC graduate, the first would-be solicitor in the family was earning a little over £12,000 a year, and running back and forth with the post or cups of coffee. She remembered the day he graduated. Uncle Javid invited them down to a celebratory dinner in the evening. His voice boomed louder than ever as he took pictures of Hamid standing around smiling away in his black robe and square cap. That had been short-lived.

'See, this one is quite good,' Hamid said, pointing at the laptop screen. 'Entry level but they want one-year's experience in Employment Law.'

He lowered his hand and sat hunched over the screen. 'But I don't have a year's experience,' he said, like a child realising he didn't have enough change for a lollipop.

Zahra watched her cousin and felt pity. He looked hopeless and disheartened.

'All your friends are in the same boat, Hamid,' Aleena sighed, as though she had reminded him enough times.

'Not all of them,' he mumbled.

Aleena held her head. 'Great, he's gonna activate his race card now.'

'Race card?' Hamid shouted. 'You don't believe me? Come here, Zahra, I'll show you.'

Zahra wandered over to the desk as Hamid logged into his Linked-in account.

'Here, I went to uni with these people. Jeff Smith,' he pointed to a profile on the screen, 'got a training contract... Donna Riley, paralegal.' Hamid pointed to a few more.

'Come on, Hamid,' Aleena murmured from the corner of the room.

'What? It's true. Every white person I went to uni with has got at least an entry-level job in the field. And us? We're all stuck in call centres or fucking photocopying.'

He pushed his computer away from him. 'They see a Paki name on the application and write you off straightaway. Or they shove us into Immigration Law,' he continued, 'so we can deal with all the foreigners.'

Zahra nodded. 'He's right.'

Aleena groaned. 'Not you as well.'

Zahra opened her mouth, ready to relay all the research she'd carried out into the subject but Hamid was on a roll. 'What if Humaira got married? Or Aleena?' he said. 'Or what if they needed help with a deposit for a house? I'm useless.'

'No, you're not,' Zahra said, hugging him. She was about to remind him of Zak and Bilal, the two eldest brothers. They were married now with kids, but Zahra was sure they would be more than willing to assist their younger siblings.

Aleena, however, interrupted her. 'There's no need to act like a big man,' she shouted across the room. 'We can look after ourselves. And there's no chance of Humaira getting married soon… Glad she's at work, to be honest. She's putting a downer on the whole house too.'

'You can't blame her,' Zahra said. 'I'd hate to be put in that situation.'

Zahra knew how it worked. Boy's family comes to see girl's family. Girl brings in the tea in Mum's best china, everyone watching as she hobbles towards the coffee table, praying she won't spill it. Boy sits across the table from girl, trying to look everywhere apart from each other. Families make small talk. Boy and girl ask each other questions in front of the whole family. Urgh, the thought of it made Zahra feel sick.

Hamid sighed. 'I've tried talking to Mum.'

'And?'

'She gets it but…'

'But what?

'Well… she's saying Humaira is getting on a bit. You know, nearly thirty. '

'Same old shit, basically,' Aleena said.

'Stop telling me,' Zahra said. 'It's pissing me off.'

'That's society for you.'

'Well, society is shit,' Zahra replied. 'They fucking want us to do everything, don't they? Go to uni, start a career, find the perfect man, get married, push out a few kids, buy a house. All before you're thirty and past it.'

'It's bullshit,' Hamid said, nodding defiantly in his own little act of feminist solidarity.

Zahra heard Uncle Javid call her name from the lounge. 'I better go and sit with the oldies for a while.'

They both nodded. 'We'll come and save you in a bit,' Aleena said.

Just before she closed the door, Zahra watched Hamid through the crack. He breathed heavily, ran his hands over his face, squinted as he pulled the laptop towards him reluctantly, and continued typing.

Twenty-Three

I bet there are no Asians around here, Zahra thought. She was sitting in the passenger seat of a car, next to a smiling English woman who was driving her down quiet roads, past pretty cafés, boutique shops and elderly couples walking their dogs. Zahra's friend Emma had broken her ankle so had taken an extension to hand in her dissertation. She pleaded with Zahra on the phone for *Ethnicity and Nationalism,* a book from the library that was currently in Zahra's possession. As she was on crutches, she couldn't travel to university to collect it. Zahra decided to help her out and arrived at Mytholmroyd train station in the afternoon. Emma's mum had kindly picked her up and was taking her to the house.

'It's only half an hour on the train,' she'd told Abbu the day before.

'But I can drop you off?'

'No, I need to get it to her by tomorrow, and you'll be at work.'

Abbu hesitated. 'You've got your alarm?'

'I'm going in the afternoon!'

'It doesn't matter, take it with you.'

'I take it everywhere, Abbu.'

Abbu had bought her the loudest, bulkiest safety alarm available on the market.

'It'll split their eardrums,' he'd said gleefully. 'You carry it with you at all times. And when it's dark or quiet, you hold it in your hands ready to pull. Like this.' He did another demonstration for her.

Emma's house was an endearing little cottage with a green door and hanging flower baskets at either side. Zahra thought back to her own terraced house on a street full of Pakistanis, something that always troubled her Abbu. The English families that had lived there when they first moved in, when Zahra hadn't even been born, had eventually moved away. Abbu muttered on about his desire to 'live in a mixed area', but with every house being sold, in moved another Asian family.

'Hey,' Emma said, hobbling towards her with her foot bandaged up in a cast.

Zahra was a little apprehensive; she'd never been fully alone with Emma before, apart from during their shared modules. There was never any time to talk properly in lectures, and soon enough, Karen and Lydia would make an appearance. The two of them stuck to their Early Modern Britain and Medieval Society electives (boring in Zahra's opinion), and took a wide berth from any lessons that involved British Imperialism, slavery or debates about race and ethnicity. After all, why would white people want to learn about race?

Emma was different, choosing option modules that would challenge her. Maybe that was why she went out of her way to stick up for Zahra.

Before Zahra knew it, all her inner feelings came pouring out. She told Emma how much she'd appreciated her support during those difficult moments with Karen and Lydia. How Emma had always backed her up and tried to calm down even the most uncomfortable of situations.

'They were plastic bitches,' Emma said, the most vocal and vulgar she'd ever been in front of Zahra. They managed to bond more in these few hours than they had done in three years. A cup of tea turned into a movie and then Emma insisted Zahra stay for a takeaway.

'Don't wanna outstay my—'

'Oh, shut up,' Emma said.

Zahra let Abbu know so that he wouldn't worry. After they'd eaten, Emma's mum offered to give her a lift back to the station but Zahra felt she had put them out enough. After saying goodbyes, she set off walking for the train at around eight o'clock.

'Abbu, chill out. Summer's started. It doesn't get dark until about nine.'

That was what she had told Abbu that morning. He worried too much. It may have been summer, but it had also been raining. The sky was dull and grey. As she reached the platform, it was completely deserted. It certainly looked creepier than it had done when she'd first arrived. There was a ten-minute wait for the train, so Zahra settled down into a seat and pulled out her phone. She wasted some time on Twitter before looking up at the platform display. The train was due now. She stood up. Five minutes went by and it didn't come. She checked again and realised her train had disappeared completely from the screen. She checked online, but there was no information. Ten minutes. Then fifteen.

Maybe she should go on to the other side of the platform? But that was the wrong direction. She looked at the time. It had been twenty minutes. Zahra didn't recognise the next train, and the one after was another forty-five-minute wait. She felt the sky getting darker. Abbu would worry. The last thing she wanted to do was tell him; he would jump into his car straightaway and drive over there.

It started raining again. Zahra thought she heard footsteps. She should ring someone. She hurriedly checked the website and searched for a phone number. If the next train was going to be nearly another hour, she may as well walk back to Emma's house. But then what if that one didn't turn up either?

'A tree's fallen down on one of the tracks so the train isn't coming.'

Zahra almost jumped out of her skin. A man in a hoodie was standing there, staring straight ahead. Half of his face was covered by a scarf. He was stood a few metres away from her. Zahra felt nervous immediately.

'If you grab the 560 bus from just out there, it will take you to Halifax. It's a bigger station so they'll probably have another train running through. It goes straight to Leeds so you can get off at… wherever you need to get off. Or you can change at Leeds obviously. Don't think anything will come by this way.'

His voice was muffled by the scarf covering his mouth. Zahra wondered where he had appeared from.

'Oh, okay, thank you very much,' she said. She'd left her bag on one of the chairs. She went to pick it up, keeping one eye on the man. She reached for her safety alarm and slipped it into her pocket.

'It'll get dark soon so you'd best wait by the bus stop,' he said. 'It's just opposite Sainsbury's.' Something strange immediately registered with Zahra.

'Right, thank you.' Zahra just wanted to get away from him as soon as possible. She made her way to the fence, knowing she'd have to walk right past him. The platform was completely deserted. There was a winding footpath which led down to the main street. Creepy enough without the hooded man.

'Erm, aren't you going to the bus stop.' She hoped he would walk in front of her so she wouldn't have to turn her back on him.

'No… I'm waiting for someone.' He carried on staring ahead, like he was determined not to look at her. Before Zahra reached him, he turned around and walked towards the shelter. With relief, Zahra scuttled along, glancing back occasionally. No one followed her. Then it registered. He'd barely asked her where she needed to be. Which direction? Which station? Yet he'd given her an entire route to follow. *It'll get dark soon…*

Zahra stood still for a while, not moving. The street was just a few yards away. Yet something was telling her to go back. Before she knew it, her legs were carrying her up the footpath again. Within a couple of minutes, she was inside the platform. Everything in her head was telling her no. But she carried on. She saw him from afar. He was in the shelter. Zahra was sure he'd whipped his hood back on as he'd seen her approach. Covered half his face with the woolly scarf.

He looked the other way when Zahra entered the shelter. Why on earth was she getting closer and closer to a hooded man who was behaving so strangely? He stood up, his back towards her. Zahra felt the colour drain from her face. Suddenly, she was breathless. She sat down on the bench waiting for a sign. It happened straightaway. The man pelted out of the shelter. Something had overcome Zahra. Before she knew it, she was running after him.

'Stop!' Zahra shouted a couple of times. He didn't and she was struggling to keep up with him as the platform came to an end.

She called after him again. He was about to dip behind the fence and down the footpath. She was going to lose sight of him when a single word spilled desperately out of her mouth: '*Saahil!*'

The man stopped. His hood had fallen. Zahra stood, trying to catch her breath.

'Turn around,' she said, her heart hammering against her chest.

PART THREE

Twenty-Four

They stared at each other.

He was quite a distance away, the scarf still covering half his face. But Zahra knew those eyes. His hand reached for it and slowly pulled it down. Zahra braced herself.

She had dreamed of this moment. Thought up different scenarios, every possible way of how they would meet again. Nothing could have prepared her, though. Nothing.

He was walking back towards her. Zahra stood rooted to the spot, unable to move, unable to breathe. Less than a few metres away and Zahra could see his eyes were swimming with tears. She could feel her hands shaking. Her breathing had quickened. Without realising she had taken a step back.

It couldn't be this easy. Her brother couldn't just re-enter her life like that. Not on this dreary platform, with the sky grey, and the breeze cold. He couldn't just walk up to her like that. It couldn't be this easy.

Saahil stopped when he saw she had hung back. But it was too late; he was an arm's length away from her. No word passed between them. Zahra couldn't help but notice, he was still beautiful.

Zahra's vision blurred through her wet eyes. He was like a ghost that if Zahra reached out and touched him, he would disappear. Either she spoke first, or she waited for him. By the look on his face, he was incapable of speaking.

They were almost nose to nose. Something had to happen. They couldn't just stare at each other like this. Zahra teetered forwards. She couldn't look at him anymore, it was too painful. She gently placed her head against his shoulder. He was real.

Slowly, Zahra felt her brother's arms wrap around her, one hand holding her head. He cried properly now. His body shook.

They pulled back. He was laughing and weeping at the same time. So was she. He cupped her face and their foreheads touched. They hugged again.

'Shhh,' he said, gently.

He kissed her on top of her head. Wiped tears away from under her eyes with his thumbs, frowning, looking concerned. He shook his head. 'Don't cry.'

But Zahra's grip tightened around him. She had to make sure this was real. She had to make sure.

They were sitting together on a train platform like two strangers. He was leaning forward, elbows resting on his knees, eyes looking down. She sat with her arms crossed, glancing over at him every few seconds.

The earlier outburst of emotion had ceased eventually and now an awkwardness hung around the air between them. Nobody spoke.

He looked older. Obviously. He was thirty-one years old. It made Zahra realise just how young he had been back then. He was wearing jeans and a grey hoodie, the sleeves pulled halfway up his arms. Zahra noticed faint scars on them. She quickly looked away.

His hair was thick and wavy, just as Zahra remembered, but he had a small beard now. It was neat and trimmed. His eyes seemed sunken in, with dark circles under them but the bridge of his nose still dipped in elegantly. Zahra resented the fact that the sky was getting darker and she would not be able to look at him.

He cleared his throat. 'Are you okay?'

Zahra nodded without looking at him. From the corner of her eye, she saw his mouth open again to say something. But he didn't.

They sat in silence for a couple more minutes. Zahra still couldn't quite believe this was happening. Was it a dream? Her phone rang and snapped her back into reality. She stared at the screen and looked up at Saahil.

'It's Dad.'

Saahil took a deep breath, his eyes widened slightly. An unspoken burden pressed down on them both.

Suddenly, he grabbed her hand. She followed him down the footpath and out on to the road. They nearly walked into a woman and her dog. The bus was already at the stop. Saahil took her phone and typed in his number.

'Text me when you get home.'

Zahra was in a daze. Saahil must have realised and escorted her on to the bus. She was still looking at him as they approached the driver. Saahil fumbled with some change in his pocket. He gave her the ticket.

'Text me when you get home,' he repeated, and stepped off the bus. Zahra followed him back.

'Are you getting on or not, love?' the driver asked, wearily.

'Go, Zahra,' said Saahil. 'I'll ring you.'

But Zahra didn't want to leave him. In the confusion and pressure from the driver, she hung back. She watched Saahil desperately as the doors closed. She rushed to the back of the bus. A girl gave her a funny look and moved out of the way. Saahil's figure became smaller. He was waving though. Zahra waved back. As soon as they turned the corner, Zahra saw him blow a kiss.

The drive home was agonising. Abbu was in a chatty mood. He told her about how one of his colleagues had been sacked for stealing something from the warehouse. She tried her best to appear normal. She didn't want Abbu to worry.

'What's up?' he asked, as they pulled up outside the house.

'Not feeling too good, Abbu. Might just go straight to bed.'

'Have something to eat first? Your Ammi's made pakoras.'

'No, Abbu, I've eaten.'

Zahra headed straight for the stairs when she got in, leaving on her jacket and shoes.

'Oi! Take your shoes off,' Ammi shouted.

Zahra ignored her. She collapsed on to her bed, crying. Then she remembered her phone. She pulled it out and looked at the number. She saved it in her phonebook: Bhai.

Zahra wrote out a text, waiting breathlessly for a response.

Saahil, I'm home.

A second later she received a message.

So am I.

Zahra frowned. But he wasn't.

Twenty-Five

Amjad rummaged through the medicine cabinet searching for his sleeping pills. He'd put the action off for as long as he could, but the clock had struck one in the morning. He'd glanced at it, over and over again, but it stayed ever present in the corner of his eye, reminding him that there would be no sleep again tonight. It wasn't good to take a tablet so late. They needed to be taken at around ten o'clock to give Amjad time to fall asleep naturally whilst watching TV. If he took it now, he would feel awful in the morning. Or, it would not even work. Amjad found the tub of pills and held it in his hands, deliberating.

There was another option. It lay in the cupboard hidden away from everyone else. A bottle of whisky that Ken had bought him.

'Medicinal purposes,' Amjad reminded him. Ken looked uneasy, his grip firm around the bottle.

'Well, I hope God dunt throw me in hell. If He exists, that is!'

'Yeah, don't worry about it,' Amjad reassured, taking the bottle forcefully and putting it away in the cupboard.

'Should probably tell Zahra so she can keep an eye on—'

'No!' Amjad had snapped. 'She can't find out about this. She'll just worry for no reason.'

Reluctantly, he put the sleeping tablets back in the medicine drawer. Without thinking too much, Amjad grabbed the whisky from the cupboard and settled down on the sofa with a glass.

He eyed the bottle with dislike. Alcohol had never passed his lips before and even the sight of it in his house without Ken being the drinker of it made him uneasy. There were other things that were worrying him too. He thought back to the meeting he'd had with his manager a few days ago. Amjad hadn't returned to his post after the morning break. A colleague found him snoozing in the staff room during work hours.

'You're not coping very well,' his manager, Dave, said.

Amjad insisted he was fine and promised it wouldn't happen again. Dave suggested extended sick leave.

'In fact, you're fifty-five now. You can even retire on ill health.'

Amjad was stunned. He'd known for a while that his job was hanging by a thread. He had taken too much time off sick, but for Dave to suggest retirement! But then again, Amjad should have seen it coming. Over the years, he had proved he was hardly the most reliable of workers.

First, his wife died and Amjad quit work for nearly a year. Ten years later, his son went missing and Amjad missed work again. Now, another ten years had gone by, and his health was causing problems. He'd used up all his annual sick leave entitlement and when he was there, Amjad was always tired due to lack of sleep. Dave had known him for a long time and was always understanding. Amjad couldn't fault him for all the support he'd received over the years due to his bad luck. They were friends, but at the end of the day, Dave had a business to run.

Amjad didn't tell Zahra or Ammi about the meeting. He didn't want them worrying for no reason. And besides, he knew nothing for sure yet. The bottle was still standing there on the table, dark and imposing. It was almost watching him. Amjad shifted in his seat a couple of times. Licked his lips and swallowed hard. He reached over, unscrewed it and poured a full glass. He sniffed it. The smell was so musty and strong that Amjad wrinkled up his nose in disgust. He downed the whole thing in one go. A burning sensation erupted in his throat. He coughed violently, clutching at his neck and ran to the kitchen for water.

Amjad stayed crouched over the sink, long after he caught his breath. He straightened up eventually and made his way back to the living room, feeling ill and defeated. He sat down on the sofa again and closed his eyes, waiting for the drink to affect his mind and body. He didn't know what to expect, but for the moment, couldn't shake off the quiver in his stomach and awful taste in his mouth, as though he had just drunk a capful of bleach. He closed his eyes, and willed for sleep. But all he could think about was Saahil.

Zahra slept fitfully that night. Every couple of hours, she jerked awake, images of deserted station platforms and hooded figures running through her mind. When she regained consciousness, she reached out and grabbed her mobile. Scrolling down her phonebook, she found her brother's number in the contact list. She reread the text message he'd sent her over and over again. *So am I. So am I.*

At five o'clock, Zahra woke again. She was incapable of keeping still. Her legs were restless and fighting a war with the bottom of the duvet. Her eyes, wide open. She blinked, but the darkness in the room stayed the same. Zahra was lying in bed, both hands tightened into fists. She sighed deeply. Why was she so out of breath?

She pulled herself up and opened the door. She peered into Abbu's room. It was empty. Zahra assumed he was still downstairs. She tiptoed to the lounge and found him sitting on the sofa, head in hands.

'Have you slept, Abbu?' she asked.

He jumped up and stood awkwardly in front of the table.

'Yeah, I drifted off a little bit,' he said quickly.

He looked awful. His eyes were bloodshot and screwed together to suggest he had a banging headache, and his face had a jaundiced appearance.

'How many hours?' Zahra asked.

'Maybe about two.'

Zahra sighed and made to take a seat next to him.

'No, no,' Abbu said, moving towards her. 'Let's go upstairs. In fact, you go, and I'm coming.'

'I'll sit with you?'

'There's no need. I want to lie down now too. Just need to get something from the kitchen.'

Abbu reached over and turned off the light. The room went dark. Zahra nodded and walked back up the stairs. She went into Abbu's bedroom. The curtains were ajar, the first signs of light were beginning to shine through. She yanked them closed, hoping to block everything out. Five minutes later, and Abbu joined her.

'Why are you awake so early?' he asked.

'Can't sleep. Are you going to lie down?'

'Yeah,' Abbu replied, rubbing his eyes. 'But I won't sleep now, Zee.'

Zahra stared at him. *You would, if I told you your son was alive.*

Abbu insisted she go back to her room.

'No,' she replied. 'I'll sit with you for a while.'

He got into bed, his movements sluggish as he peeled back the duvet and climbed in. Zahra covered him with the sheet.

'I should be tucking you in,' he laughed.

Zahra forced a smile and sat down next to him. Abbu had full view of her face so she adjusted her position and pulled herself up to lean against the headboard.

'You should go back to sleep,' he said. 'There's no point sitting here with me.'

Zahra felt the first stabs of guilt bore into her. *I could make it all better.* She mumbled a response to her father, realising she couldn't look him in the face.

Ten minutes passed by, and Zahra thought she heard Abbu snore. She watched his eyelids flutter and his jaw slacken. This was nothing more than false hope as he opened his eyes a second later.

'Don't you have uni tomorrow?' he slurred.

'No, Abbu, I finished uni last week.'

I can't tell you yet. I don't know anything for sure.

His eyes closed once more, and he started breathing heavily, his chest rising and falling. Zahra's heart was palpitating. She wanted to cry out, to release the anxiety that was clogging up her insides. Instead, she stayed frozen against the headboard, one of her hands awkwardly placed inside her Abbu's palm. Slowly, she reached for her mobile and scrolled through her phonebook again. The touch of her fingertips left small circles of sweat on the screen. She found the text message and reread it. Reluctantly, Zahra faced her sleeping Abbu.

Sorry.

Twenty-Six

A few days later, Amjad arrived home from work to find Ken's upper body buried underneath the kitchen sink as Ammi chopped onions into a frying pan. The sound in the kitchen was deafening. Ken clinked and clanged his tools, his elbows and knees arranged at odd angles. The onions sizzled loudly suggesting Ammi had heated up the oil too much. The room was too small for the three of them to fit in there and Amjad felt claustrophobic immediately.

'What the—' he began, but Ammi noticed him and cut him off.

'Bloody useless,' she said, jabbing her knife towards him. A bit of onion was still stuck to it. 'How many times have I told you to fix this?'

'Oh, the leak,' Amjad sighed.

Ken pulled himself out of the cupboard and grinned at Amjad as Ammi shouted at him in Urdu.

'Yeah,' Ken said, yelling over the sizzling onions and pointing the screwdriver at his friend. 'What *she* said!'

'And how did she tell you what needed to be done,' Amjad asked, taking off his coat. 'Or have you taught her how to speak English?'

'Nah,' Ken replied, standing up and moving his tools out of the way. 'She just pointed to it and shouted, "Fix!"'

Amjad rolled his eyes. 'Sounds about right.'

'All done and dusted for you there, Ammi,' Ken said, winking at Amjad.

'Yes, thank you,' Ammi replied in English. She turned to Amjad and switched back to Urdu: 'Tell him to eat before he goes.'

Amjad relayed the message to a delighted Ken. He walked over to the cooker and rubbed his hands together.

'What you got cooking there, Ammi?'

'Paya.'

'What?'

'Feet,' she said.

Ken turned to Amjad with a blank look. 'Trotters?' he asked. 'Like pig's trotters?'

Ammi's smile vanished. She swelled in size. 'Not pig!'

'It's sheep, I think,' Amjad said, quickly.

'Oh, I see. Lovely!' Ken touched his belly. Ammi tutted and turned her attention back to the pan.

'Let's leave Ammi to it, eh?' Amjad suggested. Ken nodded and they both hurried out of the kitchen. Amjad closed the door behind them. He sat down and quickly told Ken about the whisky nearly burning his throat the other night.

'Did you drink it neat?' Ken asked, stretching on the sofa.

'Neat?'

'You're supposed to mix it with the ginger ale.'

'You didn't tell me that,' Amjad snapped.

'Yeah, I did. In fact...'

Ken stood up and went back into the kitchen. 'I got you the bloody thing,' he said, clutching the chilled bottle.

Amjad blinked. 'I don't remember.'

Ken frowned at him. 'Well, not to worry. You know for next time,' he said. 'Did it put you to sleep?'

'Maybe three hours in total. I drifted off downstairs and Zahra found me, she nearly saw the bottle. I've locked it away in my bedroom now.'

'Oh no,' Ken said, placing his hand on his forehead. 'See, that's why I wasn't so sure about this—'

'And I woke up with a banging headache—'

'Don't have any more—'

'Shhh!'

Amjad lashed out and silenced his friend. They both listened as Zahra stomped down the stairs.

'Hi, Uncle Ken,' she said.

'Hiya, love.'

She threw on her jacket and slipped on her shoes. 'Just gonna go see Ehsan for a bit.'

'Ammi's cooking,' Amjad said.

'Yeah, I won't be long.' She disappeared off into the kitchen. 'What you making, Ammi?' they heard her ask. There was a clang of a pan lid being lifted. It dropped loudly. 'Urgh, hooves,' she said.

'Come home in time for dinner,' Ammi shouted.

'No, you're all right. I'll get a burger or summat,' she said, before closing the door behind her.

Ken turned to Amjad again. 'So what you going to do?' he whispered.

Amjad sat back, umming and ahhing, trying to choose the right response. All the while, he could see Ken watching him, eyes alight with worry.

'I'll try one more time,' he finally said. 'If not, you can have the bottle back.'

Zahra didn't panic when nobody answered the door. She snooped around into the back of the garden and moved the wheelie bins out of the way. She looked through the window and saw that Ehsan's bed was empty. She called Auntie Meena's phone. There was no response. She took a seat on the bench in the garden and stared at her mobile, willing for it to ring. It did. Auntie Meena told her what she suspected. Ehsan was in hospital. Zahra asked if she could visit as she made her way to the bus stop.

'Maybe tomorrow, Zahra,' Meena said.

Zahra stopped dead in the middle of the street. Meena had never said no to her before.

'Is everything okay?' Zahra asked, slowly.

'His oxygen levels are a bit low so we may have to go to ICU. But don't worry,' she quickly added.

'But I am worried now.'

'I'll call you tomorrow morning, Zahra. It'll be all right.'

Zahra walked back home. Ammi was still cooking her paya and handed Zahra the garlic crusher as soon as she entered the house. Zahra banged away with the pestle, not concentrating and flicking bits of garlic everywhere. A clove flew under the fridge and Ammi started to rant. Zahra escaped into the living room with Abbu and Uncle Ken. She told them that Ehsan was in hospital. Abbu's face fell.

'Don't worry,' Ken said. 'He'll pull through. The amount of times you've told me he's in hospital. Comes out fighting, does the lad.'

Zahra nodded and went back upstairs into her room, not knowing what to do with herself. Her phone buzzed. She checked to find an email reminding her to complete the application she had started to some BBC journalism scheme. Realising the deadline was in two days, Zahra reluctantly set up her laptop.

Half an hour later, Libby knocked on her door.

'Why haven't you been answering my messages?' she asked.

Zahra mumbled an excuse but Libby wasn't listening.

'Here, summat really funny happened just now. I was near that Thornbury primary school at home time and all the mums were waiting for their kids. They came running out but stopped dead in their tracks because all the mums had niqabs on so they didn't know which one was theirs! It was like this—'

Libby demonstrated for her and Zahra laughed along. 'I wish you'd been there, you'd have giggled your head off.'

Zahra nodded but her smile faded. Libby frowned. 'What's up?' she asked.

'Erm... nowt,' Zahra murmured back.

Libby turned her head to read the screen. 'Investigative Journalism graduate scheme 2014 – BBC!'

'I know,' Zahra said, slamming the screen down. 'What's the point, eh?'

'What do you mean?'

'Well, they're not going to give me it, are they?' Zahra continued.

'Why not?'

'Because they'll give it to some posh Oxbridge—'

'You've got just a good a chance—'

'No, I haven't.'

'Why?' Libby asked.

'Just forget it.'

'No, tell me.'

'No,' Zahra said. 'Because when I speak my mind everyone gets offended.'

'I won't,' Libby replied, climbing on to the bed. She put on Zahra's dressing gown and pulled up the hood, smiling at her goofily.

'You think I've got just a good chance as everyone else?'
Zahra said, secretly relieved that for the next five minutes, she
could think about something other than her returned-from-the-
dead brother. 'What, with my little blog? As if. I can't compete
with these people. They'll have tonnes of experience because
they can afford to do six-month unpaid internships and live
only a couple of tubes away from the centre of London. And
then there's...'

'What?'

Zahra shrugged. 'They're not going to give it to some little
Paki girl from up north.'

'Oh, Zahra,' Libby said, rolling her eyes.

'What? You do realise that these places recruit from the
same universities, where their students have been educated at
the same private schools? People like me and you don't even
get a look-in. Actually, I wrote a really good blog post about it.'

'Which one? Don't think I've read it.'

Zahra found it and swivelled the screen around to face her
best friend. Libby leaned over and began to read.

'Ha!' she said, pointing to a comment posted underneath.

Why are you taking a dig at white people in this post
when we make up most of the working class? I used to
like your blog until you started bashing us all the time. It's
not helpful.

Zahra's response was underneath:

Oh dear. Are you feeling really oppressed right now?

Libby leaned back. 'Yeah, you're right,' she said, looking deflated. 'I suppose I was just trying to be optimistic. I still think you should apply, though.'

'Yeah, we'll see.'

There was a moment's silence as the pair of them listened to Abbu and Ken laughing downstairs. Ammi bashed away at the garlic in the kitchen. Zahra checked her phone and absentmindedly looked at her messages. A few more had been exchanged between her and Saahil. Though it had only been a few days, Zahra didn't quite know why she hadn't told her best friend yet. She'd rushed to the phone the following morning and written out a lengthy text telling Libby she had seen Saahil. She'd deleted it moments later. It wasn't normal. Usually, Zahra had to tell Libby everything. As soon as possible. But this time, it felt wrong, that as soon as Zahra divulged the secret, it would actually become true. There would be no going back.

'Libby?'

'Yeah.'

'I need to tell you something.'

Zahra closed the door and sat on to the bed next to her friend. Libby frowned, realising it was something serious. Zahra sighed deeply and began her tale. She described in minute detail how she had encountered her brother again. Libby listened, her mouth hanging open. By the time Zahra finished, Libby looked dazed, almost as though she'd been hung upside down on a rollercoaster. She spluttered. Stopped and started sentences. Closed her mouth again. Took a moment to recollect her thoughts.

'First of all,' Libby said finally, 'I can't believe you haven't already told me. Cow. Secondly, I don't believe you.'

They were huddled together, talking away in urgent whispers, scared that somebody would hear. Zahra showed Libby the texts.

Now Zahra had had time to think about it, she'd come to two conclusions: one, that Saahil had been following her, maybe for some time. What else was he doing at Mytholmroyd station? And two, he was alive. Yes. Alive and well. And he had chosen to stay away for so long.

'You haven't told your dad yet?' Libby asked.

'No. What am I supposed to say? Saahil and I didn't even talk. At all. We just cried.'

'So what are you going to do now?'

'He wants to meet.'

Libby's eyes widened. 'Where?'

'He's staying somewhere, I have an address.'

'What did he look like?' Libby asked, a glint in her eye.

Zahra smiled. 'He had a beard… oh no, not a big bushy one,' she added quickly, after seeing the look on Libby's face.

'What else?'

'I don't know, I didn't look at him properly. We avoided eye contact most of the time. But bloody hell, he's *thirty-one*… Not like that anymore.'

She nodded towards the photo on her drawer. It was of a teenage Saahil with his arm around her. In the picture, Zahra was five.

Libby cleared her throat. 'Is he still good looking?'

'Of course,' Zahra said.

Libby grinned, sheepishly. 'I don't know if you know, but I had a huge crush on him when we were kids. That's why I was always at your house!'

'Yeah, I know,' Zahra replied. 'You'd always go bright red every time he spoke to you. And that's nice to know, I thought you were here because of our friendship.'

'That too…'

They both laughed nervously but it quickly died down.

'Should I tell Abbu?'

Libby bit her lip. 'Maybe you need to hear Saahil out first?'

'But, Libs, I can't even look Abbu in the face. I let him go to work this morning thinking his son is still missing. What if summat had happened to him on the way—'

'What are you on about?'

'—and he never found out that Saahil was alive and it'll be my fault?'

Libby grabbed Zahra by the shoulders. 'Calm down, all right? Look—' She sat up straight, ready to take control. 'We both know what this means. Saahil has been missing for ten years, but he's alive. I don't know in what circumstances, but he'll have to explain all that to you.'

Libby looked at Zahra, fiercely. 'Promise me, Zee, when you go and see him, you fucking give it to him straight, and tell him that he's put you through hell.'

Zahra blinked rapidly. The thought frightened her. 'Okay.'

'Don't let him palm you off. You want all the answers. Promise?'

'Promise.'

Zahra jumped as Abbu called her from downstairs telling her that the food was nearly ready.

'Erm, your Ammi is cooking summat really weird—' Libby began.

'I know, shall we go get a burger instead?'

'Yep. To be honest, I don't really fancy sitting across from your dad at the dinner table knowing that his son is alive.'

Zahra swallowed hard. 'Tell me about it.'

The next morning Zahra paced the room waiting for Auntie Meena's call. Flashbacks of yesterday's conversation with Libby replayed in her mind. Libby had tried her best to encourage Zahra. They planned meticulously about what to do and Zahra went to bed confident that she could deal with whatever Saahil threw at her. That passed quickly, with helplessness taking over her once more. She knew it wasn't really appropriate, but decided to ring Auntie Meena herself. To Zahra's surprise, Meena answered.

'He's the same, really. It's best if you come up now.'

Zahra quickly grabbed her things and set off for the bus. Ehsan would go into hospital often, but Zahra knew the key letters 'ICU' always set alarm bells ringing. As the bus screeched and jerked through the streets, Zahra pulled out her phone. She checked her Twitter.

Another report had been published suggesting Muslim women were the most segregated, alienated and least integrated in British society. Their poor English language skills were being highlighted. Images circulated of either burqa-clad women pushing prams or older Asian women, like Ammi, trailing along in their dowdy ethnic clothing against the backdrop of dull northern streets and huge, imposing mosques. This report led to a flurry of panic and yet another poll was being conducted to find out just how loyal Muslims were to Britain. And how proud were they to be British? What percentage exactly? Explain.

Zahra sighed and shoved her phone back into her bag, feeling even more agitated than before. She remembered Karen quizzing her with something similar. Asking her if she considered herself British, Muslim or Pakistani first. Zahra had scowled at her.

'I don't sit at home all day thinking about being British,' she'd said. 'I simply *am*.'

'Oh. Right. Of course.'

'Does that bother you?' Zahra asked, deciding to toy with Karen herself. 'How comfortable I am being me?'

'What? No, obviously not!' Karen had spluttered.

Zahra shrugged. 'Just wondered why you ask us that all the time then.'

When she arrived at the ward, she asked for Ehsan at the reception. The nurse pointed her down to the room. She dodged staff members in the corridor and found people standing around outside Ehsan's door. A young guy Zahra recognised as Ehsan's cousin approached her.

'Is it Zahra?'

'Yeah.'

'They're taking him to ICU?'

'Oh no,' Zahra said, anxiously.

'His oxygen levels are too low. But it's happened before,' he quickly added.

'Can I go in?' Zahra asked stupidly, knowing full well the answer would be 'no'. There were too many people.

Sure enough, the lad hesitated. 'Doctor's in there at the moment.'

Zahra knelt down and peered through the crowd of people. Uncle Harun was sitting in the visitor's chair. He had his arm around Meena who looked as though she was crying. For a split second they made eye contact, and Auntie Meena lifted her hand in a greeting. It was pointless. Zahra couldn't get in. All she wanted was to tell Ehsan about what had happened. That Saahil had returned.

Zahra turned her head and through a gap between two people, saw that Ehsan was lying in the bed with an oxygen mask. A doctor was standing over him holding a bulk of hospital notes. Somebody shifted and stepped in front of her, and Zahra lost sight of them. She turned to Ehsan's cousin.

'What's your name again?'

'Amir.'

Zahra pulled her phone out. 'Can you please keep me updated? When you text the rest of your family, will you text me too? I don't want to keep bothering Auntie Meena.'

'Yeah, sure.'

Amir took her number down in his phone.

'Do you think he'll be okay?' Zahra asked.

'Insha'Allah. He's pulled through worse ones.'

Zahra nodded. Ehsan had spent the last ten years of his life in and out of hospital. He'd knocked on death's door and still come back fighting.

'I'll keep you updated,' Amir said.

Zahra thanked him. She glanced back at Ehsan a couple of times, but knew it was pointless. As she made her way to the main entrance of the hospital, she spotted a familiar face in the crowd. Alisha was walking towards her with two friends. The three of them were hurrying along in white uniforms, coffee cups in hands. Part of Zahra hoped that Alisha wouldn't see her. She didn't want to have to explain why she was at the hospital; she didn't want to mention Ehsan's name.

'Zahra,' Alisha called. They hugged each other as her friends waited. 'What are you doing here?'

Zahra hadn't met Alisha before the attack. She'd heard of her, of course, thanks to Saahil constantly teasing Ehsan about his feelings for her. A couple of years later, they'd met at the hospital when Ammi had been referred for an ultrasound of the kidneys. Alisha had been the sonographer to scan her. She'd introduced herself and told them she'd been at uni with the boys. Over the years they'd bumped into each other a handful of times. Sometimes at the hospital when Zahra accompanied Ammi to her appointments, or around town. They'd never spoken directly about Saahil and Ehsan, each not knowing how to broach the subject.

'I was just visiting someone,' Zahra shouted over the buzz of the busy corridor.

'Is everything okay?' Alisha asked. 'It's not your grandma, is it?'

'No, she's fine.'

'Are you sure?'

The words slipped out before Zahra could stop them. 'Well, it's Ehsan… He's going to ICU.'

Alisha's expression changed. Her face fell and sadness flooded her eyes. 'Oh,' she murmured.

Zahra regretted it immediately. 'I'm sorry, I shouldn't have—'

'No, no. There's no need… I'm not stupid… I know.'

Alisha's friend cleared her throat. 'The evening list has started, hun, we'd better get going.'

Alisha stood up straight and glanced at her watch. 'I'm sorry, Zahra. I have to go.'

'No, I'm sorry to just spring that on you.'

'It's fine, you take care,' she replied, not meeting Zahra's eyes. 'Give my salaam to your gran.'

She rushed off without looking back. Zahra now felt even worse about everything than she already had. She'd never asked, but was sure Alisha must be married now. That didn't stop them all from wondering what could have been. Zahra walked towards the bus stop, overwhelmed by how many lives had been altered by one sharp blow to the head.

Twenty-Seven

It took another week before Saahil and Zahra were able to meet. She Google-mapped the address he had given her and planned her route. She couldn't quite believe this was happening, that she was actually going to see her brother. Zahra put on a nice dress and applied a little make-up. She didn't want Saahil to think she was a scruff, especially after the first time she had seen him. Her hair had been frizzy with rainfall and then she had cried like a baby. Not attractive. He called her in the morning to ask if she needed a lift. When she'd said no, he chuckled and said, 'That's good, because I don't have a car.' As far as Zahra could tell, his voice sounded pretty much as she remembered.

When Zahra put the phone down, she realised her heart was beating like crazy. She took a moment and sat on the edge of her bed, breathing out slowly. Ammi and Abbu were downstairs. She needed all the strength she could muster to walk past them and not tell them who she was going to see. The only thing that kept her going was the knowledge that when she returned that night, she wouldn't be alone. Saahil was coming home with her. In a fit of excitement, she checked her watch and realised she was ready too early. They had planned to meet at three. It was only half past one. She heard Uncle Ken arrive ('Ay up!') and groaned. Why did he have to turn up now? How long would he stay for? Zahra needed to make sure Abbu was alone when she returned with his son. Even Ammi's absence was preferable. She would have to call ahead and make sure everything was in place for Saahil's homecoming.

Zahra wanted to go and sit with her family before the big event. Nerves increased with every step she took. But with it, excitement. So much excitement.

Amjad watched Zahra walk slowly down the stairs. She looked as though she had made an effort, her hair was pinned perfectly in place and she was wearing a new outfit that Amjad hadn't seen before.

'You look nice,' he said.

'Thanks,' she smiled.

'Hello, love,' Ken said.

Zahra gave him a curt nod. Ammi turned to her and tugged at her dress, pulling it down.

'Oh my God, Ammi,' Zahra said, leaping back. 'It's below the knee.'

Ammi sniffed disapprovingly and turned away. Zahra took a seat on the sofa, face almost hidden behind her phone. They were all watching the news and the report was covering the influx of immigration from EU countries. A Polish man had arrived in Britain with five kids and no job or accommodation to support them. He was being interviewed by a reporter from a homeless shelter.

Amjad glanced at Ken and tutted. 'Wait until the Romanian lot come,' he said. 'Some of them are living in the house I grew up in. They've knackered the whole street up. It's a dump.'

Ken grunted in agreement.

A toothless old woman in a bingo club was also being

interviewed. 'We tolerated the Asians,' she said. 'And now we've got to put up with the Eastern Europeans. It's a small island, we're gonna sink.'

'"Tolerated the Asians",' Amjad heard Zahra mumble from the corner of the sofa. 'We tolerated you, love, when you colonised us for two hundred years.'

He hoped Ken hadn't heard, but his face turned in her direction. Zahra didn't notice and carried on texting on her phone. She looked up at them both.

'What? It's true,' she said, motioning to the TV. 'These people don't even have a clue about their own history.'

Amjad sighed. 'Okay Zahra, we don't need another—'

'And you shouldn't be saying stuff about these new immigrants either, Abbu. You're brown, you'll always be one, no matter what you do.'

Amjad looked at Ken, who adjusted in his seat to turn to Zahra.

'Go on, love,' he said, gently. 'Speak your mind.'

Zahra sighed, placed her phone on her lap and slowly leaned forward. 'I'm just sayin', yeah, we did come over here for our own economic betterment. I'm not saying we didn't. But that was after we fought for Britain in two world wars and had our land and resources taken from us. It's just so hypocritical. Only Britain would barge into other people's countries and tell them, "Oh you have to be like us." And then let former colonised people into theirs and say, "Oh, now you *still* have to be like us."'

She picked her phone up and sat back, placing it in front of her face, fingers jabbing away at the keyboard. She wasn't done, though.

'Didn't even hang around for an orderly transition of power,' she mumbled as an afterthought. 'Look at the balls-up they made in Iraq.'

'We only went there for oil!' Ken said, seemingly glad he could contribute. 'Never found no weapons of mass—'

'There's a bit more to it than that,' Zahra said, descending into a lengthy rant about 'disaster capitalism'.

Amjad watched as Ken's eyebrows travelled further up his forehead. He'd already heard about all this; Zahra had given him a few books about it, but he hadn't read them yet.

'People don't even realise just how economically focused it was,' Zahra said. 'Just so that Americans could open a McDonald's and a Wal-Mart.'

'And who actually masterminded all this? Apart from Bush and Blair, obviously,' Ken asked.

'Basically, a bunch of inexperienced people who had no knowledge of the country were given complete control.'

'That's bonkers.'

'No,' Zahra replied. 'It's white supremacy on steroids for you.'

Ken took a moment to adjust to the phrase. 'Well, I'm not racist,' he said, sitting up in his chair. 'I don't see colour, me.'

Zahra glared at him, in the same fierce way she often did to Amjad.

'Sorry, Uncle Ken, but that's not helpful. You're erasing the negative experiences of people of colour by denying that colour even exists when it so obviously does. Only privileged people can say they're "colourblind".'

Amjad cleared his throat. 'I know loads of Asians who don't like English people.'

'That's prejudice, not racism,' she said. 'I've explained this to you before, Abbu. I can't oppress you based on your gender;

you're a man and part of the dominant group. In the same way, racism isn't name-calling. It's the structural and systematic oppression of people of colour.'

'What are you going on about?' Ammi snapped. She glared in Zahra's direction. 'You're giving me earache.'

Amjad watched as Zahra looked at each of them in turn.

'Don't worry, I'm going,' she said, making to stand up. She waved at them sarcastically. 'Bye!'

The door slammed shut.

'Well,' Ken said, adjusting his collar.

'Sorry,' Amjad said. 'I know she can be a bit… too much at times.'

'No, no. I think I needed that. '

Amjad nodded. 'Think she gets impatient with me because I'm not exactly clued up about stuff. Gives me all these books to read.'

He pointed to a stack under the table. 'Don't understand a bloody word. Can hardly get past the first chapter.'

Ken chuckled but his laughter subsided when he saw the look on Amjad's face. 'What is it?' he asked.

'She just seems even more agitated than ever recently. Don't know what's up with her.'

Ken shrugged. 'She'll be fine. That's what happens when you know too much. Ignorance is bliss for numpties like us.'

Amjad nodded before turning to Ammi. 'Where did Zahra say she was going?'

As Zahra walked down the street, her heart raced. She'd stepped off the bus and was following Google Maps on her phone. She'd spent the bus journey frantically planning her meeting with her brother, fussing over her clothing and smoothing down her hair.

What would she say to greet Saahil? *How* would she say it? Would she embrace him? Or wait to see how comfortable he was? Zahra followed the blue arrow on her phone and turned into another street. She passed rows of parked cars and walked to the far end of the pavement. She slowed down as she approached the door number that Saahil had given her. She stood in front of the gate, her insides quivering as she faced the average-looking house she was about to enter. She breathed in with resolve and reached out to press the doorbell. Before she did, however, the door swung open.

They stared at each other again. Zahra couldn't breathe. She saw Saahil swallow hard, and then half whisper, half croak, 'Come in.'

She was greeted by a surprisingly modern living room with black leather furniture and white walls. Her shoes slid along the polished laminate flooring.

'It's my mate Robert's place,' said Saahil quickly before gesturing towards the sofa. Zahra perched at the end. It was cold and as solid as a wooden bench; Zahra's slender frame barely made a dent in it. Saahil insisted she get comfortable, even putting a cushion behind her back.

'Are you hungry?' he asked.

'No, I'm okay.'

Saahil looked deflated. He touched his head. 'I should have told you, I made us dinner.'

'Okay,' Zahra said, wishing to be as accommodating as possible. 'I can eat.'

'Right, well…' Saahil grabbed the remote controls from the coffee table. 'Watch TV and I'll be back.'

Zahra realised he was looking at the floor when he spoke. Now, under different and more modern lighting fixtures, Zahra thought he looked healthier than when she had first seen him. His clothes remained similar: joggers and a dark hoodie. She pulled out her phone and texted Libby.

He's in the kitchen making food. I'm watching TV.

Libby replied:

Take it easy and after dinner, go in for the kill.

Saahil re-entered the room carrying a tray of what looked like tandoori chicken.

'Do you wanna move to the dining table?'

Zahra shrugged. 'It's up to you.'

Saahil's eyes flicked to the television. Zahra could tell what he was thinking. It would be less awkward with it on in the background.

'We could just stay here,' Zahra said. 'Stoop down and eat from the coffee table, like Asians.'

Saahil smiled. 'Yeah, yeah.'

After more fussing, Saahil sat down next to her and gave her a plate. Zahra felt ridiculous doing this, but thought maybe he would want to talk after they had eaten. She suddenly felt very conscious of eating in front of him and didn't want to drop it all over her new dress. She gracefully picked up the cutlery but her fingers were trembling. A second later, and the chicken boti went flying across the table.

'I'm so sorry!'

'Oh, don't worry,' he said, moving it to one side. 'Shall we just eat with our hands, like Asians?'

Zahra nodded. They ate in silence for a while and laughed nervously at cartoons on the TV. Saahil was about to place another chicken leg on Zahra's plate when she declined.

'Did you make these?' Zahra asked.

'No,' he said, sheepishly. 'Got them from Tesco, halal counter. They already have the spices on.'

He took the plates away. Zahra texted Libby again.

He's gone back into the kitchen.

Bloody hell, tell him you're not hungry.

Mate, I can't even look at him directly.

Go and see what he's doing.

Zahra stood up and crept quietly to the kitchen door. She peered around the corner, catching sight of the silver appliances sitting on top of black granite worktops. There were no sounds of food preparation, or washing up and clearing away. As she ventured further, she saw that Saahil wasn't there. There was, however, another door which led outside. Saahil was standing with his back to her, smoking.

Zahra went into the lounge again and wrote out another text: He's fucking smoking outside.

Libby: You what?

'Shall I bring the roti now?'

Zahra jumped, 'Roti?'

'Yeah, I made saag aloo.'

'Oh... well, okay.'

Saahil dipped out of view again. Zahra found it quite endearing that he had gone to so much effort, but knew it was a good way of avoiding them being in the same room together. And the smoking? Well.

'I got the roti from this shop, they're not all that,' he said, bringing more food in on a different tray. 'They're not like the ones Abbu used to get.'

At the mention of Abbu's name, they both made eye contact.

'Shall we eat?' Zahra said, quickly.

Saahil started spooning in the curry at high speed. Zahra busied herself with the food, despite not being hungry at all.

'Nice,' she said. He smiled and nodded. It was excruciating and Zahra wished for the meal to end quickly. She took two bites and spent the rest of the time chasing the food around the plate.

Saahil stood up again to take the dishes away. Zahra offered to help. He insisted she stay. She checked her phone and saw Libby had messaged her:

Follow him into the kitchen if he's hiding in there!

Zahra took a deep breath and made to get up a second time but Saahil appeared at the door. Zahra's heart started racing again. Without thinking, she blurted out the first question that came into her mind.

'Why did you run away from me that day?'

Saahil blinked. He walked over slowly. 'Erm... I... er... I just panicked. Sorry.'

Zahra's phone buzzed again. It was probably Libby egging her on.

'How's Ammi?' Saahil asked quietly, taking a seat next to her. His head was facing the opposite direction to her.

'She's okay,' Zahra answered, not knowing how much to say.

'Abbu?' Now he looked at the floor. Zahra saw him bite his lip. She didn't speak, but just made a sound that suggested 'fine'. A minute passed by, and Saahil's eyes remained glued to the TV screen. Zahra realised she was digging her fingernails into her hand. The air could have been cut with a knife.

'Ehsan is okay, too,' Zahra said. 'He's in hospital at the moment – he has to go in sometimes because he gets chest infections.'

Saahil stared straight ahead. He rocked slightly. Zahra wondered if he had even heard her. He jumped up from the seat. 'Do you mind if I have a cig?'

He headed towards the kitchen again.

'Saahil,' Zahra called after him. 'Wait!'

He didn't stop, but quickened his steps and disappeared into the kitchen. Zahra stood up and followed him. He went through the back door again where Zahra had seen him smoking before.

'Saahil,' Zahra repeated. She almost reached him. He saw her, but with one swift movement, Saahil slammed the door shut in her face. Zahra blinked a few times, her mouth hanging open.

A new emotion awoke in her. It was no longer anxiety. It wasn't even anger. It was of pure hatred. She couldn't believe Saahil was acting in this way. Cramming their mouths with food so that they wouldn't have to talk. Running into the kitchen every five minutes. Expecting her to initiate the difficult conversations, and now that she was trying, he had run off again.

Saahil had seen her approach him. He heard her call for him. And in an instant, shut her out once more. He wasn't even bothered about how she would feel, or how the slammed door would actually feel like a slap across her face. Zahra realised that she had backed away from the room. A moment later, she'd flung open the door and was pelting down the street, wishing to put as much distance as possible between her and her brother.

She didn't know these streets, but hurried past identical houses, searching for a corner which she could dip into and catch her breath. She ran past a dog walker who whipped around after seeing the look on Zahra's face. Zahra rushed along, not wanting to be asked if she was okay. She wasn't. She needed to find somewhere she could gather her thoughts, decide what to do next.

Zahra found a snicket between two houses. She slammed her back against the wall. A group of teenage lads strolled past her, swearing loudly. She waited for them to pass, holding in her breath as they went. Once they were gone, Zahra gasped, her face flushing hot. Her hands shook as she tried to retrieve her phone from her bag. Zahra dialled Libby's number.

'What happened?' Libby asked as soon as she answered.

Zahra told her.

'He did WHAT?'

'Slammed it right in my face.'

'What a fucking—'

'What shall I do, Libs?'

Zahra listened to her best friend's silence. She could hear her breathing over the phone.

'Go back,' she finally replied.

'Back? How can I? He doesn't wanna know.'

'He does. He's just acting like a coward. You can't let him get away with this.'

Zahra bit her lip before turning around and kicking the wall, swearing under her breath.

'Listen, Zee,' Libby continued. 'There's no need to be so nice about things this time. Go and get your answers.'

Zahra put the phone down and dragged her feet back to the house. She got lost, ventured into streets she didn't recognise. She typed in the address to Google Maps again and followed the blue icon reluctantly towards the correct house. Finally, she could see Saahil from afar. He was in the garden craning his neck down the street, a cig dangling from one hand and in the other, holding his phone against his ear. She realised he was ringing her.

'Where did you go?' he asked, running towards her.

Zahra brushed past him and marched into the house as calmly as she could. She took a seat on the single chair – that way, he wouldn't be near her. He followed her and stood around.

Zahra stared at him, directly in the eyes. She could see it was making him nervous. He put his cigarette out and waited. When Zahra spoke, her voice was devoid of any emotion.

'Start at the beginning,' she simply said.

Saahil frowned, but Zahra could tell he knew exactly what she was talking about. He sat down, his movements slow and pained, as though gearing himself up for an impact.

'When you left Uncle Javid's house ten years ago,' Zahra said. 'Start from there… and tell me *everything*.'

She leaned forward, the palms of her hands clasped together, her knuckles white. Zahra continued to stare straight and hard into her brother's guilt-ridden eyes.

Twenty-Eight

'I got through the Christmas period by staying in the grubbiest hotels I could find,' he began. 'You know… the ones that don't ask too many questions, take cash payment, and are… well… mostly run by foreigners.'

He was supposed to be using this time to get his shit together, he told Zahra. Decide what to do next: either go home, or find some sort of job to keep him going. But it was freezing outside, and instead Saahil just lay for hours in bed, trying his best to forget about everything. And yet when he closed his eyes, Ehsan's bludgeoned head swam into view. Saahil could almost hear his friend letting out a long, agonising groan. Ehsan was incapable of forming sentences anymore; he couldn't tell anyone that he was in pain.

It was quiet in this new place Saahil was staying in. No one bothered him. No one checked to see if he was okay. No one tiptoed around him or seized up as soon as he entered a room. He had thrown his mobile in the bin. There were no concerned voices to be heard at the end of the phone. He had shut everybody out. Saahil was going it alone.

He would get a job after the New Year, he decided. He'd started withdrawing wads of what remained of his student loan whilst still in Birmingham, aiming to make it last for as long as possible. Now it was running out, and he'd done nothing to stop it. It was like he didn't care. The old Saahil would have thought ahead and put some sort of plan in place. That was impossible now. Saahil could no longer see anything past the present day. It was just black.

A few days ago, he'd used the internet café at the hotel and typed in his name in the Missing Persons website. He put this action off for weeks, knowing full well what he would find. There he was, in a grainy photograph. It had been taken on Eid. Saahil knew Zahra was cropped out of it because it was a picture of the two of them. There was limited information such as the date he'd last been seen, his age, hometown and a reference number. Then there was a small message directed at him:

Saahil, we are here for you whenever you are ready; we can listen, talk you through what help you need, pass a message for you and help you to be safe. Call. Text. Anytime. Free. Confidential. 116000

It unsettled him, to be addressed directly. He imagined his dad frantically searching for him, Ammi wailing, Zahra sobbing. Abbu would probably be ringing his friends: Umar, Hardeep, Kamran, Robert. Saahil hadn't even been in touch with them for months. He imagined his Abbu finally giving in and reluctantly calling the police.

Saahil tried to make himself care so much that he would pick up his things, board a train and go home. He couldn't. The last train journey had proved that. He'd left his cousin's house early and gone to the station. He'd taken a seat, shoved his rucksack in the luggage holder above as he was expected to. But something had changed in him. Yes, he *had* been withdrawing money whilst in Birmingham, but Saahil didn't think he actually had the heart to go through with it. He tried to shake off those feelings, but returning home felt like a death sentence. Every stop they'd approached filled him with dread. Saahil watched the fields and various train stations pass by. He thought of nothing. There was a time when his mind was never still. He was constantly buzzing, thinking, plotting. Now he just stared as the world flitted by, head leaning against the window, arms folded together. A pathetic, forlorn-looking figure. He felt embarrassed to be himself.

Abbu wanted him to snap out of it. Saahil simply couldn't. He could do nothing to help Ehsan either. He wasn't even allowed to see him anymore. Saahil felt annoyance every time Ammi tried to embrace him, or touch his face in a comforting way. He'd noticed his sister shrinking slightly every time she looked at him, avoiding his gaze as though they were strangers. Everybody trod on eggshells around him. Because of him, they couldn't breathe. Saahil had come to realise that there was nothing positive he could contribute to his family anymore. He knew that if he stayed, he would drag them all down to the same depths he had sunk to. Saahil couldn't do that. He needed to get away from them so that they could live again. It was the only option left.

Some people left the train, and Saahil moved to a table seat. He put his head down and fell asleep. When he woke up, he panicked. Grabbing his rucksack, he got off the train not knowing where he was. People spilled out of the carriage behind him. He turned around and looked at the sign.

Saahil was relieved to find that he was hours away from home.

He spent entire nights walking around the city centre. To keep moving was a good way of staying warm. He could walk past the same shops again and again, until finally sitting down on a deserted bench on the high street. The night had changed. It was different. It wasn't the same one he had revelled in as a carefree student. He remembered being the loudest member of the group when he was with Ehsan and his friends, walking around town after a party, shouting playful abuse at each other and making fun of drunken white people. This night was eerie. It was sinister. There were dark shadows everywhere. Saahil was in a constant state of terror.

He would jump on to a night bus to feel less exposed. It was still freezing, but at least he felt contained in some sort of way. Others would follow him on to the top deck. Saahil couldn't get comfortable. He was scared somebody would attack him or steal his belongings. Another man had the same idea. He put his feet up on the chair and snored for half an hour. Saahil marvelled at this. There was no way sleep was possible on the buses, not the way they screeched and jerked around the bends. When the man woke up, he gathered his things and glanced over at Saahil. It was just the two of them on board. He was unkempt and his smell had filled the entire top deck.

'It's the 607 you want,' he called over, packing away his things. 'It's a three-hour round trip.'

Saahil was too stunned to respond, but grateful for the information. He got through many nights on the 607 after that, along with at least ten other people sleeping rough. They would stay there for as long as possible, until the conductor would announce that the bus was ending its route and everyone had to get off. That's when the desperation would set in again. Where would he go now? That was when he contemplated whether any of this had been a good idea. That and when his money eventually ran out.

He started sleeping rough and began walking the streets every night. Saahil couldn't believe how many tramps were kipping in doorways and in dark alleyways. They were everywhere. The homeless would start gathering outside the McDonald's at 5 a.m. Saahil would too, eager for the warmth and the 99p coffees. Not that he was *homeless* homeless, of course. It was just a temporary thing. He would find a seat alone, hood pulled up, woolly scarf covering his face. It would take ages for his body to heat up. He could barely feel his fingers as they wrapped around the hot polystyrene cup. Saahil would watch the tramps rolling up spliffs on the tables, the McDonald's workers pretending not to see. He thought of the children who would sit down at the same tables and tuck into Happy Meals at more sociable hours.

When light finally came, it brought no relief. Instead, it made his indignity visible. People strutted past him. They had important places to be. Not like Saahil, who had crawled into the darkest corner of society. Groups of young people walked past, laughing and joking as they 'hung out'. There was no reason for them to acknowledge Saahil. But he tried not to notice how they went out of their way to walk around him, avoiding his gaze.

Fucking bastards. It was not like he bothered them or, God forbid, begged. He may have been a bit scruffy and smelly, but so what? He'd caught sight of himself in a shop window reflection: he was gaunt, his hair matted with the rain. He hadn't eaten properly for weeks thanks to being reduced to his last bit of change, but it wasn't like he was full-on homeless. It was just a temporary thing, he kept telling himself.

Most people just walked past him so indifferently that Saahil wondered if they would have paid more attention to him had he been an injured dog. One day, Saahil noticed, nobody looked directly at him for nearly three hours straight. The daytime may have brought with it security, but it was a stark reminder of who Saahil no longer was. Of all the things he had experienced in his life, Saahil had never been invisible before. And it hurt.

He'd wrap himself up in the layers of clothing he'd taken to Uncle Javid's house. The actual homeless people had one over on him. They had sleeping bags and blankets. Saahil wondered where they had got them from. Now the cash was gone. He was starving. He was cold. Saahil didn't know anybody in this city, nobody he could turn to and ask for help. He regretted throwing his phone in the bin. He wished he'd utilised his time better when he actually had the money and not stayed in bed, feeling sorry for himself all day.

Saahil contemplated going home. He even rang home, spacing out the phone calls to avoid suspicion. The first time had been from a telephone box. Zahra had answered, her voice chirpy.

'Hello? Helloooooooo?' she said, before slamming it down.

Saahil felt like somebody had kicked him in the teeth. What had he expected? For his family to be in a constant state of mourning? Life went on. Maybe his little sister had achieved top marks in a test, and that was why she was so cheery. It wasn't that she didn't miss him.

A week later, and Saahil called again, careful not to turn this into a regular thing. This time, Abbu answered. His voice had been gruff and weary. He said 'hello' twice. Saahil hunched over the phone in the telephone box. He bit his knuckle. There was a long silence. Abbu spoke again, but this time, his voice changed. It softened.

'Hello?'

Panicking, Saahil hung up.

He was not stupid. He knew he could go into a police station and all of this would be over within a few hours. But instead, Saahil spent entire nights walking around the city centre. He'd board the 607 bus, huddled in the back of the top deck for three hours. He'd hang around outside McDonald's willing for the doors to open, willing for the warmth to envelop him and remind him he was still human.

Saahil woke up surrounded. He thought he was hallucinating, that the five faces jeering at him were just a figment of his imagination. He reached out and grabbed hold of his bag, which prompted the men to laugh harder. Saahil realised what he had done. He'd stupidly settled down in the first doorway he could find, not far from a pub. He had seen the goray hanging around outside with their pints. First, there were one or two, then a whole crowd had gathered. From afar, they looked like football-hooligan types. The kind that would kick your head in just for fun. He was a prime candidate, of course, not only was he sleeping rough, but he was also brown. Saahil moved a couple of streets away, not realising that most of them would pass this way to get home.

'Having a kip?' one of them screeched at him. The others roared with laughter.

Saahil held his bag close like a shield, ashamed of how scared he was.

They were all carrying beer bottles, swaying on their toes, completely immersed in his humiliation. Saahil checked around quickly and saw a couple walking across on the other side of the road. They were watching, but as soon as Saahil caught their eye, they looked away and sped off down the street.

One guy kicked Saahil's bag out of his hands. Two others fell upon it like hyenas on a carcass, ripping it open and scattering his belongings all over the ground. The last of his loose change clinked on the concrete, spinning like dozens of little timers before falling flat against the floor. Saahil knew he was in for it again. Only this time it would be worse.

'Probably an illegal immigrant,' one of the men chuckled before another started stuttering in a bad Indian accent.

'Fuck off!' Saahil shouted, making to get up but they blocked his way with their stocky bodies, tattooed arms pushing him back on the ground.

'Little cunt,' one man snarled. He was at least in his forties, with greying hair and yellowing teeth. He ejected, with all his might, a great big blob of saliva and sent it hurtling in Saahil's direction. It took a moment or two for Saahil to accept what had just happened. He brought his hand slowly up to his cheek, his vision blurred by the alcohol-smelling spit that now rested on his face.

He wiped it off with his sleeve, but his tormentors had another light-bulb idea.

'Go on, Rick, go on…'

Saahil turned to find that the short, stout man stood furthest away from him was unzipping his pants. He fumbled with his underpants, cheered on by his mates. Saahil realised that if he didn't move, he was going to be used as a toilet. With their eyes diverted, Saahil bulldozed past them, knocking into the group as hard as he could. Stubby fingers tried to grasp him, but Saahil ran, as though he was running away from death itself. He didn't know if they were following him, he didn't stop to check.

When he eventually slipped into a gap between two shops, his heart felt like it was going to tear out of his chest. He clamped his hand over his mouth, lest the men hear him gasping for air. He slid against the brick wall and fell on to his knees, shaking with anger and frustration.

He'd managed to scoop up his bag from the ground as he ran away. Saahil rummaged around to see if there was anything left inside. It was empty, but his fingers felt some material at the bottom of the bag. He yanked it out, hoping to have salvaged at least one item of clothing he could use. It took him a few seconds to realise what he was holding.

His mother's pashmina shawl was curled up inside his fist. The heavy yellow fringe billowed in the icy wind.

Saahil staggered into the same alleyway two days later. The temperature had dropped to below freezing. With his belongings taken by the yobs outside the pub, he had nothing on him, except the clothes on his back, an empty bag, and his mother's shawl. No money for a bus, no emergency food and no mobile phone to call for help. The last time he checked, it was only three o'clock in the morning. He most certainly had frostbite on his fingers and toes, they felt like they were about to fall off. Frost covered his jacket. He could see his breath condense before him. Saahil lay scrunched up against the wall, it being his only comfort. He'd made a mess of everything. He had barely thought any of this through. If he survived the night, he would have no choice but to go home. What would his family think of him? This, he told himself as he lay shivering against the wall, was what dying felt like.

Half an hour passed, and Saahil heard voices. They were inaudible, until they came closer and he realised they belonged to two guys who were approaching. Fear gripped Saahil once more, but he didn't have the energy to move.

'Fuckin' freezing, man.'

They stopped when they saw him and started whispering to each other. One of them stepped forward and cleared his throat. 'You all right, mate?' he drawled.

Saahil didn't respond, but remained paralysed, the incident of two days ago still haunting his every move. And then there was the first time he had been alone in an alleyway with strange men. It had resulted in broken ribs, a fractured leg and a bloodied and bruised face. Oh, and his best friend was brain-dead.

'Come on, man!' Another, harsher voice said, making to walk away.

'Can't just leave him, you prick,' the first man replied. He addressed Saahil. 'Do you have somewhere to sleep?'

Saahil eventually looked up and shook his head. The man thought about it for a few minutes.

'Erm… you can come wiv us, if you want,' he said.

The other guy sighed and started looking the other way in a sulk. Saahil hung back and didn't move.

'Oh, come on,' the man said. 'Where else are you gonna go at this time?'

Saahil looked around. The man was right. Saahil didn't have a choice and without dwelling on things for too long, he stood up and followed them. They walked down streets, Saahil lagging behind, not really sure he could trust them. They could have taken him into another alleyway and mugged him. He was desperate, though, he needed to survive. They passed other rough sleepers, occasionally stopping to say 'hi', until the guys eventually led him to a shopping centre car park. One ventured straight underneath the ramp and disappeared. The other, friendlier bloke stopped and motioned Saahil to follow suit. Saahil hung back.

'It's all right, it's a camp,' he reassured.

Reluctantly, Saahil entered. It was pitch black. He found a free corner closest to the light and sat up against the wall, hugging his knees. He saw shapes moving beside him and figured it was the two men who had led him there. Saahil reached for the pashmina and wrapped it around his left hand. He didn't know why, but gripping it tightly made him feel better. He closed his eyes and prayed for sleep.

The next morning, he jerked awake. He heard cars passing by and people walking around. Then he looked at his surroundings and gasped in horror. Syringes, beer cans, cigs and graffitied walls. It was like he had crawled into a small war zone. He couldn't quite believe he had spent the night there. There were around ten tents and people were either sleeping or sitting around. Their appearances shocked Saahil, so did the smell. His first instinct was to turn and run. But to where? The thought of spending another night walking the streets alone terrified him.

The two men from the night before were already lighting up next to him. They hadn't even bothered to get out of their sleeping bags.

'All right, mate?'

Saahil stood up, brushing dirt off his clothes, looking disgusted.

'I'm Ben, by the way,' said one. Saahil recognised his drawling voice, he was the nicer of the two. 'This is Jason,' he continued, motioning to his friend. Jason sneered at the look on Saahil's face.

'So how long you been sleeping rough?' Ben asked.

Saahil squatted beside him and cleared his throat. He hadn't spoken to anybody for ages. That was one thing he had avoided doing, scared that once he spoke to a tramp he would become one of them.

'A few weeks,' he mumbled.

Ben nodded and carried on smoking.

'What about you?' Saahil asked.

Ben laughed, 'Since I wo' sixteen, mate.'

Saahil raised his eyebrows, 'And how old are you now?'

'Nineteen.'

Saahil tried to hide his shock. The guy looked about thirty. He already had lines around his eyes. Saahil turned to Jason. 'What about you?'

He didn't respond and carried on staring ahead as though he hadn't even been spoken to.

'What 'appened to yer?' Ben asked.

Saahil shrugged. He didn't want to go into any details with people he had just met. And he was going to be out of there soon. He just needed some help for a few days.

'Family problems?' Ben suggested.

'Yeah.'

Saahil watched the pair of them. Ben had dark hair, yellow teeth and abnormally pale skin. He seemed genuine, despite giving off the impression that he was slowly decomposing. Jason was black, so didn't look so gaunt and washed-out.

'So you don't have a sleeping bag or anything?' Ben asked.

Saahil shook his head.

'Take him to the day centre,' Jason interjected, still staring ahead.

Saahil had no idea what they were talking about, but was instructed to follow them after they had finished smoking. It was still freezing and the roads were slippery. The three of them seemed to part the crowds easily. Well dressed, well turned-out people hurried past, placing as much distance as possible between them. It was as though the boys would contaminate the air they breathed.

After ten minutes, they arrived at a glass door with no signage or reception. There was just some stairs leading up. They all shivered as they closed the door to the harsh winter weather and embraced the warmth. Saahil followed them up and through the only available door. He was surprised to find a brightly painted room with neat tables and chairs and a reception at the far end.

Ben walked over to the plump lady sitting behind the desk.

'Found this lad…' Saahil heard him say and pointing over towards him. 'Have you got any spare sleeping bags?'

Saahil stayed well away, hiding his face like he was some sort of celebrity who didn't want to be recognised. Jason had ventured over to some computers. An older man came stumbling out of another room with wet hair. As he walked past, Saahil smelt soap and toothpaste.

'Thanks, love,' he shouted and exited the room.

Saahil noticed that there was one other person in the room. It was a woman seated nearby. Her head was on the table and her arms cradled it. Saahil focused on her and realised she hadn't made a sound or moved an inch. He felt like going up and prodding her to make sure she was still alive.

'What's yer name?' Ben called over to him.

Saahil froze. 'Ehsan,' he blurted out.

'Come here, please,' the lady beckoned him over and started asking him questions.

Since when had he been sleeping rough? When was the last time he had eaten? Did he need medical attention? Did he have any friends or family that could take him in? Did he receive benefits?

Saahil mumbled his way through, dodging questions, playing thick. The lady then went on to explain the facilities to him. They provided breakfast, clean clothes, showers and toilets and they had computers too. Saahil nodded and avoided eye contact.

'If you come back tomorrow, Alan will be here. He's our adviser. You can ask him any questions related to housing and benefits. The community nurse comes on Thursdays.'

'Thanks,' Saahil mumbled, looking at the floor.

He turned to find Ben holding what looked like a sleeping bag and a blanket. Saahil took them from him. He just wanted to take the stuff and get out of there as soon as possible. As they walked towards the door, Saahil saw the girl was still seated, and her arms were still cradling her head.

That night, Saahil wandered the streets with Ben and Jason. He stuck to them like a leech. They seemed to know what they were doing. After speaking to them some more, Saahil found out Ben had just come out of prison, but didn't disclose what for. Saahil found it hard to believe, he just seemed like a harmless kid. Ben had a mum but didn't visit her.

'Don't want any trouble going to her door, man. How do you say yer name again?'

Saahil gulped, and cursed himself for taking his best friend's name.

'Ehsan,' he mumbled. Now he'd said it, he would have to stick to it.

He decided not to ask Ben any more questions. He attributed his own homelessness to 'family problems' and left it at that. Jason spoke a little more to him. He had a grandma whose sofa he kipped on sometimes, but otherwise slept rough. Saahil was confused. If his relative lived nearby, why would he sleep on the streets? Jason ignored him and Saahil soon learnt that it was from his nan's purse that Jason had nicked a tenner.

They squabbled over the money before Ben went to a shop and came back with a small metallic packet. They huddled into an alleyway and opened it like a couple of boys fighting over sweets.

Saahil peered over, but Ben turned his back on him. 'What is it?' he asked.

'Spliff, mate.'

Saahil laughed. 'You just got it from the shop.'

'It's legal, man, it's this new thing.'

'Really? Show me the packet,' Saahil asked, but Ben seemed reluctant.

'I'm not going to nick it,' Saahil sneered.

Ben held it up from afar. It had the words 'Spice' printed in gold letters.

'So what has it actually got in it?' he asked, but the boys weren't listening. They were too busy rolling up spliffs.

'Works like weed,' Ben drawled.

'*Legal* weed. You never heard of it?' Jason asked.

'Oh, yeah, think I have,' Saahil replied. 'It's that synthetic stuff, right?'

Saahil took the packet and examined it. NOT FOR HUMAN CONSUMPTION, it stated with a skull and crossbones. 'So, how is this regulated?' he asked.

'Fuck knows,' Ben replied, indignantly. 'Makes me forget about everything, that's all I know. And it's only a tenner a gram.'

Saahil shuffled over. 'Forget about everything, yeah?'

Ben nodded and crouched on the floor against the wall. He took a couple of drags. Saahil didn't have to wait long to see the effects. Ben had completely zoned out. His tatty trainers scraped against the floor as he slid down and straightened his legs out, sitting on his bum. He rested his head against the wall, a peculiar smile spread over his face. Saahil nudged him.

'Oi,' he said.

Ben didn't move or respond. The spliff was dangling from his fingers. His grip was so light that Saahil thought it would fall on the floor. He looked over to where Jason was. He'd shuffled into a corner and had barely made a sound. Saahil may as well have been alone in the alleyway.

They both came round ten minutes later.

'Give us some,' Saahil asked straightaway.

'It's only a tenner from the shop,' Ben murmured.

'You've got loads left, I only want one spliff.'

Ben sighed heavily. 'All right, but from now on, you'll have to start contributing, mate.'

Saahil rolled his eyes. 'I only want one.'

'You say that,' Ben said, staring at him as though trying to warn him of something. Saahil ignored him.

Ben rolled up and handed it over to him. Saahil took a drag. Then another. He stumbled against the wall without realising his legs had given way. Ben grabbed hold of him.

'What the...' Saahil spluttered.

Ben laughed, his voice sounded deeper. 'First time Jason had it, he was on the floor barking like a dog.'

Jason, who had now rejoined them, responded with a slight upturn of his lip.

'This is... legal?' Saahil asked, finding it difficult to form words.

'Yeah, man. Wanna sit down?'

The world softened in front of him. He sank into himself, his limbs relaxed. The harsh light at the end of the street became weaker. Warmth spread through his body, almost as if he had crawled into a cocoon. It was as though somebody had scooped all the guilt out of his brain. The negativity evaporated. So did the self-loathing. For the first time in months, Saahil felt free.

Ten minutes later, the effects wore off. They were now all seated by a doorway, emerging from the strangest of sensations.

Ten minutes later, and Saahil asked for another.

Twenty-Nine

Zahra immediately wanted to ask questions. She'd resisted cutting across Saahil whilst he told his story, afraid that any questioning of hers would put him off. The sky had become dull outside, almost as if rain was about to fall. The fluorescent lighting in the room shone down on Saahil's face, making him appear ghostly and unnatural. It was like a police questioning, with Zahra the interrogator and Saahil the guilty, the accused.

The thought of her brother sleeping on the streets was too much for her to bear. As he stared at the floor rubbing his hands together, Zahra wanted to reach out and embrace him. She didn't move. It did pain her how much he had suffered, but she couldn't let it show. After all, he wasn't the only one.

She gulped. 'I can't imagine you... homeless.'

'It wasn't easy,' Saahil sighed.

As soon as he answered, Zahra felt her face burn. Had she imagined it, or was there an accusatory hint in his response?

'Easier for you to be homeless than to come home, right?' she blurted out.

He was still looking at the floor, shoulders hunched over his chest. Zahra saw that he was holding on to one arm, awkwardly. His grip tightened.

'I've spent a lot of time looking into it, you know,' Zahra said, staring at the wall as she spoke. 'You can alert the police. You can ask them to tell your family that you're safe but don't want to be contacted. That would have been quite simple.'

This time, Saahil cupped his mouth. Zahra wanted to hit him, her mind exploding with mental insults.

'Have you ever heard Abbu cry?'

'Zee—'

'Just answer the question.'

'When... when Mum died,' Saahil mumbled.

'Yeah, it's rare, probably only a handful of times,' Zahra said. 'Obviously he doesn't as much as he probably wants to because he thinks he needs to be all manly and tough. But I've heard him sobbing in his room. I stand outside and don't know whether to go in and comfort him or just let him have his moment. He doesn't want me to see him cry. So I leave him to sob, and I go into my room and pretend not to hear.'

It was like she was working through all her thoughts out loud. Her voice lacked any emotion.

'You can't make me feel any worse than I already do,' he said, quietly.

'Just tell me why you didn't put us out of our misery and give us a ring? Or write us a letter?'

Saahil had no answer but Zahra continued to wait for him, just in case he could salvage the situation.

'Well, if you couldn't do it in those first few months away, then... you never were going to, were you?'

'I'm sorry for everything, Zee,' Saahil eventually replied. 'The longer I stayed away, the harder it got to come back. Weeks turned into months, and months turned into years—'

'And years turned into a decade.'

Saahil reached out.

307

'Don't,' Zahra said, pulling away.

'I don't know how… it happened—'

Zahra sat up straight in her chair, gearing up for a fight. 'Wanna know what we were getting up to whilst you were off being homeless? Can you even begin to imagine?'

Once Abbu and Uncle Ken's fruitless attempts at finding Saahil themselves came to an end, they exhausted every other avenue available to them. During the first couple of years, Abbu had hired numerous private investigators. He travelled down to Birmingham and tried to retrace Saahil's footsteps himself. He rang the police and Missing Persons every week, whilst Zahra, who was better at using the internet, obsessively checked the website on a daily basis.

'Abbu would drive like a maniac through the streets and stare at people's faces through the windscreen,' she almost shouted. 'Just in case he spotted you. He'd never concentrate on the road and nearly killed us all once by crashing the car.'

Saahil stood up quickly. 'Please stop,' he said, turning away and holding his head in his hands.

Zahra stood up too. 'Why? You can't bear to listen to it. You should have tried *living* it,' she spat.

They stayed quiet for some time. Saahil, standing by the window. Zahra, sitting down on the sofa. She remembered back to the first years of Saahil's disappearance. What else did Abbu's neglect let her get away with at the time? She'd just started secondary school and he was practically absent during that year. A silly thought came into her head and a chuckle escaped her lips before she could stop it.

Saahil turned around, a look of utter confusion on his face.

'I… er… This stupid thing happened once,' she began, waving her hand dismissively.

Saahil, however, appeared to wait for her to explain further.

'Abbu was out looking for you... *again*. Ammi was taking a nap. Libby was over and she decided to fake tan. I was going to, erm, dye my hair blonde.'

Saahil frowned. 'Er... why?'

'We thought we'd confuse everyone at the new school and try to look like sisters.'

Saahil, seemingly grateful for the lighter conversation, sat down beside her. 'What happened?'

'The tan Libby brought with her didn't seem to be working, she was hardly getting browner, so she emptied the whole bottle on her face and neck and arms.'

'And you?'

'I, well, needed to bleach my hair before applying the dye. It came out a disgusting orange. The blonde dye wouldn't cover it, so my hair turned into a sickly green. It looked like I had seaweed on my head. Ammi was furious.'

Saahil snorted. 'And what happened to Libby?'

'She realised the product she'd bought was a gradual tan. She'd already emptied the bottle, so she just kept getting darker and darker and darker!'

For the first time in ten years, Saahil and Zahra laughed together. It stopped almost as abruptly as it started and uneasy silence followed.

'Anyway,' Zahra said, determined to get back to Saahil's story. 'The spliff that you had. Did you try it again?'

He seemed to deflate once more, opening his mouth and then closing it.

'I'll get to that, let me make us a cuppa first,' he said.

'No, I'd rather—'

'Trust me,' he replied, before heading off into the kitchen. 'You're gonna need it.'

Saahil marvelled at how easy it was to adapt to almost any environment. He slowly lost the airs and graces he'd first possessed when he'd arrived at the makeshift shelter under the car-park ramp. He remembered wrinkling his nose up at the smell for weeks, now it festered in his own clothes and skin. He remembered laughing silently at the weirdos who sat around drinking beer and having arguments with themselves. He pitied their appearances, and the way they stared at him, probably wondering why he looked so fresh. They were gaunt and freakishly pale. He was brown and, he tried to convince himself, still handsome. For the most part, though, the tramps fascinated Saahil.

Some of them had been homeless for twenty years. At first, Saahil shook his head. *Losers*, he thought. He was going to be out of there soon, it was just a temporary thing. Most were addicts, their arms riddled with needle marks. Saahil remembered something Ehsan had told him when they were at school. That some smackheads were so desperate to find a vein, that they would go on to inject their groins, even eyeballs to get the heroin in. Saahil wanted to ask one of them if they had ever resorted to such measures, but decided it would probably offend them.

Saahil remembered sneering at Ben when he suggested the soup kitchen the first time.

'I *volunteered* at a soup kitchen when I was at uni, mate.'

'You? At uni?'

'Yeah,' said Saahil, slightly offended. *Can't you tell? I'm not like you.*

Months later, and Saahil gathered around with the rest of

the riff raff three times a week for soup. It tasted of nothing, obviously. Gora food never did. There were other gatherings as well, such as the one outside an art gallery the last Friday of every month. Volunteers would gather with donated food, clothes, shoes and toiletries. The first time Saahil visited, he immediately hung back as he saw a group of hijabis and young Asian lads walking around with volunteer jackets, directing people to the different services and offering tea and coffee. He hid behind a pillar as Ben and Jason ventured forward, stuffing jeans, coats and gloves into a tattered old suitcase that Jason had brought from his nan's house. Saahil stayed hidden, cursing the volunteers for being self-righteous, charitable little fucks who had now robbed him of this opportunity. There was no way he could be seen here by other Asians; they would take particular interest in him. He couldn't allow that.

Luckily, Ben had brought him a pair of gloves, a can of deodorant and a foil carton that contained cold vegetable lasagne. Saahil thanked him and picked away at it with his fingers as there was neither fork nor spoon. Most of Saahil's time was spent with him. Jason also joined them as well when he wasn't too busy scamming his nan. Not that they minded, they needed all the money they could get to pursue the shiny little packets.

A few months ago, Saahil had committed his first crime. He'd helped Ben break into a car to nick the spare change left visible between the seats. After, Saahil was consumed by guilt, but it was nothing the spliff couldn't sort out. He'd forgotten about it within minutes of lighting up.

They came in different flavours: blueberry, strawberry, bubblegum. It was only a tenner for a bag, and Saahil and Ben could make them last all day. It wasn't the same as the spliffs Saahil smoked with his mates at uni. This shit was much more intense and left him completely fucked out of his head for hours. Half the time, he couldn't remember what had occurred from the moment the spliff touched his lips. Saahil knew it was legal, so safer, he assumed. He enjoyed it, not having to think about what a mess he'd made of things. It was oddly liberating, to completely give up on life. There was no pressure to do this, or be that. What exactly had he done before, apart from worry about work and exams and family and achieving this and achieving that? *Fuck it*, he thought now. *Fuck everything*.

The drug gave him something priceless. Whilst he was furiously pursuing it, he forgot about his family. It made him even more selfish than he already was. Good. He needed to be selfish if he was to survive this hell. He needed to be off his head if he was to overcome the embarrassment of stealing food from supermarket bins. Even if it was perfectly edible, it was still a bin nonetheless. Then there was the humiliation of sitting in doorways next to Ben, begging for spare change. The resolve it had taken him, to sit on the cold pavement and mutter, 'Spare change?' was something Saahil would never forget. He whispered it at first, barely audible. But then his body growled for the drug. It panged. It ached. And his voice became louder. More desperate.

Again, when Saahil saw brown people pass by, he'd freeze. He'd cover half his face with a scarf. He knew they'd notice him and frown. A young Sikh guy had thrown some change into the cup Ben was holding.

'Thanks, mate,' Ben drawled.

The guy hovered around near Saahil. 'Brother,' he'd whispered, glancing over at Ben and then back at Saahil, confusedly. 'What are you doing... here?'

Saahil, not knowing how to react, told him to mind his own business. The guy walked off, shaking his head. Saahil would have felt guilty for days had he not run over to the convenience store and smoked spice for the rest of the evening.

'You lot are addicted to that shit,' one of the guys at the camp said to the three of them.

'No, we could stop tomorrow if we wanted,' Jason said quickly.

'Exactly, it's not like it's 'eroin,' Ben added.

Saahil didn't say anything, but remembered the numerous incidents that had occurred since he'd started smoking spice with Ben and Jason. There was the unpredictability of the different brands. A change of packet led to unexpected results. There was one time when Saahil's legs gave way when he tried a new packet. He lay unmoving for hours in an alleyway with only Ben to look after him. Another time, he'd been extremely sensitive to light, shielding his eyes from the sun, hearing the growl of car motors as though they were racing only centimetres away from his ear. He stayed hunched against a wall, hands clasped over his ears all night.

The worst occurred at the day centre that they often visited. Saahil had got hold of a gram of Mamba. They hadn't smoked it before. As soon as Ben took the spliff to his lips, he went ballistic, thrashing around like a man possessed. Everyone tried to control him, even the crack and heroin addicts rushed forward to help. Andy, one of the key workers, secluded him into a corner of the garden, ordering everyone to back away. He sat him down, trying to calm the situation. An ambulance was called. But once the paramedics arrived, Ben took one look at them and lunged back into the crowd. Saahil told him later that he was squinting his eyes, probably sensitive to the bright colours. Ben slipped through grabbing hands and climbed on to the shed in the corner. He headed straight for the barbed wire and razor-sharp spikes without a care in the world. It was as though he was being pursued by a demon.

'It's a fourteen-foot drop,' Andy called, frantically.

Ben didn't care. He was lost for two hours. Neither the paramedics nor any of the support workers could find him. When he returned, he remembered nothing. He was the same old drawling Ben, calm, laidback and thirsty for a cup of tea. Saahil was shook-up. He often thought back to the face of the paramedic who asked Saahil what Ben had taken. Saahil showed her the packet of Mamba, quick to tell her that he'd just purchased the *legal* high from Charlie's Newsagent's down the road. She'd looked down at the packet, then back up at him, completely baffled.

Of course, Ben was it again the very next day. The only thing consoling them all was the fact that they were staying away from hard drugs. Spice was legal, so it couldn't be that bad.

And yet those nightmares were occurring at frighteningly regular intervals. The jinn would visit him, just like it had done on the night before his graduation. Sometimes a pair of hands would tighten around his neck. Other times, it felt like his face was being slapped repeatedly. He would struggle in his sleeping bag and roll over, gasping. He'd look around and see odd, dark, twisted shapes crawling towards him on the floor. What the heck was Saahil doing out here alone, when strange things wandered around at night in deserted places? He mumbled prayers to himself. Sometimes, if they were both lying in a doorway, Saahil would end up kicking Ben.

'Are you fuckin' fighting with yerself again?' Ben asked.

Normally, Saahil would sit up and hug his knees, too scared to respond. He often wondered if Ben was in on the whole thing. Especially if they were under the car-park ramp with ten other people. Maybe they deliberately provoked him as he slept and took pleasure in watching him struggle. *You can't put owt past these nutjobs*, Saahil thought, as he came round from the nightmare.

Tonight, as Saahil tried to catch his breath, he pulled his arm out of the sleeping bag and unzipped it to let air into his lungs. Something had happened today that had left him so agitated. Was it the young woman who had left her tent and gone home with a drug dealer? The same one who supplied to most of the homeless that Saahil knew, often passing them in the street or stopping to have a chat with Ben and Jason. There was something not quite right about him. Saahil had noticed straightaway, particularly the way the dealer looked at him. His eyes would crawl up and down. Saahil would sometimes find him staring at his face. It was almost, dare he say it, perverted. Saahil felt uneasy even thinking about it. And yet he knew that the girl had gone home with him to have sex, as she and others often did, just to have a bed for the night.

Saahil watched her go, no, he'd *let* her go. He couldn't bear to think of the perversions that were being inflicted on her right now. *That* had been the dream. But instead, his own body was paralysed, hands were wrapped around his own neck. He thought he'd seen the man standing over him. Snarling. He was going to attack him. But Saahil couldn't move, he couldn't fight back.

He considered rolling a spliff and once again, be reduced to a zombie-like figure who didn't have to worry about anything but instead, he shuffled up towards Ben, who was also wide awake. Saahil's free hand found Ben's arm.

'Don't leave me on my own, all right?'

Ben grunted in response.

'I said,' Saahil whispered, 'don't leave me on my own.'

'What you on about? Am here.'

Saahil's fingers searched for Ben's hand. Their fingertips touched. Ben didn't move away, but his fingers closed around Saahil's tightly, like he too, was holding on for dear life.

The day centre was the only lifeline available to them for when things got extremely tough. Saahil tried to stay under the radar and always avoided any conversations with the various advisers and outreach officers who hung about the place. There were always plenty of people milling around, so there was no need for anyone to engage with him. Ben received some sort of benefit that was paid to him via a Paypoint card as he didn't have a bank account. He pestered Saahil to speak to Alan, the adviser who was currently trying to get Ben into an ex-offenders hostel. Saahil refused. He didn't want them to snoop around and find out that he had been reported missing over a year ago.

One day, Saahil showered and changed into a new pair of clothes. They had obviously been donated to the centre and stank of cigarette smoke. And they were too baggy, reminding Saahil of how much weight he had lost, his appetite diminishing from the first day he had smoked the legal high. He owned almost nothing from his previous life anymore, except his mother's yellow pashmina. He had taken the habit of wrapping it tightly around his fist every night, almost as if it was endowed with superpowers and would protect him from the dangers of the streets. His fingers would caress the silkiness of the material, almost as though he was holding his mother's hand. Saahil would grip the shawl tightly as he fell into a difficult slumber. Now, like baby Zahra, he couldn't settle without it.

As he returned to where Ben was waiting for him, Alan cornered him.

'Been trying to talk to you,' he said, grabbing Saahil's arm. 'Eh-san, isn't it? You seem to run away every time we make eye contact.'

Saahil denied his comment and laughed it off.

'Shall we have a chat?' Alan suggested, pointing to an empty office.

Reluctantly, Saahil followed him.

'I was homeless at the age of eighteen,' Alan said, as they both took seats. 'I now spend my time helping other people in the same situation.'

Saahil nodded, trying to look interested. Alan was probably in his early thirties now.

'How long have you been homeless?' he asked.

'About a year.'

'What happened?' he said, taking out a notepad and pen.

Saahil shuffled in his seat, 'Erm... well. Just stuff.'

Alan wasn't giving up. His grey eyes bore into Saahil's.

'Family problems,' Saahil offered up meekly.

Alan tried to uncover 'what kind of problem' but Saahil shrugged in response.

'Did you experience any form of abuse?'

'No,' Saahil shot back. Alan raised his eyebrow.

'I don't really wanna talk about it, if you don't mind,' said Saahil.

Alan dropped his voice into a whisper. 'We don't really see that many Asian lads who are homeless. I've only ever come across one other...'

His voice trailed off. Saahil frowned.

'Police had to remove him from his family because they were beating him up,' Alan continued. 'He was gay.'

Saahil rolled his eyes. 'I'm not gay.'

'No, I'm not suggesting—'

'Well, what?'

'If there are any cultural issues we can help—'

'No, thanks,' Saahil replied. He made to stand up but Alan persuaded him to remain seated.

'Okay, okay… in your own time,' he said, and continued to ask a barrage of less intrusive, more technical questions. Saahil withheld as much information as he possibly could.

'So, we can put a referral in for you for a hostel, get you off the streets,' Alan said. 'You'll be put on a waiting list at first, depends what they've got available… probably an eighteen-to-twenty-five-year-old one will be the best option.'

Saahil waited for the catch.

'They'll do some background checks and once it's all through and they've confirmed your eligibility, they'll offer you a place. Do you happen to have any ID on you?'

Saahil blinked stupidly before jumping out of his seat. 'Forget it.'

'What? Why?'

Alan followed Saahil to the door. 'Is there a problem? This is all confidential.'

'No, I just don't need your help, thanks.'

'You'd rather stay on the streets?' Alan asked.

'Yeah, leave me alone.'

Alan tried to touch Saahil's arm. Without thinking Saahil lashed out, pushing him back so he nearly tripped over the chair leg.

'Calm down, mate,' he said, sternly.

Saahil was sweating and his face felt hot. His agitation ceased and he realised what he had just done.

'Sorry,' he said.

'Do you want to sit down?'

Saahil did. Alan gave him a cup of water.

'Well, apart from the regular facilities here they offer some educational courses,' Alan said mechanically, probably deciding it was best to change the subject. 'Things like art classes, computer classes. Would you be interested in joining any?'

Despite feeling guilty for pushing Alan, Saahil sneered in response.

'What's funny? The computer classes are quite popular with people your age.'

'I know how to use a computer, did it every day when I was at uni,' Saahil mumbled.

Alan sat up straight in his seat. 'You were at university?'

'Yeah.'

'Which uni? What did you study?'

Saahil wondered whether he should tell the truth. The last thing he wanted was to spark further interest from Alan. But what the fuck, he did go to uni, he was a graduate. It was the only thing he'd ever achieved.

'Aerospace Engineering.'

Alan's eyes widened, but he composed himself quickly. At that moment, Ben tapped on the door. 'You coming,' he mouthed.

'I'm going now,' Saahil said to Alan.

'Come and see me again tomorrow.'

'Look, mate. I don't give you permission to refer me to a hostel.'

'I won't do anything you don't want me to,' Alan reassured. 'I'll be here all day. Make sure you pop in.'

Saahil avoided the day centre for two weeks. Ben kept telling him that Alan was asking about him. Finally, starvation took over, and Saahil accompanied Ben to the centre for breakfast. Most of it was gora food again. Saahil wrinkled his nose up in disgust at the bacon and sausages and headed for the toast. He took his plate and sat down, avoiding any weirdos. Ben was still filling his plate.

'There you are, Eh-san!'

It was Alan. Saahil made no attempts to hide his dissatisfaction and sighed deeply in Alan's face.

'Wanna have a chat after breakfast?' he said.

'Not really.'

'I'll be in the office.'

After he had eaten, Saahil contemplated running off again, but he decided to see what Alan had to say. After all, he had nothing to lose.

'Look, Eh-san,' Alan said, after they both took their seats. 'Why won't you let me put you in for a referral? Once you've got some accommodation you can start rebuilding your life. We can help with more permanent housing and then start thinking about employment. You have so much potential.'

'I appreciate your help. I really do. But I just don't think there's any point,' said Saahil. He'd planned on what to say. 'I'm thinking of going home soon.'

Alan nodded. 'Okay. Is that what you want, though?'

'Yeah.'

'And you'll be safe?'

'Yes,' Saahil replied, more sternly.

Alan dipped his voice. 'My mate runs a night shelter. Have you stayed in one before?'

'No.'

'Well, I don't shout it from the rooftops because they only have around twenty beds. Nowhere near enough to accommodate everyone. They only take the most vulnerable in. I'll have a word with him. If you get there on time, he'll save you a bed.'

'Okay. What about Ben? And Jason?'

'It's first come first served.'

'We'll all go together.'

'You need this referral letter before you can get in... Don't worry, it's not *that* kind of referral.'

'So they can't come?' Saahil asked again.

'It's best if you go on your own.'

Alan wrote down the details for the shelter. 'Nine o'clock sharp,' he said.

When Saahil arrived at the address the following night, he realised it was a small church. He was ushered in by a short ginger guy with a beard.

'It's Ehsan, right?' he asked.

'Yeah.'

'I'm Lee,' he said. 'I saved you a place. Can't do it every time, doesn't matter who you're mates with.'

'Erm, I didn't ask for—'

'Yeah whatever, put your name down.'

With a pang of regret, Saahil wrote Ehsan's name on the piece of paper, hating himself for smearing his poor friend's name. There were people milling around in the church. The stained-glass windows shone brightly and the lights had been dimmed. It looked like people were being led into a separate room. Lee was rushing around and told him to stay put. He came back with an odd-looking pipe.

'Breath test,' he said, pointing the thing at Saahil's face. Saahil leaned back.

'Nah, mate, I don't drink.'

Lee raised his eyebrow. 'You can't get in without passing it.'

Saahil hesitated. The inside was lovely and warm and he already felt peaceful.

'How many people have put their dirty mouths on that then?' he asked.

'It's sterilised after every use.'

Saahil took the test and was told there was a no drug or alcohol policy once inside. He'd come prepared. They had all smoked so much spice throughout the day that Ben and Jason were out of it by the time Saahil had set off alone for the night shelter. He was told he would get an evening meal, toiletries and breakfast in the morning. They had to leave by eight o'clock the next day.

Lee led him to a room away from the main hall and to a table which was full of people waiting for dinner. Saahil sat down in silence. He felt even more awkward and out of place without Ben and Jason. Some of them stared at him. Others chattered about. At a glance, Saahil saw that most of them were scruffy, toothless and slurring their words. He stared at the floor, his face burning with embarrassment.

He got a vegetarian meal. It was tomato soup, broccoli and cheese pasta and a little polystyrene tub of vanilla ice cream. He was starving and ate it all. He remembered Ammi's cooking. The ghee covered paratha she would make especially for him as he studied for his various exams, GCSEs to his degree, telling him it would make his brain work faster. Occasionally, she'd make a choori recipe, crumbling the parathas and covering them with sugar. She always gave him the first bite with her own hands, because no matter how old he got, he was still her little boy.

After, there was a pool table and some comfortable chairs where people were seated in front of a TV, relaxing. Saahil sat in a corner, alone. A few people tried to speak to him, but he shrugged them off. He didn't feel like talking. He looked around and really asked himself: what was he *doing* here?

Imagine if his mates from uni saw him now? What would they say? Umar had tried to help him, but Saahil hadn't wanted to know. The others had tried too, apart from Kamran. Saahil hadn't received a single text or call from him. There were just the two missed calls that had been recorded on his phone on the night of the attack when Kamran had apparently tried to find out where they'd both disappeared off to. If he saw Saahil now, he'd probably be happy. That's what he always wanted, to be better than Saahil. Well, that's what he got, good for him.

What about Ehsan, though? Is this what he would have wanted? It didn't matter to Saahil anymore. It was best to live this way now. He needed to suffer.

He noticed a young woman running around with bedding and pillows. The bastards were requesting all sorts from her. She was too polite to say no. She nearly tripped over a bit of bedding when Saahil asked if she needed any help.

'No, it's okay,' she said, flushed in the face.

'I can do that,' Saahil replied, taking the bedding from her.

'No, you're not allowed!'

'It'll be right.'

Before long, Saahil found himself helping the volunteers. Some noticed, but didn't say anything. He took away dirty dishes and delivered them to the kitchen and helped to distribute toiletries and bedding. Some volunteers were filling in forms for the guests, one was giving haircuts and shaves. Saahil was approached by a volunteer and was told he should be 'relaxing' and didn't need to help. Saahil brushed him off, saying he'd rather keep busy. Keeping busy made him forget about the last spliff he normally smoked just before going to bed.

At around eleven o'clock, everyone was instructed to get into their beds. Lights were turned out sharp. Saahil blinked in the darkness and smiled to himself, having forgotten the joys of sleeping inside a warm bed. He had a restful sleep and woke in the morning refreshed. Breakfast was served at seven-thirty and everyone was ushered out by eight.

Before he left, Saahil was approached by Lee. 'You were helping out yesterday,' he said. 'You shouldn't have been.'

'Doesn't matter.'

'Every day, we set up in a different church. If you want, you can volunteer again tomorrow, if you enjoyed it? You'll get a bed obviously.'

Saahil considered the proposition. 'Okay,' he said, and after taking down details for the next shelter, went off to meet Ben and Jason.

For the next two weeks, Saahil spent time helping at the night shelters. He wasn't guided out like the rest of the homeless, but stayed and chatted with the volunteers. Most of them were university students who were trying to get something worthwhile to write on their CVs. When Saahil was with them, he almost felt normal again. He avoided Ben and Jason throughout the day. If he saw them, he told them that he was volunteering at the shelters but played down the benefits of his new circumstances, moaning about how much work he had to do in order to get a bed.

There was only one catch. The more time he spent at the night shelters, the less spice he could take. He would smoke plenty throughout the day and topped himself up before arriving, but the no-drug policy meant he couldn't bring any with him onsite, or sneak out behind the building and smoke without fear of being caught. Once inside, Saahil remained functional for a few hours before slowly starting to sweat and itch. Luckily, he could use the showers at the venues and change his clothes with the donations. He'd even puked up a few times in the toilets, a pain spreading up through his stomach, but he hid this from everyone.

On one particularly bad night, Saahil was helping out in the kitchens. They'd done a full rotation and ended up back at the first participating church. He had vomited in the toilets earlier and the heat from the kitchen meant he was sweating like mad. The doors would close soon as the homeless were being checked in. Saahil felt claustrophobic. He'd smoked spice before coming to the shelter but today his body was wreaking havoc on him. He could hear every beat of his heart; it was pleading for him to put an end to the craving. He needed it. Now. He made an excuse to the kitchen staff and told Lee he needed some fresh air.

'Hurry because doors close in ten minutes,' Lee called after him as Saahil slipped out and pelted down the street. He didn't stop until he ended up in the same alleyway where he knew his friends would be squabbling over the shiny packets. Luckily, they were there.

'Oh, look what the cat dragged in,' Jason said.

'Yeah, what have you come now for?' Ben added.

'Shut up,' said Saahil. 'Give us some.'

'No, piss off and get your own.'

'Please, guys.'

'You look like shit,' Ben said. 'And you've been sleeping in a church.'

They both had a good laugh before eventually rolling a spliff up for him.

Saahil grabbed it out of Jason's hands. His own were shaking, he couldn't take a drag quick enough. He must have managed around two, because at that moment, the pavement seemed to jump up. It was inches away from his head, because Saahil had fallen back. He never heard Ben screaming or Jason swearing as his body jerked violently. Eyes rolling to the back of his head. The blood vessels bursting in his face.

Thirty

'Mind if I have a smoke?' said Saahil, standing up.

The question threw Zahra off-guard. Up until then, her focus had been so sharp she'd barely blinked.

'What do you mean, the blood vessels burst in your face?' she gasped in horror.

'Oh, it was no biggie,' he replied.

Zahra's attention turned to the lower part of Saahil's face. 'Is that why you have a beard now? To hide them?'

'No, no, they healed pretty quickly after it happened,' said Saahil, plucking a cigarette from the packet. 'It's all good.'

'No, it's not good at all. And you shouldn't be smoking now. Haven't you learned your lesson?'

'This is just tobacco.'

'I don't care what it is!'

Saahil motioned to the kitchen. 'Just have a break, make another cuppa,' he said. 'It's going to get worse before it gets better.'

He hurried out of the door before Zahra could ask him what he meant. His absence from the room gave her a chance to sigh deeply and make sense of the information dump she was receiving. Zahra knew vaguely about soup kitchens and support workers and sleeping bags and spliffs. Little did she know that her own flesh and blood had been dependent on such things for nearly two years. She tried to think of what she was doing at the same time that Saahil was fitting somewhere on a dirty street.

Around the two-year mark of Saahil's disappearance, Ammi had taken to seeking help from spiritual guides. Abbu was unconvinced at first, having already performed a pilgrimage to Mecca to pray for Saahil's return, but soon, he too gave in. Abbu followed all instructions faithfully, he wore every blessed amulet that they gave him and donated money to charity before deciding to go to Pakistan to visit as many religious shrines as he could, desperate that in one way or the other, God would accept his prayer. It was a spontaneous trip and an unsuspecting Uncle Ken had turned up on the day after his departure.

'He's gone where?' he asked Ammi and Zahra.

'Pakistan.'

'Yes, but why?'

'To do… praying,' Ammi said in English, the palms of her hands placed together.

'What's the difference with which side of the ocean you do the praying on?' Ken asked before turning to Zahra, who was only thirteen at the time, for more information.

'It's something to do with praying at holy shrines where Sufi saints and other spiritual figures are buried.'

'So it's basically praying at a cemetery?'

'Well, no, they're mausoleums,' Zahra said, relaying stuff she'd heard about in the run-up to Abbu's trip. 'If you pray at the shrine of a saint you follow, then some people believe your prayers will be answered.'

'Don't get me wrong,' Ken said, 'but what help is Amjad going to get from a bunch of holy dead guys?'

'Well, he might visit a Pir and see if they can—'

'Hold on, hold on,' Ken said, spilling tea down his front in excitement. 'What's a "Pir"?'

Zahra consulted Ammi, who went off on a long, faith-fuelled tangent that Zahra didn't think she would be able to translate. She kept it short and sweet.

'It's like a spiritual guide who claims to have a special connection with Allah.'

'Oh yeah,' Ken said, with a smirk. 'Take a nice fee, do they, to do God's work?' He made a gesture with his hands signifying money.

Ammi realised and shouted, 'No, no.' She spoke quick Punjabi, and then jabbed her finger at Zahra to translate.

'Erm, the real ones don't take money. And if they do, they use it for like charity or whatever.'

'Charity, eh?' Ken replied, thoroughly enjoying the conversation. 'And what sort of "guiding" do these Pir do? Can they tell the future?'

Once again, Ammi offered a few robust sentences for translation.

'Absolutely not,' Zahra replied, trying to match her grandmother's indignant tone. 'Nobody can tell the future or claim to have psychic abilities. That's *shirk*!'

'It's a bloody what?'

'Shirk. It's when you associate something else with Allah, like an idol or something. Only Allah has knowledge of the future, not people.'

Ken slurped from his mug. 'Don't sound like much help then, do they?'

Zahra looked to Ammi before replying. 'If you tell them your problem then I think they can offer advice on which verses of the Quran to recite, give you a taweez—'

'"Taweez"?'

'Amulet.'

'Amjad and his bloody amulets,' Ken muttered.

'Oh and of course,' Zahra continued, 'they'll also pray *for* you.'

'Sounds like awful lot of praying.'

'Well, duh,' Zahra said. 'That's kind of like the idea.'

'And God will listen to them, eh? Because they have a special connection?'

Ammi nodded forcefully and with conviction. Zahra offered a weak smile. Ken laughed a full deep-throated laugh. 'Gosh, I hope you don't mind me saying this, but you lot are bonkers!' He caught his breath before adding, 'I love it.'

The memory made Zahra smile to herself. Saahil was back in the room.

'What's funny?' he asked. 'You got another story for me?'

'No way,' she replied, motioning for him to sit down. 'The only person telling stories today is you, Saahil.'

He discharged himself from hospital as soon as he felt well enough to do so. The doctors didn't know why he had reacted so badly to the synthetic drug. Saahil was pretty pissed off too, thinking the spliff had been legal and therefore safe. All they told him was that he'd had a violent seizure and was lucky to be alive. Ben and Jason had rushed to find help as he lay fitting on the floor. He hadn't seen them since, but knew it wasn't a good idea for them to come and visit him in hospital. Saahil didn't respond to any of the questions the doctors asked; he was too terrified they would start making further enquiries and contact some sort of authority to find out more information about him.

They referred to him as Ehsan. Inadvertently, Saahil had put his best friend back in hospital.

Saahil hated hospitals. He hated the way the curtains were drawn around him, apparently for his own privacy. To Saahil, it felt more like a warning to other people that something dead and decomposing was in there and not to enter. The whole experience had brought back the memory of Alisha waiting outside the hospital. The way he had turned his back on her without acknowledgement. As Saahil lay in hospital now, two years later, Alisha's face haunted him. He could have dealt with it better. He could have approached her, asked her if she was okay. The thoughts made him restless. He needed to get out of there as soon as possible.

When the nurses left, Saahil got dressed and pulled out his venflon, like they did in films, and scarpered out of there. He knew where to head and set off towards a mosque that was located just outside the centre of town. Saahil had avoided mosques for two years. Any place populated by Asians had been a no-go area. Now he knew this had to change. He had to ask Allah for forgiveness and turn his life around, to stop living like a junkie on the streets. Saahil knew that if he went back towards the city centre, the first thing he would do was smoke spice. Knowing that it had nearly stopped his heart made him adamant that he would go nowhere near it again. But it was easier said than done and as Saahil scurried towards the mosque, his body was telling him to find Ben and smoke.

He spotted a newsagent's in the distance and stopped. He walked towards it and realised that the door was open. Saahil craned his neck to take a better look inside. Sure enough, packets of spice were lined up behind the till. The store owner saw him and stood up, frowning. Saahil contemplated going inside, but his feet dragged him away. He crossed the road and saw that the mosque door was open. Saahil ventured into the ablution area to wash himself. Then he realised his clothes were filthy. He asked a young lad who worked there if he could borrow something to change into as he prayed. The boy gave Saahil a floor-length abaya. As Saahil changed into the clothes, a shiny packet fell on to the floor. He stared at it. Some of the contents had spilled out and Saahil quickly swept it up. There was a knock on the door and Saahil shoved it back into his pocket, despite there being a bin in the room. Along with his shoes, he stuffed his belongings into a rack.

Saahil was determined to look the part. He splashed water over his face, again and again, slicked his hair back, and gargled, conscious that others would notice his smell. As he washed, he realised he hadn't read a single namaz in over two years. The streets were hardly the most appropriate place to roll out a mat and start praying. He would have freaked everyone out. He hadn't been able wash himself regularly throughout the day or obtain genuinely clean clothes either. The washing line in the camp under the car park was disgusting. It was all excuses because even soldiers on a battlefield found the time to pray two rakats. Namaz could be offered anywhere, in a palace or on the side of the road. If you were paralysed, it could even be performed lying down, for God's sake.

When he finally entered the main prayer area, he looked up. His heart warmed as he saw the gold Arabic script patterned into the mosaicked walls, the circular pillars and the domed ceiling. The stained-glass windows reminded him of the night shelter in the church. It was the same feeling. The light that shone through was otherworldly. Saahil was surprised to see so many people there. He almost expected his Abbu to be a part of the crowd. Looking down at the floor, he made his way and found a secluded spot.

He picked up some prayer beads and began reciting, 'Bismillah… bismillah… bismillah.' Saahil uttered the words as he passed each bead through his fingers. Closing his eyes and savouring the act, he could almost feel the warmth spreading through him. That was until he overheard a father and his teenage son sitting nearby.

'How long until fast opens?' the kid groaned. 'I'm starving.'

Saahil wheeled around. The father noticed and looked back at him as though he had wanted to ask a question.

'Six-forty,' he called over to Saahil, motioning to his watch.

Saahil smiled and nodded, sheepishly. So it was Ramadan. And he didn't even know. There was a calendar pinned up further down the wall. It was the same type that was given out by mosques every year. It would state all the fast opening and closing times. He wandered over and checked, realising they were halfway through the holy month. He sat back down, hating himself. Since Saahil had started observing Ramadan as a teenager, he had never missed a single fast. Everybody in the mosque was now fasting, apart from him.

He shuffled back to his spot, trying to concentrate on the prayer beads, but his mind could not escape the guilt. A few moments later, and Saahil's left leg began shaking badly. He leaned his elbow on it, but the beads rattled. He realised he was moving through them, bead by bead, but forgetting the words he was reciting. His face flushed hot. He undid his top button. His neck felt wet.

Soon, Saahil's fidgeting was attracting attention. The father and son frowned at him.

'Are you all right?' he called over again.

Saahil nodded and hastily made his way out of the mosque, grabbing his belongings on the way. As he strode down the street, his hand found the gram of spice frantically. There was enough left for one smoke. He found a nearby park and almost staggered over to a deserted children's play area. One of the two swings was broken. The bottom of the slide was filled with a puddle of green water. Saahil sat on the bench and quickly rolled up. He glanced around in case one of the mosque-goers spotted a man in an abaya and mosque hat, a man who should have been fasting, smoking in the park.

The relief spread quickly through his body. The same numbing of emotions, the dulling of senses. With each drag, the elements stopped affecting him. The raindrops that fell from the sky, the ice-cold, biting wind. Yet Saahil would rather have been out here, smoking on a freezing park bench that was decorated with expletives, than inside the warmth and comfort of the place of worship.

He let his body go limp and placed his head on the decaying wooden bench, closing his eyes. Before his mind went completely blank, Saahil wondered how he would fast tomorrow.

To an outsider, Saahil was just another young Muslim throwing himself into prayer over Ramadan. He wasn't too friendly with people, but offered a helping hand for any available jobs, knowing that the rewards were plentiful. Saahil remembered a story that

Uncle Harun had told him about an Egyptian millionaire who would spend one month out of the year sweeping the floors in Mecca and Medina. And so Saahil observed I'tikaf during the last ten days of Ramadan, which were the holiest. He spent day and night immersed in prayer, not eating, drinking or talking and sleeping in the mosque. I'tikaf, they told him, was equivalent to the reward of performing one Hajj. The mosque provided the meal at dawn, and iftari food at night. For once, Saahil didn't feel like a charity case. The young lad who brought him food every night called him 'bhai' and nodded towards him with respect. Every day that passed, he felt his dignity being pieced back together.

During the holy month, Saahil watched people swan in and out of the mosque. Friends stood, chatting together in groups. Kids ran around at the end of each congregation. Fathers shouted for their sons to hurry up and drive them home. Everyone was so busy, nobody noticed the skeletal young man crying quietly to himself in the corner. To an outsider, he was just another one of them. But they didn't notice him scurry out for breaks every two hours, down the street, throwing worrying glances behind his back as he made his way through the park and on to the same expletive-laden bench.

Saahil never thought that in his lifetime, he would break a fast. Not only had he done this *intentionally*, one of the worst sins he could commit in Ramadan, but he had broken it with something haram: drugs. It killed Saahil, knowing what he was doing. But things had gone wrong almost immediately after his first attempt at fasting, the day after he'd realised it was Ramadan. By late afternoon, his body was screaming. His stomach was tightening up in knots, crippling him from inside. His whole body was sweating. Saahil had no home, no space he could lock himself up in and fully withdraw from his addiction. He found an empty room in the mosque and fell on the floor, thinking he was dying. He heard footsteps and a burst of energy saw him pelt out of the mosque again and back into the deserted park.

He fought with his mind, every cell of his being, as his fingers rolled up a spliff, but his body was working against him. Hands shaking, eyes watering and Saahil brought it to his mouth. After it was done, he had kicked the various objects in the playground with frustration, bruising his knuckles as he vented his anger. He had promised himself that he wouldn't step foot in the mosque again. He wasn't worthy.

Making his way into the city centre, Saahil scoured the streets for Ben and Jason. A couple of hours later, he found them sitting outside Marks and Spencer. Their eyes widened when they saw him.

'What the fuck!' Ben sniggered, taking into account the mosque hat and ankle-length abaya. 'What happened to you?'

Saahil said nothing and sat next to them, disgusted with himself. He'd stayed there all day until night fell, when he realised that he hadn't eaten all day. He couldn't accompany Ben to the soup kitchen, knowing his attire would attract attention. The problem was, he didn't look so homeless anymore. Iftari time drew nearer and Saahil could only imagine the food that would be served when the fast opened. He hadn't eaten roti for two years. Shamelessly, he ventured back to the mosque. Removed his shoes and took his place in the far corner away from others.

That was when the façade began. He didn't know what was worse: intentionally breaking a fast or pretending he was keeping them just so he had food and shelter. He was duping them all into thinking he was a pious young man, immersing himself in prayer and, when he could be bothered, helping out as best he could. He had to make up for his sins somehow.

Tomorrow was Eid. They had one tarawih namaz to go – a mammoth prayer that was offered in the late evenings. It would start in around fifteen minutes. Tomorrow, Saahil would wake up with relief. He would gladly wave the holy month goodbye, be grateful to see the back of it. He sat shivering on the same park bench, concealed by the sunset. He had already eaten with the others after opening his final 'fast'.

Saahil could barely feel his fingers as he rolled the joint. He exhaled, the smoke dwindling before him, knowing that he could not sink any lower.

Once Ramadan ended, things grew quieter. Saahil, however, stayed. He still prayed all five namaz, and in between, recited the Quran in a secluded corner. That was when the imams started to notice him. They asked him questions, the one thing that Saahil dreaded. He told them he was in between jobs and his family were in Pakistan. They were delighted that such a young, handsome boy had turned to Islam in his youth. His face flushed red when the imams praised how noble he was for spending all his spare time in worship. They complained about other boys his age.

'All they care about is cars, girls and weed.'

Saahil smiled along and nodded. *Little do you know*, he thought.

The imam who was in charge of the mosque was an elderly bloke from Pakistan. Saahil loved listening to stories about the Prophet's life. He liked the way everyone smiled, how serene they became, determined to become better people. Sometimes, however, the language barrier was a problem. Not because Saahil couldn't speak or understand Urdu. The imam was old, and actually from Pakistan; his Urdu was on a higher level than Saahil's. Saahil remembered him and Ehsan were always asking Abbu to clarify what was being said. Sometimes, even Abbu needed help and would ask Uncle Harun.

There was one other thing that was similar between the new imam and the ones in his hometown. They just never seemed to engage with what was going on in the real world. Once, Saahil had walked out after Jummah and seen a group of teenagers huddled together, complaining.

'Just because you're not going to address it doesn't mean it ain't happening.'

'They think it'll blow over.'

'These old guys don't know how to deal with it.'

'Yeah, they're past it.'

Saahil was on the streets when 7/7 had occurred. He remembered reading the headlines on A-boards placed outside newsagents. He'd even sneaked into a couple of shops and watched the news on TV displays before being escorted out. Saahil dreaded to think how the mosques had dealt with it at the time. Months later, and the imams continued to dig a big hole and bury their heads into it.

'Very bad, it is not Islam,' the imam said, making a small reference to the incident during his Friday sermon. Saahil perked up, so did the rest of the young lads. He was eager for more, but nothing came. *Could have at least elaborated*, he thought bitterly, but assumed they had done when the tragedy had first occurred.

On one occasion, the mosque had acquired a microphone for a question and answer session. Though to Saahil, it seemed the staff were more excited to have the new kit than the actual Q & A itself. After a few consultations on how to work out 2.5 per cent of savings which Muslims were obliged to donate to charity during Ramadan, a young guy mentioned the word 'Iraq'. The imam shuffled and waffled his way through. Another man raised his hand and the mic was passed to him. He was dressed in a smart suit, clean-shaven and wearing glasses. He turned out to be a particularly lively fellow and stated he lived mostly in the Middle East. His voice grew higher and higher.

'You can't go to a region and destroy country after country and expect to live in peace and harmony here. *Why should you!*'

Some lads nodded vigorously, they were sitting upright, eyes alight, probably glad for some action. The imam glanced around for the mic boy who stood timidly in the corner. A few middle-aged men whispered to each other. Others grinned. The man's 'question' had descended into a full-on rant. He turned to face the congregation.

'I was there! I was there during the riots when those whites came around and attacked our homes and businesses. We were just protecting ourselves and yet I got jail time just for throwing a rock.'

Saahil leaned forward, but quickly realised they weren't *his* riots, the ones that had occurred when he had been nineteen. The ranting man, it transpired, was talking about Oldham. Saahil didn't know much about what had happened there. But he could see the imam waving his arms around and signalling for the microphone to be taken from the man.

'Me and Britannia, we go back a long way. They go on about this "Asian invasion" in the Fifties. Bugger off, I've been here for hundreds of years!'

The young members of the congregation cheered. The older

ones raised their eyebrows, unimpressed. A staff member at the mosque took hold of the mic and whispered into the man's ear. 'That's enough now, Uncle,' Saahil saw him say in Urdu. The microphone was put back into the box and not given to the audience again.

One day, Saahil was still wandering around the city centre and running late for Friday prayers. He saw men wearing mosque hats and salwar kameez heading in the same direction so followed them. They entered a tiny building that had a blank room with prayer rugs to accommodate only fifty people. It was small and claustrophobic and Saahil felt uneasy. He preferred to get lost in a massive congregation, where no one would notice him itching for a spliff every couple of hours. He was about to walk out when a scrawny-looking imam in his early thirties strolled past, speaking in a posh London accent. Out of curiosity, Saahil stayed.

After Jummah, everyone sat around with cups of tea and shushed as the young imam sat down on the stage. He spoke in English and addressed the whole congregation, who, Saahil noticed, all seemed to be below the age of forty. The imam said the talk would be about the 'youth' pronounced 'yoof'.

'Multi-million-pound mosques here in the UK, in Manchester, Leeds, Bradford. Tiles ordered from Turkey, prayer rugs from Dubai... how many of them spend even a pound on the youth? What do they do to engage the youth? Do they listen to them? Do they address the issues that are relevant to young people today? Do they spend time with them?'

Saahil thought back to the group of teenagers complaining about this very thing the other day. The imam continued:

'Some of these old mullahs, all they can say is, "the media, the media, the media." Well, sorry, but we need to get our own house in order because it's a bloody mess.'

Saahil leaned forward, captivated.

'It's a shame,' the imam continued. 'But our community isn't very good at nurturing our kids' emotional wellbeing. We don't pay much attention to mental health. They'll get you the latest mobile, or Xbox, but how many dads here take time to talk to their sons about things that matter to them, or do you just tell them what they can and can't do?

'Now I have three daughters, Masha'Allah. I worry about this toxic patriarchal society we live in. My girls are children yet, but I already worry about the limitations placed on them just because they're female. The fathers in this audience who have sons, you don't have to worry about that, everything is loaded in their favour. But those boys will go on to marry, to have children.'

The imam suddenly pointed to a lad in his mid-twenties.

'You. Would you marry a woman fifteen years older than you?'

The lad looked nervous as though he'd just been asked a difficult Maths question.

'Be honest!'

'Er... probably not.'

'Would you marry a woman more successful than you?'

Without waiting for an answer, he pointed to another audience member.

'Would you marry a wealthier woman?'

The young guy who had been asked the question looked terrified but quickly replied, 'Yeah.'

'What if,' the imam said, with a glint in his eye, 'what if she proposed marriage to you?'

Everybody shuffled around, not knowing how to respond. Saahil was glad he was seated at the back.

'That is exactly what Prophet Muhammad, peace be upon him, did. You all know this. You all know that Khadijah, the love of his life, was his employer. She was wealthy, fifteen years his senior and she approached him regarding marriage. You all know this, right?'

Everyone nodded, looking ashamed. One lad put up his hand.

'It's not just guys,' he said. 'Girls have so many demands too these days. They want Prince Charming who will spend loads of money on them.'

Several guys nodded enthusiastically. The imam lifted his hand to silence them.

'We need to go back to our roots,' he said. 'And it starts with our youth. Fathers, talk to your sons about what's affecting them. They won't say it, but they want you to talk frankly with them; I know, I've been doing youth work for years. We don't need to have the same petty theological debates over and over again. We know your salwar must be pulled up above your ankles to avoid it getting wet for namaz time. And let's not get started on the moon wars during Ramadan.'

Everyone laughed.

'What is affecting your kids right now? Talk to them about drugs, gangs, violence. Talk to them about gender. About love and relationships. Don't shy away from hard-hitting issues. Teach them what is acceptable and what isn't. Tackle domestic violence, rape, honour killings. Talk to them about sex!'

Saahil's eyes widened. He'd never heard an imam say the word 'sex' before. The rest of the congregation seemed pretty relaxed, however. They appeared to be used to it. The imam offered to stay behind at the end in case anybody wanted to discuss anything. Once things were wrapped up, the younger guys flocked to him. They ranged from late teenagers to guys in their early twenties. Saahil left the mosque in disbelief.

The following Jummah, Saahil only attended his usual mosque for two reasons: to carry out the small jobs they had assigned to him since Ramadan ended, such as cleaning and fixing things, and, to find the same disenfranchised kids who were hanging outside in their usual spot, waiting for their fathers to stop chatting. Saahil told them about the tiny mosque that seemed to be offering what they were looking for.

A week later, and he saw the same kids peeking their heads around the door of the small prayer room. They huddled together waiting for the congregation to begin. He felt a rush of affection for them. Zahra's face swam into his mind. He wondered if she was okay.

After asking around, Saahil managed to get into a shared house. The mosque had promoted him and he was now in charge of the car park, directing people to vacant spots during busy periods. It was a great job as far as Saahil was concerned; he only worked for a couple of hours during Jummah time or if there was a funeral. There was plenty of time in between to sneak off and have a spliff whenever he felt like it. He'd also started smoking tobacco, thinking it was a way to start slowly cutting down on the spice. He'd managed to drop a couple of spliffs a day, but was replacing them with cigs. It probably wasn't helping much, replacing one devil for another, but still, it was better than nothing. The mosque had been paying him, cash in hand. It was hardly enough to live on, but enough to afford accommodation in a house that was full of immigrants. There were seven of them in total. Saahil spent as much as time as possible out of there and only saw it as a place that kept him off the streets at night.

A couple of times a week, Saahil would venture out to the free langar meal that was served inside the Sikh temple. He would cover his head, and sit on the floor in line with the rest of the temple-goers. Increasingly he saw people who weren't Sikh inside the temple. They were obviously homeless. It unsettled him a little, as he didn't want to be recognised. He thought of Ben and Jason and a pang of regret followed. His meetings with them had decreased considerably. When Saahil had ventured out to town the last time, he found Jason sitting alone in one of their doorways. He'd informed Saahil that Ben had been given a place in a hostel.

'Right, when can I see him?' Saahil asked.

Jason sneered. 'He doesn't want anything to do with us anymore.'

'What? Why?'

'Trying to kick the habit,' he replied. 'Can't do that when you're hanging around the same people and doing the same shit day in, day out.'

'Yeah… but—'

'But what? Lad wants a new start. He's got on to some course, as well. Food catering or something.'

Saahil leaned up against the wall, mixed with emotions. He was happy for Ben, but also slightly envious that out of the three of them, *he* had been the one to actually take control of his life. There was also a deep sadness that Saahil wouldn't see him again. After all, Ben was the one who had taught Saahil how to be homeless.

'Will you be all right then?' he asked Jason. Jason nodded, looking in the other direction, signalling to Saahil that he wasn't too bothered about being in his company. When Saahil walked away, he knew he would probably never see Jason again.

After leaving the Gurdwara, Saahil walked past a number of parked cars when he heard someone shouting in Punjabi.

'Oi! Son! Come here.'

Saahil was surprised to see a middle-aged Sikh gentleman frantically motioning him over.

'Come here, come here,' he repeated.

Reluctantly, Saahil walked over.

'Son, my car won't start, do you have a phone?' asked the man.

'No, sorry,' replied Saahil. He hadn't had a mobile phone since he first went missing.

Saahil watched as the man jabbered away animatedly, mixing his Punjabi and English. He was a short man with a long grey beard and an orange turban. He also swore a lot. Saahil laughed.

'Why you laughing?'

'Sorry, let me try and help you.'

An hour later, a group of them were pushing the car down the road. Saahil had taken a good shot at it, enjoying the attention as he opened the bonnet and fiddled around with the engine. Temple-goers hung around. Crocodile clips were on their way. Mobile phones were passed around. The man, whose name was Mohan, kept ringing his relatives who were either at work or college or school.

'Uncle, just ring the AA,' a man said.

'No,' Mohan mumbled. 'Goray charge too much money. Get an apna.'

Two hours later, and only Saahil remained with Mohan as

the car was jerked to life by none other than a gora breakdown company. Mohan reluctantly handed over the cash, swearing in Punjabi as he did it. Saahil found him funny. He reminded him of Ammi.

Mohan thanked him. Saahil bade him goodbye and made to walk away.

'Where you going?' the man asked.

'Er... home.'

'Where you live?' he now asked in English. 'I drop you off.'

'No, it's okay, Uncle, I'll walk,' Saahil replied. He hated that street.

'No, no, I insist. In fact, come my house, we'll have chai.'

Despite Saahil's protestations, Mohan yanked him into the car and was driving him home.

'What your name?' he said.

'Saahil.'

Mohan frowned. 'Oh... Muslim?'

'Yeah.'

'What you doing at Gurdwara?'

'Helping out with the langar,' he lied.

Mohan looked impressed. 'You work?' he asked.

'No, looking for a job.'

'Really?'

Saahil nodded and watched as Mohan descended into deep thought.

'Where you live?' he asked again.

Saahil told him. They pulled up outside a building that looked like a Sixties concrete office block. Saahil wondered where they were. It didn't look like a house.

'Come, come,' Mohan said, motioning him inside. They

walked up some stairs and in through a door. Saahil was shocked to find a fully fledged gym.

'Oi!' Mohan shouted. A young Sikh who had been lounging on a computer chair with his mobile phone swivelled around. 'You said you were at college, bhenchod! Go and make tea,' Mohan snapped.

The lad jumped up and ran off into another room. Saahil sat down on a chair by the reception. The gym was filled with young guys lifting weights and running on treadmills whilst bhangra music blared to keep them motivated. Joy unleashed inside Saahil's body at the sound. He could almost feel his shoulders moving. Saahil wondered why, within thirty seconds of entering the room, he felt so at home.

Thirty-One

'I can't believe you intentionally broke a fast.' Zahra spoke slowly, her mind still trying to register the shock. 'And then you pretended you were fasting just so you could eat at iftari.'

She was surprised that Saahil had been so honest, but part of her wished he'd left that bit of information out of the conversation.

'What *happened* to you, Saahil?' she asked, looking directly at her brother. He was staring ahead, arms folded, his face emotionless. Zahra recognised that look. It was the look of someone who had gone so far ahead in a situation that they now had zero fucks left to give. Not that Saahil was remorseless. She was sure he wasn't. But he'd transgressed every boundary, every rule, every limit set in place during their childhood, that he'd almost become desensitised to all his wrongdoing. Zahra waited for an answer and Saahil eventually shrugged.

'Just another thing to add to my list of shame,' he croaked.

'What happened to those two lads?' Zahra asked, sensing a change of subject was essential. 'Did they get somewhere to live?'

'I don't know,' Saahil replied. 'I never saw them again.'

They were quiet for a while before Saahil spoke next.

'I've talked a lot now. Tell me about Ammi… and Abbu. I want to know properly.'

Zahra stood up and walked to the window. If he wanted to know for real about the state of the family, then so be it.

'I think around the same time as you were out of it on spice, Abbu was becoming more and more dependent on sleeping pills.'

'Sleeping pills?'

'Oh yeah, I forgot to mention,' she replied, unable to keep the resentment out of her voice. 'Once you disappeared, Abbu stopped sleeping.'

Saahil seemed to slump into himself once more. *What did you think,* Zahra wanted to shout at him, *that the answers were going to be easy?*

'It started off when he was out looking for you, he'd be out all night. After Ammi managed to talk some sense into him, he stopped, but the routine of sleep didn't come back so easily. In fact, it's never come back at all.'

'So he's an insomniac?' Saahil managed to utter.

Zahra nodded. 'He's been like that for ten years. Has tried everything. Sleeping pills, CBT, herbal remedies, homeopathic treatments. Nothing works.'

'How many hours does he get in a night?'

Zahra laughed bitterly. 'On a good night? Maybe four to five hours. On a bad night, he's wide awake all night. He can go forty-eight hours with no sleep, and still struggle to fall asleep on the third day.'

Saahil closed his eyes and covered his face. Zahra almost enjoyed watching him appear so guilty. The sky had darkened slightly and there was a chill in the room. It was getting late and she wanted this to be over with. She turned to face her brother.

'We don't have that much time,' she said. 'Carry on with your story.'

'We can finish off lat—'

'No.'

Saahil started off as a cleaner. He vacuumed the gym floor and wiped down treadmills after other guys his age had finished using them. They'd ignore him, but Saahil would pointedly speak to them. Some of them would fail to hide the surprise in their eyes and Saahil knew they had believed him to be a mangy, an imported spouse, fresh from Pakistan, who had probably married his cousin to get a green card and was now wiping off sweat from cross-trainers to make a living. Well, he fucking wasn't, all right? *And* he had been to uni and studied Aerospace Engineering. He was probably more educated than the whole bastard room put together.

Still, Saahil couldn't complain. Not when he thought back to the hell he had come from. He still shrank with embarrassment when he remembered begging on the street, the disgusting places he lay down and slept in, the food banks and the charity clothes he let near his body. Things had changed in the past year. Now Saahil had a home. A spare room in the back of the gym that transformed from storage space to Saahil's bedroom/living quarters. He had a job, three hours a day of cleaning. It was doable. He could be normal, stable, for three hours before retreating to his bedroom and lighting up. Switching between tobacco and spice, mixing the two together. Getting off his head all evening. No one suspected anything. Nobody checked on him once he was holed up in the room. Saahil was careful to always show up on time for his shifts. Careful to be presentable. He washed regularly, scrubbing until he was red raw. The first thing he purchased with his small wage was nail clippers. Saahil had always hated the sight of his nails when he was sleeping rough, long like women's, except for the dirt that collected underneath them. He changed his clothes often. Sometimes he'd venture out into town. Spend an evening in the mosque. But always, Saahil had a bed to go to at night. As far as he was concerned, he'd hit the jackpot.

He'd lied his way into Mohan Chacha's heart from their first meeting. Saahil asked if there was any way he could help out at the gym and if he knew of anyone looking for a lodger. Mohan frowned.

'Family?' he'd asked.

'Pakistan,' Saahil replied, figuring the best way to put an end to any questions about family would be to kick them out of the fucking country.

Mohan raised an eyebrow. 'Doing what in Pakistan?'

'Er, business.'

'What type of business?'

'I don't know really,' Saahil replied, looking flustered.

'No siblings?'

'No,' said Saahil, dying a little inside.

'Ah, so both parents there and you—'

'Just my dad,' Saahil interrupted. 'My mum passed away when I was ten.'

Mohan seemed to soften, and instantly offered him some extra jobs to do around the gym. Saahil was paid cash in hand. There was never a fixed amount at first, just whatever notes Mohan had in his wallet at the time. Once Saahil became more confident, he'd ask for more. Mohan would curse him affectionately and hand over a few more notes.

There was no need for Mohan to be so kind. Or to take in a stray from the streets. He already had his family: a wife, two children and a large extended family. Saahil spent most of his time with Amar. He was the youngest child and still just a teenager when Saahil met him. He was a skinny Sikh with a tiny face and a patka-style turban that was commonly worn by the younger boys. It tied up like a knot on Amar's head. Saahil had taken to him straightaway and willingly spent time with him after he'd finished his cleaning shift. He even promised to help Amar with tuition and assist him with his Science and Maths coursework. Guilt bore into Saahil on some of these occasions and Zahra's face would swim into his mind. Over the years, he had always documented how old she'd be. And now Amar's presence would continue to make sure of that.

Mohan had a daughter too. At first, she walked past Saahil indifferently. That was until one day when he answered the phone at the reception and dealt with a client query. That's when she noticed him and smiled flirtatiously. Pencil skirt, handbag swinging, business-like, the type of woman Saahil had imagined himself being with in the future.

Unfortunately, Mohan Chacha had noticed the furtive smiles that the pair of them exchanged on a regular basis. Not long after, he'd taken Saahil to one side.

'It's a shame,' Mohan said, watching him sadly. 'I mean, if you weren't a cleaner… *And* you're not Sikh.'

Saahil opened his mouth to say they had only smiled at each other but Mohan's face darkened and he'd leaned closer.

'Unless you want your head separating from your shoulders, then I suggest you do what your Quran tells you and *lower your gaze.*'

Saahil didn't need telling twice. He wasn't there to cause trouble. Next time Mohan's daughter came around, Saahil turned his back on her.

He realised that despite the family giving him a home, a job and a sense of belonging, despite the small things they did for him to show they cared, like helping him celebrate Eid so he wouldn't be alone, giving him Friday afternoons off so he could go to the mosque, he would never really be one of them.

And that was a fresh symptom of his new-found stability. When Saahil had been on the streets, it was difficult to worry so much about home. Survival had been his instinct. Now he was more stable than he had been in years, he could not escape from what he'd done. Nights were the worst. And that's when the ritual would begin again. He yearned for the removal of emotional feelings and attachments, and spice could give him that. At times, he'd wake up with night sweats, or the sight of something scuttling across the floor towards him. He'd scream out but no one would hear him. Often, he felt desperately alone. He could rent a room with one of Mohan Chacha's friends but he purposely didn't. Saahil needed to be around people. He needed to be woken up by Mohan tapping on his door in the early mornings. He needed the evenings where the men of the family would sit and drink alcohol in true Sikh style and laugh and joke late into the night. He knew this because when Saahil was left to sleep alone in the makeshift bedroom behind the gym, thoughts got darker. Suicide always danced around in his brain, and for a brief moment, he would really consider it. It was problematic, though, what with being a Muslim and the sanctity of life and all that. He feared God's wrath and didn't want to swap one hell for another.

That was only part of the problem. Really, he just didn't have the guts. He was scared. Scared it would hurt, scared it might go wrong and he'd injure himself and not die. Like Ehsan.

His fear embarrassed him.

There were other times when he felt the desperate need to be touched by another human, to feel the warmth of a body next to him. Sometimes, he'd find himself in a stranger's bed. He would escape the following morning and try to remember the face of the woman he had spent the night with. Most times, he didn't even ask their names, but there was one girl he remembered vividly. Saahil hoped he'd bump into her again. He'd gone to a club and she had fluttered over. Big afro, skin just a shade darker than his, heavily kohled eyes and full lips. She had been wearing the tightest dress with a tiny waist and gigantic bum. It looked like she'd just stepped out of a rap video. Saahil was surprised when she hadn't recoiled at the sight of him. He was still getting used to that. She'd flirted with him. Saahil had tried to shrug her off, but hadn't been able to resist.

Most of the time he didn't get so lucky. Most of the time, it was just him alone in a room with nothing but a couple of rolled-up joints. The only thing he treasured amongst his possessions was his mother's shawl. He still slept with it wrapped tightly around his left palm, like an amateur boxer wrapping his hands, ready for a battle. Sleep *was* a battle. When the lights went out, Saahil felt like he was buried alive. Trapped in a dark box, cold, alone, but still conscious. Very much conscious, unable to see anything, unable to move, unable to stretch out and reach out for something… someone. It could all have been solved in such a simple way. But Saahil had stopped plotting ways to return home a long time ago.

When Saahil woke up, he was covered in blood. His forearms were slashed, a knife lying a couple of metres away. He tried to stand but his knees buckled. Saahil panicked, thinking he'd been attacked. The Sikhs had burst into the room at night. They'd tried to kill him because he was a Muslim. They'd been plotting this from the beginning. Mohan Chacha had been the ringleader. He'd convinced the rest of the family, even Amar, to kill. There'd been a commotion, Saahil had probably tried to fight back, but he couldn't take on all of them by himself. This *had* happened. They'd cut him up, probably using a blunt knife to maximise the pain. Chopping him up like a butcher hacking away at a carcass. The only problem was, Saahil couldn't remember. Saahil couldn't remember.

He shuffled forward to the door, thinking he should call the police. But he couldn't. They'd send him home to Abbu. Abbu would shout at him for thinking he could trust strangers. He needed a hospital. But he hated them. The blinds that covered the glass on the door were shut. They hung, like bars on a jail cell, curtaining him off from the rest of the world.

The Sikhs were probably waiting for him on the other side, brandishing those daggers they were ordered to carry around with them. When he stepped outside, they'd fly at him, piercing different parts of his body. Saahil lunged forward towards the door, groaning with pain. Groaning with each movement. Blood gushed from his wounds. That was when he saw that the door was already locked.

From inside.

He moved into a tiny little flat not far from the gym. Mohan Chacha had kindly agreed to pay two months' rent and told the landlord, Ramu, to go easy on Saahil. It was stripped bare of any furniture, furnishings or character. When Saahil first entered, he was sure that not one, but a couple of people had probably died in there. He took his mattress and other belongings from the room behind the gym with him. But it was far removed from the comfort of hearing Mohan Chacha swearing at everyone across the fitness room in Punjabi. Or Amar coming to greet him after school. On the first night, he discovered the heating didn't even work, and the sink in the bathroom leaked gunk out from the bottom, spreading across the floor like a disease. It had to be done, of course. It was all part of Saahil's plan. A plan he concocted after he realised that *he* was the one who had slashed his own arms after smoking a joint.

To this day, Saahil was unable to remember anything. How the knife had ended up in his room? Which brand of synthetic cannabis he had smoked? He had no recollection of the pain of when the blade cut into his arms, whether the blood had spurted out, or seeped through slowly. He knew of guys who cut themselves occasionally when high, but in the four years he'd been smoking spice, he'd never gone to such extreme lengths himself. He dreaded to think what would have happened had Mohan Chacha found him. And that's why Saahil needed to get out of there.

He enquired about an alternative place to stay, making some bullshit up to Mohan about wanting more responsibility at the gym and becoming more independent. Mohan agreed and put him in touch with Ramu. There was only one condition: Saahil wasn't willing to share with anyone. He accepted the cheapest flat he was offered and within two weeks, he'd moved in.

His new accommodation was more like a bedsit with the bonus of a private bathroom. The queasy green wallpaper was torn from various places and the lampshade in the ceiling had become a cemetery for insects. But Saahil didn't care. He only had one thing on his mind: detox.

He was going to make it happen. Mohan promised to promote

him to manage the desk and be in charge of membership cards. He couldn't do that whilst he was off his head. More importantly, Saahil couldn't allow a repeat of that disastrous night. Not only had he almost killed himself, he'd nearly revealed his secret. Mohan Chacha would not be happy knowing he was harbouring a junkie. And a missing person at that.

Saahil set about things straightaway, savouring what would be his last spliff a couple of hours before setting off to carry out his cleaning duties. He then emptied the rest of the packet into the bin. It was gone from his life, he vowed, forever.

To his surprise, the first day went better than expected. Obviously, he wanted it badly, but he was able to carry out his three hours at work and continue to act normal. His body was behaving this time. Saahil remembered the many times he'd started shaking, vomiting and sweating only a few hours after trying to stay abstinent. This time, however, the physiological effects were being kept at bay. Maybe, Saahil thought hopefully, this was all it had really taken. The will power and determination to make a decision and stick to it. After all, it was only a legal high. It couldn't be that bad.

The night sweat brought him back to reality with a gigantic thud. He woke with the feeling that he'd just been thrown from a fifty-foot fucker of a building. Either that or someone had emptied a bucket of cold water over his head. Some war on terror agent had decided to waterboard him whilst he slept. The sheets and pillow were drenched.

At six o'clock in the morning, he sent a mash-up of a text message to Mohan:

Sry really poorly cnt come in2 wrk 2dy

The rest of the day he spent on the toilet, shitting like his life depended on it. Whilst holding his head, he remembered a joke he'd once made when chubby Umar had announced to the group that he'd lost five pounds in weight.

'Five pounds?' Saahil had sniggered. 'Lose that when I go to the toilet.'

For the rest of the week, Saahil dressed and undressed. Dressed and undressed. Threw on his coat, ready to march into a shop and buy a gram of spice, to put an end to the suffering. But he stopped, thinking about how far he'd come. If he gave in now, he'd have to go through this all over again. Start from scratch. He couldn't cope with the thought of that.

Some nights his stomach twisted up in knots, causing him to keel over. He lay in a foetal position on the floor, wishing he'd die quickly instead. He walked from bedroom to bathroom, back and forth, crouching over, dragging his leg as he released fluid from whichever orifice needed to be seen to. He woke up vomiting. Let his nose run without having the energy to wipe it away.

Then there were the dreams, the visions. Windows and doors would bang shut. The yellow pashmina lay on the floor, filthy and stained with the blood of his slashed arms. The images on the shawl moved, swayed and twitched. The birds danced manically, the branches twisted and curled. The shawl seemed to come to life. Saahil felt as though it would swoop down, wrap around his neck and strangle him. He saw his mother, standing in a corner, shaking her head with disgust. He mumbled to her, gurgled like a baby. When he thought she was coming over, she'd sink into the ground and become an army of giant insects scuttling along the floor. Saahil jumped on to the bed and hid under the covers.

Towards the end of his second week, he looked at his reflection in the mirror. A person who resembled him stared back. A gaunt, ghost-like figure, whose ribcage protruded, whose eyes no longer sparkled, whose hair and beard were unkempt and greasy. He remembered his old self, his old face, the time and effort he often spent applying gel to his hair and trimming his beard so he achieved the designer stubble that girls went crazy for. He stripped naked and turned on the shower. He'd been doing this for a few days now. Hot, steamy showers helped with the cold sweats. Sometimes, he even threw a towel in and sat on it to stop his bum from going completely numb from the hard surface. He placed his cold, clammy body on the floor, knees drawn, face buried into his arms. The water was scorching. But Saahil didn't care. The gushing sound helped drown out the noises in his ears and the water blurred his vision so he couldn't see things that weren't actually there.

It was way too hot, almost painful, but Saahil really did not care. Instead, he wished the water would scald him and burn through his flesh. He wished to be found by his landlord in the morning, charred and flaking away.

Thirty-Two

'Stop!' Zahra shouted, before running into the kitchen. She could feel the pain spreading through her stomach, bile rising in her throat, her mouth filling with saliva. The polite thing to do would be to throw up in the toilet, but Zahra didn't know where the bathroom was. She knew she wouldn't last if she went scrambling up the stairs trying to find it.

'Zee!' Saahil called, but Zahra kicked the door and slammed it shut. She coughed and spluttered and gasped over the kitchen sink. But nothing happened.

'Are you okay?' said Saahil's solemn voice from the other side of the door.

Zahra didn't answer. She fell into a heap on the floor and wished she could wake up in a different place, different time zone, different life even. Her surroundings blurred as she imagined slashed arms and discarded knives. Her brother writhing in pain. No one there to wipe the sweat from his brow. No one to hold him as he retched into a lavatory. How scared he must have been to go through all of this alone. How awful for a grown man to have such fearful hallucinations, and hide in terror beneath the sheets like a child.

Zahra caught her breath and turned to face the door. She knew her brother was on the other side, his forehead probably pressed against it. She hardly recognised him anymore. He had endured so much, and conquered it too. Zahra couldn't help but think that it took a special kind of bravery to put yourself through the hell that Saahil had done. His muffled voice travelled through the door:

'Zee… I'm sorry.'

She grimaced at his apology. She realised that that was not what she wanted to hear. He didn't need to apologise, not really. So what was Zahra asking of him?

When she finally opened the door, Saahil perked up, seemingly glad that she was no longer running away from him. He opened his mouth to speak but Zahra was already hugging him around the middle. The initial surprise disappeared quickly, and Zahra felt Saahil's arms wrap around her. She could feel the sadness in his embrace. But most of all, she could feel the relief.

Saahil ushered the last couple of guys out from the gym. They were hiding behind the stack of weights, flexing their muscles in the mirror.

'All right, bro,' they sighed, after Saahil went over to remind them for the fifth time. He locked up and secured the main entrance, keys jangling from his waist belt before turning the corner and making his way to the office. It had been a long day and Saahil looked forward to spending the evening chilling with Amar.

Mohan Chacha had nipped out to fetch something. Now that Saahil was helping to run the gym, Mohan often left it to him to lock up and switch off all the machinery. Sometimes he manned the desk, other times he gave personal training lessons, and if anything needed fixing from a faulty rowing machine to the boiler, Saahil was the go-to person.

Saahil had a new life now. He had been drug-free for fours years. During the first few weeks of being clean, he'd regressed into a child-like state, having fits of anxiety or lashing out with tantrums. It wasn't just a case of kicking the habit; Saahil needed to learn how to live again. It wasn't easy. The family noticed his strange behaviour and eventually, he had no choice but to tell Mohan Chacha the truth about his drug problem. It was easier to talk about it, easier for them to accept him, now that he'd overcome it on his own.

Still, despite knowing the family for so many years, Saahil never disclosed his biggest secret. That he was a missing person and, he had a beautiful, wonderful family that were probably still waiting for him. Hanging in limbo. Regretfully, selfishly, Saahil convinced himself there was nothing he could do to put that aspect of his life right. Not right now, anyway. Nearly nine years had gone by, times had changed. *He* had changed. The things Saahil had done, the things he'd endured and overcome. Even he didn't recognise himself anymore. He couldn't just flounce back home. Just because he wasn't on drugs anymore, it didn't mean it was over. It was far from over. Saahil ached at the thought of turning thirty in a few weeks' times. How could he be entering a new decade of his life with none of his family around him?

Saahil had a new life now. This is where he would stay. But that didn't erase the fact that he had a little sister called Zahra who was in her late teens now, practically a young woman. He had an Abbu, who was over fifty. And Ammi… was Ammi even around anymore? He imagined a funeral. Ammi's body wrapped in white cloth. Her warm, love-filled embraces no more. With no drugs to help him forget about things, Saahil had no choice but to learn to live with himself.

He immersed himself into the workings of the gym. Training hard to rebuild his body after years of drug abuse. He looked like his old self now, but more muscular. He enjoyed helping Amar with his college coursework. He loved bantering with the other guys at the gym. He even had 'friends' now, not that anyone came close to that friendship he'd shared with Ehsan. It was still better than having no one. Yes, he did wake up sometimes with horrific nightmares, sweating all over. But nothing like before. Saahil was integrated back into normality. The only problem was, as much as he ignored it, there was nothing normal about his situation.

He could hear the sound of laughter coming from the office as he approached.

'What's so funny?' Saahil asked, as he entered the room.

There were three of them in total, Amar and two of his friends, sitting behind the laptop screen giggling like hyenas.

'Finding people we went to primary school with on Facebook and laughing at their pictures,' Amar said. He was due to start university in a few months.

'Oh.' Saahil wasn't really into the whole social media thing. He glanced around for somewhere to sit when a thought suddenly occurred to him. He strode over to the friends.

'Zahra,' he said. 'Zahra Sharif.'

'Who's Zahra Sha—'

'Type her name in.'

Amar turned around and typed in the name. A list of faces appeared.

'There's loads,' said Saahil.

'Yeah, it's Facebook,' he said, rolling his eyes. 'It'll be easier if you gave us the city.'

Saahil hesitated. 'Have a look first.'

Amar flicked through the images. The more he did, the less comfortable Saahil became with the idea. There were a lot of girls. Some of them were pouting, their lips pursed together suggestively, faces caked with make-up. Some had their chests sticking out, heads thrown back. One girl had taken the picture from above, the lens giving a clear view down her top and the crease of her breasts.

Amar's friend pointed at one particular group of hijabis huddled together wearing tight-fitting maxi dresses, a series of bums, boobs and pouts.

'I thought they were supposed to be "modest",' he said, confused.

'Can't make their minds up, can they…' the other chimed in.

Saahil could say nothing, he agreed with them.

'This one?' Amar pointed at a pretty girl who was smiling with actual teeth.

'No, she doesn't wear hijab,' Saahil replied. But then, how the hell did he know? Maybe she did.

'Give us the hometown and we'll find her.'

Saahil told them.

'Who is she?' Amar asked, before realisation flooded his eyes. 'Your sister?'

Saahil had had enough.

'Let me know if you find owt.' He regretted even asking. What if his sister was like one of those girls – pouty, chest sticky outing, self-obsessed types of the younger generation? Suddenly, he wasn't so sure he wanted to see anymore.

'Of course, she might not have a profile,' Amar said. 'Which is highly unlikely. Or it might be set to private. But I can try.'

'Thanks.'

A couple of weeks later, Amar and his friends called for him. He said nothing but pointed to the picture on the screen, smiling. Saahil's heart dropped.

'She looks just like you, that's why I recognised her. But obviously she's a girl so she's pretty. And I was gonna ask—'

'Shut up,' the friend nudged Amar in the stomach.

Saahil's nose was almost touching the screen. His heart was beating so fast. His fingers passed over her face. The boys had gone quiet but Saahil forgot that they were even in the room.

Saahil studied the picture. His sister was smiling (with actual teeth). Her hair was tousled and long. She had big brown eyes, high cheekbones and a small nose. He was staring at his mother's face. But he wasn't. It was Zahra. Little Zahra. Zee. She was so beautiful that Saahil's heart fluttered. He wanted to laugh out loud, and cry at the same time. He had last set eyes on his sister when she was a child, not long before her eleventh birthday. Staring back at him was a young woman. Nineteen years old, almost the same age he had been when he had abandoned her.

'You going to tell us what this is all about?'

It was Mohan Chacha. Saahil turned and stared at the four bearded faces watching him. They were waiting for him to answer. But Saahil had to get out of there.

Nine years of despair came tumbling out. Saahil was back in his old room behind the gym. He bit into his knuckle so the others would not hear him. His tears soaked the fabric on his shirt. He held his head, clutched at his hair. He kicked at a number of stacked boxes and toppled them over. Mohan Chacha wouldn't be pleased.

The enormity of what he had done hit him like a train. He

thought of the little girl he had helped raise, and again at the face of the stranger staring back at him through a glass screen.

For the next few days, Saahil barely ate. Amar printed off the photo and passed it to him silently. He stared at it all day. Kissed it. Cried again. When he slept, it visited him in his dreams.

Saahil wanted to know everything about her. When he looked at the photograph, he looked for clues about her personality. What had she been through, what had shaped her? Her ambitions, her insecurities. When was the last time she had cried? He wondered what the impact of his disappearance had had on her specifically. He knew she would miss him, but what of her state of mind, her own wellbeing? Dealing with an absent brother and a broken father. It wasn't that he hadn't thought of these things before, but now he could put a new face to the young girl he had left behind, everything became more real.

There was one thing he knew for sure: Saahil wanted to reach out to her. He wanted to know her. Suddenly, there was a purpose to his life. One day (a day that seemed sooner than it had done in years), Saahil wanted to walk up to his sister, take her in his arms, and ask her if she would still love him.

Over a year had passed by since Saahil had seen Zahra's picture. He hadn't returned home, but regularly checked the Facebook profile to see what his sister was up to. She wasn't social-media obsessed, he'd figured that out quickly. Rarely did she add any new pictures or post meaningless statuses. She shared many posts including one about UK arms sales to Middle Eastern dictatorships, and links to articles vilifying the austerity measures imposed on the poor by the coalition government. Not long after he discovered her online, Zahra posted a link to another webpage.

She did this every two weeks and Saahil discovered that she had a blog. It was packed with posts dating back to 2011. There was a brief 'about me' page with a small photo of her wearing oversized glasses and looking bookish and wise. His eyes widened when he read that she was a History and Politics undergraduate. That explained a lot.

Saahil beamed as he read post after post. She seemed to be so sure about what she was writing about and tackled big, uneasy subjects that Saahil barely ever spared a thought for. In one post, she ranted against the caste system and colourism in India and Pakistan. In another, against misogyny in the Arab world. Readers commented underneath each post: 'Stay woke!' Saahil couldn't believe that this was his little Zahra. His little girl, who was now using words like 'intersectionality' and getting into arguments about 'white feminism'.

'Microaggressions I have experienced as a woman of colour in white feminists spaces,' read the title of one post. A girl called Sana had commented underneath:

Also while feminists, regarding the headscarf, I'll tell you what's more oppressive. The fact that YOU keep telling me how oppressed I am.

Another lively post entitled 'An open letter to men who get HYSTERICAL about feminism' kept Saahil's eyebrows pinned up his forehead. Out of curiosity, he scrolled to the comments section. Someone called Waqar with Arabic writing in his profile picture responded:

I've never met a feminist who had a loving dad growing up lol.

The same girl called Sana wrote back:

Oh dear. Looks like another mansplaining Muslim brother.

He replied:

Sister, fix your hijab. Your hair is showing.

Zahra:

Self-righteous fucks who halal-police Muslim women in one breath and take six-pack mirror selfies in another are not tolerated here. Shoo.

Sure enough, when Saahil checked, Waqar had numerous gym selfies posted all over his Instagram.

Saahil loved reading the blog. He waited eagerly for a new post or share. They came regularly at two-weekly intervals and never failed to entertain and educate him. They became the highlight of his week. But he still hadn't returned home. He often went to the railway station, lingered around and watched the trains speed off without boarding them. A few times he'd actually got on and then jumped off a couple stops later. If he needed any more confirmation of just how cowardly he was, this was it. Saahil just didn't have the heart to go through with it. He spent his time planning the logistics of the whole thing. How would he contact Zahra? Would he just tap on her shoulder and reveal himself? What if she wanted nothing to do with him? What about Abbu? And Ammi? How would he reach out to them? Most of all, Saahil worried about one thing, and it kept him up at night. How on earth would he explain his absence of ten years to his little sister?

Another weekend arrived and Saahil was at the train station near Mohan Chacha's house again. This time, he was determined to go through with it. It wasn't a half-hearted attempt; Saahil had actually packed an overnight bag. He would check the situation out first. Even if it took a couple of attempts before he finally contacted his sister. Saahil would go and stand outside his home and watch Zahra's movements. Was she studying and working? What was her routine? Once he had figured all this out, Saahil would pluck the courage and approach her.

These were the thoughts racing through his mind as he boarded the train. It was a familiar feeling. Every stop they approached filled him with dread. His hands shook. His heart beat hard in his chest. Closer. And closer still. A few hours later and he was the nearest he had ever been to his family in years. Just two stops. Just two stops.

At the last moment, Saahil buckled. He leaped off the train and spent the rest of the evening wandering around the centre of Wakefield. He was less than twenty miles away from home. The evening turned into night and Saahil sat alone on a high-street bench. He knew he had to get that last train back to Mohan Chacha's in less than two hours. There was a mosque in the distance and, absentmindedly, Saahil began walking in that direction. He was almost there when a group of old men in salwar kameez walked past him. A few minutes later, a younger man followed.

The light fell on the side profile of his face. He walked swaying from side to side, his arms positioned at an odd angle as if he was carrying heavy shopping bags. Saahil squinted and looked harder. He felt his insides tighten and his breathing quickened. Saahil knew that walk. He remembered it vividly. Only last time, the walker had been marching directly towards him, accompanied by five other men. There was only one person who possessed that swagger and Saahil quickly realised that he knew this man.

After following him to make sure he had got it right, Saahil felt compelled to act. If he turned the corner, Saahil would lose him. There was nobody around and it was dark. Without hesitating, Saahil ran up behind the man and grabbed him. He wrestled him into an alleyway and began pummelling him with all his might. Saahil punched and kicked until the guy stumbled. There was nothing cool or calculated about his attack. It was ferocious, desperate, almost like a teenager struggling to get the most hits before being restrained by teachers during a school fight. The man fell against the wall, his knees buckling.

Saahil squatted down on the floor, trying to regain his breath. A line of blood fell from the man's head. He was panting and his arm lay limp by his side. Saahil observed closely. His eyes followed the bright green turban, only adorned by the most devout followers of faith, the two round marks on his forehead to suggest he never missed a single namaz, the fist-length beard and the white floor length abaya. Saahil looked him up and down.

'So what,' he said, sneering, 'are you all religious now?'

The man struggled to speak as the blood ran down the hook of his nose. He had the same stare, the same creepy eyes that had bored into Saahil's nearly ten years ago. The ringleader who'd destroyed his life. Majid, his name was. Majid Khan. The man tried to move his arm and he groaned in pain. Saahil hoped he'd dislocated it.

'I suppose there's no point asking you why? You just did it for a laugh, didn't you?' Saahil asked. His eyes never left Majid's face. He didn't want to miss a single detail.

Majid mumbled something. Saahil listened and could make out a faint 'sorry'. This angered him even more.

'Save it,' he said, viciously.

'I...' Majid started. 'I ask Allah for forgiveness every day.'

Saahil laughed. 'Don't you know how it works? Allah will forgive you, no need to worry about it. But if you wanna escape hell, you need to gain forgiveness from those you wronged. Without that, you're doomed, mate.'

Saahil watched Majid squirm before continuing. 'Let me tell you something. I will *never* forgive you. Even when we're both dead and you're begging me on Qiyamah, I will laugh in your face and I will make sure you burn in hell.'

Majid's face fell. 'I spent eight years in jail,' he whispered, feebly.

Saahil rolled his eyes in disbelief. 'You're pathetic.'

'I've changed.'

'Changed?'

Majid nodded eagerly, as though the harder he shook his head, the more he could convince him.

'No, you don't get away with it so easily.'

Saahil picked up an abandoned glass bottle and smashed it against the wall. It scraped along the uneven brickwork, the sharp edges sticking out menacingly. It was the perfect opportunity. Nobody was around. They were in a secluded alleyway in the dark. Even if he screamed, no one would hear. Saahil could run to the station and grab the last train out of there.

Majid whimpered and tried to shuffle away. He couldn't move. Saahil could avenge Ehsan. He could sink the glass straight into Majid's throat. He could watch curiously as the blood spurted from the wound like a gory horror film and line his white abaya red. Saahil could wait, and make sure the job was done properly, until his face went blue and his head fell limp, the green turban falling off and rolling along the floor.

But Saahil realised that the hand that was holding the glass bottle was shaking. His own life was flashing before his eyes. His life before the attack. His mother's death. Ammi holding him when he was little. Abbu telling him off for wearing his pants too low. Play fights with Zahra. Saahil teasing Ehsan about Alisha. The pair of them looking through university prospectuses, discussing their plans for the future. The ambitious, playful Engineering graduate who had wanted to make aeroplanes.

Then there was God. If Saahil went through with this, there would be no going back. He would burn in the same hell he had condemned his victim to. Allah would not forgive him, not for taking a life.

'There's something you should know,' Majid gasped.

Saahil held his hand up. 'No more pious bullshit,' he said. He didn't want Majid to know he was faltering.

'One of your mates followed us,' Majid blurted out.

There was silence. Saahil wasn't sure he'd heard him right. 'You what?' he asked.

'I swear to God it's true, I saw him.'

'Saw who?'

'He was watching us as we followed you—'

'Who was watching?'

'I don't fucking know,' Majid spat. 'Just one of your mates. I recognised him from outside the club.'

He seemed to have drifted back into his natural voice, and dropped the holier than thou image. Still, Saahil wasn't buying it.

'You're just trying to worm your way out of this—'

'I'm not!' Majid almost screamed. 'When you and Ehsan walked off after our argument outside the club, he wo' stood there staring at us. I asked him, "What the fuck are you looking at?" He wo' off his head, you could tell.'

The bottle had slipped from Saahil's hand. He didn't know what to make of this unexpected outburst.

'When we all walked off after... you know... he wo' there again,' Majid continued. 'We went right past him. I stared the fucker out, I knew he'd followed us.'

'Liar,' said Saahil, reaching for the broken bottle once more.

Majid began talking fast. 'I promise... I promise it's true. As we turned the corner, he ran off in the direction of the alleyway where you were both lying. We legged it, thinking he would call the police straightaway. But nowt happened.'

'Ken found us,' whispered Saahil, menacingly.

'What? That old gora?' Majid waved his hand dismissively. 'Nah. Your mate found you hours before. He found you pretty much straightaway... Obviously didn't help though. Did he?'

Saahil was shaking his head, not wanting to believe the words that were coming out of Majid's mouth. But something niggled at him. He needed concrete evidence. Some form of confirmation. Not random, made-up stories.

'Describe him,' snapped Saahil. 'The person you saw. Describe him.'

Majid searched the air for answers. 'Erm… It was a long time ago.'

Saahil launched himself at the man and grabbed a fistful of his clothes.

'You piece of shit, don't fuck with me!' he shouted in Majid's face. They were almost nose to nose.

'Er… er… Paki… Glasses,' Majid stuttered. 'Ugly-ass birth-mark on his nose.'

Saahil stared into his enemy's eyes. They didn't falter. He could feel his own grip of Majid's clothes loosening. Why did he seem so sure of himself? So certain of what he was saying.

Speechless and dazed, Saahil left the alleyway. He left Majid alone and struggling, certain that someone would find him sooner or later. He felt like his life had just been turned upside down once more, like a sandglass being jolted the opposite way.

The next morning, Saahil packed his bags and thanked Mohan Chacha and Amar for all they had done for him. A lump rose in his throat as Mohan tried to convince him to stay. Saahil said he had to leave and kissed Mohan's hands. He'd been like a father to him. Amar grabbed hold of him and wouldn't let go.

Saahil boarded a train, his mind still spinning from the previous night's revelations. This time, he was going home for sure.

Saahil pressed the doorbell of the modest-looking terraced house. He prayed silently that the next fifteen minutes would go his own way, though wasn't counting on things to go too smoothly. He knew the occupant inside the house well enough not to believe that.

A shadow appeared through the glass and Saahil's old friend opened the door. The confusion on his face quickly turned into shock.

'What the—?' Robert stared at him.

'Can I come in?' said Saahil, already halfway through the door. He pushed past and disappeared into the lounge.

Robert followed him inside. He looked as though he could barely speak. Saahil loitered around the room, face almost covered with a hoodie. Robert cleared his voice. 'Saahil?'

He turned to face Robert. 'Yeah, sorry about that. Was a bit rude of me to just invite myself in, eh?'

'Saahil, what the—? Where—?' Robert was struggling as to which question he should ask first. He settled on this: 'What are you doing here?'

Saahil opened his mouth. He'd rehearsed his speech beforehand, knew exactly what he would need to say to make this work in his favour, but his mind just seemed to go blank.

He'd been staying in a hotel for the past week, trying to figure out how he, as a missing person, could acquire some temporary accommodation for the next few months. He could not enter into any formal agreement with an estate agent, nor call upon any old friends. Each would blow his cover. Whilst walking the streets and peering half-heartedly into the windows of letting agencies, Saahil had spotted a familiar face from the corner of his eye. The man left the shop and jumped into a gleaming black Audi, briefcase in hand. When Saahil glanced at the name of the agency, everything fell into place: ROBERT LISTER, ESTATE AGENT.

Saahil marvelled at his own luck. What were the chances of him seeing his old university pal within a week of returning to his hometown? He wondered why his friend had moved away from Engineering, but figured this could also be a side business. *The cocky bastard had made it after all*, he thought.

Saahil hung around near the agency for the next couple of days in the hope of seeing Robert again. He showed up eventually, and instead of jumping into his Audi, he left the shop and began walking. Saahil followed him and a few streets later, they were both standing inside a well-decorated, modern living room, not knowing what to say to each other.

'I... er... I need your help, Rob,' Saahil finally said.

Robert held up his palms. 'Hold on a second, where the bloody hell have you been for the last—'

'Look I'll explain everything later, but I need to know if you can help me—'

'And how on earth did you find me?'

'I saw your name on the estate agent's.'

Robert put his briefcase down on the floor with a thud. *Probably getting late for a meeting,* thought Saahil. He'd put a few pounds on around the middle. Even his hair was thinning.

'I need somewhere to stay,' said Saahil, quietly.

'And why have you come to me?'

'Let me stay here.'

Robert burst out laughing. 'You can't stay here.'

'Fine. I'll stay somewhere else then. I'm sure you've got loads of properties. Just put me in your shittiest, most worthless rental.'

'I don't think so, mate.'

Saahil fiddled around in his bag. 'I've got cash, nobody will find out,' he said, pulling out a wad of twenty-pound notes. Robert hung back as though the money was infectious.

'If you've got money go to a hotel.'

'Too much hassle.'

'Where's your family? As far as I know they still live around here.'

Saahil began pacing the room. 'Look, my situation is a bit difficult—'

'Understatement of the fucking year,' mumbled Robert.

'I've just come back to the area and I need to… reconnect. I just need somewhere to stay whilst I get my shit together.'

Robert picked up his briefcase. 'I'm sorry, but I can't get involved in this.'

'Rob, look, this place is unoccupied,' pleaded Saahil. 'If I'm here, no one can break in or try and squat here. It's a win-win situation.'

Saahil seemed to have captured Robert's attention, but he shook his head. 'I can't let someone stay here illegally. You know how these things work.'

'Oh, come on. You're the motherfuckin' boss, it's your name above that door.'

Robert barely managed to conceal his grin. Saahil decided to polish a bit of the old ego some more. He knew what buttons he needed to press to make his old friend tick.

'No one's going to question your authority on this. None of your staff will even know.'

'I'll have to think about it,' Robert said.

'Can I wait for you here?'

Robert hesitated. Saahil slouched on the sofa, scruffy looking and half hidden behind his hood. Rob's face seemed to soften, almost with pity.

'It's raining outside,' Saahil mumbled.

Robert sighed before replying, 'If anything is out of place when I get back—'

'It won't be. Believe it or not, I'm good at making myself invisible.'

An awkward silence followed. Saahil regretted pointing out how lowly he'd become.

'Fine,' Robert quickly said. 'I'll drop by in a couple of hours.

Then I want to know where you've been for the past…' Robert's voice trailed off. 'Bloody hell. It's been ten years since we graduated.'

'And then I can stay?' Saahil asked.

'I said I'll think about it.' Robert grabbed his briefcase and headed towards the door. He stopped and turned around.

'You know we thought you were dead?' he said.

Saahil breathed hard from his nose. 'I'll lock the door behind you.'

'Nice try,' Robert laughed. 'If you're gonna wait here, then I'm locking you in mate.'

Saahil spent days hanging around in an alleyway, waiting for a glimpse of his family. It was the same one where he and Ehsan had first tried a cigarette. The same one they would hide in after playing knock-a-door-run as children. Now it was empty, apart from the flattened plastic bottles and other rubbish lying around on the floor.

He crept just behind the wall, fagging it. One after the other. Craning his neck towards his house. The first time he saw Zahra, he smiled and his heartbeat quickened. When he saw Abbu, he hurried all the way back to Robert's house, saving his emotions for when he was firmly inside. Abbu was podgier, his hair peppered with grey. Black, unnatural circles cloaked his eyes. The following day, he saw Ammi hobbling up the garden with her walking stick. He sighed with relief. Laughed out loud to himself.

After watching them for a while, Saahil found the courage to travel to Ehsan's house. As soon as he arrived, he spotted two nurses leaving. Uncle Harun emerged too, looking tired and sad. Saahil squinted into the window of the semi-detached. A shadow resembling Auntie Meena drew the curtains closed in the evening. A car pulled up outside the house, just as the sun disappeared from the sky. Two more nurses hurried up the driveway. Saahil inhaled. *Ehsan was alive.* He exhaled. *What was he like?*

The following evening, he went back to the alleyway near his home. He was just in time to see Zahra limping down the street carrying a huge bag filled with books. One of them fell out. Saahil watched her struggle to pick it up as she clung on to the rest of them. He wanted to go and help her. Sometimes she was accompanied by a friend, who would almost always go into the house. Saahil felt jealous at times. There he was, hiding in a stinking alleyway and stalking the house whilst other people just wandered in and out of *his* home with ease.

It was hard predicting when Zahra would go to uni and when she would come back. One day, he decided to follow her. She caught the same bus to uni he had always done, ten years ago. He watched her walk past the same streets; she stopped to buy a coffee. His uni had obviously received some funding; the collection of buildings had changed entirely and now loomed over the once simple campus. Saahil waited outside patiently as she attended lessons. For two hours he hung around against the wall, smoking. When Zahra finally emerged, she was surrounded by friends.

He took a few steps closer. It was a silly thing to do, but he couldn't help it. Hiding behind a wall had not been near enough. A little further, and Saahil could almost hear Zahra's voice. He wondered if it sounded like his mother's. As he casually walked past the group of friends, his mobile phone fell out of his pocket. *Idiot*, he thought. Some of the talking had quietened down. Saahil picked it up and straightened. He didn't hesitate. He put the phone away in his pocket and quickly sped off in the opposite direction.

When he was a safe distance away, he checked to see if Zahra had seen him. She hadn't. She was laughing with her friends. She was happy. Saahil hadn't turned her life upside down just yet.

Thirty-Three

It was done.

Saahil sank back into his chair, his muscles aching as though he'd just run a marathon. His mouth was dry and the beginnings of a headache were starting to set in. They were sitting on the sofa side by side, Zahra finishing off the dregs of another cup of tea that she probably hadn't wanted to drink. Night was falling fast, but his sister's expression remained calm. Dare Saahil imagine it, or had forgiveness started to bud?

He'd been completely truthful about his experiences, but the last segment of his story had been the hardest to tell. Even more so than having to describe withdrawal to his little sister. Or explain in detail how he'd slashed his own arms, begged for loose change and slept like a tramp on the streets. There was certain information he'd omitted in the last half hour. The meeting with Majid he'd completely obscured, including the revelations of that night. Until this point he was still up battling with whether or not he should keep that news to himself.

Zahra placed her cup on the table and tapped it with her fingers. She appeared deep in thought and slightly overwhelmed.

'I... don't know what to say really,' she mumbled.

Saahil remained silent, because he too, didn't know what to say either.

'You didn't have to stay away for that long,' she said, turning

381

to look at him. 'Whatever problems you had, whatever you were going through, we would have worked through it, we could have helped—'

'I know all that but… it wasn't you, it was me.'

All reassurances and consolations seemed meaningless. They were just searching for words to fill the silences.

'Oh, that reminds me,' he said, jumping up from the sofa. He ran upstairs and grabbed his mother's pashmina from the bedroom. Zahra's eyes widened when she saw it. 'I have something of yours,' he smiled.

Zahra took the shawl in her arms and pressed it against her cheek. 'You,' she breathed. 'I looked everywhere…'

'I'm sorry,' he said, reddening with shame. 'It wasn't mine to take. It belongs to you. But it just ended up in my bag somehow.'

Zahra touched the floral border. She followed the length of the tree and its branches with her fingers, caressed the birds and the falling petals. She shook her head, the tone of her voice hardening, 'Well, that's another thing you're going to have to explain to Abbu when we get there,' she said, reaching out for her coat.

Saahil frowned. 'Where?'

'Hopefully he'll be home alone, I'll ring beforehand and check,' Zahra continued. Saahil felt the colour drain from his face. He wasn't expecting *this*.

'Zahra. I can't come home yet.'

She stopped putting on her coat, and glared at him. 'What are you talking about?'

Saahil stood up and started pacing the room. He could feel Zahra's eyes following him. She was frozen in the same spot, the collar of her coat still unsmoothed.

'I need more time,' he eventually said. 'I can't come with you right now.'

'Why?'

'Just… there are a few things I need to sort out.'

'Like what?' Her voice rose. 'What things do you need to sort out?'

Saahil stared at his sister. *Should he tell her about Majid?* He didn't want to restart their relationship with lies, and so opened his mouth to speak. But his voice faltered. He couldn't do it. It would just complicate his plans.

'You know, just stuff,' he found himself saying. 'Once it's all done I'll come home. Until then, you can't speak a word of this to anyone.'

'For how long?'

'Maybe a few more weeks.'

Zahra exploded. 'Are you being serious? It's killed me to hide this from Abbu. I can't keep it from him anymore. He needs to know!'

Saahil reached out and held her by the arms. 'Please, Zahra, you have to.'

Zahra pushed him away, knocking her fists hard into his chest. 'Your dad thinks you're *dead*. Does that mean anything to you?'

'We have to do this properly,' Saahil replied, not looking at her directly. 'I can't just waltz in there, Zee.'

'We will do this properly. Come with me.' Zahra held her palm out for him. '*Please*,' she added.

Saahil stared at her hand as though it was something poisonous.

'I need more time,' he said, weakly.

'You've had ten years, Saahil.'

Zahra's hand remained outstretched.

'Last chance,' she said.

Slowly, Saahil shook his head. 'I can't do this right now.'

The words escaped his lips in one swift breath. It polluted the air between them. The hopes and expectations that Saahil had seen in Zahra's eyes diminished. He could only see the pain and misery she'd carried around with her for ten years, and it was all because of him. It encircled them, in every molecule, in every particle. There was nothing left to say or do. Saahil followed her as she picked up her bag and headed towards the door.

'Zahra, come on. Be reasonable.'

She turned around, hesitating, but then she spoke, almost pushing the words out. 'I wish you'd jumped off a cliff and they'd told us you were dead,' she said. 'That would have been easier.'

Saahil felt as though he had been kicked in the stomach. Zahra rushed past him, stopping only to snatch the yellow pashmina from the sofa. She set off down the street in defiance. The night engulfed her. Had Saahil imagined it, or did he hear her break down once she was safely around the corner?

Thirty-Four

Amjad was alone at last. He had just hurried Zahra up the stairs, commenting on how tired she looked and was in need of an early night. He turned out the lights and drew the awful wine-coloured curtains closed before tiptoeing to his bedroom. Amjad headed for his wardrobe. He took one last glance at the bedroom door, making sure all was still, before pushing aside his clothes and reaching into the back corner of his wardrobe. He felt the cold glass against his knuckles and wrapped his fingers around the neck of the bottle. He withdrew a glass from his underwear drawer and sat down on his bed. Amjad couldn't pour the drink into the glass fast enough.

Somewhere, in the few weeks that Ken had provided him with the whisky, it had become part of his nightly routine. Amjad was drinking every day. His sleeping pills lay forgotten and once he managed to get rid of Ammi and Zahra, Amjad would settle down with a glass of whisky, sure that neither of them would pop their heads into his bedroom to say 'goodnight'.

'Medicinal purposes,' he reminded himself before gulping back the drink, pushing out of his mind the fact that he had started to enjoy the way it made him feel. It no longer burned his throat, the smell no longer made him screw up his nose in disgust. When the liquid entered his mouth, his taste buds would start buzzing. If the sensation persisted, he would sneak into the bathroom and mix in a capful of water, a tip given to him by a wary Ken, who had no idea that Amjad was drinking more regularly than he let on.

Amjad sank into his bed and finished the drink. The same warmth spread through his body, his muscles relaxed. Amjad smiled to himself and poured himself another. More than helping with the sleep, the whisky took away the anxiety that ensued whenever night fell. When Amjad lost control of his mind, he could stop worrying about whether he would sleep or not. He had told Ken this.

'That's because you're drunk,' Ken shot back.

Amjad flinched. 'No, no, I don't have that much that I'm "drunk". It's just enough to help me relax my mind.'

'Yeah, whatever.'

Amjad didn't like it being put that way. He wasn't 'drunk' or 'hungover', as Ken put it. Amjad never thought he would ever be associated with those two words in his life. He tried to convince himself that it just affected him more because he wasn't used to it. But he did wake up dizzy and sickly nearly every morning. Dave, his manager, had noticed and called him in for another meeting. Amjad fobbed him off, but Dave mentioned 'retirement' again.

Amjad still hadn't told Zahra about the meeting. He wanted to, but for the past couple of weeks, Zahra had been acting strangely. She never seemed to want to stay in the same room as him and Ammi. Normally, they would all sit together and watch telly. Now she stayed shut up in her room. She was always on her mobile, the screen right up in her face. Amjad would catch her smiling coyly as she texted, and other times, she would tap away furiously and frown as though she was having an argument with someone. Lately, Amjad noticed, Zahra wouldn't make eye contact with him. It was as though she wanted to avoid him at all costs.

Amjad decided it must be a boy, and this worried him. He never came across any decent young men of Zahra's age. Most of them were ill-mannered and badly dressed, speeding around in their blacked-out cars and nodding their heads to that awful rap music. They just weren't in the same calibre as his daughter.

Amjad used to catch Saahil with girls all the time, either on the phone to them or walking down the street hand in hand with one. He used to tell him off for being such a scoundrel. He'd never had any problems with Zahra. She seemed so focused on her education and future career. Zahra was always too busy getting angry whilst watching the news than worrying about boys. Obviously, Amjad knew she would eventually meet someone in her own time. Someone she would go on to marry and spend the rest of her life with. She was twenty-one, hardly a child, but Amjad still thought it was too young.

He rubbed his temples and imagined Zahra leaving home. The thought of his daughter not being there terrified him. Selfish as it was, Amjad depended so much on her. She was his life.

He heard the floorboards creak next door and jumped, spilling the whisky down his front. He stumbled over and placed his ear next to the wall. He could hear Ammi groaning as she switched the bathroom light on. He hurried to the wardrobe and hid both the bottle and glass. Amjad dragged himself back into bed, holding on to furniture as he walked, his head spinning. He sat down with a thud.

Ammi's bedroom door closed. Amjad thought about Zahra and decided he was getting carried away. He knew nothing was going on for sure. He needed to give her the benefit of the doubt.

Amjad closed his eyes and prayed for sleep.

Saahil checked the time. It was two o'clock in the morning and he couldn't sleep. His legs were restless. There was a pounding in his ears. He sat up in bed quickly and breathed hard through his nose. The pain in his jaw subsided as he unclenched his teeth. Instead of lighting a fag, Saahil decided to go for a walk. He jumped out of bed and threw on his jacket and shoes. He pulled up his hood and headed out of the door and into the night. Saahil knew exactly where he was going. It was the same place he always went to when he couldn't sleep at night. Hiding behind the tree across the road. Staring at the house.

As he walked, the same anger gushed through his body. Somebody had found them. No, Saahil and Ehsan's 'friend' had found them and done nothing to help. Why? Saahil didn't need to search hard for the answer to that. When he lined up all the guys who had been with them on the night of the attack, the same name cropped up again and again. The same bespectacled face. The same bitterness. The same jealousy.

Ugly-ass birthmark on his nose...

Saahil lamented the fact that he hadn't known this information earlier. How different would life have been? It was his own fault. He made no effort whatsoever to find things out for himself. He had shown no interest in the investigation. Instead, he had withdrawn and spent months feeling sorry for himself. Even now, Saahil was lying to himself. It wasn't rage that propelled him out of bed every night to visit Kamran's house. It was guilt. It was shame. It kept him up at night, knowing that he'd done fuck all to avenge his best friend.

Saahil needed to slam down and shut the emotions off before he harmed himself or anyone else whenever he thought about it. He *always* thought about it.

Why?

Why had Kamran done what he'd done? Did he bypass the

alleyway and take another turn? Was he so drunk that he hadn't even seen them? But whenever Saahil thought back to that night, he was sure he'd felt someone approach them after the gang had left. He'd previously dismissed this as nothing but a figment of his imagination, but now he needed to know the truth. At times, he felt like his life depended on the answer. Other times, he fretted about whether the whole thing was even true. Had Majid tricked him? Was this all just a ploy to distract him? Was he being played? Saahil wrestled with these thoughts. He didn't know which way to turn. What should he do? Saahil always returned to the same conclusion. This was no accident.

He could still remember the hatred for him in Kamran's eyes. So much so that Saahil could almost feel it. But why, oh why, had Kamran sacrificed Ehsan in the process?

It wasn't easy, standing opposite *his* house without barging straight in there. Saahil had watched his children playing in the living room. There were two. A boy and a girl. And a wife, whom Saahil recognised as the girl who Kamran had accused Saahil of flirting with. But that didn't deter Saahil from his plan. Nothing did. There was only one thing on his mind as Saahil watched his old friend play happy families whilst he stood alone in the dark with an empty house to return to that didn't even belong to him. As Ehsan lay once again, in a cold, unfeeling ICU ward.

Saahil imagined how he would do it. Not just for his own pleasure; the logistics of the operation were important. The pain needed to be maximised, not just the physical, but the emotional. That's why Saahil had rejected the idea of a quick death. Kamran had to know why.

Saahil contemplated kicking him to death in an alleyway. Just as Majid and his mates had done to him and Ehsan. He could smash his skull in. That's how it worked, didn't it? An eye for an eye, a brain for a fucking brain. Or, to really hit hard, Saahil could snap his spine and paralyse him. That way, he could keep his brain but endure the humiliation of shitting in his pants and have somebody else clean it up. He could watch his son play football and not be able to even move a toe. To stay bed-bound whilst his wife got bored and shacked up with another man.

However Saahil chose to execute his plan, it had to be spectacular. He couldn't cower away or chicken out at the last minute. Not like he had done with Majid. No, Saahil would see this through. He had to do this for Ehsan.

Thirty-Five

Zahra stared at her phone and paced manically around her bedroom. She flicked through her messages as though expecting a text to magically appear from her best friend. She'd been waiting for a response from Libby all morning. There was nothing new in her inbox, apart from the three texts from Saahil asking her if she would meet him in the park in the afternoon.

It's nice and sunny. I'll get you an ice cream.

Zahra reminded him that she wasn't ten years old anymore and couldn't be coaxed into doing things by sweets. He hadn't replied after that. It was harsh, but she still hadn't forgiven him. In the week following their meeting at the house, Saahil bombarded her with dozens of apologies and suggested meet-ups, all of which she rejected. But as the days passed by, she realised she was secretly eager to see him again too. Saahil was her brother. Zahra had spent the past ten years desperate to be near him, to listen to him talk, to laugh with him and casually throw her arm around him. She finally gave in and met with him in the park on the other side of town. He showered her with empty reassurances: *Everything's going to be okay.* Convinced her to stay quiet: *Please don't tell Abbu, Zee.* Told her that he would fix things quickly: *Just hold tight.* One day, she even took Libby with her who burst into hysteria when she saw him from afar.

'Remain calm,' Zahra had ordered. 'Don't be too friendly with him. Remember what he did.'

Much to her disgust, though, Libby laughed gleefully and hugged him upon arrival. Zahra lied about needing the bathroom and stared at Libby to remind her of her mission. She could feel Saahil watching her as she went.

She wasted time in the toilets before emerging to find Libby wagging her finger at Saahil in a theatrical way. Saahil stared at the floor, nodding solemnly. Zahra decided to wait until the bollocking was over, but doubted it would have much impact. Sure enough, they'd left the park fifteen minutes later, with Saahil refusing to accompany them home. She'd not seen him since.

Every time Zahra plucked up the courage to go to Abbu, she stumbled. How could she tell her dad that his son had returned, but he didn't want to see him right now? Reuniting with his father was at the end of his priority list. He had urgent fucking business to sort out first. Sorry.

Zahra was growing increasingly restless. She pulled her mother's shawl out from her bottom drawer, having hastily stuffed it in there when she arrived home that night. She spread it out over the duvet, ready to examine. She felt uncomfortable immediately.

Evidence of Saahil's trauma could be spotted easily. Frayed edges, faded colour, holes in the material, and even blood that had stained the fabric and not washed out. The image of slashed arms invaded Zahra's mind. She had to look away. Even the family tree seemed different. The birds were no longer positioned in the same way that Zahra remembered. Their mother still flew high above. But now, Abbu and Zahra were the two birds facing each other on the bottom branch. Ammi was there too, stood slightly apart, but level to them. Ehsan was mid-flight, taking off, almost as if he was preparing to join Zahra's mother. And Saahil? Where was Saahil?

Zahra looked closer, her eyes darting around. She found him eventually, halfway down the tree, nearly obscured by blossom. He was neither flying nor interacting with any of the other birds, but just hidden away in his own little corner.

Zahra scooped the shawl up in her hands. It didn't even feel the same. It was so integral to her childhood that Zahra could remember the silkiness of the material. Now it felt rough and coarse. The kind that was ready to be donated to Oxfam. She shoved it back into the bottom drawer with renewed agitation.

She needed to ask Libby what to do, but she was still sleeping from her night shift at the hospital. Her phone vibrated. It was Amir giving everyone his daily update about Ehsan:

Oxygen levels still quite low. Same as yesterday, not much change. Keep praying.

Zahra looked at the message. She'd been receiving them in a WhatsApp group that included the rest of the cousins and friends since the day at the hospital. The main thing was that Ehsan's condition hadn't worsened. Zahra had experienced many of his hospital visits to know that this was a good sign. He was sticking it out. Fighting. Just like he always did.

Yesterday, she argued with Ammi, who suggested that maybe it would be for the best if Ehsan drifted away this time. It was out of kindness. At least the suffering would stop. Sometimes Zahra agreed. But it was always in secret, in a corner of her heart that she had closed off even to herself. She couldn't bring herself to say the words out loud: that out of compassion, Ehsan was better off dead. But Zahra couldn't let him go. Not when he was the only brother she could go and visit any time she liked. The brother she could talk to, even though he didn't answer. The brother she could actually see, even though his eyes never focused on her. The brother she could touch, despite the fact that his fingers never tightened around her hand. Ehsan had been reduced to a shell. But being true to his nature, he was still always there.

Zahra decided to go downstairs and wait for Libby to get in touch. She regretted this as soon as she entered the lounge as Ammi was sitting with one of her friends, an elderly lady who she'd known since she had first arrived in the country. The friend was accompanied by her daughter-in-law, who had kids that were the same age as Zahra.

Zahra did the compulsory hugging and kissing before jumping on to the sofa and switching on the news. She couldn't hear a word. Ammi and her friend were complaining about all their medical ailments.

Ammi seemed to have pain in her kidneys today. Not in her stomach area, but her kidneys specifically. Her friend topped that with pain in her legs, her shoulders and her head. Zahra concluded that this was 'total body pain'.

'I'm swollen around my belly because of my asthma,' the daughter-in-law chipped in. 'Look how big it's got!'

Zahra wanted to point out that this was scientifically impossible. Asthma did not cause any type of swelling in the stomach. *You're just fat, love!* she wanted to say. Instead, Zahra turned up the volume to listen to the day's headlines.

'Turn it down,' Ammi snapped. 'We're trying to talk.'

'It's important,' Zahra replied. 'I need to listen.'

'Ahhh, yes, Zahra's all into politics, isn't she?' the daughter-in-law said in Urdu, grinning from ear to ear.

'No, I just wanted to see the headlines,' Zahra said, trying to be polite.

The daughter-in-law made a face. 'Boring,' she said, shrugging it off with a wave of her hand.

'Oh, it's far from boring,' Zahra retorted. 'A terrorist group considered too violent by Al-Qaeda stormed through Mosul in Iraq last week. The military fled and the ones that were caught were thrown in a ditch and shot dead.'

The room fell quiet before erupting in, 'Oh, what has the world come to?' before they quickly lost interest. As expected, nobody asked Zahra to explain further. She didn't care, and carried on:

'It's not just something happening in a faraway land. People my age, your son's age—' Zahra said, pointing at the daughter-in-law, '—from *here*, Britain, are leaving to join them in Syria. Look, that's what they're talking about.'

'See,' the daughter-in-law said, waving her hands melodramatically. 'This is why I don't watch the news. It's so depressing.'

'Terrible things happening in the world. I'm too old for all this,' Ammi's friend wailed, holding her head.

'Well, maybe you are, but you're not, Auntie,' Zahra said, nodding her head towards the daughter-in-law.

Ammi hissed at her. 'We get the point, Zahra.'

Zahra shrugged. 'Just sayin'. You've got kids growing up in this country. Things are going to affect them. *Especially* them.'

The Auntie looked over at Ammi and sniffed disapprovingly. Zahra's phone buzzed. It was Saahil asking her if she would change her mind. Ammi and her friend were mumbling to each other. Zahra could feel the Auntie watching her.

'So, what are you going to do after your graduation, Zahra?' she asked. 'Become prime minister?' The malice in her voice was overwhelming. She giggled away for quite some time.

Zahra stood up and reached for her bag. 'I didn't mean to offend you. Just think everyone needs to show a bit more interest in what's going on in the world. Especially when some Muslim kids would rather be in a war zone than here at home.'

'Who said I was offended?' she snapped back.

'Are you still talking about that?' Ammi growled, breaking away from her conversation.

'Yeah, because it's important. In case you haven't noticed, none of you are in a remote Pakistani village anymore, where the biggest news of the day is that the neighbour's goat has given birth.'

Ammi gasped as Zahra marched out of the room. She knew she was being extra harsh as she slammed the door shut, but she had more important things to think about. She cursed herself for giving in to Saahil again so easily. Her mind hadn't even decided what she wanted to do for sure, and yet her feet carried her towards him with such ease. She gave herself a good telling off as she walked briskly in his direction.

Saahil had just about given up hope when he spotted Zahra stomping towards him in the park. The last time they had parted, Zahra had given him an ultimatum: to return home by the end of the week or never contact her again. He hadn't. Saahil continued texting her with apologises and reassurances, and suggested another meet-up. He wasn't sure she would come, but here she was. She sat down on the bench next to him with a thud, arms folded, legs crossed. She didn't speak a word. Saahil cleared his throat and told her that he was going to buy ice creams. She shrugged and stared ahead. When he returned, they ate in silence. This didn't bother Saahil. For the first time in years, he was the most content he had been in his life. Sitting there on the bench, eating ice cream next to his little sister. Even if she did give him a funny look for smiling and watching her as she ate.

They'd seen each other a handful of times since the day they'd met at Robert's house. They took walks in the park and met in a little café. She asked him questions, further details about his absence. Was he scared when he was homeless? Did he ever tell Mohan Chacha about his family? Did he ever have a girlfriend? But Saahil always shrugged her off. He'd done enough talking on their first meeting. From now on, he only wanted to know about her.

She told him that Abbu's insomnia was getting worse. So was Ammi's health. That amongst all his other problems, Ehsan ground his teeth constantly. The sound was awful, Zahra said. He almost choked once by drawing blood and nearly swallowing a loose tooth. Apart from that, they made small talk. Even the silences were getting less awkward. Most of the time, though, Saahil just observed her.

He had loved her as an infant, then as a child. Now she stood before him as an adult and he felt such a pang of regret that he had missed out on watching her grow. It startled him a little when she strutted off in front of him, hips swaying, handbag swinging from her arm. Saahil would have been lying if he didn't wish she was a little girl again. Now, her eyes stared back at him challengingly. There was no idolisation in them anymore, just disappointment.

Saahil liked her style. The last time she came to see him, she wore a yellow kurta, rolled-up jeans, Converse and a silver chain around her ankle. This, Saahil realised, as she piled her hair up on top of her head in a bun, was her scruffy look. And yet she was still unbelievably pretty. She possessed the same high cheekbones and elegantly arched eyebrows as their mother. She didn't need to cake on lots of make-up. Every time Saahil saw her, she was bare-faced, casual and still stunning.

'Have you seen them?'

Saahil motioned to group of guys standing nearby. They were wearing running gear and were stretching against the park bench. They were talking amongst themselves, but only a few seconds before they were glancing over non-stop.

'What about 'em?'

'They keep looking at you.'

Zahra shrugged.

'So… what do you think to guys then?' Saahil asked.

'Oh dear,' Zahra replied, rolling her eyes.

'Come on, Zee. We can talk about stuff, right?'

'Yeah, but you have this type of conversation with teenagers.'

'Well, I didn't do it then so I'll just give you my advice now,' Saahil began, clearing his throat. 'There are some decent guys out there, but they're rare, y'know. Most of them at your age are just arseholes. They just wanna mess you about. I should know,' he paused and added. 'I was one of 'em.'

Zahra looked at him, eyebrows raised.

'But I wasn't completely shameless! I had boundaries,' he said quickly, seeing the look on her face. 'Anyway, you can always tell me if you like someone or—'

Zahra shook her head. 'No, there isn't anyone. I'd tell you if there was, promise.'

'Hmmm.' Saahil decided to take the conversation further. 'So… what type of person do you like? What are you looking for?'

Zahra sighed. 'Do we have to do this?'

Saahil nodded. 'Yeah, it's fun,' he said, trying to be convincing.

'I'm not really *looking*, I'm too busy.'

'Oh, come on.' He nudged her, smiling.

Zahra sat up straight. Her handbag was resting on her knees. She wrapped her arms around it, hugging it.

'Apart from being a decent human being,' she started. 'Someone who… believes in something. You know, he has to be passionate about something.'

Saahil nodded encouragingly and waited for more, but Zahra looked at him, all done and dusted.

'What? Is that it?' Saahil asked. 'I thought you were going to say something along the lines of "good-looking and good sense of humour".'

'That too! But I'm just sayin', I'd rather be with someone who… has something to say, who is interested in things, and isn't afraid to question what's going on.'

'Ah right. So you want someone who is "deep",' he said, smirking.

Zahra giggled nervously. In that moment, she was almost his little girl again.

'Well. Be careful with… yeah don't settle for anything less than you deserve.'

He decided to take it easy. She was a clever girl and he didn't need to insult her intelligence. Zahra nodded and Saahil was glad she let him have his say without too much of a fight. She obviously knew it was important to him. Saahil's heart warmed. She had turned out exactly as he would have hoped. Even better. The only thing that pained him was that he had played no role in it.

Despite this, a small part of Saahil's observations troubled him. He still tried to remember a time when he had seen his little sister smile. Mostly, she was stressed out, and looked pretty pissed off all the time. Saahil knew he was a big reason for that. But there were other things. One time, Zahra spent ages arguing on the phone with the doctor's surgery for not producing Ammi's prescriptions on time. Another time, she admonished a plumber who had wasted their time and not turned up to fix a leak in the bathroom. Saahil waited patiently as she gave everyone what for. He watched as his sister rushed around, sneaking away to see him for a half an hour, here and there, before heading off home to run errands.

Today had gone better than expected; Zahra seemed to have really relaxed with him. It had almost been 'easy' to be in each other's presence. Saahil invited her back to Robert's house again. As he returned to the room with coffee, he noticed she was watching the news and simultaneously checking her phone, brow furrowed, eyes darting back and forth. Saahil asked her what she was doing.

'Nothing,' she replied.

The newsreader was talking about the NHS. Saahil sat down next to Zahra who was stuffing the mobile back into her pocket. She looked bright red in the face.

'What's up?' he asked.

Reluctantly, Zahra pulled the phone back out.

'I've been following this story for a few weeks. Two Syrian journalists, they were injured quite badly in a bomb attack on their homes and have been in hospital ever since. One of them

was a photographer documenting the war. I've just seen it now…
he died from his injuries.'

Zahra showed Saahil her phone, which was already displayed
with a picture. Saahil stared at it.

'He was twenty-four,' she added. He looked up at his sister
abruptly. Taking the phone from her, Saahil studied the photo,
lost for words.

The guy in the picture could easily have been in a boy band.
It was a black-and-white photo of a man with dark, serious eyes,
trimmed facial hair and a strange air of dignity for someone so
young.

'Twenty-four?' Saahil repeated. Zahra nodded.

He swiped for the next photo. This time he was in the car
with his friend. Both were wearing press jackets and bandaged
heads, looking directly into the camera with steely resolve. Saahil
swiped again. They were standing in a dusty Syrian street, with
fists pointing in the air, undefeated.

'What about his friend?' Saahil asked.

'Still in hospital, but stable.'

Saahil felt like someone had grabbed his insides and twisted
them. He didn't know why, people died in Syria every day.
Including young children. But Zahra seemed to understand
his expression as he handed the phone back to her. She looked
straight ahead and spoke:

'Not fair, is it? When it's your generation's turn to grow, to
create a legacy, to pursue dreams, to fall in love, to build a life,
you get stuck in a war.'

She paused, flicking through the pictures again.

'And the only way you can contribute to the world is by taking
pictures of rubble and burnt-out cars and dead bodies. All the

time hoping that someone, somewhere will care and help put an end to it... But it ends you first.'

Saahil grunted in response. He couldn't speak.

'That's gotta be even worse, right?' Zahra asked, looking at him intently. 'When you've dedicated your whole life to a cause but then... you die. So you'll never find out how things turned out. If your family survived. If there was ever peace. If your country rebuilt itself. '

Saahil reached out and touched Zahra's hand. She didn't pull away, but closed her fingers around his. He thought about the picture again. It was all a matter of geographical lottery. These people were their counterparts, other young Muslims in the world, whose only mistake was to be born in countries that had been turned into infernos. Saahil looked at his sister and the same unspoken words passed between them: *It could so easily have been us.*

If only on a dramatically smaller scale, Saahil knew something about lives being cut short by violence. He thought about his own youthful aspirations, thoughts and desires he had locked away. He sometimes wondered what it felt like to dream.

Something else struck Saahil. Zahra cared about these things like they were her own personal problems. The way she spoke about them, the way she worried about the future. He thought about himself, wasting years wallowing in self-pity. He felt ashamed. There was the time when he felt the same foreboding about the future when he'd seen Zahra innocently watching the 9/11 attacks on TV. He'd sought to protect her. Instead, he had left her to fend for herself.

Even now, he wasn't being entirely truthful. At times, Saahil thought Zahra was softening towards him, but if she knew the real reason he'd returned, the actual reason that had forced him to sit on the train and come home, it would kill her. Saahil was still walking the streets in the dead of the night. He was still hiding behind the tree across the road. Staring at the house. Watching Kamran. Watching his family.

It destroyed him, but despite ten years apart, Saahil still couldn't envisage a future with his family. Despite everything he had put her through, it was inevitable that Saahil would go on and break his little sister's heart.

Thirty-Six

When the email from the BBC recruitment team landed in her inbox, Zahra gasped, bringing her hands to her face. It was an invitation for an interview in London and detailed the next stages of her application to the investigative journalism scheme she had applied for a few weeks ago. Zahra read and reread the email, convinced there must have been some sort of mistake. She made to grab the phone and ring Libby, but her bedroom door opened and in walked Ammi. She groaned in pain, as she usually did, and struggled to sit down on the single bed. Zahra rushed forward and helped her.

'Guess what, Ammi?'

Zahra pointed at the laptop and explained to her grandmother about the BBC email.

Ammi's eyes widened. 'BBC?'

'Yep. It's only an interview, there are loads of stages. I'd be lucky if I get past this bit... But still. I'm amazed they even contacted me. *Me!*'

'Why shouldn't they ask you, my beautiful girl?'

Zahra sat on the floor next to the old woman. Ammi pulled at Zahra's cheek and muttered more sweet things in Urdu. But all the excitement seemed to wear off and a panic rose in Zahra's chest.

'Do you think I can do this, Ammi?'

Ammi peered at her through her glasses and frowned. 'Yes. Why not?'

'They're going to be really posh.'

'So what, you speak the same language.'

'Yeah, but my accent is *not* posh,' Zahra said. 'And I might be the only brown person in the room. What if I say something really Asian and embarrass myself?'

'You won't,' Ammi said, waving her hand dismissively.

'If I get it and that's a big *if*, I'll have to move down to London,' Zahra said.

Ammi's smiled faded. 'Move? On your own?'

Zahra nodded.

'And where will you live?'

'I'll rent a room somewhere.'

Ammi didn't speak for quite some time before finally mumbling: 'Okay.'

Zahra gulped and quickly pulled the laptop towards her. 'It says I have to do a presentation on a topic of my choice.'

'Presentation?' Ammi asked.

'Yeah, it's where you have to stand and present your work in front of an audience. Like a speech.'

Ammi made a face.

'That's why I'm worried,' Zahra laughed.

'So you have to talk about yourself?' Ammi asked.

'No, about something relating to the news,' Zahra said. 'The training is to become an investigative journalist. You know, the type that go out and, erm… investigate things.'

'Like what?'

'Erm… crimes, corruption, wrongdoing,' Zahra said, excitedly. 'There'll be something I can talk about in my blog.'

Ammi peered at the laptop. 'Is that all the writing that you do?'

'Yep.'

'What's a blog?'

Zahra looked at Ammi, and realised she'd never shown her grandma the blog. She picked up her laptop and snuggled next to Ammi.

'This is a platform where I publish my own work,' she explained. 'Nearly everyone has a blog these days. You can have a blog about fashion, make-up, cookery, absolutely anything you want.'

'And what is yours about?'

'Relating to my degree. History and Politics. This post is about neoliberalism and how it's expanded throughout the world through war and poverty.'

Ammi looked at her blankly. Zahra thought to explain but the phone rang and she handed Ammi the laptop before running downstairs. It was a wasted journey. It was an automated machine informing her about PPI. Zahra slammed the phone down and walked back to her room. She found Ammi scrolling down the page before turning to her.

'You wrote *all* this?'

Zahra nodded. Ammi began scrolling back up the page. Zahra sat down on the floor next to her.

'I wish you could read it,' she said, softly.

Ammi stared at the screen through her glasses, her frame hunched over, the laptop touching her big belly, her bony finger tapping the only button she knew how to use. The alien words and letters swam past her. A pang of regret passed through Zahra at the fact that Ammi could only be impressed by the length of the essay Zahra had written, not at the actual content.

Zahra always tried to pass on all the new things she learned to Ammi. But she found it so difficult to explain in Ammi's language.

Zahra often waffled her way through. Frustration led her to switch back to English when she couldn't find the right words to articulate properly. All she was ever left with was Ammi's blank expression. She tried to tell Ammi about the Bengal famine and the Amritsar massacre being obscured from history books. Of the Milton Friedman school of economics that had shaped the world they lived in now. Of the proxy wars being fought by Saudi Arabia and Iran that had devastated the Muslim world. But she stumbled and stuttered her way through in mismatched Urdu, Punjabi and English and often gave up, not sure Ammi had understood. Or if Ammi even cared. After all, her eighty years on Earth had always encompassed family members, four walls and not much room for anything else.

'Who else reads this?' Ammi asked.

'Not that many people. Maybe about fifty people a month visit it. And that's including Libby, Sana and the others from uni. I get the occasional racist, misogynistic piece of shit—'

'Fifty people? You're slaving away and writing all this for fifty people?'

'This is just the beginning, Ammi,' Zahra said. 'It's a portfolio that I can show to people when I apply for jobs. To prove I can write.'

Ammi nodded and smiled with realisation. 'So when you show them this, they'll give you a job?'

'Well, it's not as simple as that. I have to fight off all the competition. There are lots of people out there who are better than me, more resourceful, graduates from better universities, cool work experiences on their CVs—'

Ammi pursed her lips. 'Nusrat's granddaughter has a lovely job. She works at this office, a ten-minute drive away from home and has a company car and everything.'

'I'm not bothered about all that.' Zahra waved her hand dismissively.

'So what do you want, then?'

'I wanna make an impact,' she blurted out. Ammi watched her, frowning. Zahra suddenly felt very embarrassed. Ammi grunted, suggesting she continue.

Zahra sighed. 'What I mean is, I have things to say. All these things that I've written about, it's my opinion. And my opinion matters.'

Zahra realised she wasn't doing a very good job of explaining. Ammi looked even more bewildered than before. Her head was tilted to one side, lips parted. Zahra understood the old woman's confusion. Why would *her* opinion matter?

'Do you remember that speech I once showed you?' she asked Ammi.

One day, after Ammi had been gossiping about a neighbour's daughter eloping with a boy she had met at college, Zahra stopped her in her tracks.

'Ammi,' she'd said, pacing the room, 'we need to dismantle the notions of shame and honour.'

Zahra found Chimamanda Ngozi Adichie's 'We Should All Be Feminists' speech on YouTube and played it. She paused on the significant parts and translated it line by line for Ammi. She eventually sat on the floor and looked at her grandma, tired, her head hurting.

'Do you understand, Ammi?'

Ammi thought about it for a few moments, applying it to her own situation, in the only way she understood.

'My father didn't want me to marry and go so far away to England,' she'd told Zahra. 'And the men in your granddad's family had a reputation for being strict. All men were like that in those days. My father argued with my mother throughout the night, who told him to face reality. They had five daughters. And we were really poor. Who would marry them? Where would they go? He spent the whole night crying. I could hear him.' She'd dabbed at her eyes, like she did every time she told this story before continuing: 'A few days later, he gave my hand in marriage.'

'But things turned out okay?' Zahra asked eagerly. 'My grand-dad was a good man. You loved him.'

'Of course,' Ammi said. 'But we didn't know that for sure at the time.'

Zahra remembered the story and felt a wave of affection. Ammi came from a different time. It was impossible for them to truly get each other and Zahra understood this. There was another story that always stuck in Zahra's mind too. This time, it was 1978 and a letter had come through the post.

'The boys were at school,' Ammi recalled. 'I waited all day for them to come home and read it for me.'

Zahra's insides clenched. The letter would have been written in Urdu. But Ammi was completely illiterate, her parents never having enough money to send them to school. Although Zahra never knew her grandfather, he only knew basic words too, enough to get him a job in the local mill with all the other Pakistani immigrants.

'I handed the letter to Amjad as soon as he came home. He started reading. I remember I was stood by the sink…'

Zahra imagined a young Ammi, holding the letter against her chest when it arrived. It was word from her family, and had travelled by air for thousands of miles to reach her. But despite her now clasping it in her hands, her fingers tracing the red and blue border, she couldn't access the beautiful Urdu script, the secrets the words contained. It would inform her of her father's death who, by the time the letter arrived ten days later, would already have been buried. Zahra imagined Ammi bundling the letter into Abbu's hands as soon as he came home from school. Her young dad reading to the second line of the letter, his words faltering. Looking up at Ammi. Her face crumbling.

Zahra cleared her throat, bringing herself back to the present. Ammi's gnarled fingers were still jabbing at the laptop, the BBC email displayed on the screen. Zahra touched Ammi's wrinkly hand and looked up at her. Her glasses were perched at the end of her nose, her varicosed feet firmly in slippers. Zahra realised just how close they were and at the same time, so different from each other.

Ammi sighed and placed the laptop on the bed. She cupped Zahra's face. 'You're so able, so capable,' she said. 'You can do anything.'

Zahra smiled and hugged her grandmother. Even if Ammi never really understood what Zahra did, or wrote about, even if she couldn't tell her about the desires and ambitions she possessed. It didn't matter. They were bound by other things, things that only the two of them could understand.

Their embrace was only interrupted by Zahra's phone vibrating. It was Amir:

Ehsan had a good night. He is much better today. Oxygen normal and may move him back to general ward. Alhamdulillah. Thank you all for your duas.

Thirty-Seven

Saahil was awake again. His instinct was to get dressed and go for another one of his nightly walks. To stand outside Kamran's home once more. He would definitely be awake. Only he was up at this time, poring over work late into the night. Drinking. Saahil had seen him drinking, shifting, hiding the bottle away when his wife came down in her dressing gown, calling him to bed. In the daylight hours, Saahil watched Kamran pull his Mercedes out of the drive and head to work. He watched his wife strut around through the windows of the four-bedroomed detached with the trimmed lawn. Not that either of them did that themselves. Saahil had seen a gardener tending to the flowers. His wife had a separate car. An Audi. She didn't work. All Saahil had ever seen her doing was pull up with shopping bags. Not high street ones, but bags from designer shops. Saahil was pleased to see she had put on a lot of weight.

Saahil was awake again, but this time he couldn't find the same anger that propelled him out of bed. For the first time since he had found out, the hatred was vanishing from his heart. And Zahra was the reason.

He sat up and swung his legs over the side of the bed. He walked over to the mirror and stared at his reflection. Zahra forwarded him a text last night regarding Ehsan's condition. He was doing much better and Insha'Allah may come home soon. Nothing would change though. Saahil couldn't go to him and ask:

Do you want to be avenged?

He already knew the answer. Ehsan would tell him to shut up and sit down. No, he would tell him to shut up and go home. Ehsan would talk him through the consequences. If Saahil carried out what he was planning, then it meant jail, and more anguish for his family. If he wasn't caught, he'd be running for his life. He'd been tormented about what to do. Should he avenge his best friend or go home and be with his family? Could his love for Zahra outweigh all the hatred he harboured in his body? These thoughts haunted him as he tossed and turned in bed. He eventually fell into an uneasy sleep.

He was in a room with a hospital bed. There was a body underneath the covers. Saahil rushed over and pulled back the sheets. It disappeared. There was nothing there.

He glanced around and saw cuddly teddy bears arranged on the drawers. A train set on the floor. Toy cars and broken Action Men with arms missing. Saahil had been here before. It all came back to him. He could hear the sound of a woman's voice calling them from downstairs. The taste of sugary sweets, fizzy Coca-Cola bottles and white chocolate mice. A child laughed. Saahil whipped around.

A small figure was crouched down on the floor, racing a toy truck. It sped along and bumped against the bedside table.

'Boom,' Ehsan said, smiling, pleased with himself.

'What you doing?' Saahil asked, scrambling towards his best friend. 'Why are you out of bed?'

'I'm chillin',' he replied.

He looked up. Saahil stopped and realised. He had to hold on to the bed for support. The face of his childhood stared back at him. Ehsan was ten.

He jumped up from the floor and upturned the collars of his little shirt. Smiling goofily, Ehsan strutted around the room. He pointed at his mouth.

'Look, my teeth are okay now.'

Saahil nodded, his voice choked. 'Zahra told me…'

There was a weakness in his legs. He fell on to his knees and held on to his stomach, certain that this time, the pain in his heart would kill him.

'What's up with you?'

Little Ehsan was eyeing him with a frown. Then he burst out laughing.

'My teeth are okay now,' he repeated, pulling back his cheeks and revealing his gums.

Saahil reached out. 'Come here.'

Ehsan shuffled over. Saahil touched his small hands, both of them, and pulled him forward. They were level now, eye to eye, nose to nose. Like a parent having a word with his young child.

'I'm sorry, Ehsi,' Saahil whimpered.

Ehsan was humming and looking around the room.

'Ehsan,' Saahil said again, more forcefully. 'I'm sorry.'

The little boy shrugged. 'My teeth,' he said. 'They're okay now.'

Saahil woke up crying. It took ten long minutes for him to adjust to real life again. Ten long minutes for him to realise that Ehsan was no longer young, innocent and whole. Saahil sat up in bed for a while, huddled together, his arms cradling his head. Eventually, the sun began to shine into the room. He stayed in the same position as it grew brighter, until a glint hit his face. He peeked at the window through his arms. The curtains were slightly ajar. The gap was at an odd angle. A triangular shape, like two double-ended arrows. Saahil didn't remember leaving them like that.

He imagined the little boy from his dream bounding across the room and yanking them back, failing to draw them fully apart, like all children who were unable to reach the top end of the curtains. He'd done the job, however, that little boy. He'd let in just enough light to stop Saahil from drowning in his own darkness.

He realised something new. A decision had been made for him. A decision he could no longer fight against. Tomorrow, Saahil would go home.

Zahra almost knocked Saahil over when he told her. She held him in a tight embrace. He picked her up from the floor and spun her around, the pair of them laughing.

'This is for real?' Zahra asked him, when he put her back down.

'Yeah,' he replied, holding her face. 'It's happening.'

She screamed out with excitement and hugged him again. Her brother was finally coming home.

'I'll make us a cup of tea,' he said. 'We can talk about how we're going to do it.'

Zahra could hardly contain herself. She paced the room as Saahil went into the kitchen. Jumped up and down on the spot, laughing to herself. There was so much to plan. Zahra decided it would be best if she told Ammi and Abbu beforehand, rather than Saahil emerging from behind her like they did in films. It would push them over the edge! Would she tell Abbu she'd known for weeks? Probably not. She'd have to ask Saahil what he thought.

Abbu was ringing her. She didn't answer it, thinking she would see him in one go now, with his son. She was about to put her phone away when she noticed he had already called twice. There was an unopened text message on her phone. Zahra read it and her world changed instantly. She stared at the phone, not knowing what to do with herself, thinking her legs were about to give way. Abbu called her again. She watched the phone ring and made her way to the kitchen. She peered around the corner, dazed. Saahil was smiling to himself as he stirred both cups.

'Saahil. Come here,' she said, gently.

'Yeah, hang on, let it brew,' he replied, happily.

'No, you need to come here now.'

Saahil looked up from the mugs. 'What?'

Zahra walked away, knowing he would follow. 'Sit down,' she said, when he entered the room.

Saahil did so, not taking his eyes away from her face. 'What is it?' he asked.

Zahra couldn't speak, but motioned to her phone. She clamped her hands over her mouth as tears fell from her eyes. Saahil grabbed the mobile and stared at it. It dropped. The screen smashed but the text message was still visible, despite the cracks:

Salaam,
My cousin Ehsan has passed away.
Funeral tomorrow, Jummah time. Will be in touch with more details soon.

Inna lillahi wa inna ilayhi raji'un.

Thirty-Eight

Zahra never fully appreciated being only a day old when her mother had died. She did now. As she watched the scenes at the mosque play out before her, Zahra dreaded to think what it must have been like. A young death was always the worst. A death of a mother with small children. A death of a young man of only thirty-one years.

The trauma of the previous evening was only exacerbated by the fact that, in under twenty-four hours, Ehsan's coffin lay at the centre of a large room. It was bare, except for prayer mats that added splashes of colour. Zahra had always heard of how quickly Muslim funerals took place. She'd never really participated in one so close to her heart. Ammi normally took charge and represented their family at such times. Zahra always managed to stay in the background. Not today.

She thought back to yesterday, teatime. She was getting ready to plan the future with her brother. Today, at midday, they were burying Ehsan. Women were clinging on to the coffin at all sides. The men were curtained off in a separate area. The imam had already performed the funeral prayers. They were transmitted through a speaker in the ladies' section of the mosque. After that, the crying started up again. The sounds made Zahra want to slap her hands over her ears and scream. Women wailed. Others recited the Quran loudly. Auntie Meena stood weeping at the top end of the coffin. Ammi sat on a chair, as close to the casket as she could. She turned and beckoned to Zahra.

Zahra stood up, her legs numb and wobbly under her weight. She approached cautiously.

'Go and see Ehsan,' Ammi said in her ear.

Zahra hesitated. A small glass panel gave the funeral-goers one last chance to view Ehsan's face and pay their respects. Ammi nudged her.

'Go on,' she said. 'Before they take him.'

Zahra hung back. She tried to take a better look over the crowd. There was so much activity. So many people. Some familiar, others not. Zahra thought she saw Alisha amongst the mourners. She was weeping, hand against her chest. They made eye contact and raised hands in acknowledgement, but somebody stepped in front of them, blocking the view. Zahra didn't spot her again. In between the bodies, she could see the pine coffin carrying a bouquet of white flowers that lay on top of a navy blue sheet adorned with Islamic calligraphy.

'I don't think I can,' she said to Ammi.

'What?' Ammi shouted back, not able to hear her.

'I said, I don't think I want to see him… like this.'

Ammi nodded sympathetically. 'Sit down beside me.'

Zahra almost hid behind the chair. She wondered why her hands were shaking. Ten minutes later, Zahra noticed that people were now pointing towards the exit. Men gathered there. Whispers began spreading around the room. Wooden doors were flung open. The crying grew louder.

Zahra knew what was coming. Six men strode inside. She recognised them as family members. Ammi stood up and instructed Zahra to do the same.

'This is the end,' she whispered.

The women moved aside as the men gripped the handles of the coffin. Auntie Meena reached out frantically, trying to touch her child's casket for the last time. But the men wheeled it away. Zahra clamped her hands over her mouth. Ammi grabbed hold of her in a tight hug. Though her vision blurred with tears, Zahra could see women consoling one another. Some waved in the direction of the coffin. Just as it disappeared through the wooden doors, Auntie Meena fell to the ground.

Amjad watched Harun struggling inside the grave. The rain had subsided eventually. The sun shone through a parting in the clouds, its rays reflecting against the wet floor. The water slid down black headstones that were engraved with gold Arabic writing. Amjad adjusted on the spot. There was a squelch. Mud coated his shoes. He raised his head, still overwhelmed by the size of the crowd. Men and women, all dressed in salwar kameez, stood around the hole in the ground. Some held their hands together, eyes closed, muttering prayers under their breath. Young men were consoled by older ones. Women dabbed at their eyes. A white man in the tractor shouted out instructions in Urdu: 'Place the wooden strips down... Align them... You need to cover the glass at the top... No, no... align them first.'

The same man had shouted instructions out to Amjad when he had buried Neelam. Only that time, he spoke in English. After twenty years of organising Muslim funerals, he'd eventually picked up the lingo. Amjad remembered the day again. Standing inside his wife's grave, not wanting to go home alone to a newborn baby and young son. Wanting to shake Neelam awake and tell her to come with him.

Harun was also struggling. Only half his body was visible as he stood on top of his son's coffin. He looked shattered. Amjad could see his dry, cracked lips and dark eyes from yards away. And yet when various family members charged forward he refused help, holding out his hand in a warning. *He's always been a stubborn git*, Amjad thought.

'Let them help!' Meena shouted. She was being held up by two younger women. Her eyes were wet and bloodshot.

Harun ignored her and continued.

Amjad's fingers were interlocked with Zahra's, but when he turned to look at her, she appeared distracted. In fact, she was looking into the distance, craning her neck behind her as though searching for somebody. Amjad nudged her.

'What are you doing?'

'Nothing,' she croaked.

Amjad knew Ehsan's passing had hit her really hard. She would go every fortnight, without fail, to visit him. Read him books, sit with him. He'd filled Saahil's place. Amjad placed his arm around her. She hugged him tightly.

Several minutes passed by, and it appeared everyone was losing patience with Harun. Amjad had approached him a few times in the mosque, but things had been so busy like they usually were with Muslim funerals that he hadn't been able to reach him. Amjad knew it wasn't his place, especially after the pair of them hadn't spoken properly for ten years, but his legs were twitching. Before he could stop himself, he was marching forwards towards Harun.

'Abbu?' Zahra's voice followed him, as did whispers from the funeral-goers. Amjad didn't care. Out of all the people who were in attendance, he was the only one who knew how Harun felt. Amjad may not have physically buried his son, but he had done it mentally every day for the past ten years.

Amjad knew he was taking a huge risk. He hovered over the grave. Harun was bent over trying again to rearrange the wooden panels and hadn't noticed. Family members looked at Amjad with wide eyes, either impressed or offended by his nerve. But he was here now, and there was no going back. Amjad took a deep breath and slipped into the grave next to his old friend. Harun saw him from the corner of his eye and straightened up quickly. Amjad reached for the wooden plank in his hands. Harun's grip tightened around it. They stared at each other, though Amjad was sure Harun's face had softened. Nobody spoke. Zahra rushed over to the grave and was watching, mouth hanging open.

Amjad pulled hard again, trying to take the wooden plank from his friend's hand. Slowly, Harun released his fingers. His body went limp as two young men grabbed him by the underarms. His gaze never moved from Amjad's face as he was pulled out of the grave.

Amjad thanked God that there'd been no commotion. He bowed his head and busied himself with the work ahead. He placed one plank after the other, knowing the hard part was yet to come. Eventually, he reached the square glass on the coffin that provided him with a last glimpse of Ehsan's beautiful face, shrouded in white cotton. Amjad knelt down, holding the final plank in his trembling hands. He brought his hand to his mouth. Bit his lip. Amjad remembered the two little boys he had loved and raised.

'That's right, place the last one,' called the white man in the tractor, almost in slow motion.

Amjad looked up, squinting his eyes to block out the sun.

The sea of faces blurred before him. There was a soft buzzing in his ears. The misshapen clouds were crawling past, slowly. The blue sky, infinite, expansive. Amjad felt so small. Time was standing still.

He couldn't buckle now. Amjad had to do it. He lay down the plank reluctantly, covering half the glass. He could still see Ehsan's closed eyes. He remembered the countless sleepovers the boys had had when they were children. Amjad remembered throwing mattresses on to the floor in the lounge and covering the boys with duvets as they giggled and promised they wouldn't talk and play games once he'd switched the lights off.

That was what he was doing, he told himself, as he finally committed Ehsan's body to the ground. Tucking Ehsan into bed. Telling him to sleep tight. Only this time, forever.

Thirty-Nine

Zahra waited for two weeks to hear from Saahil. Her messages went unanswered. Her calls, straight to voicemail. She'd even ventured out to the house a couple of times, but he wasn't at home. Zahra wasn't trying to nag or pester him. She knew he had been there at the cemetery, hiding behind a tree and watching his best friend's funeral from afar. Despite all the anger she had directed towards her brother in the past few weeks, she knew now was not the time. She just wanted to make sure he was okay.

Zahra sat back against her desk and sighed. She thought about how the entire situation was now back to square one. They had been so close. Zahra had almost reunited them all, but life didn't stop for things to pan out so perfectly. She'd been silly to think it so. Ehsan's loss broke them all. Even though he'd left them a long time ago, things were now so final.

Her phone buzzed. She grabbed it anxiously, thinking it might be Saahil. It was Sana, telling her that elsewhere in the world, all hell was breaking loose.

The murder of three Israeli teenagers was kicking off the latest round of bloodshed in the Israel and Gaza conflict. The Free Palestine hashtag had gone into overdrive on social media. People were picking sides. Rockets were being launched by both parties. Plans for a ground offensive were beginning to take shape. Death tolls rising. Ceasefires being broken. Human shields.

People accused each other of anti-Semitism for saying the Israeli government was wrong. Hamas was a terrorist group so anyone who supported Palestine was clearly a terrorist sympathiser. Yet signs praising Hitler had been spotted at pro-Palestine rallies.

She'd avoided writing about the subject on her blog. Not just now, but ever since she had started it at college. There was no topic that stirred such passions as Israel and Palestine. She threw her phone on to the bed and started pacing the room again, wondering whether she should go and knock on Saahil's door for the third time. Instead, she went to check on Ammi and helped her chop onions, peppers and tomatoes for tonight's supper. An hour later, Zahra went back and retrieved her phone from under the bed covers.

This time, there *was* a message from Saahil. She had texted him earlier on in the day to ask him how he was. She read it quickly. It contained only one word:

Fine.

'Where are the girls?' Ken asked, looking around the room as he settled down on to the couch. Amjad followed him into the lounge with two mugs of tea.

'Ammi's lying down. And Zahra...' Amjad's voice trailed away. He made a face.

'What?' Ken asked, frowning.

'Upstairs. As per usual these days.'

'What's that supposed to mean?'

'Well,' Amjad began, taking a sip of tea, 'she's been acting really strange recently.'

'How?'

'I don't know… Like avoiding me.'

Ken snorted. 'What do you mean?'

'She's always upstairs. She won't make eye contact with me. And… I know this sounds daft, but I can hear her pacing the room. In fact, I've seen her do it. I caught her.'

Ken took his time choosing between a Jammie Dodger and a custard cream from the plate. Amjad wished he'd take what he was saying more seriously. He cleared his throat to hurry him up a bit.

'What did she say?' Ken asked quickly, realising.

'Just shrugged me off,' Amjad replied. 'Summat about waiting for her friend to get back to her. And that's the other thing, she's always on her phone.'

Ken chuckled again and waved his hand dismissively. 'Oh, well, you know what these young 'uns are like. Glued to their mobiles.'

'No, it's different, Ken. *She's* different. When she's texting, she's smiling differently. And sometimes she's arguing with someone, I can tell.'

Ken's eyes twinkled. 'A boy?'

Amjad nodded.

'Well, that's nothing to worry about then, is it?' Ken laughed.

Amjad shuffled in his seat, grimacing.

'Look, I know your culture is different and all that,' Ken began, but Amjad cut him off.

'It's not that I'm worried about, but whoever it is, he seems to be causing her more hassle than anything else.'

'Young love,' Ken smiled, though subsided after seeing the look on Amjad's face.

'Ask her?' he suggested. 'She's probably worried you might… you know… kick off about it.'

Amjad sighed deeply before nodding, 'Yeah, I should really, before making assumptions.'

He glanced at his friend who was busy dunking two rich tea biscuits into the cup at the same time.

'Ken?' Amjad said, tentatively.

'Hmmm.'

'Will you get me another bottle of whisky?' he blurted out.

Ken turned to him, the soggy biscuits suspended in mid-air, mouth hanging open.

'You what?'

Amjad brought the cup to his mouth, trying to hide behind it. He avoided eye contact.

'You've finished it already?' Ken asked, his voice rising. 'What the bloody hell—'

'No, no,' Amjad said. 'I've got loads left. But my mate came over the other day and he had some—'

'Which mate?'

'Dave, from work,' Amjad lied.

Ken raised his eyebrows. 'Oh really? You never drink wi' me. Always fob me off with tea.'

'Don't be daft.'

'Well, it's true. And anyway, you shouldn't be bloody drinking for no reason. You said it was for medicinal purposes. And only occasionally when you're really desperate. '

Amjad leaned forward, feigning offence. 'I don't drink it for pleasure. Have you gone mad?'

Ken sulked in his seat. 'So why do you need another one? I hope you're not getting carried away. I warned you not to—'

'I just meant, by the time you get me one it'll be a few more days and it'll be there for when I need it. It's not rocket science.'

Amjad regretted the way he said the last sentence.

'Don't patronise me,' Ken muttered.

They stared at each other. Amjad knew that if his friend was going to get him another bottle, he would need to salvage the situation. Quickly.

'Oh, come on, mate.'

But Ken cut him off. 'Thanks for the tea,' he said, standing up. 'Where are you going?'

Amjad followed Ken to the door. He touched his shoulder. Ken whipped around.

'I don't know what you're up to, mate,' he said. 'But I don't want to be involved in it. Sorry.'

He slammed the door shut behind him, leaving Amjad standing there, deflated. He moped his way back to the couch, knowing that he deserved his friend's anger. Ken, however, only knew the half of it. The truth was that the alcohol was starting to take over everything. It didn't affect him as strongly as it used to. So Amjad needed more.

The other night, Amjad had done a bad thing. He'd taken a sleeping pill and then drank a glass of alcohol straight after. Amjad was no expert, but he knew that that wasn't quite right. The problem was, it worked. He had at least five hours of sleep without waking up. Amjad promised himself he would not do such a thing again. But he did, a couple of nights later. And again, and again.

He tried to convince himself that he was still in control of the situation. But something told him that he was unravelling. And the worst part was, he couldn't confide in anyone because they would stop him. Amjad couldn't be stopped, because sleepless nights were starting to terrify him. As soon as the sky darkened and Ammi drew the curtains, Amjad felt like a noose was being tightened around his neck. They hung there, those awful curtains, heavy and velvety, blood-red, like a pair of strung bodies hanging at either side of the window.

Feeling alone and agitated after Ken's abrupt departure, Amjad went and stood at the bottom of the stairs. There was nothing he wanted to do more than call for his daughter and speak to her. Find out what was wrong and figure out a way of navigating through this new phase of their relationship. One that, Amjad thought uncomfortably, involved another person. A man. He wished so desperately that Neelam was here to guide him. *It could be anyone*, he thought. Amjad didn't think he had it in him to trust anyone else with Zahra.

After standing quietly for a while at the foot of the stairs, he abandoned his plan. He switched on the telly and tried to focus on *EastEnders*. Five minutes later, he muted the volume.

The floorboards were creaking upstairs.

Forty

'They've shot an aeroplane out of the sky.'

Abbu's voice travelled from the lounge and into the kitchen where Zahra was washing the dishes. She dropped a mug into the sink and ran with wet hands into the living room.

'What! Where?!'

'It's all right, it's okay!' Abbu said, holding his hands up reassuringly. 'It's not... it's happened over Ukraine.'

Zahra sat down next to Ammi and sighed with relief before realising this was not quite an appropriate response.

'Malaysian Airlines MH17,' Abbu said. 'It was flying from Amsterdam to Kuala Lumpur. They're saying Russian soldiers shot it out of the sky.'

'How?' Zahra asked, dumbfounded.

'Don't know.'

Zahra leaned back on the sofa, reluctantly pulling out her phone. If this had happened a week ago, Zahra would have been on her Twitter within an instant to check what everybody was saying. But she'd laid off for a while after people were posting the most gruesome pictures of the escalating conflict in Gaza. There was a constant flow of them. People hashtagging popular trends and posting pictures of mangled bodies to unsuspecting Twitter and Facebook users. Suddenly, everyone had become a politician.

428

Zahra usually managed to avoid anything of a 'sensitive' nature, thanks to placing the right settings on her account. Yet a few days ago, she had logged on to Twitter and pictures of dead children with missing body parts splashed across her mobile screen. She scrambled to move it out of the way and had accidently clicked on the user's profile. Somebody admonished them for posting graphic images. A response came within seconds hitting back:

Says you? Who posted this the other day of Syrian soldiers…

An image of dozens of decapitated heads courtesy of ISIS filled the screen. They were thrown in the back of a truck, piled on top of each other, like rubble. Zahra threw her mobile away from her. It landed on the bed. She stayed hunched in the corner of her room, shaking. Luckily, Ammi found her. She held her tight, and then told her off for being on the phone all the time. The image haunted Zahra throughout the night. She was unable to get it out of her head. She didn't tell Abbu about it. She wanted Saahil. But he hadn't replied to her for days again, despite her sending him numerous messages and missed calls.

Even when Zahra tried to stay away from it all, she couldn't escape it. Sana had called her yesterday.

'Did you see Cameron's statement this morning?' she asked urgently as soon as Zahra answered the phone.

Sana erupted into a lengthy description of what the prime minister had said. She was speaking so fast that Zahra could only focus on snippets: *strong support for Israel, condolences to soldiers, no mention of Palestinian death toll, four kids were blown up on a beach yesterday…*

They'd both stayed on the phone in silence. Something un-spoken passed between them. Zahra ended the call and jumped on to her laptop. Without thinking, she started a blog post.

Here is our country, storming around the world, telling off North Korea and Iran for their nuclear testing, invading entire countries to 'save the women', condemning human rights atrocities everywhere. And suddenly, hundreds of children have been blown to pieces in a matter of weeks, and the government can't even find the right words.

It matters when people who look like you are killed – liter-ally vaporised – and your own government is not enraged enough to speak out. And then you wonder why people feel like they don't belong here…

Zahra didn't even check it over after she'd written it. It was probably a mess, but that was how she felt.

Libby called her an hour later. 'Er, Zee, that what you've just posted. It's a bit… crazy, isn't it? You know the BBC will be looking through your online profiles for that job.'

'I actually don't give a shit, Libby, they can stuff their job,' she'd replied, thinking about the BBC's unfair and biased report-ing of the whole thing.

Abbu was still shaking his head at the TV screen as Zahra deliberated whether or not to go on Twitter. She imagined pictures of plane crash victims would soon start resurfacing.

'This is like something out of a movie,' he said, before turn-ing to Zahra. 'So what exactly is going on between Russia and Ukraine, Zee?'

'Don't really know, Abbu.'

Abbu frowned. 'You don't know?'

'No.'

'How come?'

'Because I don't, Abbu,' Zahra snapped. 'Can't bloody keep up with everything now, can I? Why don't you try and find out for yourself?'

She stormed off upstairs and slammed the door shut behind her.

Two hours later, Zahra put on her jacket. She was leaving for Saahil's house again, and this time she was determined to get in. He'd done enough hiding around. They were all grieving. He wasn't special. She was in an agitated mood and planned on channelling all that in his direction.

Ammi had some more friends over. Zahra didn't bother with niceties and headed straight for the kitchen. Abbu was in there making a cup of tea.

'Abbu, I'll be back in about an hour, just seeing a friend.'

As she opened the door, Abbu reached for the handle. His cold hand clamped over hers. He slammed the door shut. Zahra looked at him, startled.

'Where are you going?' he asked, confrontationally.

Zahra mumbled something about a friend.

'Which friend?'

She fidgeted. 'Sana, from uni.'

'Tell me the truth, Zahra.'

'I am,' she said.

Abbu took a deep breath and grew in size, as though he'd been preparing for this moment for weeks. 'You've been acting really strange.'

'No... I haven't.'

'Yes, you have. You're always in your room, you're constantly checking your phone—'

'No, Abbu, I—'

'Is it a boy? Are you seeing someone?'

Zahra frowned, then realised what Abbu meant. She laughed with relief. 'No, not at all! Abbu, seriously—'

'Then why are you avoiding me?' Abbu asked, his voice softening. Zahra averted her gaze. She stumbled over her words, unable to form sentences.

'It's okay if it is, I won't shout,' he said. 'I still think you're too young. You're only twenty-one and you've just finished uni. Don't you want to focus on your career?'

'Yes, absolutely!' Zahra began. 'That's why it's not—'

'But I get it, times have changed and young people want to get to know each other. I agree with it. But there are still certain things you have to be careful with—'

'Abbu , you've got the wrong end of the stick.'

'... someone worthy of you. I'm not sure about guys these days, they're of such a low standard.'

Zahra grabbed hold of Abbu's hand. 'Abbu, stop! It's not what you think.'

He sighed and stared down at his feet. 'Just don't go behind my back, Zee.'

'I won't. Just...' Zahra looked at him, helplessly, not knowing what she could say to make things better. 'Just trust me on this... Please.'

Abbu frowned as though he didn't quite understand that statement, but he never said anything. Zahra almost told him the truth. If she had, the next couple of hours might have panned out differently. Instead, she muttered more reassurances and left her father standing by the kitchen sink.

Today, she would bring Saahil home even if it killed her.

Zahra waited outside the house for five minutes before she started shouting out Saahil's name.

'I know you're in there. Open the bloody door!'

Another couple of minutes passed and Zahra started banging her fist hard. 'I'm not moving from here, so it's up to you,' she said.

Slowly, the lock turned and Saahil's eye peeked through the small gap where the door was chained.

Zahra frowned. 'What you doing? Stop being a weirdo and open it.'

'Go home,' Saahil said, before slamming the door shut again.

This infuriated Zahra even more, and she pressed the bell and didn't let go. The sound was ear-splitting. She kept her finger on it until the lock turned quickly and Saahil, this time angrily, opened the door again.

'You little shit,' he said, hand placed over his ear.

Zahra brushed past him quickly. He tried to grab hold of her but she was too quick, trampling on his toes as she bulldozed past. She turned around to face him.

'Right. I'm not being funny or owt but why haven't you...' Her voice trailed off.

Saahil looked a mess. He was sweating and seemed not to have washed for days. He was wearing jeans and a white vest that looked as though it was stained with blood. He stared at the floor, his head bowed submissively, as though Zahra was pointing a gun at him.

'Are you all right?' she asked.

'Yeah,' he said, glancing over at the door of the living room. 'What's going on?'

'Nothing,' he replied. 'I'd rather just be alone if you don't mind. Can I call you tomorrow?'

As he spoke, he opened the front door again and motioned for her to leave. Zahra didn't move.

'Why do you keep looking at the door?' she asked.

He didn't answer, but just stared at her, wild-eyed.

'Go please,' he said, more forcefully.

'But why are you acting like this? And I've been ringing you day and night. What's wrong?'

This time, he shouted: 'Zahra, fuck off out of here. Now!'

Zahra flinched. She stared at him, convinced that something big was happening. There was no way he would speak to her like that. He'd never done so even when they were kids and she'd been an annoying little brat.

She moved quickly. So did he. He managed to grab her arm but she pushed him away and crashed into the living room, looking around for the cause of the problem. It wasn't hard to find. It was right there, lying in a crumpled heap on the laminated floor. Beaten black and blue. Hands tied behind its back. Unmoving. Still.

Zahra clamped her hands over her mouth.

'Saahil,' she gasped. 'What have you done?'

Forty-One

Amjad dug his knuckles into his forehead, squinting as Ammi's friends laughed loudly in the next room. His head was banging. He had had another forty-eight hours without any sleep and was desperate for some rest. He decided he would have a lie down and get out of the way whilst Ammi enjoyed her company. Zahra had left to meet her 'friend'. Amjad still didn't know whether to believe her or not, but decided to give her the benefit of the doubt.

He needed to go to his bedroom to get to the bottle of whisky that was hidden in his wardrobe. He'd bought it himself. Ken hadn't been in touch since the day he'd got the hump and stormed off. Amjad went to the supermarket, and for the first time in his life, ventured into the alcohol aisle. He'd never felt so strange and out of place as he stared at the rows of brown coloured bottles. It was like being a vegetarian and accidentally wandering into the meat section. Nervously, he asked the assistant for the one he needed. He'd written the name down on a piece of paper.

Then came the difficulty of getting it out of the store without being spotted. It seemed that hijabs, mosque hats and beards had doubled at every corner and at every checkout. It was the most uncomfortable supermarket visit of his life.

He rushed past Ammi and her friends and stood at the foot of the stairs. He wondered how he would reach the top. Amjad remembered the night after Neelam's burial. Zahra's cries had woken him as he slept on the couch. The hopelessness made climbing the stairs seem a momentous task. He felt the same now, dragging every step, heaving himself up with the banister. It was almost as if twenty years had not even passed by. His life was still seeped with loss, and now he had to face the reality of Zahra no longer being his little girl.

Only the other day she had strutted past him with a scarf tied around her neck. When Amjad had peered closer, he recognised the familiar teal blue and mustard yellow colours. When he called after her and she turned around, Amjad did a double take. He may as well have been staring at Neelam. Zahra did resemble her mother in looks, but the addition of Neelam's shawl wrapped around her shoulders surprised Amjad. They could practically have been the same person. When he'd enquired about the shawl, which he realised he hadn't seen for years, Zahra had been hesitant to discuss. She made an excuse and left quickly. Amjad couldn't stop looking at his wife's picture after that encounter. He couldn't stop thinking about how Zahra no longer snuggled into her birdie blanket for comfort. She wore the pashmina around her neck, like a woman.

Amjad was convinced this was no ordinary 'friend' that she was meeting. Something wasn't quite right about the whole situation. Either way, his daughter had started lying to him and that meant he'd already lost a small part of her.

Amjad passed the portrait of Jinnah hanging in the hallway. The father of the nation was rumoured to drink alcohol himself. Every night when Amjad passed the photo on the stairs, his secret became less terrible.

He reached the top and realised he was badly out of breath.

Zahra's bedroom door was ajar. She had kept all her cuddly toys from childhood. They were arranged on the drawer in a perfect line. Her bedroom walls were still pink and girly. Amjad had been meaning to decorate it for her. Zahra eventually gave up asking him. He regretted this now.

He closed his bedroom door and retrieved the bottle from behind the wardrobe. He poured the drink and downed two full glasses, wanting to receive the maximum effects.

She was a good kid, was his Zahra. Insha'Allah, she would succeed in whatever she went on to do, and was intelligent enough to only involve herself with good people. If Zee had chosen this 'friend', then he had to be someone special. Even Amjad's eighty-year-old mother was having a great time with her friends. The sound of laughter was travelling up to his bedroom. Amjad groaned as he took a seat at the end of his bed. He looked at the two pillows arranged at the top and wondered why he'd never got rid of one. He always slept on the right-hand side and faced the window. If Amjad was blessed with sleep, he sometimes woke up surprised to find the bed next to him cold and empty. A couple of seconds later, he would remember. He'd worry about what Neelam would say if she saw him drinking. What would she think?

It was too early. Only eight o'clock in the evening but Amjad washed down two high dose Diazepam pills with water. He felt nauseous but noticed that the curtains were slightly ajar in his room. He limped forwards, drawing them fully to block out all the light, and lay back on the bed with a thud.

Twenty minutes later and Amjad's mind started spinning. When he woke up forty-five minutes later, he'd forgotten the last thought that entered his mind before he'd fallen asleep. That nobody really needed Amjad anymore.

*

'Is he dead?' Zahra asked, trembling.

'No, not yet,' Saahil replied.

'Who is it? How long has he been here?'

'Two days.'

'Who is it?' Zahra repeated.

'Did I ever mention a mate of mine?' Saahil asked.

He stood by the doorway, eyes fixed on the figure on the floor. Zahra had never seen her brother like this. He appeared vicious, almost as if he was possessed and no longer had control of his mind and body.

'Jealous fucker,' he continued. 'Always having a go at me because I beat him at everything. He even started on me that night...'

Zahra watched as Saahil sat down on the sofa, holding his head. The coffee table they had both hunched over and eaten from was pushed up against the wall. A large space vacated, it seemed, for the body.

'It was him,' he said, talking into his cupped hands.

'What was him?'

'Kamran,' Saahil snapped back. 'He found us on the night.'

Zahra frowned, before realising what 'the night' meant. 'No, Uncle Ken found you.'

Saahil shook his head. 'This piece of shit found us two hours earlier. He didn't help us because he was off his fucking head drunk. And because he hated me.'

'I don't understand.'

'Ehsan is dead because of him. Ehsan might not have been as brain damaged if this bastard had called an ambulance when he found us.'

Zahra was lost for words. Saahil was spitting venom, but the revelation could wait. 'Saahil, look, we can sort that out later. We need to get him out of here, to a hospital or something. We'll just say we found him or…'

Saahil ignored her but she carried on blabbering: 'Then I can call Abbu, I'll explain everything to him. We can clean this place up. No one will know.'

'Go home, Zahra.'

'What?'

'I'm going to finish this.' Saahil stood up and faced her. Zahra did too.

'What do you mean you're going to "finish this"? This isn't a gangster movie, Saahil.'

'You shouldn't have come here. I told you to go home.'

'"Finish this"?' Zahra repeated, incredulously. 'What's that supposed to mean?'

She stared at her brother. He stared back and Zahra understood. She broke into a shaky laugh.

'Are you being serious?' she said. '*You* can't kill anyone. You're not… you're talking crap. I'm calling Abbu.'

Zahra pulled out her phone but before she could type anything, Saahil grabbed it and threw it on the floor, smashing the already damaged screen. He kicked it under the sofa and out of reach. Zahra was too stumped to speak. Saahil walked over and nudged the body on the floor. His foot was on the man's face.

'Saahil, you're scaring me,' Zahra said, meekly.

He turned to look at her, wild-eyed. 'Will you please just go?' he said. 'Go home and forget I ever came back.'

Something occurred to Zahra. 'How did you find this out?'

Saahil wasn't listening. He was kneeling down next to Kamran and analysing him almost with a sick, sadistic curiosity.

'Saahil, I asked who told you about this?'

Saahil stood up, though he didn't turn to face her.

'Majid.'

'Majid?' Zahra asked. 'What, you mean Majid Khan, the guy who...'

'I ran into him,' Saahil replied.

'What happened?'

'He told me. I was... Talking to him. He said they'd seen our mate – apparently Kamran had come out of the club after us and called us. We didn't hear him. After they battered us and were walking off, he passed them and was heading in our direction. They legged it thinking he would alert the police. "The guy with an ugly-ass birthmark on his nose," that's what Majid said. There was only one of them in our gang.'

Zahra listened carefully. She felt anger towards the man on the floor, part of her thinking he deserved it. 'When did you find out?'

Saahil didn't answer.

She asked him again.

'A couple of months ago,' he eventually replied.

Zahra felt like the ground had moved from beneath her feet. She sat down on the edge of the sofa. Her mind was exploding, the puzzle of the past few weeks slotted into place. Zahra didn't want to believe it, but it all fitted together perfectly.

'Is that why you came back?' she breathed.

Saahil fidgeted around and didn't face her. Zahra felt tears swimming in her eyes when she realised that everything had been about Kamran. That's why Saahil pressured her into keeping quiet. That's why he put off meeting Abbu. He'd had this planned all along. Ehsan's death had just pushed him over the edge. Saahil hadn't returned for them.

Zahra could feel him throwing glances in her direction. He didn't even have the courage to turn and face her directly.

'You don't call me Bhaijaan anymore,' he said, quietly before shrugging. 'Why would you? Haven't been much of a brother to you, have I? Still, can't pretend it doesn't... hurt.'

He was right. Zahra didn't refer to him as Bhaijaan, not like she did when she was little. It just hadn't felt right. And now more than ever, she knew she'd done the right thing.

'You can't just go around calling strangers "brother", can you?' Zahra said. She took a deep breath and stood up. 'If you only came back for your pathetic little revenge,' she shouted, 'then why did you meet me? Why didn't you just leave me alone?'

Saahil stared into the distance for a while. 'I missed you,' he eventually said. 'I saw pictures of you and read your blog. I wanted to know you.'

'Then don't do this. Come home now.'

'I need to speak to him first,' Saahil said, nodding towards Kamran.

Zahra went and stood in front of the man.

'Move,' said Saahil.

'No.'

'I'm warning you.'

'Think about Abbu,' Zahra said.

'I can't think of anyone right now! Just Ehsan.'

'Oh, get a grip,' Zahra snapped, pushing Saahil back. 'What

did you ever do for Ehsan when he was alive? What have you done for his parents? You just buggered off for ten years and left us all to deal with it. I'm the one who visited him. I read books to him, I held his hand. I volunteered at the head injury charities. I spent time with Auntie Meena. I tried to talk to Uncle Harun. What the fuck did you do?!'

'Exactly,' he shouted back. 'I've never done anything good for anyone. That's why I have to do this now for Ehsan and you need to get out of my way!'

He grabbed her by the arms and tried to shift her to the side.

'No, I won't let you!' Zahra yelled.

Before she knew it, she was slapping and punching him all over his body. She pulled at his hair. It didn't seem to make much of a difference. He was at least a foot taller than her. He just scrunched his face and shielded his stomach with his hands. Zahra's feeble attack barely made him move an inch. This pissed her off even more, and without thinking, she aimed for his face.

Zahra regretted it as soon as it happened. It even took Saahil by surprise. For the first time, real anger flashed in his eyes towards her. Older siblings were like parents. You weren't supposed to slap them across the face. Zahra had done the unthinkable.

Before either of them had time to react, they heard a groan behind them. Kamran was waking up.

Forty-Two

Amjad jerked awake. He sat up in bed and realised he'd slept for only forty-five minutes. It was nearly nine o'clock. He could hear movement downstairs and assumed Ammi and Zahra were making roti. He felt sick, and rubbed his eyes. His vision blurred.

Amjad felt stupid for thinking the whisky alone would put him to bed. He should have taken a sleeping pill as well. Mixed the two of them together like he had been doing recently. Maybe he had?

He stumbled over to the medication drawer. Had he taken one? The packet was completely empty. He stood for a few moments trying to remember but concluded he mustn't have. The pills were quite powerful. They usually knocked him out and left him ridiculously groggy the next morning.

He had others. Older ones he didn't take anymore. He rummaged through the drawer and found a bottle of Zopiclone pills he'd stopped taking a few months ago as the effects were wearing off. He struggled to open it and went to the bathroom to fetch some water in a glass. He didn't want to go downstairs. Ammi would start fussing over him.

He swallowed some of the pills, washing them down with water. He replaced the glass on the cupboard and knocked over the bottle in the process. The tablets spilled everywhere.

Leave it, Amjad thought. He would clear it up in the morning. He stumbled back into bed and closed his eyes.

Zahra ran into the kitchen. She poured water into a glass and hurried back into the lounge as Kamran's coughing fit grew louder. As soon as she entered the door, the glass was knocked out of her hands by Saahil. It smashed on to the floor, the water lay in a puddle on the ground.

'Shut up and sit down,' he said.

Feeling guilty for whacking him across the face earlier on, Zahra did as she was told. Saahil nudged Kamran with his foot again.

'You know why you're here?' he asked.

Slowly, Kamran nodded. His breathing was heavy and croaky. Zahra felt uncomfortable listening to it. Her eyes travelled down to his chest, he surely had a couple of broken ribs.

Saahil marched over to the wall. There were a series of four switches, all of which were turned off. Saahil yanked at them forcefully. Two harsh beams lit up directly above them. The light fell on Kamran's face. He averted his eyes.

'Right,' said Saahil, standing over him. 'Get on with it, then.'

Zahra held his arm and pulled him down on to the sofa next to her. He sat right on the edge, as though ready to lunge at Kamran at any moment.

'Just relax,' Zahra whispered.

Reluctantly, Saahil sat back. He crossed his arms and stared intently ahead.

Kamran struggled to hoist himself up. Zahra wanted to help him. Not because she was so concerned for his welfare. She just didn't want him to die on them and ruin everything for their family.

'Talk,' said Saahil, losing patience.

Kamran cleared his throat.

'I didn't see him…' he whimpered. 'I saw you having a go at them… and then they followed you and—'

'You didn't see who?' Saahil snapped. 'And you saw who having a go at who? Tell me everything!'

Zahra winced as she saw Kamran's face properly for the first time. It was bloody and bruised. His eyes were swollen and purple, his lip cut. Blood had dried black under his nose. Zahra glanced from him to Saahil and couldn't believe her brother was capable of causing such injuries. Part of her hated him for it, and yet the other part just wanted to protect him from himself.

'You argued with them lads and were getting gobby—' Kamran began.

'I didn't argue with anyone,' Saahil shouted. 'They pushed Ehsan on to the floor so I was sticking up for him… See this, Zahra. He's still acting like a fucking prick. Maybe I didn't hit you hard enough, dickhead—'

'Saahil, leave it!' Zahra pulled him back on to the couch. 'Just let him talk.'

This time she turned to Kamran herself. 'Can you just tell us what happened, please?'

Kamran seemed to shrink slightly when she addressed him. He nodded and took a deep breath.

'They stood around for a bit after you'd gone,' he said. 'You both went off towards your house. Ehsan lives the opposite way.'

'Yeah, I know where my best friend lives… lived,' Saahil mumbled.

'I was watching them. They asked me what I was looking at, so I went inside. But then I saw them head off in your direction.'

'What did you do when you went inside?' Zahra asked.

Kamran hesitated. 'Had another drink.'

Saahil muttered swear words under his breath.

'You didn't tell anyone about what had happened?' Zahra asked.

Kamran shook his head. Zahra thought he was going to burst into tears.

'I knew summat wasn't right,' he said. 'So I came out and walked off in the direction you were heading. But to be honest…'

Kamran stopped and groaned in pain as he shifted on the floor.

'What?' Zahra asked.

'I was a bit out of it. My head was all dizzy.'

'Well, who told you to act like a fucking pisshead,' Saahil spat. 'Just because I was talking to that slag you fancied?'

'Saahil!' Zahra was horrified.

'But it's true,' he said. 'This is why he had it in for me. Over that fucking girl who I didn't even like anyway.'

Zahra didn't have a clue what he was talking about. She turned to Kamran. 'Keep going.'

Kamran was looking at Saahil and even through the swollen eyes she could see the hatred. His posture stiffened. His shackled hands balled into fists.

'That's my wife you're talking about.'

'Like I give a shit,' said Saahil.

'So you followed them. But you were dizzy?' Zahra interrupted.

'Yeah, I didn't even know where I was at one point. But then I heard them. A big group, really noisy. They saw me… he was there.'

'Majid?' Zahra asked.

'Yeah. Stared me out as he walked by. As soon as they all got past me, they ran off down the street and around the corner.

446

I knew something had happened so I headed towards the alley and…' His voice trailed off and he looked at the floor. 'I saw you,' Kamran said, quietly.

Saahil breathed hard from his nose.

'You were unconscious and… and you didn't move.'

Zahra imagined the scene in her head. Her brother's body lying spread-eagled on the floor, limbs shifted at unnatural angles. The blood on his face interlaced with grit and mud from a shoe. She shuffled in her seat, willing for the conversation to be over.

'I knew it, I knew I felt someone,' said Saahil. He turned to Zahra. 'I never mentioned it before because I thought I must have been imagining things. At one point when I was lying there, I could feel someone watching me. But I was out of it. And now I realise it was *him*,' he spat.

'I'm sorry,' Kamran mumbled.

'How far away was Ehsan from me?' Saahil asked slowly. He spoke every word with pain.

'No, you don't understand,' Kamran began.

'How could you have walked away from that?' Zahra said, shaking her head.

'No, I didn't—'

'If you'd called an ambulance straightaway.'

'I didn't see him!' Kamran blurted out.

'What?' Saahil said.

'I didn't see Ehsan. It was dark, my head was spinning. Ehsan wasn't there.'

Saahil looked at Zahra. 'What is this shit?' he asked.

'I swear on my children's lives. I did not see Ehsan… otherwise I would have helped,' he added.

447

Zahra grabbed Saahil's arm. 'That's what Uncle Ken said, remember?'

Saahil shook his head.

'That he found you, but never saw Ehsan. Those students found him because he was—'

'Lying face down, in the shadow,' Saahil finished her sentence.

They looked at each other, unable to speak. Saahil seemed to have gone pale, his posture slumping. Zahra faced Kamran.

'That doesn't excuse you,' she said. 'You still found my brother. It was okay for you to let him die there on his own. How could you have put a petty grudge before something like this?'

Kamran wasn't listening. He just repeated one word over and over again. 'Ehsan… Ehsan… Ehsan.'

Saahil and Zahra watched as he cried to himself on the floor. His hands were still tied, so he could not wipe away the tears.

Libby knocked on the door again, this time with more force. She was going to kill Zahra when she saw her. She'd been trying to ring her all evening, but there was no answer. Despite being tired from her shift at work, Libby had decided to run out and check to see if her best friend was okay. She knew Zahra was having a tough time at the moment. She needed to be there for her.

She sidestepped a plant pot and peered through the curtains. Everything seemed to be still. Normally Amjad would be sitting in his armchair, and Ammi pottering about in the kitchen. Even the lamp in the corner of the room was switched off.

That's unusual, Libby thought. Zahra hadn't told her they were going out. And Zahra told her *everything*, even the pointless, miniscule stuff.

She knocked for the last time and was about to head off back home when Libby heard the sound. The hair on the nape of her neck lifted. Her heart started drumming against her chest. Libby seized up in fear and looked up to the source of the commotion. It was a shriek. A desperate, anguished cry, followed by a female voice speaking frantically in a language Libby only heard when she was at Zahra's house. Libby didn't understand it, but she could make out one word: Allah.

Libby started kicking at the door. She shouted as loudly as she could in English. The bedroom window flung open.

Forty-Three

'Save the sob story,' said Saahil, jumping up from the sofa. He started pacing around the room again and dragged his hands through his hair repeatedly. Saahil stopped as though he had just remembered something and turned to face Kamran.

'I haven't told you the best bit, have I, Zee?' he said. 'I got two missed calls from him on that night, hours after the attack. He called me, twice.'

Kamran gulped and started looking at the floor again.

'Why did you call me?' Saahil asked.

Zahra could tell he was getting increasingly agitated. His face was reddening, his hands jerked around in sharp, edgy movements. It looked to Zahra as though he needed to punch something.

'Why did you call me?' he repeated, but there was no response from Kamran. Saahil bent down and shouted in his face, 'Why!'

Zahra flinched. Kamran started talking quickly. 'The boys were wondering where you were and they were all telling each other to ring one of you so I just pulled my phone out and did it. I wasn't thinking straight…'

'You sicko,' Zahra said.

'I'm so sorry, Saahil,' Kamran said. 'I've had to live with this all my life… what I did to you and Ehsan. I cut myself off from everyone. Every morning I wake up and I think of him. I lash out at my wife all the time, can't even play with my kids…'

'Boo-fucking-hoo,' Saahil sneered. 'Because of you my best friend is already in his grave and you want me to feel sorry for you because you can't play with your fucking kids. Fuck you and your wife and your kids!'

Zahra gasped as Saahil kicked Kamran straight in the stomach. He fell back before turning over on his side and spitting out blood.

'Saahil, stop it, please,' she whimpered.

'Ehsan was my friend too,' Kamran shouted, once he had regained his breath. 'He used to include me in everything. You thought you were fucking *it* at uni, and everyone did whatever you said. No one ever told me when you were meeting up. Ehsan was the only one who invited me along to stuff. He even helped me with work sometimes. He was…' Kamran's voice trailed off.

Zahra looked at Saahil and noticed that his eyes were filling up. He seemed lost for a second and turned his back on them both. He took a few steps forward before falling on to his knees. Zahra jumped up and enveloped him. He covered his face and Zahra could feel him shaking.

'It's okay, it's okay,' she repeated.

As Zahra held Saahil, she realised he was muttering something. 'What are you saying?' she whispered.

'Do something… have to do something.'

'Saahil – what?'

In a split second, Saahil broke free from her embrace and lunged forward. He reached behind the sofa and pulled out a metal rod. Zahra stared.

'What's that?' she asked.

Saahil turned to Kamran. 'This is what they hit him with. Just once. And then they left him to choke on his own blood and become brain dead. That's what's gonna happen to you.'

Kamran's eyes widened. He shuffled back against the floor, pathetically. Zahra tried to grab her brother.

'Last chance, get out of here, Zee,' Saahil said, holding her back.

'You'll go to jail,' Zahra cried.

Saahil shrugged. Zahra knew she needed to throw everything she had at him. She grabbed a fistful of his vest. 'You'll burn in hell,' she shouted.

'Fine,' he said. 'I'll do it in front of you.'

He grabbed hold of her and pushed her into the kitchen. She fought against him, but he was too strong. The door was slammed shut. When Zahra tried to open it she couldn't, meaning Saahil had barricaded it from the other side. He was completely out of control. Zahra knew she could do nothing. She needed Abbu. She backed against the wall, helpless. She could hear Kamran begging: 'Please, please… no!'

Zahra tried to find a phone, but there was bound to be nothing in the kitchen. Still, in her fretfulness, she yanked open drawers, clanging cutlery together and rummaging through bottles of Fairy Liquid and detergent. From the corner of her eye, she noticed a heap of material on the floor next to the stainless-steel bin. She reached for it and realised it was a suit jacket. It was Kamran's and, to her relief, she pulled out a mobile phone from the pocket. There were nearly a hundred missed calls and messages displayed on the screen.

Zahra rang home. Nobody answered. *Where were they at this time?* It was nearly ten o'clock. She called again. And again. She couldn't remember Abbu's mobile number off by heart.

Zahra heard Kamran shriek in the other room. She placed her ear on the door and shouted for Saahil to stop. He'd obviously hit Kamran with the rod. There were thuds of metal hitting flesh.

She had to act fast. Her fingers lingered over the number nine. *Could she really? To her own brother?*

Kamran screamed again. There was no time. Zahra typed in 999 and almost dialled when a loud thumping noise made her drop the phone in shock. She could hear a female voice shouting outside.

Suddenly, everything went deadly quiet. She pushed at the door again, but this time, it opened itself from the other side. Saahil was crouching on the floor, his fingers placed in a shushing sign over his lips. Kamran seized the opportunity and started yelling for help. Saahil grabbed him and covered his mouth. Outside, the person was kicking the door and continued shouting to open.

'Zahra,' Saahil whispered. 'Is that—'

'Libs!'

Zahra ran and opened the front door. Libby burst into the hallway. Saahil ran out too, forgetting to conceal Kamran. He could be seen in full view and after spotting Libby, begged for help. Saahil slammed the door shut. Libby looked gobsmacked but was breathing heavy.

'You bastards,' she said 'Why didn't you answer the phone?'

'What's going on?' Zahra asked, rushing to her side.

Libby looked at them both, from Saahil to Zahra. Her face changed.

'It's your dad,' she said. 'He's overdosed.'

Zahra had never seen anybody move so fast. Libby had arrived in a taxi which was waiting outside. They all jumped in with Saahil telling the driver to put his foot down.

'What happened?' Saahil asked Libby.

'Who the heck was that guy—'

453

'Forget that, tell us what happened?'

'I went to your house because you weren't answering the phone,' Libby said, motioning to Zahra. 'And I heard your nan upstairs. She was hysterical.'

Zahra's eyes bulged. She was shaking her head, in denial. *This couldn't be.*

'When I got in, your dad was in bed… there were pills all over the floor. He was unconscious.'

'Is he gonna be all right?' Zahra stammered.

'I… I don't know,' Libby replied. 'The ambulance took him and I came straight here.'

Zahra's hands crept to her face. She gripped the sides of her head.

'Oh God… my Abbu,' she wailed.

Libby hugged her but nothing could console her. All Zahra could think of was her last conversation with Abbu. His desperation as he tried to understand why she had been so distant in the past few weeks. She had left him there on the doorstep, rushed away from him without a decent explanation.

Sometimes Abbu would ask her if she knew which pill he had taken. It was just precautionary in case he forgot. But one thought plagued her as they drove towards the hospital. *Could this possibly have been deliberate?*

Ten minutes later, and they pulled up to the A&E department. Libby paid the driver whilst Saahil and Zahra pelted inside. Saahil asked at the reception and grabbed Zahra's hand, leading her to the direction in which they were pointed. The beds and closed curtains whizzed past them. Zahra could hear the moans and whimpers of miserable patients. A man complained about the waiting time. A woman vomited into a bowl. The familiar scent of antiseptic and bleach flooded Zahra's nose. It was the same smell she often inhaled from Libby's uniform.

Outside one such cubicle, Saahil stopped and found a nurse. He was speaking so fast, but the nurse was talking slowly. She had one hand on his shoulder and was holding the other up reassuringly.

'We're doing all we can,' she said.

Saahil and Zahra were directed to a waiting area and told they would be updated as soon as possible. Zahra watched as Saahil backed away against the wall, helplessly. They made eye contact. She burst into tears once more and clapped her hand over her mouth. He reached out but before he could touch her, a shaky voice interrupted: 'Saahil?'

Ammi was standing behind them.

Forty-Four

They waited the entire night for news. Huddled together in a mismatched seating area. Zahra couldn't get comfortable. Some of the chairs were rigid and plastic with metal arm rests, others were overly padded and too heavy to even move. Saahil grabbed hold of nurses as they strutted past. They promised they would provide an update but never returned. When the doctor eventually came out, it was the news they had been waiting for: 'We've stabilised your dad,' she said.

Zahra, who was digging her nails into Saahil's arm as the news was finally delivered, let go. Ammi cried as they translated to her. Saahil held it together whilst the doctor was there, but as soon as she disappeared around the corner, buckled over with relief and sat on the floor, holding his face.

Ammi clung on to Saahil in the waiting room. They stayed like that for a while, Ammi overwhelmed and muttering feeble enquiries. She spent most of the time crying and kissing her grandson. He didn't respond to any of her questions, but just repeated that he was 'sorry' over and over again.

Now they had been transferred to a medical ward where Abbu was given his own room whilst they observed him. Zahra watched with Libby as Ammi towered over Saahil. The initial shock of seeing him again had eroded. She sat opposite him, her tears drying and her face darkening. Her grip tightened around her walking stick, and she began questioning Saahil in true Ammi style. When Saahil failed to respond satisfactorily, she started pacing in front of him. Now, she had resorted to full-blown Punjabi curses.

'So, what's she saying now?' Libby muttered into Zahra's ear.

'Summat about frying his liver,' Zahra replied, casually. She was too busy ringing Uncle Ken, who wasn't answering his phone.

'Oooh, that's harsh.'

Zahra shrugged. 'He deserves it.'

Libby pricked her ears up, as though somehow the words would magically translate for her. She opened her mouth but Zahra interrupted: 'She wants to set dogs on him.'

Libby's eyebrows shot up her forehead. 'Really?'

Zahra grinned. 'It sounds worse in English. She normally says stuff like that to my dad when he's bought the wrong can of chickpeas for her.'

'Ah, right.'

At that moment, Uncle Ken answered the phone and Zahra disappeared off, away from the commotion. When she returned, she decided to put an end to Ammi's rant. Saahil had transformed into a ten-year-old again, his head pointing at the floor as Ammi's anger rained down on him. Zahra insisted he take Ammi home for a rest. She was elderly and had been waiting around all night in the hospital. Now that they knew Abbu was stable, she needed to take her medication and have a lie down. Saahil gulped and nodded. He held out an arm for Ammi who pushed it away. She stormed off as fast as her walking stick could take her, with Saahil making to follow.

'Sort the house out,' Zahra whispered to him. He nodded in acknowledgement.

An hour later, Uncle Ken ran up the corridor towards her shouting, 'What happened?' before he even reached her. She explained about the overdose, saying they suspected it was accidental and were waiting for Abbu to come around.

'Oh God,' Ken said, touching his head. 'It's my fault.'

Zahra frowned.

'I gave him whisky to try,' he continued. 'He asked me for it, for medicinal purposes, thought it would help with the insomnia.'

Zahra felt more guilt bore into her. It was another thing she didn't know. Just as she hadn't paid proper attention to the fact that in recent weeks, Abbu was struggling more with his sleep. She'd neglected him and was too busy with Saahil. Zahra had left him entirely alone, and Abbu had collapsed completely.

'Can I see him?' Ken asked.

'There's something you need to know first,' Zahra replied.

Ken motioned with his head for her to go on. Zahra bit her lip.

'You might want to sit down.'

'So,' Ken said, pacing the corridor, 'not only did he come back after a decade without a good enough reason to explain his absence, but he manipulated you into not telling Amjad, kidnapped a guy, tortured him and then tried to kill him in front of you?'

'Er… yeah,' Zahra said, glancing at Libby who had joined them mid-conversation. 'Sort of.'

'Wait 'til I get my hands on him!'

'He won't be long,' Libby said, grinning.

'Do you know what's happened to that guy then?' Ken asked.

'That's the problem,' Zahra said, jumping up from her seat. 'He's here! Libby saw him.'

'Yeah, he was in A&E with his wife. You should have seen the state of him, looked like he'd been run over by a car. I've been stalking him thanks to this,' she added, holding up her ID badge and pointing to her student nurse uniform.

'Oh, bugger,' Ken said, sitting next to them.

'He's going to tell the police,' Zahra said. '*Obviously*, I don't blame him. But once he does they'll get Saahil and everything's gonna go tits-up again!'

'Okay, calm down,' Ken said. 'Let me think.'

He pinched the saggy skin at his throat, eyebrows drawn together. It was a while before he responded: 'Let me go down, see if I can get Kamran on his own and speak to him.'

'But he doesn't know who you are,' Zahra said.

'I could come with you,' Libby suggested. 'He might recognise me from the house.'

'Where's Saahil?' Ken asked.

'Sorting the house out in case Robert drops by and finds blood everywhere,' Zahra replied.

'Okay, come on, Libby. We'll just go and suss out the situation.'

'Are you sure I shouldn't come?' Zahra asked. 'I feel awful making you do this… but I didn't know who else to call.'

'Don't be silly.' Ken patted her shoulder. 'You stay here with your dad.'

Zahra watched as they set off down the corridor, her heart racing.

Half an hour later, Saahil returned to the hospital.

'I've sorted it,' he croaked.

Zahra nodded. She didn't really feel like talking to him and wandered off to sit in the private room designated for family members. She could feel her brother's eyes follow her, but he never asked her where she was going. She sat alone in the room for a while, knowing that whatever happened next all rested on the news that Ken and Libby brought back with them. She flicked through a stack of women's magazines and read the celebrity gossip sections before throwing them aside.

Feeling restless, she ventured back out to the ward to check on Abbu when she saw the pair of them bounding down the corridor. Saahil seized up. Ken charged at him and grabbed him by the scruff of his neck. *Be easy on him,* Zahra wanted to say, as Ken dragged him off into a quiet corner for a good telling-off. Despite everything that Saahil had done, Zahra couldn't help but love him.

Libby shook her head.

'He was surrounded by nurses. And his wife was waiting outside the cubicle. There's no way we'll get to him yet.'

Zahra's heart sank.

'We walked past a couple of times,' Libby continued. 'I pretended I was helping Ken find a family member, but to be honest, I can't really hang around there too much. I'm not stationed there, you see. The staff will think something dodgy is going on. We'll just have to wait until he is moved to a ward—'

'Or until the police come for Saahil,' Zahra said. She dropped into a seat next to her best friend, wondering what it felt like to be at peace.

The next morning, after another fitful night, Zahra stood outside her father's room. She uttered a few prayers under her breath and pushed at the heavy wooden door, bracing herself for another day of worry and dread. She jerked to a halt upon entering and saw Abbu twitching his arm and trying to reach for the nurse's buzzer.

'Abbu!' she shouted.

She ran over, yanked down the side rails on his bed and almost fell on top of him, hugging him. She felt his hand stroke her hair.

When she pulled back, Zahra could see his eyes were blood-shot and it was taking him all his strength to keep them open. One side of his head was sweat-soaked and hair was stuck to his forehead. A raspy noise came from his oxygen mask; short, sharp breaths. He was trying to say something.

'Abbu, what is it?' Zahra asked softly, as though talking to a child.

After a few attempts, he finally pushed the word out: 'Accident.'

'I know, Abbu, don't worry,' Zahra said. She kissed his hand, the relief flooding her once more. In that moment, all the worrying she had done over the past few days seemed minuscule, insignificant.

After calling the nurses, Zahra ran out of the room to find Saahil. She told him that Abbu was awake. He laughed out loud, but just as quickly, retired into a corner and didn't speak a word. Yes, his father was alive and well, but he still couldn't walk into the room and put his arms around him. Zahra knew this, and didn't say a word.

Over the next couple of days, Zahra felt the exhaustion take its toll. Hope sprang in her chest when Uncle Ken arrived at visiting hours. He would take a stroll past Kamran's cubicle to see if he could find him alone. With each failed visit, Zahra's hopes were dashed. She jumped every time the wooden doors opened, expecting uniformed men to stride through looking for Saahil Sharif. She prepared herself for what she'd say to her brother if that happened. 'Run' came to mind. *But what the heck*, she told herself, *this isn't a movie*. Saahil would eventually have to take responsibility for his actions. Even worse was the imaginary

461

conversation she would have to have with Abbu. That his son was now going to prison for kidnap, imprisonment, battery or GBH. He had come home a couple of months ago, but Zahra hadn't bothered to tell him. If she had, maybe none of this would have happened. She was just as much to blame.

On the third day, Libby burst in through the door, telling her that Kamran had been moved to a ward. Zahra waited for Uncle Ken again.

'I'm going with you this time,' she told him when he arrived.

Libby said she would stay with Abbu, as Zahra and Ken made their way to Ward 13. It was on the other side of the hospital. They walked down flights of stairs, took a lift, past the Costa coffee shop in the main entrance. Porters wheeled around trolleys, doctors hurried past them with patient notes. Zahra even spotted Alisha carrying a lunch carton, and hurried away quickly, not wanting her to ask why she was at the hospital again. When they finally reached the ward, Ken pressed the buzzer. The receptionist asked who they were here to see. Zahra gulped and mumbled Kamran's name.

They were let in and Ken hovered around the reception.

'Is he alone?' he asked the woman. 'Don't wanna intrude if he's with family.'

'No, his wife just left now. Visiting closes in twenty minutes.'

Zahra's heart panged. This was it.

Ken led the way to the room. It was already ajar. He tapped on it with his knuckle.

'Ay up,' he said.

As Zahra turned the corner, she saw the confusion in Kamran's face evaporate as his eyes rested on her.

'I'm sorry,' she said, quickly. 'We're just here to see if you're okay.'

Kamran nodded and motioned to the chairs. Ken closed the door behind him. Zahra sat down next to Kamran. He looked awful, bloodied and bruised with a cut lip, black eyes, and bandages around his arms. She glanced at Ken who was too stumped for words. He gathered himself quickly and clearing his throat.

'So,' he started. 'How… er… are you?'

Kamran ignored him and turned to Zahra. 'Saahil?' he croaked.

Zahra averted her gaze. She quickly relayed the story of Saahil's return. How he had warned her to keep quiet until he resolved 'unfinished business'. How she'd lied to Abbu for weeks, but had no idea what her brother was plotting. How Libby had burst into the house just in time to tell them that their dad had been found unconscious and was rushed into hospital. They were currently waiting on Ward 30. Abbu still didn't know Saahil was here, Zahra hadn't told him.

'If I'd known this is what he was planning…' she said, desperately.

Kamran's swollen eyes gave nothing away. Zahra couldn't tell whether he was angry or bitter. Or whether he wanted revenge and had told the police. She waited with bated breath.

Ken stepped in again.

'Look, mate,' he said, moving towards the bed. 'We need to know where we stand here. We assume you've told the police?'

Kamran shook his head. Zahra frowned, unsure whether it was a 'yes' or 'no'. She was almost leaning into the bed. Ken interpreted it as a 'yes' and his voice rose.

'My mate Amjad is recovering from an overdose, he doesn't even know his son is back. They've suffered for ten years. All of them. And poor Ehsan is lying six feet under. As far as I know, you're very much to blame for a big part of this.'

This time Kamran shook his head more vigorously. He tried to speak, pursing his chapped lips together.

'Mm-mugged,' he stuttered. 'Mugged and don't remember a thing.'

Ken almost jumped back. 'You what?'

'Haven't told police… anything.'

Zahra stood up. She didn't believe it. 'What? Why would you do that?'

Kamran blinked but said nothing.

'But I was there,' she continued. 'Saahil was going to hit you over the head with that thing and—'

'Okay,' Ken said, loudly. 'If the lad's made his decision.'

Zahra took a seat next to Kamran again. She didn't know this man. The first time she had met him was when her own brother was trying to beat him to death. But Zahra needed to know the truth, *and* she needed his help. She leaned closer, feeling an urge to reach out and touch Kamran, to make him understand.

'Please tell me you're not lying,' she asked, both of her hands gripped around his bandaged arm. 'Please, don't—'

'I want… put it behind me,' Kamran sighed.

Zahra glanced back at Ken, who laughed nervously.

'Zahra?' Kamran whispered.

She turned to him.

'Does he… he forgive me?'

Zahra thought about it before giving a curt nod. 'He *will*. I'll make him.'

Forty-Five

A few days later, the nurses spoke of discharging Abbu. Everyone had visited him now. Ammi barely left his bedside, switching from scolding him for not paying attention to his medication, and muttering prayers under her breath. Zahra was the same, only returning home at night to sleep. Ken and Libby came during visiting hours. One person stayed outside on the corridor, waiting for someone to come out of the room so he could ask, 'Is he all right?'

Up until now, nobody had told Abbu about his missing son. Even Ammi kept quiet, though not without a fight.

'Just let us think about the best way to go about this,' Zahra pleaded with her. 'He's been through a lot already, don't wanna send him into shock again.'

She turned to look at Saahil, who hadn't spoken much since they'd first arrived at the hospital.

'Do you mind helping me out here?' Zahra said, trying to be discreet and motioning with her eyes to Ammi.

'Yeah, sorry.'

He put his arm around the old woman and suggested they go for a walk. Ammi resisted but Saahil led her away, offering to buy her a cup of tea and cake. They came back an hour later, with Ammi in a more relaxed and agreeable mood.

Now with talk of Abbu returning home, Zahra was itching to

465

get things out in the open. Abbu was feeling much better. He was talking, eating and getting out of bed on his own. There was only one thing Zahra was certain about, that *she* couldn't be the one to tell him about his son. Even though Ammi would have gladly walked in and blurted out the truth to Abbu, she was hardly the most tactful. Being gentle just wasn't in her nature. And so Zahra waited again for Uncle Ken's visit that evening, he being the only 'proper adult' she could rely on at the moment.

He arrived at his usual time. Zahra asked for a quiet word and explained that Abbu would be discharged tomorrow morning. She couldn't hide it for any longer.

'I can't bring myself to tell him,' she said, eyes averted with shame. 'I lied to him for weeks. If something had happened to him now… He would never have known.'

'Don't worry,' Ken said, placing his arm around her. 'I'll explain it all to him properly. He'll understand.'

They stood for a moment outside Abbu's room, preparing themselves for the task ahead. Bringing his shoulders up in resolve, Ken pushed open the door.

'It wasn't your fault,' he said to Zahra. He nodded to her reassuringly. Zahra couldn't work out whether he was genuinely optimistic, or just putting on a brave front for her. He disappeared into the room.

Zahra took a deep breath and stood around facing the door. She realised it would reveal no secrets and decided to take a seat. Both hands were placed over her fluttering heart. Her stomach growled. Zahra's face flushed hot. Her knees shivered. She was taking long, slow breaths. Her body was reacting to an event that she had been waiting for for half her life.

Twenty minutes later, and Ken appeared at the door.

'You better get him in here now!' he shouted.

Zahra ran around the corner to where Saahil had gone to get coffee. She found him carrying two plastic cups back carefully from the vending machines.

'Forget this!' Zahra said, putting the cups on a table. 'Come on!'

They sprinted together down the winding corridors, hand in hand. They ran past the nurses' station and dodged other waiting relatives who were lounging around in the available seating. Ken was pacing outside Abbu's room.

'In!' he simply said.

Saahil nodded as he realised what was about to happen. He was breathing hard. His shaking hands smoothed down his collar. He swore. And then apologised.

'Go on, Saahil,' Zahra said, nudging him.

Saahil closed his eyes and scrunched up his face. He pushed open the door, and disappeared off quickly inside. It slammed with a thud. Zahra and Ken were left to stare at each other.

For the next half hour, she walked around the corridor in a daze. Visiting hours closed and Ken was ushered out by the nurses. Zahra was left alone to worry. She placed her ear against the door. She could hear nothing. They were thick and wooden, and no sound escaped them. There was a window, but the blinds were drawn. Zahra didn't know if they were arguing or reconciling.

Eventually, she could take no more. She teetered towards the door, placing her head towards it. It was cold against her ear. She shivered. Her fingertips touched the wood, she pushed slightly. It was too heavy to be opened with just her fingers. She arranged her palms to lie flat against the door. Her forehead was also leaning in. Zahra pushed harder. There was a barely audible swoosh. She tilted her head and peered through the tiny crack. There was no sound. Further still, and Zahra saw Saahil's legs dangling from the side of the bed. Another inch, and her dad and brother both came into view.

Abbu was lying down. Saahil was curled up next to him, head resting against his shoulder. Abbu's arm was cradling his head. Clutching him tight. Both had their eyes closed, almost as if they were sleeping. Almost as though the past ten years had never even happened. Zahra let out a small cry. The machine in the corner of the room beeped. Her shaky hand reached over and turned a circular switch on the wall clockwise. The light dimmed.

Slowly, Zahra closed the door. She stood outside, guarding the room for half an hour, shooing away the busybody nurse, telling her that Abbu's eight o'clock medication could wait.

'Excuse me?' the nurse asked, head tilting from side to side with attitude.

'It can wait,' Zahra said, smiling with dreamy eyes. 'Everything can wait.'

Forty-Six

'Nasreen said I hadn't put enough butter in my sweet rice,' Ammi said, peeling pomegranates on to a plate. 'Silly cow.'

'I think they're gardening, Ammi,' Zahra said, peering out of the window.

'Gardening? It's January.'

'Oh… no, they're doing something to the car.'

'That's good,' Ammi replied. 'You should have tasted her rice pudding. Fat, lumpy bits in it. Mine is beautiful and smooth.'

'Probably washing it or something,' Zahra said, adjusting her head to get a better look. 'They're not talking, though.'

Ammi placed the pomegranates down and looked up, exasperatedly. 'Zahra, stop worrying. Please come and sit down.'

Reluctantly, Zahra backed away from the window. She took a seat next to her grandma, fidgeting and unable to sit still. It wasn't the first time Ammi had said that to her. The agonising past six months had gone by with Ammi repeating the same words to her over and over again: *Zahra, stop worrying.*

But Zahra couldn't stop worrying, because something was supposed to have happened by now, and it hadn't. She often thought back to the crazy summer of last year. Her brother returned after a decade, and Zahra had been so determined to reunite everyone that she hadn't given much thought to what

469

would happen after he came home. All the problems would end the minute he stepped in through the door. Six months on, and Zahra was still waiting for things to get better.

After Abbu had been discharged from hospital, he was referred for a newer, more intense Cognitive Behavioural Therapy programme for sleep problems. He would visit the therapist on a weekly basis and return home with new instructions on how to reset his 'internal sleep clock'. They provided him with a sleep window: to go to bed at midnight, and to be out of the house by 6 a.m. sharp, even at weekends. If he was unable to drift off, he could only stay in bed for fifteen minutes before returning back downstairs and starting all over again.

'Apparently it conditions your brain to associate the bed with sleep and nothing else so you're not tossing and turning,' Abbu told them miserably.

Things got worse before they got better. Weeks passed by and Abbu stomped up and down the stairs throughout the night. The whole family tiptoed around him, talked in whispers and shushed each other as soon as he entered the room.

'You *can* talk in front of me, I'm not an invalid,' he'd snapped.

Slowly, things seemed to work out. His sleep improved, inching forwards by fifteen minutes at a time. So did his mood. Abbu hadn't spoken to Zahra properly for a few weeks after he'd been discharged from hospital. She didn't blame him. She knew she shouldn't have hidden Saahil from him. It had taken time, but things eventually returned to normal between them.

'I know it was his fault,' Abbu said. 'He made you.'

'Well, he didn't have a gun to my head,' Zahra replied. 'But I just wanted him to come home... because he wanted to. Not because he had no choice. I was too busy trying to make him understand, and weeks just went by.'

After things were patched up between them, Zahra waited for the same thing to happen with Abbu and Saahil. It never did. The two of them could hardly be in the same room together without an atmosphere. Six months on, and Saahil still looked guilty all the time. Six months on, and Abbu still looked hurt. Zahra knew that he couldn't really accept that his son had deliberately gone missing, and willingly stayed away from them for a decade. Saahil put them through ten years of hell, and Abbu wasn't so forgiving.

Neither was society. Once news of Saahil's reappearance passed around, the 'well wishers' came to visit. They'd ask insensitive questions in front of everyone.

Where had Saahil been? Why did he stay away from his own family? Did he realise what he'd put them through? His Abbu had nearly died in hospital with worry! The family needed to look after Saahil properly this time.

Saahil squirmed his way through. Ammi tried to change the subject. Zahra was told off for opening her big trap and being rude to guests. When it was all over, Abbu stomped off upstairs and slammed his bedroom door shut.

Even without annoying guests, things were far from rosy. Because Abbu and Saahil could barely talk to each other, Zahra was always left to deliver messages between them both:

'Tell Abbu that…'

'Say to Saahil that…'

Zahra insisted they speak to each other themselves. So they did, but even that almost always went wrong. A few weeks ago, the DVD player had stopped working. Zahra watched as Abbu and Saahil squabbled over who should fix it.

'Let me do it...'

'No, Abbu, it'd be easier if I—'

'No, move out of the way...'

After discovering that it was simply a wire that had come loose, Saahil said, 'If you'd just let me reach behind the telly I could have sorted it out ages ago.'

Abbu exploded: 'We don't need you to sort things out. Who do you think did things around here when you disappeared for a decade?'

Saahil stared at Abbu. Ammi shouted at him for 'saying things to the boy'. Saahil stormed out of the house and didn't return all day. Ammi was hysterical, believing Abbu had chased him away. Zahra's calls and texts to Saahil went unanswered. Three agonising hours later, the whole family sighed with relief when he walked in through the door that evening.

Zahra found an opportune moment to quiz Abbu alone when Saahil took Ammi to a hospital appointment. She sat next to him as he watched the news and held his hand.

'Abbu?' she asked.

'Hmmm?'

'Are you happy?'

Abbu looked at her. 'Yeah, why?'

'No, I mean... you know.'

Abbu sighed. 'As long as... as long as he's in front of my eyes. And I can see him... Both of you.'

'But I want it to be better than that,' Zahra said. 'Why can't it be like—'

'It'll take time, Zee. Anyway, no need for you to worry.'

And there it was again. Everyone telling her to stop worrying. Just like Ammi had done again now for the hundredth time.

'Will you get me my Metformin tablet?' she asked, chopping another pomegranate in half.

Zahra went into the kitchen and brought back some water for Ammi. She couldn't help but take another glance out of the window.

'Ammi!' Zahra shouted. 'I think they're laughing.'

'Really?'

'Yeah, Saahil is and… hang on, I can't see Abbu.'

She pulled the ridiculous curtains out of the way and craned her head through the window. 'Abbu's smiling!'

'Well, leave them to it. Give me my tablet.'

Zahra did so.

'I wonder what happened,' she said, beaming.

Ammi swallowed the tablet with a hiccup. She brought her hand to her chest and regained her breath. 'Stop worrying.'

'I know.'

'It'll take time,' Ammi said, holding Zahra's chin. 'Just give them time.'

Forty-Seven

Saahil sat alone by the window of the depressing café. Hood pulled up and earphones in. He was dead to the world. He watched commuters run past to catch buses as he drank his tasteless coffee. The windows were steamed up, the air cold. Saahil wondered what he was doing there. Alone at the bus station, where only weirdos hung out. The chavs with their prams, the alcoholics, the homeless sitting on the floor with plastic cups waiting for change.

There were loads of them. They were a lot more visible than when he himself had been on the streets. Zahra informed him that homelessness had risen by 60 per cent due to benefits cuts imposed by the government. Funding was also being slashed to services that provided help and support for rough sleepers. The government wanted to save money. Not people.

'This spice thing,' she told him one day. 'It's lethal. Look at this.'

She swivelled her laptop around and played a video for him. A man was staggering around on a busy high street. People were avoiding him and he stumbled over himself, walking around in circles. Eventually he collapsed on the floor, his head bouncing off the pavement. No one helped him for a full five minutes. Saahil pushed the laptop screen away from him.

'Oh, sorry,' Zahra said. 'I didn't mean to upset you.'

She sent him numerous articles via WhatsApp, tagged him on various Facebook and Twitter posts. Legal highs were no longer just a new thrill that people were experimenting with anymore; it had become a nationwide epidemic amongst the homeless. Everyone was at it. The chemical compounds were being altered to keep within the law, people were collapsing in city centres, A&E departments struggling to cope with the strain. One disturbing article spoke about users being gang-raped and trafficked. Some were having mental breakdowns and being sectioned, twenty-year-olds were having heart attacks and dropping dead in day centres.

'You beat this,' Zahra said to him. 'You can help do something about it.'

Saahil shook his head. 'No, I can't.'

'Why?'

'Because it's gotten worse than when I was on it. That was just the beginning. Now the drug is more potent, more dangerous.'

Zahra didn't push him any further. It was still difficult at times, navigating their relationship. They were all still getting used to knowing each other again, adjusting to one another's space. On some days, Saahil needed to get out of the house and spend some hours on his own. Not that he had loads of spare time now that he was working at the warehouse. Abbu had returned on a part-time basis, only working three days a week as he tried to control his insomnia. Saahil always drove, even when Abbu was with him. They set off together in the cold, dark mornings. They spoke at work, about things relating to work, and drove home again in the evenings, in silence. It was okay. It kept Saahil's mind busy.

At the weekends, he would fix things around the house, take Ammi shopping, or go out with Zahra for lunch. Sometimes he would meet up with Umar and the old gang from university. One day, Saahil spotted Kamran. He'd been at the supermarket, waiting around as Ammi fussed over the prices of fresh fruit. He'd glanced over his shoulder and seen Kamran watching him from across the aisle. Saahil didn't know what to do. Kamran had hesitated, then raised a shaky hand at him. Saahil's eye fell on the child in the trolley seat. It was Kamran's little girl. He remembered what he'd almost done and considered raising his hand in acknowledgement. Something stopped him and a second later, Saahil turned away.

As he finished his coffee, he received a text message from Zahra. He knew what it would be before he even opened it. As much as the family tried to be normal around him, they failed miserably. They would freeze whenever he told them he was off out and only breathed easy again when he walked back in. Zahra sent him random messages to ask what he wanted to eat that night. Did he want to go to the cinema? Or would he prefer to watch one of those addictive TV shows on Netflix? It was just a way of checking to see if he was coming home or not. This time, however, she told him the complete opposite, as a neighbour had dropped by and was being nosy about him. He was about to reply when a voice made him jump.

'Saahil?'

He looked up and couldn't believe his eyes. 'Alisha?'

She smiled and nodded. They both giggled nervously before Saahil asked her to take a seat. She declined and said she was waiting for a lift that would be here at any moment.

'How are you?' she asked.

'Good,' Saahil replied. 'How are you?'

She had barely changed from the days when Ehsan would pine

476

after her down university corridors. The only difference was she was wearing a hospital uniform, white with a blue border. Her hijab matched the blue and Saahil had forgotten how beautiful her eyes were. They were green. Saahil thought of Ehsan with a pang.

'I heard you were… glad you're back,' Alisha said.

'Yeah… are you a nurse now?' Saahil asked, wishing to change the subject.

'No, a sonographer.'

'Right.'

'How's your little sister?' she asked.

'Oh, she's good,' Saahil replied, surprised Alisha would ask about Zahra.

She realised and rushed to explain, 'I've met her a few times at the hospital, she's a lovely girl,' she said. 'Plus Ehsan was always mentioning her.'

They both stared at each other. Saahil thought he saw Alisha's lip quiver.

'I'd best be off anyway,' she said, moving away. 'Nice to see you.'

'Wait,' Saahil said, standing up. 'Would you like to meet for a coffee sometime? We could have a proper catch-up?'

He watched as Alisha thought about it for a second. Eventually, she nodded. They exchanged numbers and Saahil watched her disappear from the station. It was probably more out of courtesy that she had agreed to meet him. It wasn't like they really knew each other. But the day that Saahil had seen Alisha at the hospital and ignored her had haunted him over the years. He wanted an opportunity to explain himself and apologise.

As he walked home, he thought about Alisha's reaction to

Ehsan's name being mentioned. She'll have moved on. It was only natural. As people who were now in their early thirties, Alisha would probably be married and have a family of her own. It was strange, that after so long, she would still become visibly upset by the mention of his name. It comforted Saahil that a small part of his friend's memory still remained in her heart.

Saahil sent Alisha a text a few days later and they agreed to meet at the weekend, this time at a much more upmarket café. It was awkward at first, because despite her link to Ehsan, he had always remained in the background, mocking Ehsan and laughing at him. He could, however, take credit for most of their correspondence, as Saahil was the one who counselled Ehsan through the writing of text messages.

'Shall I put a kiss?' Ehsan would ask.

'Yeah, put one,' Saahil replied.

'But she put two.'

'Idiot, put one,' Saahil snapped.

'Maybe I should put three, because she put two, one more than last time,' Ehsan pondered.

'Three? Are you off your head? Three is overkill, mate. Put one!'

After making small talk and over-stirring their coffees, Saahil went straight to it.

'That day I saw you at the hospital,' he began, not looking directly at her. 'I should have spoken to you. I'm really sorry.'

'Don't worry about it,' Alisha said. 'I know it was a really hard time for you.'

'No, I've never been able to get over what I did that day. I just left you there and you were standing alone.'

'It was probably for the best,' she reassured. 'I don't think he would have wanted me to see him… like that.'

She sipped her coffee, the cup lingering in front of her face longer than it should. Nobody spoke for a while. Something niggled at Saahil. *Why was she so sad?* He assumed he was the only one who was still so hung up about the whole thing. Since his return, Saahil had spent time with Umar and the rest of the guys from uni. Everyone seemed to have moved on. Saahil didn't blame them, it had been over ten years now. But Alisha seemed to withdraw at the mention of Ehsan's name. And in all fairness, Saahil thought, they hadn't even been a proper couple at the time. That chance had been snatched away from them.

Saahil steered the conversation away from Ehsan and asked Alisha about her job. After laughing about horror stories of smelly patients who she would have to perform intimate scans on, Alisha asked Saahil if he was working.

'Just with my dad, at the warehouse for now.'

'But what about your degree?' she asked.

'Might as well flush it down the toilet,' he replied.

'But can't you—'

'No. Don't think I could get away with the ten-year gap on my CV,' he laughed.

As the conversation ran cold, they distracted themselves with a cute baby that was sitting near them in a high-chair. It was a little girl, with blonde ringlets. She waved at them and hid her face.

Saahil looked at Alisha. 'Have you got children?' he asked.

'No, I'm not married.'

Saahil quickly concealed his surprise. Early thirties and unmarried? That was heart-attack-inducing in the Asian community. The only reason they hadn't got to him yet was because he hadn't bloody been around for the past ten years. And Saahil knew women had a much harder time with the marriage police than guys.

He quickly asked if she wanted another coffee as he didn't want her to think he was prying. It was none of his business.

'I almost married a few years ago,' Alisha continued, unperturbed. 'But I called the wedding off.'

'Oh,' Saahil said, not sure just how much interest he should show. But Alisha carried on.

'We met at work, he was nice. But everything went downhill once the families got involved.'

'Sounds about right,' said Saahil, only too aware of interfering Asian family politics.

'As the wedding drew closer, their demands were just getting more and more ridiculous.'

'What about him, though?' Saahil asked.

'He just started doing whatever his mum said. So I told him to get stuffed three weeks before the wedding.'

'Nice,' Saahil smiled.

Alisha smiled back.

'So now I suppose everyone's going on at you because you're over thirty and not hitched?'

'My family have got over it,' Alisha replied. 'But it's everyone else. The women, they come over and say stuff to my mum.'

'They can piss off,' said Saahil, thinking about his own experiences with so-called 'family friends' since his return.

'Exactly, I'm not getting married just for the sake of getting married,' she said, grimacing.

Saahil's phone vibrated on the table. Alisha went silent and waited for him as he checked it. It was Zahra asking him if he'd ever watched *Prison Break* while he was 'away'. It had first aired in 2005, she told him.

Saahil replied: 'No, I was homeless then.' He added a sticky out tongue emoji.

'So, what happened to you?' Alisha asked, tentatively. 'When you were... gone?'

Saahil wringed his hands under the table. The question still made him anxious. 'Erm... It's a long story.'

Alisha raised her eyebrows.

'Right,' she said, making to stand up. 'I'll get more coffee then.'

Forty-Eight

Saahil was old news by the time spring arrived. Not just for the family, but also for the wider community. He sat alone in his room, free to ponder over his latest dilemma. Zahra was tapping away on her laptop next door. Abbu and Ammi were watching an old Amitabh Bachchan movie downstairs so no one would disturb him. An email was displayed in front of Saahil telling him he had reached the third stage of applications for a job. The problem was, it wasn't just any old job. Over the past three months, Saahil had spent his evenings and weekends undertaking extremely hard online tests. He'd been one of the 3,000 applicants, proceeded on to stage two with 1,700 others, and now, unbelievably had passed again as one of 600 applicants. Saahil had reached the interview stage to become an Air Traffic Controller.

There was a slight problem. From the first time when he had casually googled it, Saahil started the application out of curiosity. It was an open opportunity, anybody could have a go, as long as they possessed five GCSEs. But out of 3,000 applicants, five assessment and interview stages, a three-year training programme, only twenty people would go on to qualify. Saahil definitely only started an application through curiosity, but the more tests he passed, the more immersed he became. It was varied. The assessments ranged from reaction time, visualisation, planning, processing, alertness. When he was doing them, Saahil felt like his old self again. His fingers jabbed away at the keyboard. His focus was razor-sharp. He worked on it late into the night, careful that no one would hear him. Now that he'd got to the interview stage, Saahil knew he still had it in him.

But in all his headiness, he made one fundamental mistake. Without properly researching what the role required, Saahil had got way ahead of himself. Now, a lump appeared in his throat as he read the job description properly. A relocation to Hampshire, to study for three years at the NATS college was essential. Saahil popped it into Google Maps. His heart sank when he saw that it was on the south coast of England near Bournemouth and Portsmouth. After this, he must be prepared to be posted to any air traffic control unit in the UK. Flexibility was key, and that was the one thing Saahil didn't have.

He couldn't go now, not after only being at home for six months. He was needed here. He still had to make it up to his family, to prove that he was here to stay, to look after Ammi, to rebuild his relationship with Abbu. Not go off to Hampshire to pursue his own dreams.

Nobody knew. And Saahil wouldn't tell anyone. If Zahra got a whiff of this, she would make sure he completed his application, and do whatever it took to achieve his ambition. So would Ammi. Saahil was sure that even Abbu would agree too. In the long term, it would benefit them all.

'Long term' was something Saahil could not think of right now. He was living day by day. Maybe it was something he could do in the future. But right now, no matter how many tests he passed and how many people he surpassed in the applications, Saahil could not pursue it. It was Zahra's time now, not his. She had pelted him with a few emails of her own, detailing vacancy positions for substance abuse support workers, similar to the kind of work Alan, the man at the day centre, did. Saahil read them with great interest. The roles involved outreach work, counselling and rehabilitation. Saahil knew he could do it. He had the bonus of having been there himself. But still, he wasn't sure he wanted to re-enter that world. And it wasn't the same as being an Air Traffic Controller. That was something that was part of his initial dreams, his passion, before his life had fallen apart.

He thought about it. Really wrestled with what to do. In the end, Saahil moved the mouse and lingered over his account details. With a heavy heart, he clicked on the button.

Withdraw application.

'You okay, Zee,' Saahil asked, entering her bedroom. She was sitting at her desk.

'Er... yeah,' she replied, slowly closing her laptop.

'What you doing?'

'Oh, nowt.'

Saahil raised his eyebrow.

Zahra sighed. 'Just applying for this job.'

'Hmmm. What is it?' he asked.

Zahra shrugged. 'Forget it.'

'No, tell me,' Saahil said, sitting down on the bed.

'Well, it's a bit... out there. It's an internship for this current affairs show that comes on in the early mornings. People debate stuff,' Zahra said, trying to trivialise it. 'But it's only open for BAME people, which may help.'

'BAME?' Saahil asked, feeling stupid.

'Black, Asian, minority ethnic,' she replied. 'It says, "Open to

BAME candidates from underrepresented and disadvantaged groups."'

'Right, who is it with?'

'ITV.'

Saahil nodded encouragingly.

Zahra laughed at him. 'You can just tell me not to bother,' she said.

'Why would I do that?'

She shuffled on her chair. 'Well, I haven't had much success so far, have I? And I have applied for some really crap jobs too.'

'Look,' said Saahil, pulling his knee up on to the bed and getting comfy, 'I've told you not to worry about rushing to find a job. You see it on the news all the time, graduates can't get jobs at the moment. You're all in the same boat.'

'Yeah, but I graduated six months ago,' Zahra mumbled. 'And I've done… nothing.'

'That's not true. You're trying at least. All I see you doing is filling in these awful application forms out, day in, day out.'

Saahil watched as Zahra rocked in her chair, biting her lip. She looked at the floor. 'I just don't want people to think I wasted my time doing a worthless humanities degree and—'

'It's not worthless at all,' said Saahil, touching her arm. 'You know about stuff I don't even have a clue about.'

Zahra shrugged it off.

'Give me the laptop,' he said. 'You talk, I'll type it up for you.'

'Well, I was just watching the programme, to see what it was all about.'

'Cool,' he said. 'I'll watch it with you.'

Saahil held the laptop on his knees as Zahra snuggled next to him. It was nearly midnight, and they both settled down to watch a politics show that normally aired on Sunday mornings.

People were seated on both sides of the room. A presenter wandered around the studio with a microphone as questions appeared on the screen. Members of the audience offered their opinions on topics. To say that things got a bit heated was an understatement. Saahil wore a permanent scowl on his face as people debated the niqab/hijab and what Muslim women wore. A man spoke about Pakistani grooming gangs operating in northern cities and announced that 90 per cent of sex attacks were committed by Muslims. People hit back in outrage. They shifted topics. Immigrants were a favourite. So were cuts to the NHS and Britain's role in the European Union. Things, however, always seemed to roll back to one thing: Muslims, Muslims, Muslims. Their views on free speech. On women. On homosexuality. On Palestine. On anti-Semitism. On Isis. On terrorism. By the time the programme was over, Saahil was biting his nails.

'Hmmm, interesting,' Zahra said, putting the laptop away.

Saahil was shocked to see that she was completely unruffled. 'Zee?' he asked. 'Are you sure this is what you want to do?'

'What?'

'*This*,' Saahil replied. 'I mean… bloody hell. Don't you want a quiet life?'

Zahra smiled. 'Libby says stuff like that to me,' she said. 'But despite how close we are, she just doesn't get it. She doesn't know what it's like to be hated.'

'Zahra, stop it,' Saahil snapped. 'Stop saying stuff like that. People don't hate us.'

Zahra stared at him. Eventually she answered. 'In case you haven't noticed, terrorist attacks are happening more regularly. In the past two months there's been Sydney, Peshawar, Istanbul, Paris—'

486

'I know.'

'Fanatics are beheading aid workers in Syria who have sacrificed their Christmases—'

'I know, Zee.'

'—and you don't think people hate us?'

'Fine, whatever. But just because there's a fight happening doesn't mean you have to go and throw yourself in the middle,' Saahil urged. 'You don't have to engage directly with all of this. You could just… I don't know… keep your head down.'

Zahra laughed. 'Everyone is out there trying to keep their head down, but it still comes and finds you. Every day.'

'I know—'

'No, you don't.'

'Why?' Saahil asked.

'Because you remember a time before 9/11. I don't.'

In a few words, Zahra had completely shut him up. He was stumped, lost for words. She was right. He had managed nineteen normal years before everything came crashing down on them all.

'Look,' she said. 'I know what you mean. I've got friends who I go out with, and we never discuss any of this. We sit there and talk about boys and clothes and make-up. And that's all good. But at the end of the day, I'm not that type of a person. I'm nosy. I want to know what's going on.'

Saahil smiled.

'It's true,' Zahra said. 'I will read all those awful *Daily Mail* comments to find out what everyone's thinking about us.'

'People talk crap online.'

'No, that's where their true feelings come out. And I won't feel happy sitting here wrapped up in my own life when I can be doing something about it.'

'But there's nothing we can do about it,' said Saahil.

'It's not about whether I *can* do something or not, I *want* to,' Zahra replied, adjusting herself on the seat. 'Think about it. Has anyone ever asked you how you feel? No, because everyone is too busy *telling* us who we are. It's time we spoke for ourselves.'

'Yeah, I get that, but it's just not very effective, it is?'

'Because we don't get a platform,' Zahra cried. 'What about the people that don't become radicalised? There are more of us, and they've just completely written us off. Why? Because we're not interesting enough? It's the same cycle every time. Terrorist attack happens, start apologising, condemn everything. Repeat.'

Saahil reached out and took Zahra's hand in his. He wanted her to understand, but she wore a frown that didn't seem as if it would budge so easily.

'This whole thing is so… big,' he began. 'And we're so small. For every good thing that you or I do, there are ten people out there in a training camp somewhere, undoing it at the same time.' He sighed. 'We can't win.'

Zahra stayed quiet for approximately ten seconds.

'But look, Saahil, at the moment everyone is "Je suis Charlie", right? And a few weeks ago, the Taliban massacred a hundred and thirty-two kids in a Pakistani school. No one changed their Facebook profiles then, did they? And then they actually want us to grovel every time something goes wrong. They conveniently forget that we get killed too. By the same people. In fact, if they want a competition, we get killed more!'

'Well, yeah, we're too busy killing each other,' said Saahil. 'Look at the Middle East. It's a complete shit show.'

'But we're not from there,' Zahra shot back. 'We're here. *This* is where we come from. Whether they like it or not, we're British.

488

And you just watch, one day, something massive is going to happen here. And we won't be able to just stay under the radar.'

'But I don't want...' Saahil began. 'I can't bear the thought of anybody hurting you, and the abuse people receive online, especially women...'

His voice trailed off. He couldn't quite sum up his fears. He admired people who were brave enough to tackle difficult things head-on. But when everything bad in the world seemed to be directly connected to them, it was a different story. Zahra seemed to read his mind.

'A lot of the things that are happening to us, only *we*,' she said, motioning to the space between them, 'know what it's like. Our opinions and perceptions are unique. They matter and who knows, they may even help. Nobody can tell things from our point of view better than us.'

Saahil watched his little sister's eyes narrow and focus on him, face resting against her palm.

'I'd just hoped for something better for you,' he eventually said. 'Something easier.'

He wanted to grab hold of her and ask her if she could just start caring less. *Be selfish like me*, he wanted to say. He didn't and instead Saahil just watched her, realising that it was like looking in a mirror. He'd been like that at her age. Buzzing, angry, passionate, bouncing off the walls. Thinking he knew everything, thinking he was important and was going to change the world. The only difference was that Zahra was more intelligent than him. And her grievances, legitimate. The old Saahil would have egged her on. Pumped her. Exacerbated the problem. Now, as he listened to himself, he just sounded grumpy and a tad bit boring. Any type of rebellion had been knocked out of him good and proper.

As he lay in bed thinking about their conversation, he heard Zahra knock something over in the next room. She was awake too. He wondered when exactly fear and foreboding had become so ingrained in their lives. So normal.

I'd just hoped for something better for you. Something easier.

When he'd said this, Zahra opened her mouth but didn't say anything. She sat back and stared ahead, sighing deeply. Saahil knew what she wanted to say. That 'easy' just wasn't an option that had been given to them.

Forty-Nine

A few weeks later, Saahil woke up in the morning and cursed under his breath. He turned to his side and pulled the bed covers over his head, wishing he'd not woken up at all. The previous day's events replayed in his mind. Saahil tried to shut it out, but the images whizzed through his brain, vividly. He felt worse about the situation than he had done yesterday. He'd fallen into an uneasy sleep, tossing in bed, berating himself for his actions. Saahil reached under his pillow and checked his mobile, but there was no text message to say 'Don't worry about it'. Just silence.

He sat up, hugging his shoulders and wondering how things had ended up this way. How a genuine concern for Ehsan's love interest had evolved into something else.

Alisha

Saahil felt strange about her. That was how it had started. Text messages turned into lengthy phone calls, which turned into regular meet-ups. There was a time when Saahil wouldn't have even dreamed of thinking about her in that way. He cared for her because of her link to Ehsan. That was all. But now, he was not so sure.

Saahil tried to push those thoughts out of his head. He tried not to notice how pretty Alisha looked when she came to see him. How her hijab was loosely tied and always coordinated with the rest of her outfit. How her eyes were always lined with kajal, perfectly framing the elegant dip of her nose.

491

Even Zahra seemed to have noticed. She said something a few weeks ago when Saahil had received a text message from Alisha. He was replying when he saw that Zahra was watching him.

'Who is it?' she asked.

'Just Alisha,' he replied, smiling.

Zahra smirked at him.

'What?'

'Nothing,' she said, in a teasing, drawn out way.

It niggled at Saahil for the rest of the evening. He wanted to ask his sister what she meant by it, but didn't. Yeah, he was communicating a lot with Alisha at the moment. But it was no biggie. They got on, that's all. He liked spending time with her. At first, they spoke mostly about Ehsan. It was comfortable, Alisha seemed to loosen up a bit. She told him about things the two of them spoke about all those years ago.

'Every single thing he talked about,' she said. 'You were always there with him. So if we'd ever… you know… got together. Me and Ehsan. There would have been three of us in that relationship,' she'd laughed.

Saahil informed her that they already were, as he had been the architect of most of Ehsan's correspondence with her.

Slowly, though, Ehsan began slipping away.

Not just from the conversation, but from their minds too. When Saahil really thought about it, it consumed him with guilt. It wasn't the first time, after all, that he had left his best friend behind. But after weeks of getting to know Alisha, Saahil knew he was too invested in her. He would wait for her messages, her phone calls, her suggestions that they meet at the weekend. He brushed it aside, as nothing more than 'just friends' but deep down, Saahil knew it was transforming into something else. He was even sure that Alisha was feeling this too. There were signs, he thought. The way their eyes lingered for longer than was appropriate, the nervous giggles, the furtive glances. How their hands seemed to brush unexpectedly and neither would pull away.

Saahil felt it was wrong. It couldn't be right, not after Ehsan's love for Alisha in their youth. And yet Saahil couldn't resist. He couldn't pull back. He still replied to every text, answered every call, rushed to spend time with her. She was calming and laidback. When he was with her, things softened. One moment she would be thoughtful and wise, and the next she would drop the 'C' word into their conversation like a bullet. When Saahil thought about her, he smiled unintentionally. He'd spent the last six months waiting around for things to get better. As much as they all tried, it just wasn't possible with his family. He had hurt them too much. Alisha was an outsider, so things were different.

Yesterday, though, he had taken things too far. Alisha was talking. Saahil couldn't remember what about. Then he realised she had stopped and was staring at him. Without thinking, he leaned in and kissed her on the lips. They were full and soft. When he pulled back, she was staring at him still, but this time in shock. He didn't see it coming, but her palm made contact with his face. Hard. He watched her storm off and didn't follow.

Later on, at home, he'd written out a text apologising, but didn't send it. There was no point. He'd blown it, and it was probably for the best.

Now, as Saahil sat up in bed, he loathed himself for being so stupid. It was classic *him*, to make a mess of everything. Nothing changed there. Feeling depressed, Saahil got up and dressed to go downstairs. He would probably go for a run to take his mind off things. His phone buzzed.

When he checked, his heart dropped. It was Alisha. She'd written:

Can we talk?

Saahil looked at it for a while. A small ebb of hope sprang into his chest. He knew this much about women, that if Alisha really thought he was a creep and couldn't stand the sight of him, she would not have reached out. Still, he needed to make sense of things. If they were going to 'talk', where did he stand?

After wasting ten minutes pacing around, Saahil realised he needed Zahra. He made his way to her room and knocked on her door. It was already slightly ajar. She was still in bed, her curtains drawn closed.

'Zee,' he whispered through the crack.

'I'm awake,' she croaked from under the duvet.

Saahil told her not to get up and sat on his knees on the floor, facing her.

'Are you okay?' she asked, making to get up.

'I need to tell you something.'

'I knew it,' Zahra hooted, pointing at him and laughing.

'How?'

'Because you're like this all the time.' She imitated him texting on the phone. 'Like a teenager,' she added.

'Oh no,' he said. 'Was it really that gross?'

She shook her head. 'No, it was kinda cute.'

Saahil looked unconvinced.

'What's the problem?' Zahra asked.

'Be honest with me, Zee,' he said. 'Is it... wrong?'

'Wrong?'

'Well, weird… Because of Ehsan?'

Zahra pursed her lips. She clipped and unclipped the buttons on her duvet, thinking. Saahil waited patiently for her response.

'You don't think,' she began, slowly. 'After everything that's happened, it's sort of… meant to be?'

Saahil frowned. 'No, not really.'

'Hear me out,' Zahra said, touching his arm. 'You loved Ehsan. She loved Ehsan. You're single. She's single. You're unhappy and, I don't know her but, assuming everything that happened with that previous bloke, she's unhappy too. Kinda makes sense.'

'I'm not unhappy,' Saahil shot back, sitting bolt upright. 'Why would I be unhappy? I'm finally at home, I'm with all of you.'

Zahra looked at the floor. 'I know, but there's something missing, isn't there?' she mumbled. 'You don't have to pretend.'

Saahil gawped at her. How did she know him so well? Better than he even knew himself? Saahil could have denied her comment, but knew there was no point. One thing he'd learned since returning home was that he couldn't fool his little sister. About anything.

'I understand where you're coming from,' she continued. 'But it's not like they were married or even a proper couple. The way you've described it to me, it sounded like a high school crush. I mean, they'd only just started talking on the phone, right?'

'Yeah, Ehsan took his time.'

'Bless him,' Zahra said, smiling as she thought about him.

'It could have been, though,' Saahil suggested. 'For both of them.'

'We can't change what happened. But we can make the best of it.'

'And you're sure *this* would be making the best of it?'

'Saahil, stop worrying,' Zahra said. 'I don't know, but I think Ehsan would be totally cool with it.'

'Really?' Saahil raised his eyebrows, marvelling at Zahra's wild imagination.

'I'm serious. Two people Ehsan loved could make things work – together. Why not?'

Saahil sighed. Even with his sister's reassurances, he couldn't quite make peace with the idea. Not yet.

'It depends on what she says tomorrow,' he said. 'How she feels?'

Zahra smirked and started looking the other way.

'What?' asked Saahil.

'Well, you did deserve to get slapped,' she replied. 'Not being funny, but you can't just go and snog a hijabi without her permission.'

'Oi!'

Saahil prodded her in the ribs. She pulled his hair. The play fight ensued for approximately thirty seconds, until Ammi shouted at them from the next room to keep the noise down.

Fifty

Amjad could hear his children whispering behind the kitchen door. He glanced over and shook his head, unimpressed with their feeble attempts at trying to hide things from him.

'I'll start, then you jump in,' he heard Zahra say. Saahil shushed her and hissed a response, but Amjad couldn't make out what he said.

The past few weeks had carried on in a similar manner. The two of them talking in low voices, going quiet when Amjad entered the room. Nudging each other, exchanging private smiles, passing mobiles phones around. Going into different rooms, whispering again.

Amjad didn't know what it was all about. He didn't need to. He was just relieved that the two of them had slotted right back in. That they were close and could talk to each other. Rely and trust in one another. Their relationship seemed to grow stronger every day. Amjad watched as Saahil and Zahra laughed and goofed around, they even had play fights like they did as children. And yet when it mattered, as he was witnessing, they could share secrets and be there for one another. That was all Amjad had ever wanted.

By now, the muttering was out of control. Amjad sighed and called over: 'If you've got something to say can you do it now, please? *Crimewatch* is coming on in five minutes.'

The door opened and Zahra entered the room sheepishly. She took a seat next to Amjad. Saahil sat opposite, as far away as he possibly could.

'Erm... well...' Zahra began. 'You know Saahil?'

Amjad pointedly looked at his son. 'Yeah, I know him.'

'Well, he's sort of getting on a bit,' Zahra said. 'He'll be thirty-three at the end of this year. Give it a few more years and... no one will wanna marry him.'

Saahil looked at her from across the room. 'Thanks,' he said, smiling.

Zahra ignored him. 'So yeah, Abbu,' she continued. 'Maybe you should start thinking about getting him wed.'

Amjad's eyebrows shot up his forehead. 'Really?' He looked over to Saahil, his voice became sterner. 'You're ready for that, are you?'

Saahil shuffled around. 'Erm... I suppose.'

Amjad leaned back, his mind racing immediately as he thought about any eligible young women he knew of.

'Rashid's daughter is a lovely girl, she's similar age to you, I think. Could introduce you to her. Or there's—'

'Oh no, you don't need to worry about that,' Zahra said. 'He's already got someone.'

Amjad's face hardened. 'Oh, he's already got someone, has he? I should have known.'

'No, Abbu,' Saahil quickly said. 'It's not like... that.'

'Yeah, they've known each other since uni,' Zahra replied, jumping in to save the day. 'And she's really nice, I've met her a few times.'

Amjad looked at the pair of them. 'So you're telling me now, after you've already decided?'

'We want you to meet her,' Zahra said, before dropping into a whisper. She spoke into Amjad's ear. 'I had to make sure she was *all right*, you know what I mean, Abbu? She could have been a right cow.'

'What?' Saahil asked from across the room, craning to listen.

'What's her name?' Amjad asked.

'Alisha.'

'What does she do?'

'She's a sonographer,' Saahil replied.

Amjad nodded, impressed. 'Parents?'

'Dad does the night shift at the supermarket, and Mum is some kind of family liaison officer.'

Amjad asked a couple of more questions. *Where did they live? How big was the family?*

'So are they quite... well off or are they like us?'

'Like us,' said Saahil.

Amjad was secretly relieved. He waited for a moment before answering. 'Bring her over at the weekend.'

Immediately, he stood up and walked over to his drawer where he kept all his bank statements and important documents. He found his little bank book for his savings account. Like most Asian parents, he had started saving as soon as the kids were born, putting away some money every month. They had no choice. It was a necessity, knowing how notoriously expensive Asian weddings were.

'It's not a lot, compared to some people,' Amjad said, flicking through the pages. 'But it's enough for a decent-sized wedding. My friend's son got married at that new venue that's opened in town, what's it called again, Zee?'

'There's no need for all that, Abbu,' Saahil interrupted. 'I don't want a fuss. Neither does she. Just a nikkah at the mosque is fine. In fact, forget the mosque, call two witnesses and an imam and we'll do it here at home.'

'You might have to push the boat out and go to the registry office as well,' Zahra said, rolling her eyes.

'Yeah, whatever.'

'But you're sure she doesn't want the whole shebang?' Zahra asked.

'No, I told you, she nearly married once before and has been through that nightmare. And as for me… I'm happy with anything that doesn't involve people.'

Amjad listened quietly before speaking. 'But this is your money,' he said to Saahil. 'For your wedding. Ammi won't be happy if we don't do anything for you. And… you're my only son. We need to have a celebration.'

'No, Abbu, please. I don't want it,' Saahil insisted.

'Fine, you can put it towards a deposit for a house—'

'No, we're living here.'

Amjad's eyes bulged. 'You what?'

'Yeah, we're going to live here. Both rooms in the attic are ours. Nobody uses them anyway.'

Amjad looked at his son, stunned. Yes, living with the in-laws was common in his day, but the trend was not as popular with the modern generation.

'And she's okay with that?' he asked.

Saahil nodded. 'I'm not going anywhere,' he added, quietly.

Amjad turned to Zahra, unconvinced.

'I asked her about it, Abbu, when we were alone,' she said, throwing a glance at Saahil. 'She doesn't mind. Said she has a younger brother and hopes when he marries they will live at home

500

and look after her mum and dad. Plus, we get on really well. It'll be fun to have another girl around here.'

Amjad stood for a while, holding the bank book to his chest. 'It's up to you,' he said. 'This money is still yours. You can do—'

'Give it to Zahra. I don't need it.'

Zahra made a face. 'I don't want it, I hate big weddings.'

Amjad stared at the pair of them and anger rose in his chest. He hadn't worked all his life to save up for his kids just so that they could turn around and say they 'didn't want it'.

'*You* don't want it and *you* don't want it,' he said, throwing the book to the side. 'If you'd told me that before I wouldn't have worked so hard all my life. Would have just sat on my arse and let it be.'

Before he had chance to move, Zahra was hugging him around the middle. 'I'm sorry, Abbu.'

Saahil stood up too. 'We didn't mean it like that.'

Zahra looked up at him, her eyes full of concern. 'Spend the money on yourself.'

'Yeah, go on holiday,' Saahil chimed in.

'Do something nice for yourself, for once.'

'Don't be silly,' Amjad said, trying to free himself from his daughter's grip. She didn't let go.

'There must be somewhere you've always wanted to go?' Zahra asked, her face resting against his chest.

Amjad thought about it for a second. 'Well... the mosques in Istanbul are nice. Apparently all the calls to prayer are in sync with one another. Each muezzin gives the other a chance to say their verse before carrying on. Must be beautiful to listen to. But still, I'm not sure.'

'I'll sort it out. I'll book it online,' Zahra said, excitedly. 'And I'll find a really nice hotel. Near the blue mosque!'

Amjad's frown turned into a smile and he put his arms around Zahra. He glanced at Saahil who was standing around like a spare part.

'Do you have a picture of her?'

'Who?'

'Alisha, who else?'

Saahil pulled out his phone and handed it to Amjad.

Amjad looked at the photo. She was a pretty girl with a beautiful smile that lit up the screen. She seemed relaxed and laidback. Amjad found it strange, but he already felt a pang of paternal affection for her. Slowly, a smile spread across his face.

'So, she's coming over at the weekend?'

Saahil nodded.

'I wonder if she likes biryani. Have I got any ginger?' Amjad asked, strutting off toward the kitchen. His children followed him.

'Or I could make my signature dish, achar gosht.'

They heard footsteps and Ammi's voice ask, 'What's going on?'

She stomped down the stairs. 'Why are you all in my kitchen?' she said, with a hint of suspicion.

'Saahil's bringing a girl home,' Amjad said.

Ammi's eyes widened. 'Oh, really,' she asked, hobbling toward them.

Amjad watched as Ammi and Zahra began whispering away. Only Saahil stood around looking reserved, his eyes glued to the floor, hands in his pockets, biting his lower lip.

Amjad reached out and touched his face, but Saahil flinched.

Their eyes met. Amjad frowned. So did Saahil, but he quickly realised that it was a gesture of love and his face relaxed. Amjad cowered with shame. He had never wanted this. For his own son to be on tenterhooks around him. To confuse his father's love for aggression.

A second later, and they were both bound together in the strongest of embraces. Amjad pulled his son into a desperate hug and Saahil responded eagerly. Zahra and Ammi both took a step back, jamming into the kitchen sink simultaneously. They watched with open mouths as Saahil cried like a small child. Amjad squeezed him tight.

'I'm sorry,' he said, stroking his son's hair. 'I'm so sorry.'

Fifty-One

August 2016

'Are you sure this is a good idea?'

Saahil's eyes met Zahra's in the rear-view mirror. He didn't answer her for a second.

'What's the worst that could happen?' he asked, starting the engine of the car.

'I don't know… Uncle Harun flips and kicks us out of the house.'

She was sitting in the back seat with Neelam, whose little hand was wrapped around her pinky. Saahil glanced outside the window. Abbu stood in the garden, hand shielding his eyes from the sun. A huge smile on his face. He craned his neck to get a view of the back seat.

Saahil and Zahra waved at him. Alisha appeared at the door wearing her pyjamas. She waved too, probably glad to have some baby-free hours to herself.

They drove in silence until Zahra cleared her throat.

'So, your plan is to just go and drop the baby on Uncle Harun, and everyone is going to live happily ever after?'

'Yeah,' Saahil replied.

Zahra opened her mouth to respond but thought better of it. She began cooing at Neelam, who gurgled back. Saahil drove with a lump in his throat, unsure of whether he was doing the right thing. It had been three months since the birth of his daughter and only Auntie Meena had visited them. She appeared embarrassed that she was alone, but nobody asked her where Harun was.

Saahil, however, was determined. He remembered the lonely days spent at random cafés just after he returned home. He had been waiting around for things to get better, for some magical moment, an epiphany to occur that finally made him feel okay about things. It never came. Even after he married Alisha in the small ceremony at the mosque, there was never an utterly carefree moment for the two of them. He concluded that they weren't like most newlyweds, joyful and madly in love. There was too much history. Too much of a burden that Saahil just couldn't seem to shake off, no matter how hard he tried.

As soon as Neelam arrived, though, things changed. All the anger and pain just seemed to drain out of him. The whole house was transformed. Abbu became a doting grandpa. Ammi boasted to all her friends. Zahra couldn't step out of the house without returning home with cute little dresses and trendy shoes for her niece. It was perplexing how everything now just seemed to revolve around this tiny little baby.

'We'll have to start a new growth chart soon!' Zahra said, almost as soon as the baby was born. 'We can measure her on my side of the door.'

'One thing at a time,' replied Abbu, smiling. 'She's literally just arrived.'

The biggest impact was on Saahil and he remembered the precise moment his life changed for the better. He had fallen asleep on the couch with Neelam lying on his belly. She was warm and cosy, with Zahra having wrapped her up inside their mother's shawl. When Saahil woke up, the afternoon sun rays shone through the blinds. Neelam snored, her tiny nose placed next to a button on his shirt. Her skin was soft, like cotton wool. Her chest rose and fell. Saahil remembered his arms had been wrapped around his baby girl and he had held her tight. For the first time in years, he had woken up smiling.

Ehsan.

Saahil still thought about him every day. He visited the grave every Friday after Jummah with Abbu. He prayed for him. Talked about him. Wanted to tell him things. But there was one thing Saahil needed to do more than anything, and that was why he pulled up outside Harun and Meena's house, determined to set things right.

'I'll hold Neelam,' Zahra gulped. 'You go first.'

Saahil knocked on the door and waited. He placed both hands on his hips and tapped his foot, matter-of-factly. He meant business. When Meena answered, her eyes widened when she saw them.

'Can we come in?' Saahil asked.

She nodded and led them into the lounge. The curtains were drawn shut. Meena flung them open, letting light into the room. A prayer mat was spread out in the centre. Meena folded it away, hastily. Prayer beads jangled in one of her hands. With her back turned to them, Zahra pointedly stared at Saahil. Saahil looked away. Meena had been praying in the dark.

They stood around awkwardly for a while. Meena asked how Abbu was and busied herself with Neelam. She picked her up and cradled her in her arms.

'Is Uncle home?' Saahil asked.

'Er, yes he is,' Meena began. 'Saahil, I don't know if...'

'Don't worry about it. Can you call him?'

They didn't need to. Uncle Harun's cough signalled his appearance. His heavy, burdened footsteps were making their way down the stairs. Heads turned in the direction of the door. Saahil braced himself. So did the rest of them. Harun entered the room and did a double take. Nobody spoke for a while.

Zahra's words echoed in Saahil's head. *Drop the baby on him.*

He grabbed Neelam. 'Look who it is, Neelam,' he said, quickly. 'Your other grandpa.'

He put the baby in Harun's arms, who seized up. He stared ahead, unmoving, wooden. Neelam gurgled and hit him on the nose. She pulled at his beard. Everyone laughed nervously.

Harun looked at Neelam as though he'd never seen a baby before. His brow was furrowed. His lips parted, the corners of which seemed to be upturning. Harun held his finger up for Neelam, who wrapped her little hand around it. Suddenly, he was smiling.

'Shall I put the kettle on?' Auntie Meena blurted out.

Zahra followed her into the kitchen. Saahil's mouth was dry. He didn't know how to react and began fidgeting on the spot. Harun seemed to notice him and motioned with his head to the sofa.

'Sit down, beta,' he said. *Son.*

Saahil could feel his eyes welling up.

'Yes, okay!' he said, nodding enthusiastically. He felt a sudden lightness in his head. He wanted to laugh out loud.

Saahil watched Harun play with Neelam and his heart panged. He remembered all the times Harun took care of him when Abbu got stuck in traffic on the way home from work. How, when Saahil was with them, Harun barely distinguished between him and Ehsan. Saahil knew Abbu felt the same.

'He never let me comfort him,' Abbu often said. 'It would have helped us both, I think.'

Abbu's eyes dimmed whenever he spoke about Harun.

'I don't like the way he reacted to everything. And even after all these years, when I see him, he turns away,' Abbu said. 'But at the end of the day... I got my son back. He'll never get his.'

Two hours later, Saahil carried a sleeping Neelam out of the front door. There was a slight drizzle outside and Saahil covered his baby's head with a blanket. Meena stood by the door and waved. Harun hobbled forward too.

'Saahil?' he called.

They turned around.

Harun scratched his nose. 'Erm... I might come over tomorrow... after Jummah. See Neelam again... And your dad?'

'Yes, of course, definitely,' Saahil replied, speaking so fast he barely took a breath.

'Yeah, good,' Zahra chimed in, from underneath her hood. 'You come as well, Auntie.'

Meena nodded. Zahra squeezed Saahil's hand as they walked to the car.

Saahil checked his mirrors as they made to set off down the streets. He did a three-point turn and stopped midway, the back tyres almost touching the opposite side of the street. The rain was falling thick and fast now, blurring his windscreen. Saahil fumbled around and switched on the wipers. The water swept to one side and Harun and Meena came into view directly opposite them.

Saahil breathed out, slow and mournful. He bowed his head to get a better look at Ehsan's mother and father. They had aged so much. But Saahil's heart warmed as he saw them both smiling and waving. He could have watched them forever.

A gentle hand touched his shoulder.

'What's wrong?' Zahra asked. She looked at him, thoughtfully.

Saahil shook his head, pressed the gas pedal and drove off down the street.

Fifty-Two

'Bhaijaan, are you sure you've got everything?' Zahra asked.

'For the hundredth time,' Saahil said, fiddling around with his backpack. 'Yeah, I have.'

'Just making sure.'

'And anyway, even if I haven't, you're coming home in two weeks,' he said. 'You're only in London. Not Los Angeles.'

'Shut up.'

They both stared at the display boards at King's Cross station and waited for details of the Bradford train to show. A crowd had started gathering. Nearly a hundred faces were upturned towards the screens, eyes glazed and lips parted as though they had all just spotted a UFO.

'This is bloody stupid,' Saahil muttered. 'Train's in ten minutes and they've not even announced the platform yet.'

'Apparently they always do this.'

'Twats.'

There was a constant buzzing in their ears. Urgent footsteps thudded past them, the occasional screech of suitcase wheels. People talked to each other over muffled music. The packaging of hastily eaten sandwiches lay abandoned on benches. Commuters tutted as they moved them out of the way as they searched for available seats.

Zahra glanced at her brother. 'Are you gonna miss me?'

Saahil kept his eyes on the platform screen and opened his mouth to answer but Zahra cut him off.

'Actually,' she said, eyeing him mockingly, 'you're used to taking extra-long breaks away from your family, aren't you?'

'Don't get funny with me,' he retaliated. 'I used to wipe snot from your nose when you were a kid.'

'What's that got to do with—'

'I'm just reminding you, that's all.'

'Well, I don't remember,' Zahra spluttered.

'Well, I do.'

They both giggled. It was the second time since Saahil had accompanied Zahra down to London that they had cracked a joke about his years in the wilderness. The first had been when they were arguing over who should take the decomposing single bed in the box room Zahra would be renting from now on.

'You're my elder,' she smirked. 'You should sleep on the bed.'

'No,' said Saahil, rolling out his sleeping bag. 'You're a girl, you take the bed.'

Zahra continued fussing about it being uncomfortable on the floor until Saahil reminded her about his past:

'I slept on the streets, under car-park ramps and in doorways for two years. Shut up and take the bed.'

They looked at each other for a moment before descending into laughter at his outburst. The fact that they could joke about it now was another huge step forward.

Saahil had helped her scrub mould off the skirting boards, disinfect the bathroom and vacuum the stale carpet in the small room. After cleaning, they visited a nearby Tesco and Zahra bought her own dishes, pots and pans.

'Keep them in your own room,' Saahil instructed her.

'But there's no space,' she complained.

'It doesn't matter, you need to. Or you'll wake up one day and find them goray frying bacon in your pan.'

There were five other girls in the house-share. Two were foreign students from Spain, one was from Wales, and there was a fellow Yorkshire lass who Zahra connected with instantly.

Once the room was organised, they spent the weekend being tourists. They visited the London Eye, Buckingham Palace, and took a boat down the River Thames.

'It's beautiful, isn't it?' Zahra said, her eyes twinkling as they stood on the bridge watching the Houses of Parliament light up at night.

'I thought you were anti-establishment,' said Saahil.

She laughed and linked arms with him as they strolled up to Piccadilly Circus. They took a seat by the Eros statue and watched the screens shine down on the crowds at night. It was just the two of them.

'We've never really chilled out like this before,' Zahra said to him.

Saahil nodded and bowed his head. Zahra hadn't meant to make him feel bad. She just couldn't believe she was actually there, with *him*. When they got to the flat, Saahil slept on her floor in a sleeping bag and they talked throughout the night.

'You don't have to worry about Abbu,' he reassured her. 'It'll be hard at first, but he'll get used to it. And you know what it's like nowadays. Neelam won't leave him alone. She's glued to him.'

They chortled in agreement before shushing each other.

'Ammi?' Zahra asked.

'She'll probably cry for a few days, but she'll be fine too. And she has Alisha to boss around now,' Saahil said, snorting. 'You have to remember, they're both really proud of you. I'm proud of you.'

Zahra turned over in bed to face him. 'And I'm proud of you.'

Saahil made a noise to suggest *'what for?'*

'I could never do what you do,' she told him.

After her persistence, Saahil had eventually applied for a few drug support worker vacancies at local homeless charities. A few failed interviews later, he secured a job, never realising how fulfilling and satisfying it would be. Zahra beamed with pride as he came home every day with new stories. Sometimes they were grim, such as the time Saahil had gone running down the street chasing one of his clients who was having a psychotic episode. Other times, they were hopeful, when Saahil knew he had played a small role in supporting someone out of addiction. He received calls from all over the city, telling him that somebody 'known to them' had collapsed, here or there. Saahil would drop everything, even after he'd finished his shift, and run out to help.

One morning whilst still having breakfast, he'd received a tip-off that a local convenience store was still selling suspicious-looking packets that could be spice. Legal highs had been banned the previous year though the situation had undoubtedly worsened. Riskier and more potent versions of spice were constantly being developed and sold on the black market. A simple ban by the government had never been the answer. After all, it was easier to control the owners of headshops than underground drug dealers.

Zahra watched as Saahil jotted down details of the convenience store and stood up, leaving his unfinished breakfast.

'Don't worry… I'll sort this out,' he said to the person at the other end of the phone. A ban was still a ban. Spice was illegal now, and this was something Saahil could actually investigate himself.

Alisha had cleared away the food and rolled her eyes at Zahra. She, however, couldn't be happier for her brother. Even if it hadn't been the life or career Saahil had imagined for himself, there was no denying he finally seemed to have found a purpose.

Zahra's future had taken a little longer to figure out. There had been many schemes and internships in the past two years that she'd applied for, including the ITV programme that Saahil had watched through gritted teeth. She missed out on them all, including the BBC interview she'd excitedly told Ammi about. She worked at a depressing bank whilst applying for every type of job she thought she could do. She made it to interview stages and buckled with nerves.

'Most of the time I just throw CVs in the bin,' one interviewer at a big company told her. 'They annoy me.'

That's nice, Zahra wanted to say, considering the mammoth application form, online questionnaire, two assessment days and telephone interview it had taken her just to get there in front of him. *And people brand* my *generation as lazy and entitled,* she thought.

'I haven't seen yours though so you're lucky,' he continued. 'Sandra here picked them out.' He motioned to the lady sitting next to him. 'So, what can *you* do for our business?' he asked. 'What can *you* bring to the table?'

Probably a lot more than you could when you were 'hired on potential' for your first job thirty years ago, Zahra wanted to say.

Eventually, she saw an opportunity on Twitter to write for an edgy, online platform written solely by women of colour. She was already familiar with the magazine; it was rapidly gaining

514

popularity as an alternative voice against the mainstream media that did not reflect their experiences.

'This is so you,' Libby told her.

Zahra applied right away, working for months on a part-time, freelance basis from home. Six months later, she received a phone call from the magazine telling her they had big plans for the following year and were very impressed with her work. Zahra couldn't believe her ears when they offered her a job as a political editor. As expected, though, she would have to relocate down to London.

Ammi and Abbu had plenty of time to mentally prepare for Zahra's move, but when the time came for goodbyes, reality set in. It was only London, hardly a different country, but they had always been a close-knit bunch. Zahra would still be apart from them all. Libby's goodbye had been the worst.

'FaceTime me every day, you cow,' she said through tears.

Since they arrived in London, Zahra had already spoken to her every few hours. In fact, they'd made plans for Libby to visit her overnight in the coming weeks.

An announcement went off in the station and finally, the platform details for Saahil's train appeared on the screen. Travellers began making their way. Saahil had approximately five minutes to get on to the platform.

'Oh no,' Zahra said, looking back at the long queue that was gathering behind them. 'You didn't get a picture at Platform 9 ¾!'

'Next time,' Saahil replied, picking up his rucksack and readying himself.

'Are you going?' Zahra asked, quietly. She suddenly felt small and lost.

'Yeah, you're going to be okay, though, right?'

Zahra realised she was choked up. 'Tell Abbu I said…' Her voice drifted away.

'You don't have to worry about anyone anymore,' said Saahil. 'I'm… *there* now. I'll sort it. Do you know which tube you're getting back to the flat?'

'Yeah.'

Saahil held Zahra by the arms. He lowered himself to her level and looked her in the eye. 'It's *your* time now. You're going to do amazing things… important things.'

'Don't, Bhaijaan,' Zahra said, pushing him away. 'I'll start crying.'

Saahil smiled. 'Okay. I'm off then.'

'Wait.' Zahra searched inside her bag and pulled out their mother's yellow pashmina. She placed it in Saahil's hand.

'Let Neelam's shawl go back to Neelam,' she said.

Saahil frowned.

'I want it to comfort baby Neelam, just like it did me as a child,' she explained. 'And like it comforted you… when you were away.'

'Are you sure?' Saahil asked.

Zahra nodded.

Saahil cupped her face and kissed her on the forehead. Zahra watched him walk away. Her heart always fluttered with uncertainty, just like it always did whenever she saw the back of him leaving to go anywhere. That feeling had been cemented when he'd waved them goodbye and walked out of the house, not to return for ten years. This time, though, Saahil stopped.

'See you in two weeks,' he called back to her, reassuringly.

Zahra nodded. She realised that this time, there was no uncertainty, only trust.

Before reaching the concrete pillars that would curtain him from view, Saahil stood and waved from the distance. He placed two fingers on his lips.

'Love you,' he mouthed.

Zahra couldn't respond. She just watched him turn away. The swarm of travellers was overwhelming, obscuring Zahra's vision. She craned her neck to catch a last glimpse of her brother before he disappeared on to the platform. Zahra stood for a while, unmoving.

'Love you too,' she breathed, but her voice was lost, even to her own ears, as the crowds swelled and beat around her.

Acknowledgements

Thank you to my parents, Mahmood and Perveen, and my sister, Rahema, for all your love and support. I will always be grateful for your patience, reassurance and understanding over the years and would not be where I am today without you. I love you.

A massive thank you to the team at HQ, particularly Lisa Milton. You changed my life one day by offering to read my work after our meeting at the Bradford Literature Festival, and in the process, became my biggest champion. Your desire to reach out to those who don't feel represented in literature is truly inspiring. Thank you for being a great publisher and a great friend.

My deepest gratitude to my agent, Christine Green, and my editor, Clio Cornish, for being so kind and nurturing throughout the publication process. Thank you both for all the time and energy you have invested into making this novel the best it could be. Your belief in the book has never failed to elevate me during the difficult times. I am so lucky to have you on my side.

Thank you to my PhD supervisor and mentor, Michael Stewart, who has been with me on this journey from the start. Thank you for going through multiple drafts of this book with the upmost care and consideration. Your enthusiasm has kept me going for the past five years and it has truly been a privilege working under your supervision.

I am grateful to the University of Huddersfield for awarding me two scholarships that allowed me to progress on to postgraduate study. This gave me not only a supportive environment in which to work, but also the time and space I needed to dedicate to this novel.

Huge thanks to Pam Drake from the Headway charity in Bradford for sharing with me her immense knowledge of brain injury. And to Rebecca O'Gorman for being a lovely friend and, luckily for me, a drug and alcohol counsellor! I really appreciate all your help in answering my questions on homelessness and spice addiction.

And last but not least, thank you to Claire Chambers, Shawni Dunne, Alexandra Cook, Hassnain Haider, Fehzan Jamil and Romesa Jamil for being amazing friends throughout this journey.

ONE PLACE. MANY STORIES

Bold, innovative and
empowering publishing.

FOLLOW US ON:

@HQStories